VILLAGE HEIGHTS

L.R. CLAUDE

1

To the educators, the fight against ignorance takes all kinds, it is a never ending uphill battle, but it serves the greater good of mankind, one that all must fight.

-L.R. Claude

Special Thanks to:

COVER DESIGN:

Heidi Hobde Dailey

EDITING:

Bonnie Swartz

Theresa Vandendriesche

Village Heights

I need to explain how everything happened, this is one hell of a series of events that is almost too much to truly believe, like Forrest Gump but without the retard, well, we have a few retards but not medical retards like Will Ferell, just white trash retards, like those Jersey Shore twats. I suppose I can start this with the striking of a match, a wooden kitchen match that leads up to a crooked Newport cigarette, it's the first smoke of the day for Aimee, it's Friday July third and the day before the whole trailer park gathers to party like no one else in the state can imagine. Village Heights is a small encapsulated trailer community, it's a ways from the inner city but they have what they need.

Aimee is a thirty-four year old medical assistant, she is healthy in size and the mother to Brittini, a quiet stringy fourteen year old that loves to doodle and read quietly to herself. Aimee has shoulder length auburn hair, and has been dating a burned out ex-con roofer named Tod for several years. Lot eighty-four is where Aimee and Tod call home; it's a two bedroom single wide, beige on the outside with dark brown trim and a small aged wood deck at the front door. Aimee had a crush on Tod back in high school where he was a running back for the team until mid-senior year when he was expelled for steroid use and distribution among the rest of the football team. Tod now spends most of his days roofing, his afternoons drinking and most weekends passed out or searching for the best high he can get for as cheap as possible, but we'll get back to him. Aimee struggled to find her feet before giving birth, she bounced and floated around but she cleaned up her act enough to fight through school in her early twenties in an attempt to provide for her toddler and secure housing. Tod was not only arrested in high school and expelled from it; he spent two years in jail because he was eighteen when he was caught in the locker room shooting up his fellow jocks with steroids before a game.

Big Ken lives a few lots down from Aimee; he is the size and shape of a gorilla, drives an old busted ass Chevy that you can hear from the entrance way as it idles to the stop sign. Big Ken has a little boy named Jonny, Ken is a concrete trucker and at the ends of long days, he's often glued into his recliner and finishing off a second six pack. Jonny is fifteen, he's a meek quiet blond haired boy, he has light freckles on his cheeks, he has a hard time looking people in the eyes when he talks and has poor posture. Jonny was awarded to Ken a few years ago and the whole dispute has left Jonny in a miserable state of existence. Ken was married to Michelle, Jonny's mom, when the feds busted in on them, charging them for meth production, Ken spent his few years in prison, somewhere up north called Ionia, and when he was released it was Michelle's turn, seeing's how Jonny didn't have anyone to watch him, the judge split their sentences and Michelle still has two more years left, and till then, Ken drinks and Jonny bleeds. Jonny has gotten to the point over the last few months that he tells Big Ken he stays at friends' houses to avoid getting slapped around, all the while he sleeps in other peoples cars, or behind the skirting of their trailer, he has a sleeping bag and some scavenged camping supplies hidden up under his house so he can retreat there most nights when Ken decides to take out every last bad decision he's ever made on Jonny. Ken is probably three hundred and seventy pounds, when his giant baseball mitt sized hands land on Jonny's ninety pound frame; it leaves welts from one shoulder blade to another, and his nose bleeding from the whiplash. Big Ken wears a dirty black Kanga hat with a slight side kick to it, usually a wife beater and Dickie pants to and from work, his time in prison left him with a lot of faded ink across his arms, shoulders, and neck.

Ken and Tod often chat about getting their neck tattoos acquired while on the inside. Ken has a flaming sword on the left side of his neck with black flames licking up behind his left ear. Tod has a Chinese symbol on each side of his neck, one side is allegedly "War" while the other is "Love" he also has the monster "M" on the back of his neck. Tod has short reddish hair and a bony face, probably from years of sorted drug use and choosing an altered reality to moderate nutrition, but compared to the shorter stature of Aimee, his six foot-three height is towering. Kids at school often teased the kids from

Village Heights, poked fun at them over the last fifteen years since it was established, "hillbillies" and "white trash" were just the tip top of the pyramid of slurs that were slung towards the "*Meth Heights*" kids and so on, but to their credit there may only be a handful of GED's and even less diplomas in the entirety of the park. Each night, no matter how much you smoke or how hard you drink, there is no escape from reality but when you spend each and every night jacked up, and in a small community that is just like you, that becomes your reality; but anyways. So this story is rife with sex, drugs, partying and some rather twisted up shit, if you can't handle it than you'd better go put on your Disney princess marathon, if not, crack a beer, take a Midol and settle in for a story that might just get you higher than an eight ball of Black Shadow and a mouth full of Roxy's.

So in lot eighty-two is Don and Shelley, Don is the brother of Roger, whom was the prick that knocked up Aimee before disappearing. Don is a stocky black haired guy, he doesn't bother to shave regularly but his wife Shelly doesn't mind, she is a waitress in town and he works as a drill operator in some non-regulated circuit board company that exposes all of its' employees to a mix of noxious chemicals, shit like copper chloride which will turn your facial hair blue. Shelley is fairly heavy set, you wouldn't guess she spends a majority of her days on her feet with the look of her, nor serving food, her hair is mostly blonde with dark roots and is usually tied back, when she's out of work she is rarely caught without a Newport hanging out of her mouth. Don and Shelly have lived in the *Heights* most of their marriage, Roger impregnated Aimee a few years out of high school when Don and Roger were living together in the trailer right after Don married Shelley. Don and Shelly hadn't heard from Roger since before Brittini was born, Aimee lived with them through the pregnancy and then some, it was a little later when she moved to the lot next door, Brittini didn't have her father but Don and Shelley stepped up in a big way, but we'll come back to that too.

This story is about a party, a Fourth of July party, the annual *Heights* bash for its' residents, thrown by its' residents for the residents to enjoy. The park manager is a cavernous cunt named Karen Winshmidt, she has a cunt daughter that lets her come out for the Fourth each year and when the rotten snatch leaves for the holiday, Village Heights tears shit up. Last years' party was so out of control that when the police responded; a single patrol car rolled into

7

the single driveway entrance and was met by the usual crowd. Two officers exited the car and attempted to break up the gathering, big mistake, a big damn mistake. The crowd began to "*BOO*" the pathetic attempts of the two officers, it turned from booing to shouts rather quickly and then rocks began to fly from the back side of the crowd as the speakers pounded into the dark night and the mortars streamed into the air. As the officers began to unleash the small piss streams of pepper spray, the two quaking cops were facing fifty or so *Heights* residents, plus guests with several hours of drinking and other assorted drug use behind them. One officer was a short stocky guy; he stood with a wide stance and attempted to be at the ready, his partner was a taller thinner guy with a shitty dirty blond mustache, an ill-fated attempt to fake authority, or at least the confidence.

Stones turned to rocks, rocks to bricks and within two minutes of their arrival, the patrol car was damaged to the point that the officers that drove it in, couldn't drive it back out. The wrecked squad car became a blockade into the park, the red and blue flashing lights shattered into pieces as bricks bounced off of various places of the car, the shattering glass sounds further excited the mob as the explosive fireworks overhead changed the colors that reflected off of the faces near the officers as they began to walk back from where they originated. The cops were offered a beer for their troubles and one large tattooed man with a thick wallet chain hanging from him tried to play nice by offering up a cold beverage and a seat to watch the firework show, the officers lamented and were extremely nervous about the crowd and withdrew their feeble attempts to disperse the crowd.

So Aimee sucked on her Newport to start her morning, she had to get moving to get to the doctor's office that she works at, she was trying to load up enough nicotine to encourage herself to rise up out of bed. Tod already heaved himself out of the home, work boots unlaced and on his feet, stained jeans filled with torn holes and worn through spots running up and down the legs. Aimee couldn't even tell if she had panties on or not, when you pass out near Tod it's hard to tell what he may have done to you, as she sat up she felt the pain in her backside to better make sense of which hole he finished in overnight. Tod packed a thermos full of Kryptonite: two parts mountain dew; one part of vanilla vodka, it tastes like superman ice cream and it fuels his hot days spreading tar or nailing down shingles.

8

Tod works with a small crew, there's Tuner, a skinny tall dark haired scrubby guy that always smells like piss and cigar smoke. Billy who has reddish haired guy, medium build and mostly quiet, Billy always smokes Marlborough's but never seems to have a lighter and is always bumming lights. Karl is a bit of a sleaze, he always just stares at Aimee's tits, he also sneers at Brittini's ass if he's near the house when she walks near him, he stares at her ass looking for pantie lines or hoping to get an eye down her shirt and talk about supple mosquito bites every chance he gets, just a real slime ball. Anyway, so Tods' roofing crew is just a bunch of lowlife high school dropouts, all tattooed like you'd imagine, they all smoke and drink the day away while aimlessly moseying the tops of people's homes on hot afternoons. There used to be a Jerome on the crew until late last fall when he was watching a girl take a piss through her skylight, he swore he saw bush and tried to get a better angle to snap a picture with his cell phone when he tripped on the air hose leading to a nail gun, causing him to fall from the roof. Jerome didn't fall down both stories but he did land on the ladder which then projected him onto a saw table, by the time he hit the ground he had been impaled with the claw of a hammer, a branch of some sort and had been busted up pretty badly. The guys joked that Jerome got what he had coming to him because he used to steal stuff from clients when he went in to use the restroom, not to mention peeking in on women pissing.

The day before the fourth party was always busy with set up; the middle road was usually the hardest party while the two adjacent streets helped to insulate the wildness from the outside. The outer perimeter of the park was lined with a grass berm embankment and just beyond that is a sidewalk lined with windscreen trees to hide away the eyesore of the trailers that lined up inside. The prep for the party took all involved; each house was to supply a case of beer, a food tray of sorts and to tune their radios to 104.3, an empty station that would receive the tunes that were transmitted by DJ Wriggle, a local kid that can spin party beats. Wriggle has an easy set up but with a mild receiver set up that he can broadcast his beats to all of the radios sitting in windows around the whole park, it was easier than bringing in a concerts' worth of speakers to pump up the party. Each trailer set up their outward facing speakers and Wriggle sets up his gear on the red wood deck with a few party woofers right in the center. Wriggle is a private school kid, his parents actually make good

9

money but he tries to stay real by spinning at a few parties here and there to keep up his street credit, despite the fact that he has himself a prissy private school education. Wriggle comes to get drunk and high and maybe laid, he puts on a good show and it didn't hurt that he knew several kids from the neighborhood.

So the few days leading up to the party was usually somber, Karen was an evil bitch with a rotten snatch, the kind that would snitch to the cops over the smallest drop of piss that lands anywhere other than the porcelain. Tod swears that the bitch is a lesbian and that she was so miserable because she hated herself that she spilled it out to everyone else, well she needs to put her Timbo's under someone else's bed for once. When Karen goes to see her manly looking daughter once a year, she eases up a bit afterwards but if someone shits sideways and risks her not going to see her grandkids, it would piss all over her plans and then ruin the party. Karen is an unhappy bull-dyke and she would love to foreclose on each trailer, boot each resident and have each one hauled the hell off of the cement slab they're parked on, it would probably lubricate something on her that has been a desert for fifty years.

Karen loves to cite residents, she walks with a scour look on her face, counting piles of dog shit in each yard, if the shit doesn't get picked up every other day she puts a citation in the mailbox, each time an infraction occurs it's a five dollar fine, it's not about the money but she loves the power of it all. Karen lives in a pea green single wide at the opening of the park, she had a chair propped up to keep an eye on all of the comings or goings and was suspected of popping playground balls just to watch kids cry. The week leading up to the party is quiet, each resident chatters a bit about what to make and who is bringing what tables and shit to help facilitate. Kiddie pools are filled with beers and ice and they line the main center street for people to conjure around, the younger kids usually fill up on sodas while the adults get tanked, each group of people mingle and listen to the jams blare from the speakers until it gets dark out, then the pyrotechnics begin to fire off from the side streets over top for all to enjoy.

Aimee finishes her cigarette before she stands up from her bed, she rubs her stomach, swollen from age and gravity, lifting parts of her to stare at stretch marks, pits, and scars in the mirror, she remembers being a smooth bodied sixteen year old cheerleader, less

10

than half the size she is today, she stares at her naked body in the mirror, wondering when exactly her nipples had stopped pointing forward and now towards the ground. Aimee has worked for the same doctor's office for almost eight years, she was fired from a part time job last year as a morticians assistant, she was siphoning off formaldehyde for Tod and his crew to smoke, she needed the money but Tod is an abusive junkie and it's easier to please him rather than get slapped around. Aimee turned to see bite marks and handprints in the ripples of her ass, Tod must have done a number as the welts were still pretty prevalent, she does her best to pass out before he gets too riled up and carried away. Like I said, everyone in the *Heights* has regrets, this ain't a story about that, it's about a party. Aimee searched for clean scrubs to wear to work, half of her clothes sat in the corner, some of them were clean enough to wear again, the pair of pants she wore yesterday didn't fit in that category, they were used by Tod as either a rag to blow his nose, or to blow, well something else. Aimee washed her face and rolled on deodorant as she fumbled to half brush her teeth and apply light makeup to cover over small scars around her face before fumbling out of the small bathroom on her way to the living room. Aimee shouted through the other bedroom door to Brittini to make sure she was moving; she had chores to do as well as babysit later in the day. Opening the door revealed the small teen asleep and half draped off her bed, her hair looked like a rat's nest, her tank top stained and a pink sheet hardly covering her midsection, the girl just nodded in response.

It was early yet but around the complex there was plenty stirring, Big Ken had already been up and gone for the day so Jonny could be seen down the street heading into his home to sleep or finally eat. Darryl is a kid that lives towards the end of the street, he's twenty but still rides a BMX bicycle because he's a broke ass but most know to hit him up for weed, it was about all he was good for. Darryl is short and stocky; he keeps his short hair matted down onto his head if he isn't wearing a flat billed hat, usually Pistons. Darryl claims Detroit to keep it "real," real "what" is the question. Darryl has spent two different stints in county jails for drug related sentences, he'll never learn but that's the sort of lives that reside in the mobile community. Darryl got his start in high school, he used to spray graph paper with Raid bug killer and sell it as acid, he was real low rent but always kept his Shinola watch in view, regardless of the fact that he usually

11

doesn't change out of his Pistons' Rodman jersey from the 90's. Darryl sounded black most of the time, at least within a crowd, you get him alone and he fronts much less, but he has to keep up his rep. Darryl is usually found riding around the trailer park, he has no limits and will try to bed anything that resembles a warm hole, Brittini has had to swat his hands as he lets them roam towards her if she's near. Darryl always manages to find smoke or drink if he needs it, but he's more skilled at doing it all without having to pay a damned dime, his prepubescent mustache always raised when he smirked and unless it was dirty, it was near invisible.

A few lots down from lot eighty-four is sixty-seven, leased by Shameeka Knopes and her daughter Dez'rae. Shameeka was some form of receptionist; she often hung around with a few of her people and hardly caused much of a stir. Dez'rae was a beautiful light skinned girl; she had a dancers' form with matching long legs and a body that everyone wanted to drool all over. Dez'rae has a best friend named Tammi, Tammi is also fifteen but a jealous little bitch and has a tendency to let her jealousy turn into desperately vying just about anyone for the attention. Dez'rae and Darryl flirt back and forth a bit, she likes the attention from the older boy but other than blowing him once for some pot, she rarely has anything to do with him. Shameeka on the other hand, she'll get naked and freaky with Darryl twice a year or so, she'll smoke down with him and when they are both stoned, she'll get touchy and horny for the younger boy, and like I mentioned earlier, he'll screw anything with a wet spot. Dez'rae holds good grades, she works hard both in school and out, afternoons she and Tammi work at a fast food joint in town called "ChickLips" it's a greasy fried chicken joint but the afternoon manager is some seventeen year old pimple ridden twerp and his hard-on for Dez is so big that he'd probably hand her money from the till if she asked.

Tammi lives in an apartment complex a few miles from Village Heights, closer to town and she usually made the walk to the Heights to hang out, or rode the bus which runs in the morning and in the late afternoon, Dez'rae often rode the bus to and from work. Down the road from the park entrance is an Amoca gas station; it has overpriced everything and is the central hub for most of the trailer park residents to purchase alcohol or smokes. The usual attendant is a pudgy homely douche named Gary Rousley, he still lives with his mom and it's rumored that he sells anything to underage girls and anyone willing to shake their ass or pop out a titty for him. Gary has curly black hair, thick glasses and the body of Rosie O'Donnell, despite being in his mid-twenties. Gary usually sits on a stool playing video games to pass the time, or probably jerking off in the backroom. Gary also went to school with most of the rest of the trash from the Heights, just at different times, the entire cesspool that keeps it breeding and infecting itself with more lower- IQ'd wanderers. So last year's party left a squad car destroyed, three people hospitalized from a fight, one from the pepper spray and a car firebombed, and that was just what was reported. So last year leading up to the party, Tammi wanted a few bottles of Boons Farm, it's a cheap hillbilly wine that tastes like fermented piss but the high school girls that don't know any better, drink it, it's real cheap so whatever. Tammi is a thicker girl, blonde hair and green eyes, probably a size twelve or fourteen, usually has a muffin top squeezing out of the top of her yoga pants and her shirt that rides up atop of her belly, this girl will put anything in her mouth, she's a lot like that a Kardasian that way. So anyways, the day of last year's party, Tammi goes in to buy a few bottles of Boons to party with and Gary is nervous to get hit for contributing to a minor so he holds off at first.

Tammi is hard up to get some alcohol so she can become deluded from her pathetic little life. Tammi walked into the gas station where Gary was perched behind the desk. The store was devoid of other patrons so Tammi felt she had the opportunity to purchase her booze. Gary propositioned the desperate to fit in girl, Tammi was desperate to not only fit in, but to find any sort of way to dignify herself among her peers so she turned and flashed the back of her thong for Gary, he didn't find it amusing enough despite the chubby in his trousers for the young girl. Dez'rae once told Tammi that he blew Gary, once, and told him it was only the one time in exchange for buying anything anytime from him, Tammi offered up the same bargain.

Gary didn't buy into the blowjob this time despite Tammi pleading that she could suck him off better than Dez'rae; her primary competition in life. Tammi could see the bulge in his pants as she curled her shoulders close to amplify her cleavage in her tank top, further enticing Gary to get what she wanted from him. Gary ignored the throbbing beast in his pants and continued to angle getting the girl naked, which worked according to stories. Gary locked the front door

13

and lead Tammi to the back room where she removed her black tank top to reveal a leopard print demi-cup bra to the older man. Gary was more than excited to get this young girl naked, she removed her jean skirt with some struggle over her thick thighs to expose herself in a beige thong to the man wearing a sweaty wife-beater under an unbuttoned blue work shirt and khaki's. Tammi still thought that if she knelt down and unzipped him that she might escape actually letting the gross slob inside of her by taking him into her mouth instead. Gary let Tammi put him in her mouth for a few minutes as she gagged on the stench of his balls and the tangled mass of thick black pubic hair that wreaked of sweat and body odor, Tammi was gagging too much to breathe through her mouth but the smell was so bad that she could taste his filth through the smell before even touching the small wrinkled penis to her tongue.

Tammi hoped that the wrinkled balls of the man were wet from being washed but by the sticky sweaty scrotum smell, they hadn't been washed in days and were soaked from being a fat slob and the sweat building up in his crotch. Tammi closed her eyes and fought her best to suck off the gas station attendant in order to buy a few cheap bottles of booze, she thought it was jacked up that she was all but naked just to purchase the liquor, not even to get it for free, she sucked and waited for his cock to harden all while thinking about the strawberry flavored booze and how badly she wanted to get wasted and forget about everything. As Tammi bobbed and jerked she thought about Dez'rae doing the same thing, she wanted to be better than her prettier friend so she cupped the swinging balls and tried to make up for the fact that she had thinner white lips instead of Dez'rae's thicker sister lips. Tammi tried her best to ignore the thick black curly pubic hair tangling around her fingers as she jerked and stroked, the nasty taste in her mouth was beginning to create a film that felt like she smoked a pack of unfiltered cigarettes and then fell asleep without brushing her teeth. Tammi tried to look up and see if the face Gary was making was anything close to orgasm, she'd much rather swallow down his salty load than have to have sex with him but if he wasn't close to getting off, she wasn't sure how much more she could take, her view was blocked by his big hairy stomach, sweat beading up and beginning to run down his belly and towards her mouth.

14

Gary grabbed handfuls of Tammi's hair and bobbed her head back and forth as he got into the action better, she hoped he was close as he suddenly stood her up and bent her forward on a bench in the back room. Tammi reached behind her and continued to jerk Gary off as he fidgeted with a condom wrapper. Tammi took a moment to moisten herself with her right two fingers so his entry wouldn't be as painful while he rolled the latex down onto his shaft, Tammi just couldn't fathom why his dick was half of what she had thought it should be, maybe his girth had inhibited it from extending very far? After a moment of fumbling with the rubber he pushed her forward and straddled up behind her, one hand on her waist the other pulling the back of her hair.

Tammi felt her boobs hanging down and swinging as he thrusted at her, she tried to lift so she didn't pinch a breast between her stomach and the counter edge, Gary still fumbled his way into her, he kept poking at her inner thigh or near her ass, he wasn't that close to his target hole, she had to reach under herself to help facilitate his uncoordinated attempt to hump the underage girl. Tammi felt his sweat begin to run down her thighs, his stink was musky and filled the back room as he grunted and panted heavily, she dreaded how much longer he would take. Tammi had been with several boys by the time she gave up her snatch to Gary for the right to buy alcohol but she hoped that because he was obese and a dork that he would have just creamed his pants at the sight of her bare tits, she hated herself even more as he stroked at himself staring at her exposed body standing in the backroom, she wanted to cry but knew that being able to show up with her own contribution to the party meant status.

Frankie is the name of the kid that runs ChickLips, he is the afternoon manager and only really worked to that level because most of the rest of the shift was caught pissing in the fifty-five gallon drum of pickles before serving them on the burgers and then were fired, Frankie was out casted from the afternoon shift and wasn't invited to crack some whippets and piss in the pickles so his outcast status kept him from getting fired when the day manager walked in and noticed the group of people pissing in a bucket and busted all of them, except him. Frankie was also out casted at school, his parents were lower middle class and this was his first job so when he was promoted it not only went to his head, he had a hand in being able to hire the hottest sophomore at school; Dez'rae, which then he tried to arrange himself to any sort of social standing just by knowing her.

Frankie usually spent time staring at Dez'rae's ass in her tight pants as she worked the window, he was still extremely awkward but he put on a different face when it came time to manage the small chicken place. Earlier this spring it was noted that Frankie was trying every trick in the book to take a peek at Dez'rae when she was changing, he even placed a small pinhole camera in the ceiling to get to watch her change into her smock. Towards the end of this school year Tammi had enough of his pining for Dez'rae so she finally traded with someone else to stay late and close the restaurant in order to seduce the boss. Tammi had cornered Frankie in his office as he was counting the night's register; sure enough she pulled down her pants to show him her shaven snatch, which he told classmates, looked like a knee with road rash.

Jonny and Brittini were in some of the same classes, they chatted and hung around the neighborhood together, they were both quiet and very reserved and that brought them something in common. Jonny kept his hair short so he couldn't be pulled by it by his father when he was getting slapped around, Brittini felt safe enough to confide in Jonny when Tod was on a bender or Aimee was being slapped around by her boyfriend of six years now. In the middle of the park was a small set of metal play structures and a picnic table. Most of the younger teens often hung around near the picnic table, some that began to smoke did so sitting at the very same picnic table, same as their older siblings did, and their older friends did so also. Jonny and Brittini sat up some warm nights when neither wanted to go home and slowly drag on swiped cigarettes as the nights grew late but remained warm. Karen hardly maintained anything in the trailer park except the entrance sign, it was a stone sign and she often hand planted flowers near the base, the swings and monkey bars on the playground hadn't seen paint since it contained lead. Next to the playground was another single wide that contained the Mexicans, hardworking lot of them sure but a bunch of spics nonetheless. The parents were Jose and Maria, there was an older teen named Tara, a pretty but a dumb broad, a younger teen boy they called "*Bonito*" he was known around the block as "Blunt" or "Lil B."

Tara had a killer body that many of the older boys stared at when she flaunted her form in a bikini during the hot summer months, Lil B

16

was often hanging around trying to smoke weed with anyone he could find, he also often hung out with Darryl trying to score pot to sell to his classmates for a quick buck. Lil B wore a thick gold chain with crucifix dangling from it, for a kid that wears a hearty cross around his neck and probably having an uncle named Jesus or some shit, you wouldn't believe the mouth of the kid, a real righteous little prick. Curtiss is a kid that lives with an older cousin down the front road. The cousin is named Monte or something and is hardly around, every once in a while the young thirties guy is seen in his Oldsmobile Eighty-Eight but other than coming or going, it's hard to say much about him. Curtiss is usually seen with Darryl, he's maybe seventeen or eighteen but is on the verge of dropping out of school and spends his time finding all sorts of things to smoke, snort, or inject. Curtiss found some concoctions of cancer drugs that he palmed from his ailing grandfather and if you mix this or that with this or that, "you get tore up," he thought of himself as some sort of street pharmacist. In April during spring break Tammi was avoiding being home as usual and with no one else to keep her company, she found herself huffing formaldehyde and nitrous, the nitrous cracks in through the liquid in a balloon and really jacks you up, Tammi found herself awake in the middle of the night without most of her clothes and Curtiss sprawled out on top of her sweaty body.

So you have a brief introduction to a few of the cast members that can be found in the Village Heights trailer park, these are your run of the mill hillbillies and assorted social trash, this party is where all of the members come together and forget about the day before or the day after the party, the Fourth of July is the epitome of the year, the culmination of all their bodily tolerances for abuse and drug use, all to get jacked up and forget about living one check away from eviction, one check away from foreclosure, and one payment away from repossession. Karen used to be some crooked law clerk before her deviant sex life got her kicked out, not to mention she was releasing private information on court cases to other girls ladies had crushes on. One night Karen was partaking in a group session with a few other swingers when some of the veterinary tranquilizers and Quaaludes that were being passed around gave one of the men a heart attack, with the amount of penis pills he ingested for the evening of debauchery Karen was hosting, it became too much for him and he stroked out; not in the good way. When the ambulance got the man to the hospital he was brain dead, his wife sued Karen and lost but the lawyer fees and accusations had skewed Karen's life and landed her in the Heights, managing peoples' small plots of grass and dog shit.

The local cops are plenty aware of the goings on in the Heights but figure that as long as the problems stay contained within the confines of the park and not bleed out into the community, there was only so much that could be done. The morning in spring break when Tammi woke up with Curtiss half inside her left her truly feeling ashamed, she didn't tell anyone about what had happened but she wasn't certain it was consensual but she lacked the ability to recall how or what happened to her panties, or why she hurt so badly "down there," but she did know that if she told anyone then her vague reputation would be further tarnished and lead to more desires to drink away who she was.

Shameeka often made purchases from Darryl, they occasionally got naked and freaky but that was between the twenty year old boy and the woman that was twice his age, they were consenting adults so whatever, the weirdness comes from the fact that Darryl always tries to convince Dez'rae to hook up with him regardless of the fact that he had sex with her mother. The stories that escape the solidarity of the *Heights* are endless and surprising; the occasional resident gets caught up in some of the same nonsense outside of the community limits and gets caught. Over the winter a kid named Martin was picked up for pedaling dope in the high school, the bastard was scamming on some freshmen girls after a basketball game and got caught up trying to impress them rather than watch the sheriff walk up behind him to catch him red-handed. Martin got his pot from a Heights resident but failed to admit which one, he was given probation after all was said and done because he was a minor but his drug charge wasn't enough to give the department enough cause to start patrolling.

So enough with the story, A.D.D shut up and let me get this story underway, like I was saying, this isn't about the stories behind why all the white trash is white trash, this is about the Fourth of July party, this is an attempt to piece together all of the events, shit got out of control and there needs to be some order to something so here we go. Aimee climbed into her Caprice and eased her way out, over the big yellow speed bumps, past the painted stop sign and out of the park. Once past the border lined wind screen trees you could make out the far road just past the Amoca gas station, the car was white with navy blue interior; the fabric that lined the ceiling had begun to fall as the cigarette smoke dissolved the adhesive used in the factory to attach it. Aimee tried her best to use the rear view mirror to smooth out her blush and concealer as she drove toward the sun on her way to work. Aimee had to deal with the pounding headache of a hangover from the night before, there was a warm half of a mountain dew in the console that would have to do to help rehydrate her throat, maybe the caffeine would also help quell the pounding head of hers as she turned right towards the city limits, and to work.

The Friday didn't offer any change to the monotony of her life but the next day's party was often a good way to blow off steam and get pissed in the fire drunk. As Aimee continued to look in the rear view she still tried to compare how she remembers looking in her teens to how worn and aged she looked now, deep crow's feet, specks of graying hair at her scalp, her teeth stained from smoking and drinking coffee, her body tired easily as well. Aimee remembered being a cheerleader and having the ability to cheer on the team for hours with her girlfriends before going out to an after game party for the rest of the night, now she gets winded just trying to get dressed.

Aimee was a sophomore when Tod was arrested at school for steroids, he was tall and muscular and all the girls of her grade were willing to spread their honeypots for him, he had a wiry chin patch and strawberry blond hair that coupled with a cocky grin and broad shoulders from playing football. Aimee isn't sure why she let him stay over the first night six years ago when they crossed paths at the bar, she should have kept her head down and focused on her daughter, instead she thought back to how gorgeous he was in high school and maybe this was the chance to hook up with him: it was. Tod spent almost two years in jail for his distribution and needle use with other jocks in high school, after he got out of jail he was sent out of state to some work furlough program that was to remove him from any contacts or temptations, he ended up in New Mexico for three years before finally making his way back. Aimee wasn't sure she was still as sexually attracted to Tod when they re-met, he had acquired many tattoos, had lost a front tooth and taken on a really weather-worn look to him but he still had the cocky smile and she kind of assumed her snatch still craved a shot at him at least once for old times' sake. They were in their later twenties when Tod and Aimee hooked up, Brittini was six or seven and now had to deal with the notion of sharing her

19

mother with this gruff roofer and she was less than amused. Aimee looked into her own light brown eyes as she glanced at the view behind her as she drove, she often wondered how she got to such a place in life, it was hard to pin point that one moment where the shit slid off the shingle and landed on her life.

Everyone has small moments, those slight inching's from the universe, or fate, or whatever you want to call it, they are those small moments that may seem minuscule but create a cosmic shift in one's universe. Aimee thought she had a good thing going with Roger, he was smart and hardworking, his ethics were appealing and she was taken over with love for him. Aimee and Roger seemed to start strong and with lust as their glue, they felt invincible to the warnings they had received. Aimee had felt strange one morning after a long sorted night of illicit bedroom activities, she hadn't seemed to bounce back like she had been expecting and thought nothing of it at first. Women know that if you're running late for your monthly that you can sometimes trick yourself, take a stick test and once it comes back not pregnant then your period is only hours behind, except this time it wasn't negative. Aimee told Roger about the sudden surprise, he insisted she try one more test to be certain as he began to sweat, she headed to the pharmacy and when she returned, he had fled. Aimee was distraught when she returned to only find a scribbled apology on a used envelope, it was hard to believe and she turned to Don. Don had only gotten a voice-mail from his brother that simply said that he couldn't do it and was "out like a pocket of one's at a strip club."

Don was ashamed of what Roger had done; he felt a sense of duty to help care for the family bloodline, even if he hadn't propagated it himself. Aimee spent her pregnancy alone, before her belly grew she had gotten her cravings for men satisfied with a few one night stands, it was after her daughter had come forth from her that she learned that she was the only one in the world that could get her to where she could ever want to be in life, or whom she could ever want to become.

The history of the park is as sorted as its' residents, one of the longer residents is a heavier set middle aged woman named Gelica Ewts. Gelica was once married to a trucker whom she almost bled dry by the time he realized she had plundered most of what he had made during the long hauls, she provided well for their children but she also ate very well, always had to have a new car and show off wealth to her friends. Gelica's husband was partial owner in a development company that had leveled the land and begun to lay down the cement slabs to start parking trailers on. Gelica splurged on food and gambling while she often left her older daughter watch over the other kids while was out doing things to validate her life. During the divorce the development company was sold for extremely cheap to the other partner so the judge wouldn't garnish the sales amounts to split with Gelica, whom hadn't lifted a finger to assist in providing for the household. Gelica ended up with the trailer she resided in and enough of a retirement to pay most of her bills while slipping further into section 8.

Gelica's trailer was next to Karen's and the old hag and she were civil to one another. Gelica hardly ever wore anything but a flowered Mumu, her wide hips often got stuck in the chair on the front porch. Karen sometimes shot a sly eye towards Gelica, whom was rather tifflee in regards to the lives of others, nosy. Gelicas' ex-husband James improved his life significantly once he dropped the several hundred pound Gelica; she was an anchor around his neck in marriage and undermined his hard work for her own personal gain. James had gotten free and after some slow progress, he got back to putting his children first and flourished once he was away from Gelica.

Two years ago Aimee had slowed her Caprice down in front of Gelicas lot to ease over the large speed bump, Gelica had gotten some notion that there was an issue, as if Aimee was mocking Gelica's trailer, of all things. Gelica hadn't taken her time struggling down her six steps to level ground on her aching feet before she began yelling and throwing her porcelain garden gnomes at the car. Aimee didn't even realize what was going on until the third gnome actually made contact with the vehicle because she was blasting "Paulina Jayne," a new country music star Brittini introduced her to. As the fourth gnome shattered against the hood, Aimee was clambering out of the driver side door and barreling towards the older hunched lady in a Mumu As the two hefty broads clashed, Gelicas curlers had begun to untangle from her brown hair as Aimee swung to assault the gnome chucker. After a brief minute bout, each woman knelt winded on the ground, huffing and puffing and praying for enough breath to live another day. Gelica had a much harder time rising to her feet than Aimee, whom was running late for her work and worried about having to conceal the beginnings of a black eye from her work. Gelica often laid low while perched on her wooden stoop, hardly minding her own business but hardly in the way at the same time.

Two lots down from Gelica is another "Section 8" resident, Carsey and her son Brodan. Carsey is in her younger twenties and is bipolar as all hell. Brittini often babysits for Carsey and watches Brodan, Carsey rarely has a social life but once in a while she'll turn a trick or two to make quick cash, she has three or four regulars, about one a week or so and when it's intimate time, Brittini gets a text. Once a month on top of everything Carsey sometimes forgets her Lithium and after two days of non-medicated Carsey, Brodan was once in a while found wandering the playground which was across the street. Carsey is biracial; you can always tell what kind of a day she is having by looking at her hair, or Brodan. Brodan is probably seventeen months or so by now, he shouldn't still be in diapers but if the diaper is clean, so is she. When Carsey is on her meds her hair is often combed in some various pattern or design, when her hair is frizzled and disheveled, you need to stand a step or two back as she is a hard crazy to anticipate.

The last time Carsey went without her meds, Brittini ended up watching Brodan for almost a week, a week in which Brittini missed school because the child needed some sort of guidance and care, it doesn't help that in the middle of the bender, Carsey showed up banging on Aimee's door at four in the morning looking to see if Brittini stole her son and she was willing to physically fight the young teen to get him back. Tod came storming to the door, pecker waving as he was up to who knows what when he confronted the raging woman, if Carsey had been any more with it she might have remembered who slapped her and how she ended up face planting into the ground. It was two days later when Carsey was released from a mandatory forty-eight hour hold after she was picked up by the cops wandering topless shortly after being slapped.

The morning after Tod got to slap the random bitch on his porch was a rough morning for Aimee, Tod decided to keep the party going after Carsey left and once he boozed up in the wee morning, he was feeling aggressive and decided to keep the party going with Aimee, she awoke to a rough beginnings to her day. Tod lost one job in order to take on a whiskey fueled day session of slapping around Aimee. The day Tod spent slapping around Aimee to get his rocks off was a particularly rough one for Brittini; she was maybe twelve at the time and had to leave her home in undies and a t-shirt to Don and Shelley's next door while it was low teen temps outside.

So if you take inventory of the lives that live in skirted mobile homes, you'll probably soil some Depends when you look at the whole collage of goings on. Darryl lives with his mom Annabel. Annabel was a biker in her teens, she hung out with a group known as the *Lucifer Squadron*, and it was mostly guys whom had spent time in various military branches then rebelled against society and the government when they formed. The Lucifer squad ran Ecstasy and methamphetamines from Florida through the Ohio river valley, they were over a thousand members strong through the end of the nineties until in 2003 the DEA and ICE conjoined to royally corn-hole the group of bikers, there were over eight-hundred arrests and convictions over the following five years as trials came and went.

Annabel was lucky enough to avoid being named despite having transported several baggies of "product" in various places within her body and so forth. Darryl never left the Heights, he was raised through the nineties by drunken grandparents and learned various trades from some of the older boys around the neighborhood, as a young teen he was responsible for picking out the blue crystals from that cat litter to help make crystal meth with. Annabel looks and sounds like a 3 pack a day smoker, whom grew up in a basement dive bar or some mess like that. Annabel is some night worker at some recycling factory in the next town over, she's hardly around but Darryl is twenty and hardly pays no never mind anyways. Annabel is often gone for weeks on end, she often resides with various men she meets but occasionally shows up at home, Darryl is the one in charge of his trailer but her room is always there for her.

The little beaner or "Lil B" is now that cat litter picker that Darryl was, Lil B was scouted several times hauling bags of kitty litter out of the Amoca station, Gary the attendant stocks and supplies every needed item to produce meth, he adheres to the regulations of combinations in that he can't sell certain combinations by law to one person, but if you get a twelve or thirteen year old to purchase match books and cat tidy, or hydrogen peroxide, each simply harmless household items, but also each a small ingredient in the shady manufacturing of methamphetamines. Lil B was pretty slick when it came to what he was doing, he was stopped and searched a few times for tagging random buildings in town, Newports in his pockets and white residue near his fingertips as he worked, there was no denying, but also no proving what the kid was up to. Last spring there was a weekend party at Darryl's lot, it was still cold out as spring had barely begun to thaw the ground and the trees started to bud. The party was small as Darryl sometimes cuts batches with random chemicals or pills that he scores in trade, this specific batch was cut with some cancer fighting pills Curtiss swiped from his ailing grandfather, and the handful of pills were ground up and added to the concoction in his wood paneled single wide. Don't let the irony stop on a drug making kid that wears a gold chain with a crucifix but swears like his imprisoned family members over in Chino.

The party that happened the first weekend in April was a small but kicking ordeal. Dez'rae and Tammi often rolled to all parties in the neighborhood, they have a weird friendship, Tammi always tries to retain her popularity by proximity to the taller much more slender Dez'rae, yet when she gets any chance to get naked and distasteful with anyone before Dez'rae does in order to retain superiority, she takes it. Last year at the Halloween party there was some Ecstasy passed out to anyone that braved the cold air to stand near the burn barrel and drink down some igloo cooler brewed jungle juice. The care-bear Ecstasy was laced with some medical grade *Suchs* something or another, supposedly it's a type of paralytic, as the hours counted down and the flames blurred into the night, so did the senses of each partier. Theresa is a schoolmate of Tammi and Dez'rae, Theresa is a healthy built girl, a bit of a tomboy whom played basketball in school with Tammi last year. At the party Theresa sucked off Darryl for providing her with the jaded ecstasy, the care-bear drug was a small white pill with a portly blue bear on one side.

24

As Theresa followed Darryl to the side of the lot and pulled her shirt and bra up over her tits for him, he dropped his sagging FUBU jeans to expose himself to her. He blamed the cold but she couldn't help but laugh at his less than ideal pecker size, enraging him and giving him cause to punch the distracted girl in the face, quickly rendering her unconscious.

Due to the medical lacing on the drug, there wasn't an easy trace as to why Theresa didn't remember much, at least with GHB and Rohypnol, both date rape drugs, they are traceable when it comes to blood testing, with medical grade paralytics, even in small amounts, there was no test for it and it numbed the senses. Curtiss had a cousin that caught and kept a couple of Copperhead snakes both as pets as well as to milk them for their venom. Tyrone wasn't a dumb kid, he was a broke kid and broke kids often became desperate, ingenious kids. Tyrone mixed the acquired venom with potent and high proof alcohol, let it sit and then sold it to his peers in school a little further south. Tyrone was a bigger success once he began to peddle his patented tincture, than he was at being an all-state wrestler and with much less effort. Tyrone was a self-taught chemist; the kid could recite chemical equations and formulas not to mention balance NASA type shit, even while blown out on some fuzzy smoke. Tyrone had a father in jail and a mother that worked two jobs, he was mildly bitter to say the least but he took to the socially accepted means of causing trouble for a black kid, it was easier than being heckled by other boys for being smart.

Tyrone failed at his attempts to make good grades and become anything with his life, he let his homeboy pals further encourage his pot use and he didn't even bother to graduate high school. Tyrone had street smarts, he figured out how much of the venom needed to be mixed with how much alcohol, since next to pure alcohol denatures the toxins and changes it enough over time to make it a wild drink, one shot is cheaper and longer lasting than bath salts, and less chance of the brain damage from the use. Once your body goes numb and you only feel like a pair of wandering eyeballs to roam the cosmos, or the female genitalia that you are trying to impress, you can't feel your legs, you can't work your arms, and since your tongue is the first to go numb, your teeth buzz around the rigid taste buds in your face hole, all you can do is slur and listen to the "woohwha hooaaahhh" of your heartbeat and pulsing near your ears, kids love it. Tyrone was playing amateur gynecologist with some little tart and took a strong shot of "Zebra Milk" (what he called is venom and 180 proof mixture) with her when he wanted one more shot as he and his date watched the poisonous snakes slither their cold coarse bodies along one another in their enclosure, the date wanted to pet one of the long cold blooded wetland creatures. Tyrone poured his shot then opened the terrarium without enough care to prevent getting his hand bit.

Tyrone hoped to drink a few more straight shots of his white lightning to offset the toxins coursing through his veins within seconds of being bit. Panic set in but the vision he had on the tight cooch of his date was a higher priority as the Zebra Milk set in. Tyrone passed out face deep in the teen when his heart seized up a few minutes later. Curtiss didn't make it to the funeral but his aunt Cherice was inconsolable, everyone dressed in their best velour jumpsuits, the pastel colors probably looked like the Easter bunny had the shits all over a bunch of chocolate chips. Tyrone must have had something right, he made batch after batch of his bedroom snake wine, he often had five five-gallon buckets fermenting at a time, one for each week of each month as each bucket had to sit for six months, he kept a few breeding mice to feed the snakes and his chemical diligence and due care when handling the serpents was paying off for him. Tyrone enjoyed the ease that pot brought him, he hated the pressure that being black brought, he hated that he was expected to just be another hood nigger, older kids wanted him to just be a thug like they were, he hated the notion of just being another rapper wannabe with no future or skills, he had an IQ that could have carried him through M.I.T, instead he was force fed the black culture, it was hard to swallow, like broken glass.

Curtiss didn't learn anything from Tyrone, he always made excuses anyways, Curtiss assumed that Tyrone got caught up cause he wasn't gangster enough to get away with his dealings, stuff that Curtiss was too smooth to do. The night of the Halloween party Curtiss was laying his lines down to get into the torn and well-worn panties of Tammi, it didn't matter that it was cliché to get himself a white girl, even a thicker girl like her that had some jiggle around the middle, he wanted to get a nut off. So Curtiss propositioned the rather wasted Tammi, they ducked behind lot seventy-nine, and half lazily removed articles of clothing from each other, Curtiss was clumsy as he pulled and tugged down the pants and undies off of Tammi, their bodies steamed in the cold air, she enticing herself to prep her parts for his entry as he continued to fall and stumble over his own dropped trousers. The session was over within minutes, the drug had made a minuteman out of Curtiss and he was too wasted to bother much else of any of it. Curtiss fought his best to crawl back around the north side of the lot and back towards the burn barrel in the middle of the street. As Curtiss crawled around the corner he found himself another half-naked topless white girl laying on the ground, with very little effort it didn't take much to put his half flaccid little weasel inside of the unconscious Theresa, she didn't say no and he was too wasted to pass up the chance to slither on top of another girl.

Tammi fell a couple of times as she pried and fought to pull her tight pants up over her still moist thighs, her inebriated state made the usual task of dressing absolutely uncoordinated, she fell forward to smack her face on the ribbed siding of the trailer she was pressed up against a few minutes before. Tammi reached down to run her hand through her snatch and wipe half of the wet goop out of her gash and wipe it on the grass as she bent over again reaching for her clothing. Tammi finally wrangled her clothes up and rounded the same corner shortly after Curtiss had shoved himself into the girl he happened upon, just Theresa passed out behind the pallet pile and Curtiss spasming on top.

Theresa had her pants yanked down around her knees, a purple hoodie with pink undershirt wedged up over her tits as she laid there partially atop the cement walkway leading to the wood stoop she braced herself up with. Tammi focused on the small Dorito chip shave job in the pubic hair of Theresa as she lay there, motionless under Curtiss, it seemed funny for some odd reason to Tammi, whom began to laugh with the drug addled coercion on her side. Tammi knelt down to shake and wake Theresa, shooing Curtiss away, she must have been cold with her naked ass riding the walkway, her belly and breasts shook in opposite rhythm of the shoulder Tammi pushed on her to try and wake her up. Even with a shoulder shake, a nipple flick and even Tammi spitting into the mouth of her friend to see if she was faking, there was no rousing Theresa.

Tammi enlisted Tod and Aimee to help carry Theresa inside, there was no recollection of events, just a swollen cheek with black eye, and grass clippings imprinted into her exposed backside. Aimee and Tod left Brittini to tend to Theresa after helping to maneuver her clothes back on so they could return to the gathering. A week after Thanksgiving Theresa found herself in a real tough situation; she had missed her period and really began to panic. Theresa had pretended Halloween didn't happen when they were all at school, there was no admitting to following Darryl around to the side of the trailer to suck him off, there was definitely no recall of Curtiss climbing into her either. Tammi wasn't positive enough of any of it so she didn't initiate a conversation and Theresa started to fret over unknown events and began to withdraw a bit over it all. The party spent a majority of its events hovering around the burn barrel; the drug addled gathering was naive to the non-consensual sex just a few yards away. The flames licked high into the night as the dried pine boards were pried from their braces of the pallets and fed into the old steel drum causing crackles and embers to rocket to the sky while warming the park residents that turned out. King Cobra and Mickey's Malt forty ounce bottles were often the cheapest way to get drunk for most of the partygoers; cases were often ordered straight from the Amoca and often brought in by the trunk load.

Down around the corner in lot one twenty-nine are a couple that have had several disturbances of their own. Angel Johnson was engaged to a man named Joey, they dated for almost five years before they decided on a wedding date, and once a date was settled, things within began to heat up and boil over. With one year to go before the wedding, Joey finally decided he looked better in her clothing than she did, she was convinced that they were to be wed and have children until he started going by the name "Lilly" and insisting that he walk their small Chihuahua in her pink hot pants and tube socks rolled up over his calves.

Half of the guys in the neighborhood spat slang of all sorts like "*fag*" and other adoring names like "Dr. Frankenfurt" to the man, er' woman. Big Ken loved to bench press his weights on his front porch, wedged into his wife beater tank and sit up to shout "*pussy faggot*" out at Lilly, despite the fact that he'd go inside and palm his python to pictures of Carmen Carriera on TV commercials. Jonny avoided his own father for such hostility in the home, Ken was an angry and violent man, when he was in prison he near beat a fellow inmate to death, except the man slipped into a coma from allegedly "falling over the railing" so there was no proof that Ken was behind the assault.

Lilly still kept his short crew haircut and had to buy triple-X size sweaters so the neck hung down off of one shoulder, Angel didn't understand it and was rather heartbroken over the situation. Angel's parents lived in Florida and hardly spoke with her, she partook in Fentanyl patches and cocaine to help cope with the mess that Joey caused when *HE* slowly became a *SHE*. Angel often had the hiccups as a result of the Fentanyl, she was an entertaining conversation when she found the nerve (or need for more coke) to leave him behind at home. Angel still held onto hope that Joey was just stressed, except that he was socking away money for the necessary steps for his gender reassignment, which meant that he couldn't afford to move out. The night before the Halloween party Joey had decided that he was going to the party as Lilly to prove to Big Ken and Tod that he wasn't ashamed of whom *she* was, which irritated Angel right before a hearty line of 80's disco powder. Angel was irritated with the hiccups as she tried to persuade Joey to just drop the whole spiel, which sent him into a tangent as well. The argument between Angel and Joey went from heated, to enraged, and then to throwing things, police were never far behind. By the time the police showed up there were torn ladies shirts, in two different sizes, and a thick glass ashtray that had rocketed through the front window. The police locked up Joey for the night for the domestic disturbance, giving her the night alone with her hiccups and a little shit dog named Trujillo.

With fifteen residents gathered around the burn barrel for the late evening Halloween gathering, Angel kept Trujillo nestled into her cleavage, the dog kept its' head popped out from the neck hole of her hoodie to watch the other people swig their beer and enjoy the chaotic buzz from the chemical concoction meant to replace their realities with altered delusions. Ken and Tod jostled ironies they couldn't wrap their heads around, such things like "*it's called sloppy seconds in the real world unless it's in Hollywood, then you just get the whale pregnant and name the kid after some business*" or "*how such ugly white trash hillbillies just get a little coin in their pockets and suddenly Pam Anders is sharing Hep C with you in a sloppy pile of groupies,*" things that didn't make sense in any part of the world, certainly not in their small corner either. The real world was way too depressing to handle sober all that often in the Heights, the power company made weekly rounds to reinforce that they were serious when shut off notices were mailed out, anytime anyone won more

29

than a hundred bucks in a scratcher then the nice meal out was at Cracker Barrel or Shoney's and when premium liquor was purchased it was *Buffalo Trace*, not Mohawk or *Five O'clock*. The cheapest drunk was one that could be acquired on a daily bases rather than weekly for special occasions, it is the way of life and there was no other way to cope with the way things are.

Standing around the burn barrel with stacks of pallets piled up on the curb was a *Heights* style family meeting that happened fairly regularly throughout the year. When Bridge cards refilled, some of the residents would pop for a case of hot dogs and all would stand around and grill and chatter up stories about the week. When Tyrone passed due to the accidental snake bite when he was preoccupied with the young girl on his bed and got himself bit, the topic of how much his Zebra Milk would be missed. Zebra milk was chemically sound and as long as the venom sat in the alcohol to denature and break down enough to become less fatal, it was one hell of a trip, it caused hallucinations similar to Peyote according to Big Ken, the body buzz of Ecstasy and you didn't have to take Dramamine to ward off the spins like when you drink too much. Tod missed the Zebra Milk; he would binge for weeks at a time in one various stupor inducing drug or another.

Two summers ago Tuner, a co-shingler of Tod's, decided he was going to dip into some recently acquired Meth for a quick gutter job. The four guys sat around the humid rainy summer living room and partied like eighties rockers while Aimee ran back and forth making sandwiches for the crew with a fortunate day off and her twelve year old daughter doing extra math study assignments in her bedroom. Tuner was a little wilder, he had no remorse about snickering at the small ass of the twelve year old girl that ducked out of sight whenever he came around, and he also passed crude comments towards Aimee and her ample cleavage that he lusted after. Once the crew was zooted out of their minds on meth cut with who knows what as it changed hands from some greasy Mexican, up through Texas on a non-English speaker and through any assorted route and finally to the aluminum sided trailers that made up the Heights. Each time Tod got ahold of cocaine it was always a crap shoot to what it was cut with, a few months prior Karl landed himself in the hospital with heart damage when he took an eight-ball to the schnoz that was cut with some industrial cleaning powder, but this time he trusted his good time high to his coworker Tuner.

After the meth had gone and the men fell into lethargy with the anxious giggles of energy, the notion came up that the men were rife with energy and angst when Aimee made the mistake of crossing the living room again after she left Brittini's room, the men were feeling horny and none of them felt like going out to do anything about it. One meager suggestion that started out as a joke with very little substance fueled into an out of control situation for Aimee. Tod found it arousing that his boys wanted a part of what he called his; so with the meth riddling through his veins he jumped on the bandwagon and "encouraged" Aimee to participate, against her will. Aimee tried to refuse the suggestions to blow Karl; first, he was more than willing to let her go down on him and quickly lost his temper when Aimee tried to brush off the harsh advances and physical coercion as he pulled her shoulders towards him. Tod grew impatient when Aimee continued to make him look like an ass when she refused, the first slap convinced her to take the crew in to her mouth one at a time, Tuner found it hilarious that her tears added to the lubrication when he was getting his turn, his hand was fisted full of her hair as he thrust into her throat, despite her gagging and running mascara, he was utterly amused

Billy was much rougher when he had his turn, he pawed and groped at her as she unsuccessfully tried to shut out what was happening to her over the arm of the chair, he pulled at her and left many bruises for her to find a few days later. Tod grew angry as Aimee first made him look like an asshole that didn't have control over his girlfriend, he then grew even more frustrated when she was already tired, had swollen lips and had been crying when it was his turn, he tried to take her right there in the living room to show off his control in front of his friends, to prove he was the alpha male. Aimee tried to fight off his advances as he pulled and tugged at her clothing as he wasn't going to take no for an answer, he wanted to have sex. Aimee fought Tod off pretty well at first, her concerns were for more than just her pride, her concern was about her daughter down the hall that was probably hearing all of the foulness that was going on, which made her cry even harder. Aimee fought and struggled, she cried out for him to stop and to just leave, he kept grabbing at her wrists to

31

prevent her from slapping him, and his men laughed at the skirmish and encouraged Tod not to lose his upper hand.

Tod finally had enough when Aimee continued to fight him off and keep some of her clothes on in front of Tod's crew. Tod managed to rip half of her top down and as she tried to corral herself for some small sort of self-respect. Tod finally lost his temper and swung a hard as he could, his meth increased rage connected with her jaw, fracturing it. Aimee woke up on the floor gargling her own blood as Brittini knelt near trying to shake her awake while frantically crying and freaking out that her mother was half undressed and passed out on the living room floor.

Aimee was near delirious as she couldn't figure out why her head felt like it was trying to explode and her eye felt like it was going to fall out from being slapped. Brittini helped her mother get dressed and then to the car for a trip to the emergency room. The emergency room nurse Gloria knew the truth just by seeing the hand print on Aimee's cheek before she even mumbled out the tale of tripping and hitting the table with her jaw on the way to the floor, Gloria had seen enough to see right through it. Gloria was a knowledgeable nurse with a long history of dealing with spouse abuse, domestic violence victims and woman making excuses to put up with the assaults. Aimee convinced herself that Tod had only been riled up because of the drugs and pack mentality in the midst of his crew and having to show off his manliness and virility.

Aimee spent almost eight weeks with her jaw wired shut, Tod didn't even come back home after he left until after three days on a party bender with his crew, secretly Aimee hoped that he had died and maybe he would be found in some gutter and maybe she would just get a call to identify his scraggily tattooed carcass. Aimee came home from work to find Tod rifling through the fridge when she stood in the living room and waited for him to look up and lock into eye contact. When Tod looked up there was no recollection of what had happened, he saw her swollen face and had the balls to ask her what happened. Aimee broke into tears all over again because not only did he not show up after her night and day in the hospital, but he was the bastard that had caused the injury to begin with. Tod hardly made any emotion that he felt sorry for what had happened, he did help to blend smoothies and shakes for her but he didn't even try to bother to make amends to Brittini, whom didn't begin talking to him until after the summer was over and she was back in school, and only out of necessity.

Brittini knew her mother was afraid of Tod, it was obvious each time she flinched when Tod made the smallest sudden move, but she knew more than anything her mother was much more afraid of being alone, or even dead if she tried to kick him out. Aimee didn't know what she was getting into when she agreed to meet up with the kid that once had a Jerry curl back in high school and that she once had a crush on. The first few months Tod and Aimee were seeing each other, he was charming and desperate for a place to stay so he stayed the nights almost from the get-go. Aimee was hard up for a second income and that in conjunction with being lonely raising Brittini for the first eight years and was tired of doing everything on her own. Aimee had put herself through school to become a medical assistant and when there was no life changing benefit to all of her hard work in school, she had to remain in the Heights next to Don and Shelley, whom helped endlessly with Brittini. Aimee was grateful for all of the help and companionship of her neighbors. Don was a rather stand-up guy despite that his brother bailed on Aimee and had never resurfaced, Aimee was grateful and Shelly was a decent friend, except that neither of them had any tolerance for Tod.

Tod did work fairly hard when he had work, he spent his days in the hot sun hauling bundled shingles up and down ladders, he spent winters on a crew shoveling and busting his ass in the cold or doing anything he could for money. Tod spent time in community jail and missed the last bit of high school; he was injecting other jocks with 'roids' so he could be the big winner of his football team. When he was caught, he didn't bother to spend his time learning to read or even polishing off a G.E.D, or "*Good Enough Diploma*" he just remained a loser. Tod spent his probation out of the state; he just lived in a half-way house and painted street curbs for the city to "repay society." Most of the *Heights* residents had some form of history with the law; they all seem to congregate to lower income places such as the village. With the Amoca station so close it wasn't uncommon to find some of the up and coming delinquents trying to snag hubcaps from cars parked out front or Gary calling the police on someone trying to walk out with a *forty* tucked into their pants, unless the girls flash enough skin to persuade him to just give it away.

Dez'rae gave Gary one blow job a few weeks before the end of this school year; he often licked his teeth at her and sneered while making it more than obvious he was staring at her body when she wandered around the store. Gary was always ready to pop a chubby whenever any form of split tail wandered in. Dez'rae was smart enough to realize the power her athletic body held when it came to boys at school, plenty of them bought lunch or brought her snacks. Dez'rae would often squeeze her shoulders together to pop her cleavage towards the top of her tank tops and sports bras when she was out buying Newports underage, Tammi did the same thing, and she was heavier set so she had more cleavage to work with. Dez'rae was at the gas station almost every day and it was just easier to go along to get along when it came to the acne ridden curly black haired weasel. She mentioned in passing that she liked well bathed men and that he would be more attractive with some mousse and cologne, she preemptively suggested the shower ritual so she wouldn't risk dealing with nasty nuts when she did him the favor. Gary was reeling that the younger girl Dez'rae even mentioned the idea; she struck the bargain that once was it and that she could forever buy whatever she wanted without any problems, she secured herself safe passage to make her purchases.

Dez'rae wasn't the type to just go down on anyone out of boredom, that was Tammi, but she calculated the benefits of a one-time charitable act and it seemed like a small sacrifice. Gary kept his small store well stocked, there were plenty of shelves crammed together to make money off of anything he could, counters crammed with gadgets and everything you'd find that you might need, he also kept on hand plenty of household supplies to provide for the *Heights*. Gary kept plenty of cigarettes, booze, rolling papers and those little glass vials that would second as a glass pipe, he also kept a small supply of "bath salts" and other synthetic drugs that were gaining popularity. Booze was the biggest commodity behind fuel for Gary, he was aware of his proximity to the trailer park and to the city so he went through many deliveries a week to keep the coolers stocked, it was also common to see many of the same kids from the Heights, so there was very little concern for undercover narcs or the police trying to bust him for selling to minors.

Gary knew that the boys would easily purchase for the girls so he was much more reluctant to sell to underage boys, he was much faster to let his guard down for a young girl that was willing to linger while bent over for him to peer down her shirt, or even be a little more forward to show him something of interest. Gary knew how to manipulate many of the customers that were already tiptoeing on trouble by buying beer or cigarettes so he propagated the risk by creating the idea that they'd have to be willing to do "something to prove they weren't out to get him in trouble too."

Gary lived in his moms basement, he had no ambition to do anything other than run a shitty gas station trying to sleep with any girl that tried to buy alcohol or smokes underage from him, he looked like an overweight Jerry Seinfeld, except he didn't have that voice that would make you want to beat puppies to death with a lead pipe, that nasal draining noise when speaking. During the summer Gary often sat hunched behind the counter and played video games on the security camera monitor, sweating through his shirts and packing his cheeks with Slim Jims and Combos. The Amoca was the central hub for a majority of the groceries and supplies for the trailer park, smokes and snacks not to mention all the alcohol that could be ordered and brought in on a daily delivery. Tammi and Dez'rae were often buying Boons Farm; it was a trailer park piss wine that the rookie drinkers were akin to, long before they could tolerate real booze to delude themselves with. The park was not a place for success and with each new member born or moved in, there was often the need for police presence except that if officers showed up after dark they end up with a destroyed cruiser and a long walk back to the department to figure out what happened. There was always hustle and bustle, Curtiss wasn't nearly half as intelligent as Tyrone, say what you want about the drop out black kid a city over but Tyrone balanced the chemicals to make sure that nothing was poisoned or at least poison enough to kill anyone getting wrecked on his homemade Zebra Milk.

Zebra Milk started out a potent tincture, one shot instantly numbed your lips and teeth, once your tongue touched it, it was an instant anesthetic. The body buzz was slow once the first shot of Zebra Milk soaked into the bloodstream, your skin came to life with goose bumps and all of your body hairs stood on end. One shot of Zebra Milk was a good mixture to begin your night with, the buzz kept low key if you nursed more drinks, but a second shot of the Milk further made your skin numb and some of your fingertips followed suit. Two shots of booze weren't enough to get you plastered but three through five took you to another world. Your brain began seeing light shows, your ears droned out sharp noises but a humming accompanied other unworldly sounds and the lights and sounds danced in your brain. Shot four and five were the party shots, your heart seemed to climb a hill and then jumped off with each beat, your adrenaline made your entire chest swell with each heart beat and the down surge of blood gave you a cooling rush that was borderline orgasmic. Drinking the Zebra Milk was a must for anyone who hasn't felt it, it was unlike any other drug out there but it also depended on the social events going on around it. Drinking the Milk at a party enhanced the party over one million times, drinking it while silently sitting in the grass watching the stars overhead, was philosophical enough to change your grasp on life.

Curtiss heard from Tyrone fairly regularly and was jealous that he was pedaling his booze, he was jealous that he was even able to figure it all out, not to mention being a brother that wasn't scared to death of snakes. Tyrone even built a large terrarium for a few snakes in his room so he could milk them often and have much better control over the entire process. Tyrone mixed his venom, he handled the reptiles carefully and was very successful with his mixture, and it gave consumers a whole new wild high that you couldn't really replicate along with the body numbing joys of a medical anesthetic. Curtiss was a low level scumbag, he pinched pot here and there to sock away on the side to sell an extra baggie to the kids at school; he was a tall athletic kid at school and was able to pedal small amounts of "*Pharmaceuticals*" to kids for spare money. Curtiss played himself up as a baller among all the white kids while flossing his Shinola watch and squeaky white sneakers as he sauntered up and down the hallways.

When Tyrone passed away there was hardly one small poke in his right hand near the snuff box. The coroner first assumed that the wiry kid passed away from heart conditions possibly acquired from years of drug abuse. The terrarium was filled with murky water, composting leaves and a dim heat light, the officers inspecting the scene of death were oblivious to the poisonous snakes that lurked within. Tyrone's mother had a neighbor drop the pets off to a local swamp and no one was the wiser what was going on. The room was Tyrone's final resting place, the girl loaded up the few gallons of zebra milk hidden in his closet before she bailed after she thought he had just passed out. Once the coroner's report was finally released on Tyrone and his cause of death any and all evidence of the small brewery and reptiles had been cleared out, luckily the master chemist who also was the only person with the right balance of hooch and venom to ensure whirly lights and buzzing noises resonating within the ears of the drinker as they mentally fled from reality.

Zebra milk was on the verge of becoming the largest drug to hit the market since meth, easy to make, quick to take effect and much less dangerous than having a potential bomb sitting around the house waiting for all of the rocks to bubble out, with the exception of having to catch a rattle snake and milk the little bastards without getting snagged by a fang. The Feds were decent at keeping certain items of the meth production list so those whom purchase certain combinations would alert authorities and risk bringing in drug enforcers and what not, when Tyrone began experimenting with his Zebra Milk he would test the first few batches on the neighbors Rottweiler, waiting to make sure the venom was broken down enough to prevent cardiac arrest. When Tyrone tested out the milk for the first time he was nervous but it was cut enough with high volume alcohol that it took a several shots before the venom even kicked in, so the mixture was tweaked and worked till it was just enough to send the brain riding the solar flares through the universe and beyond, all while leaving a clean feeling morning and no scary anxiety.

Curtiss felt fairly solo in the Heights, he hung out with Darryl often and the two of them just palled around and smoked dope or drank away mornings. Curtis and Darryl both avoided walking near Karen's lot as she was a sore excuse for a vagina and a wretched evil harpy, she knew they were trouble and for that she was right, but she was on the phone with the cops more than a police dispatcher. Karen and Gelica were neighbors so they naturally confided in each other, Gelica hardly had reason to leave her comfy Mumu, which looked like a flowered shower curtain with a head hole in the middle and her curler filled head popping out. Gelica filled her flower bed with gaudy knickknacks and porcelain critters, Karen despised the woman, as did most people who met her. Curtiss and Darryl referred to Gelica simply as "section 8" because she was unbalanced and would often shout at the bushes.

Gelica would always brag about her lavish lifestyle, or at least the life she used to have when she was married and had a husband, now her own kids won't even visit her. When Gelica finally took her curlers out it was "to go to the beach" which was a weekly occurrence, which entailed that she would hobble across the road and stick her crusty feet into the sand of the playground and continue to talk to herself, unless she was hurling garden gnomes at Aimee's caprice and starting fights with people that didn't even know they were in the fights anyways. Gelica was white trash and it exuded from her, low class and too ignorant to know anyways, her fake bragging about trips to Jamaica or feasting it up in Germany while she kept herself obese on sausage and kraut. Gelica kicked around the sand and didn't give much mind to the mounds of cat turds; she was delusional enough to actually believe she was in Jamaica.

Karen hardly saw her daughter or grandkids, she was that noxious of a person and her few friends were of the same low caliber, they all belonged in the Heights and it was shamefully obvious, and as a matter of speaking, Karen being the self-appointed leader of the trailer park was almost destined. Gelica was ditched into her ex-husbands' trailer park ironically, the loony chick was too preoccupied with spoiling herself in his money and bragging to her fake friends to notice that he was noticing her spending the money that he was making to keep up her lifestyle. Gelica thought she was cruising as she bought her kids new cars to keep them loving her, she got a face lift despite being over a hundred pounds overweight, kind of like changing the tires on the single wide when the siding was warped and mossy.

During the Halloween party last year Gelica complained vehemently about the noise booming from the speakers the next street over, she raised her hands and shook her arm skin without the ability to comprehend that her voice wouldn't carry over Ton Loc coming through the woofers. DJ Wriggle often played the tunes for the parties, he came over to hang with Darryl and see who he can sleep with as he searched through his mp3 player and through most upbeat jams to get the girls shaking their asses, which also pleased the guys. Wriggle didn't mind watching Dez, Tammi, and Theresa all jiggle it up and writhe on each other, Aimee would sometimes get enough to drink to neglect the notion that she might have to return home to Tod and his tattooed drug addled body, not to mention his abusive and aggressive nature. At the Halloween fire Joey, "aka Lilly" spent the night in a holding cell, Angel Johnson spent her time swaying to assorted tunes with her small yappy dog nestled in the cleavage of her hoodie, ice cold *40* in hand and doing her best to hold onto the delusion that he ex-fiancé wasn't becoming a woman, her body disliked the Fentanyl patches she was wearing to cope with depression, they caused hiccups, which gave others fodder to laugh about while she grew more frustrated with her situation.

Curtiss brought some residual Zebra Milk to pass around the party; Theresa took a few heavy swigs of the bottle before passing it around. Aimee, Tod, Big Ken, Jonny, Darryl and all of the others that stood around dropping Darryl's Ecstasy and sending the remainder of the evening into the blur of oblivion. Tod and Ken usually spoke about their stints in prison, neither ever mentioned having to shower with dozens of other guys, which everyone knows happens in prison, but Tod and Ken stood tall and tatted and tried to play up how tough they were because of prison instead of how they were really just the states' bitches. Darryl had several bouts of probation so he thought that made him tough, Tod and Ken just looked at the short stocky kid with freckles and short hair matted down onto his head, and they knew that in jail he would have been the catcher and they would laugh it off. Jonny would often stand around near Brittini at the gatherings, Ken wouldn't let Jonny drink and if there was to be any partaking in drugs it would have to be without his father seeing it or else it would result in a beating.

During the Halloween party Jonny and Brittini hid out in Aimee's caprice, the windows were dark tinted and gave them a hideout from the rest of the prying eyes of the partiers. The night boomed on, some of the younger kids sat around and filled up on gas station candy bought by their parents, no one trusted their neighbors enough to accept candy from them anyways. As the music carried on into the background, Jonny and Brittini spoke and consoled each other, they grew up near each other, just a few lots apart, and had several classes together at school. Brittini couldn't figure out why she didn't have any other friends but he was also quiet and both of them felt comfortable enough to be shy together. The Caprice was the their clubhouse and they could hide, it was also were she let Jonny sleep most nights when he had to stay away from Big Ken, Jonny was good about

39

ducking out before Aimee had to head out for work and make sure he didn't leave any proof that he was even there.

Brittini was physically budding and as most young teens are, curious about the opposite sex. While everyone was milling around a half rusted burn barrel staying warm, Brittini was asking question to Jonny, whom she could trust, what it was like to deal with erections, how weird it must have been to have a *"package"* there, they exchanged weird bodily questions that they wouldn't dare ask anyone at school or have any ability to look up on the computer. Brittini shared her new breasts with Jonny and tried to get his opinion; he wasn't sure how he felt while there was still a sense of dread that he might get caught with a topless young girl and finally send Ken over the edge enough to get beat to death. Brittini was lonely, she was hardly a blip on her own mothers' radar, especially when Tod was around, he would pass comments about her *"mosquito bites"* and make each and every interaction between them more and more uncomfortable, she was good friends with Jonny and coming from the same upbringing, they had many common roots.

Brittini felt ever so uncomfortable exposing herself to Jonny but she also was curious and a bit warm blooded at the idea of a boy touching her, she grabbed his hand and coerced his touches, from everything she had heard she was expecting a more visceral response from his anatomy. Jonny groped and pawed at Brittini's chest, she wasn't exactly sure what she was doing but they were both ignorant to why her chest flushed with blood and her heart rate pulsed, she was feeling as if something inside of her was catching fire, maybe her womanhood perhaps. Jonny was deathly afraid of his father, his mother still had several years of her sentence in some slammer in some butthole Montana city, leaving Jonny under the supervision of Big Ken.

Brittini persuaded Jonny to remove his pants and let her see first person what all the girls all raved about. Jonny was extremely shy about what was going on but it was only fair to show her since she showed him. It was cold and Jonny finagled his pants down and fought his best to ignore the cold fabric on his small pale body, Brittini had seen pictures of boy parts and was really expecting a lot more than what he had to offer, he was flaccid and unimpressively shriveled, *"due to the cold"* according to him but she felt further let down by the fact she couldn't arouse him, yet any other boy wouldn't

40

be willing to turn their head towards her either. Brittini and Jonny hid out and quasi explored one another visually as the adults further drank away their lives. The kids often looked out for one another, Brittini had a crush on the blond haired boy when she was younger, he had freckled cheeks and kept his hair short and tank tops tight during the summers.

The St. Patrick's Day party was another rip roaring blast a few years back; everyone was swilling Mickey's and heehawing the afternoon away. Tod and Ken had come up with an idea to screw with Darryl because he had gotten pretty cocky with his community jail stint. Darryl had gotten a lightning bolt tattoo on his wrist, it looked like some crackhead with cerebral palsy had inked his wrist while having withdrawals, once he realized how ghetto the shaky tattoo looked, he then began hiding it under his Shinola watch and making sure he kept his pants pressed and hat bill flat. Darryl talked like he was black, his favorite idea was that if a company created "fried chicken flavored sex lube, niggas be eatin pussy all day long, no more sixty-eight and I'll owe you one." Darryl had an annoying "*yaww*" when he laughed and when he was high, he laughed a lot, which meant he was always laughing, and carrying on about his sex lube idea that could make him millions.

Darryl was raised by extended family while his bipolar biker mom roamed the country bouncing from one biker to another until Darryl became a teen, long after it was too late to attempt to parent. Darryl dropped out of high school, a common denominator among the *Heights* residents, he mostly hung out with Curtiss but also had a few other pals in and out of his mother's trailer, and she was hardly there anyways. Tod had taken a big money job in a bigger city; he and his crew needed the early spring that wrapped up in time to get back for the St. Patty's day party. While Tod was out of town and Brittini over at Don and Shelley's for an evening, Aimee was finding that she was lonely, and terrified of such.

Aimee had a hard time dealing with the loneliness of her life; she had only made one miserable decision after another, over and over again since she graduated high school and then got knocked up a few years later resulting in Brittini. Aimee wanted to find a way to better handle herself, she texted Darryl for some non-prescription "uppers" and he dragged his feet leaving his home. Darryl cut Aimee a deal in hopes of just "hanging out" to loosen her up and see what he could score from the lonely gal. Sure enough Aimee was easily persuaded to be comforted and consoled by the derelict wannabe thug. Darryl put on some booty bounce music and let Aimee enjoy her magic white pills to escape her reality.

Being the sole breadwinner and the only person to keep up the home, it was burdensome to have to make all of the decisions for the home, Tod pitched in some money here and there but often drank his money, he sometimes picked up some mediocre groceries so he had snacks or lunch items, if he was feeling sorry for being too rough with Aimee or just trying to butter her up he might grab takeout and not expect repayment from Aimee. Aimee let her drugs turn off her permanent anxiety, she began to cry wondering how her life had dribbled to such circumstances, she was forever overwhelmed and nowhere near what she imagined her life would be like by this point in her life. Drugs and alcohol were an easy escape from being herself, she hadn't been wooed, she hardly received any attention of note, she was eyed from half of the other women in the park and she hated being who she was. Darryl wasn't a knight in shining armor, not even a decent thug with a shiny chain but he was a warm body and close by at the time.

Darryl waited for some of the tears to dry up before he had the notion to move close to Aimee and rub on her hand, hoping to warm her up to his middle school advances. Aimee was quick to let the goofy looking kid run his hand up her shirt as he slobbered on her neck, she hated herself but that mental state hadn't changed since she was sixteen when her thighs out grew her chest and she was much more round than busty and her insecurities ruled her life. Darryl would sometimes palm his mother's lithium and convince some of the younger teens around the park that the tweaked head from the lithium was the high they were looking for. Darryl continued his advances onto the inebriated Aimee as she slouched to give Darryl more access to her body under her clothes. Aimee slunk down and let Darryl work her sweater up over her chest before he began to work down her pants next.

Aimee was self-conscious about her belly and tried to hide as best as she could as Darryl fumbled to kiss her stomach before moving further down on her. Darryl fronted that he had all the prowess in the world but other than having made it with a few young high teens that didn't know any better, he was as nervous as a virgin and just as clueless. After a few minutes of slobbering between

Aimee's dimpled thighs Darryl assumed he was still in the running to have sex, he worked himself out of his jeans, which were already half way to the ground anyways. Darryl wrangled his unimpressive self out of his name brand boxers and rubbed himself against her, she was *pie eyed* drunk and whirling the skies with her drugs, she couldn't function enough to bother saying no or making sure he even hardened up before heaving on top of her for both short winded minutes. Darryl had the foresight to pullout and finish on her bare stomach, he didn't even bother to offer a washcloth or to even dress her; instead he pulled himself together after he got his nut on and let himself out. Darryl strutted down the sidewalks towards his own trailer and kept an eye out for Dez'rae, hoping she was out and would let him climb onto her much more firm and ideally younger body.

If Tod had found out that Darryl screwed Aimee they both would have been the recipients of a prison shower welcome, and probably with a lot less than water for lube. Aimee woke up the next morning; she had rolled onto the floor while her pants still remained around her ankles and her bra half undone with her tit hanging out. Aimee rubbed her thighs a bit to get the carpet impressions to go away as well as return some circulation to her cold blue legs. Aimee started her coffee maker and then the shower, she had a stomach covered with crusted man sauce, and within that man sauce were carpet fibers and assorted cigarette ash from the floor.

Darryl never boasted about his conquest, only that there were many and that the younger boys should worship him for being a sex god among them. Lil B was always glad to run errands to pick up supplies for Darryl to mix his two liter bottle meth labs, Lil B was always trying to sneak a peek at Brittini changing in her room from outside or up-skirt any of the girls at school, when he went. Darryl was Lil B's idol, Darryl was always spouting out the necessary skills and requirements to being a hardcore thug in the neighborhood, how to be a real gangster at school and how to pull girls left and right to be a real pimp. Lil B ate up each and every word that Darryl doled out, even carried a rusted kitchen knife to try and act big around his mentor.

Aimee stared at her reflection in the mirror, her eyes were puffy, her belly button had a crusty cork of dried spunk in it, her legs were still bluish purple and her stretch marks stuck out even more in the cold skin, the woman hardly recognized herself, she just wanted to cry when she looked upon the pathetic woman hunched forward in the mirror, the steam slowly blurred out her image, the steam helped to warm her skin but began to make her joints ache. As her image in the mirror faded much like her self-image had many years ago, it was time to climb into the shower and hope that her legs held her up sturdy enough to keep from slipping in the shower. Aimee did her best to wash; she scrubbed as hard as she could in an attempt to scrub away her shame and guilt, a very familiar practice that hadn't ever worked before. Aimee leaned against the cold wall as the water ran down her body, she was too exhausted to cry and there wasn't anything that she hadn't cried over hundreds of times before, but she was stuck and had no ability to change her life now. Brittini was the sole reason Aimee didn't end up in the gutter, she may be half in now but she at least held a job and a shitty community college associate's degree.

Don and Shelley felt responsible for Brittini, they loved her like the niece she was and tried their best to look after when they could. Don didn't approve of Jonny, kid wearing sagging jean shorts, a faded Metallica shirt and the grammar of a fourth grader, Don did his best to stare down most of the trailer park guys, even if you took the best attributes of each one you still couldn't come up with a high school graduate. Don wasn't Brittini's father but he wanted so much more for the small girl than the small confines of the Heights, he hoped that she might make more of herself than her mother did, if he had the ability to do anything to improve Brittini's life, he would. All he could really do was be there for her and help encourage her in any way possible, he and Shelley both.

The St. Patty's day Barrel burner was another not to miss occasion for Big Ken, he was a gorilla sized man, and Angel assumed that if he hunched any farther forward than his knuckles would actually drag on the ground, he looked like the second from the left in one of those evolution of man posters. Big Ken pulled an extra couple of cement jobs on and off during the drier than usual previous winter, his company let him bankroll his hours to keep milking the winter unemployment so when his first check finally rolled in after the winter hiatus he was able to pad his pockets a bit with some green. For St. Patty's day Big Ken sprang for the corned beef for sandwiches and got himself a bottle of Buffalo Trace to precede a bottle of Jameson to keep his Irish pride in full swing. Jonny was under the impression that he could sleep in his own bed after Big Ken cracked is second bottle of pricey booze to share, Big Ken began in on how much of a burden it was to be the sole provider for himself and Jonny, he was adamant that Jonny was plenty old enough to get a job and pitch in around the house, Jonny explained that there wasn't anything close enough to hire at his age, even the *Chick Lips* where Tammi and Dez'rae worked part time.

Jonny crept into his room as Ken continued to swill his bottle between sips, growing ever more impatient with his life. Ken was doing well until he and his wife were sent up for manufacturing and distributing narcotics, it was supposed to be a hefty charge for the married pair but because no one would have been left behind to care for their young son, each parent served in opposite times, doubling their time apart. Ken was more than unhappy that he was left to maintain the home and try and keep Jonny on the straight and narrow, the problem was, he was miserable as a parent, he didn't have a clue in the world what he was doing and he despised his own seed for making him have to be responsible, or sober most of the time. Big Ken was enjoying his Irish heritage, not to mention liquor when Carsey roamed closer to him by the barrel. Big Ken tried his best to escape his circumstances as often as possible, he would often drink a case of nasty ice during his work day slinging cement, then when he got home his actual drinking would commence, sometimes he would stride his weight bench set up on his front porch, it was a simple barbell, similar to the ones that kept him occupied while incarcerated in Ionia prison in mid-Michigan.

Big Ken struggled to cross his massive arms over his large chest and gut, he was enjoying the tingling teeth and gums as his second bottle was finally beginning to do its' job. Carsey was enjoying the time without her son, she was also looking to supplement her income with some after-hours activity and Ken seemed to be willing to shell out twenty bucks or so for half an hour of her assorted company. Carsey was a very pretty girl; her manic changes in mental states made her tough to handle in sections of time larger than a few days, being bipolar made her an interesting conversation as well as stories of her life to laugh about. As Ken and Carsey got cozy, no one was about to pass judgment around the barrel if Ken was going to take his turn for a once around with the girl. While back at home Jonny was treating himself to a hot shower instead of a washcloth bathing

47

outside past the tree lining. As the bottle of Jameson neared its'
bottom Big Ken was winking and giggling along with Carsey, the
much smaller girl by comparison, he was lined up to have himself a
good ole time and was on the verge to taking Carsey back to his
place, she planned on being done with him in time to be back to the
barrel to finish making dinner money.

The two residents headed towards Kens trailer, people around the
burn barrel averted their eyes, no one was bothered enough to say
anything, let alone to Big Ken, he was a large man with a small bit of
tolerance for any school yard bull crap. Ken waddled towards his
trailer at the end of the street, Carsey close in hand as he ran his giant
meat hooks across her back shoulders, brushing her hair off her back
and waiting to get her blue fleece off and play with the toys
underneath her top. Carsey was thinking about the quick twenty bucks
she'd make by showing some skin and easily going down on the
brute, then return back to the barrel side and see who the next taker
might be.

As the frisky couple let themselves into Kens single wide, Ken
was solely focused on finishing undressing Carsey, she was fairly
slender and retained most of her c-cups after birthing Brodan; Ken
was looking to spend more time with her chest than her son did.
Inside the door Ken was removing the fleece spring jacket to leave
Carsey standing in just a white bra with red pinstripes, Ken was laser
focused on the breasts of Carsey, she was trying to think about being
anywhere else except under Ken. Carsey stopped for a moment as
Ken continued to fondle away at her and pulled her towards him so he
could bury himself face first into Carsey's cleavage, she grabbed his
left ear for a moment to gain his attention to the background noise
coming from down the hall. Ken couldn't understand why he was
being pulled away from two ample boobs as his strained to use his big
plump fingers to pull and tug at some stubborn bra clips that weren't
easily unclipped due to the size of his fingers. As the breasts parted
from the reach of his tongue he was still neglecting the ambient
sounds from down his hallway until it clicked that he was hearing
running water. Big Ken had an epiphany, lightning struck his brain
and an explosion went off in his chest, fueled by a large amount of
alcohol.

Ken pushed Carsey to sit on the recliner and instructed her to
stay put, and unclothed as he turned his rage and attention on the

origin of the noise as he stormed down the hallway and barged into the bathroom where Jonny was finishing his first hot shower in weeks. When the door imploded after Ken's fist sent it straining the hinges, the concussive blast of the hollow veneer door startled Jonny to the point that he slipped and fell in the shower, taking the curtain and rod with it. Jonny landed in a pile of shower curtain and soap suds as Ken reached in to grab the scrawny kid by his neck and remove him again from his home. Jonny was to tangled up in shower curtain to get his bearings or even gain any awareness as to what was going on before Ken wrapped his large hands around the neck and shoulder of Jonny and ripped him up from the floor of his warm shower. Ken didn't even bother to avoid shoving half of his body into the stream of the shower, his rage kept his eyes locked on the little leach that hardly ate his food or used his electricity, but the little bastard was using his warm water for five whole minutes in the middle of the afternoon and risked voiding Ken's guaranteed nookie.

Jonny was heaved up over the shoulder and headed towards the front door in nothing but a shower curtain, Carsey was too drunk to stop the commotion but she was surely startled, she needed to make sure she made her twenty dollars in order to make lot rent in two weeks so she sat idly by and let Ken deal with his issues before returning to her. Ken stormed out from the hallway, hunk of naked flesh wriggling from within the blue and white plastic wrapping propped up on his shoulder, as Ken braced his footing Jonny slipped out the back portion of the shower curtain, landing hard on the floor. Jonny was scared out of his little body and didn't let the hard landing on the floor take the wind out of his long enough to keep him off his feet for any longer than a moment before springing back up and heading towards his room for a chance at getting some clothes. Jonny was near embarrassed to tears as the girl not much older than him from down the road was sitting topless on the couch and had her eyes fixed on the wriggling nude boy as he hit the ground. Carsey tried her best not to laugh as the small white ass ran like a Kenyan down the hall away from the giant man. Kens eyes crossed momentarily as he tried to register what had just happened, his inebriated state slowed his ability to realize that his wet slippery nuisance had just gotten free from his grasp.

Jonny had enough of a head start to be able to leap into his room and grab a pair of pants and shirt before Ken wrapped one hand all the way around his thigh, his fingers touched when he grabbed Jonny just above his knee, his right leg dragged against the carpet leaving a nice rug burn along the unprotected skin as Ken dragged Jonny from the room that Ken paid for. Jonny screamed and pleaded with his entire little body as Ken held him by one leg and reached for the door with his available hand. Jonny held on to his clothes as he was trying to wriggle free to avoid landing on the front steps, or the weight bench, Ken kept his eyes locked on the hanging tits of Carsey as he stood next to her while fumbling with the doorknob and readying to heave his own son out to the cool afternoon so he could return to the girl waiting close by on the recliner. Big Ken hurled Jonny towards the weight bench, far enough to clear the door so the flailing limbs didn't break anything on the door on his way out. Ken wasn't always as aggressive towards his own progeny all of the time, sometimes it was a mere yelling; sometimes Ken was just too tired to even chase Jonny out.

Ken blamed Jonny for his prison time, it was Jonny that had some meth in his backpack to show what his parents did at school that lead to the initial drug raid that landed Ken in prison to begin with, now Jonny inhibited Ken from being able to live drunk or high, he still had to maintain a home of sorts and even feed the kid once in a while. Half of the time their tolerance was enough to live in proximity, Jonny felt brazen enough to sleep in his own bed once or twice a week, that was about as much as Ken could tolerate the kid, the summers were longer working days, Ken hauled and poured cement and the hot summer days, it made his blood boil throughout the steaming summer. When Ken had to work seven long hot days a week, his exhaustion shortened his ability to remain tolerant of Jonny and he often let his temper explode into a physical assault to "*toughen up*" his son while he was at it. Jonny was less bruised during the school year, it kept child services off his ass, and porch, the summer didn't matter and Ken usually convinced his sober self that his sons bruises weren't from his own drunken self but from Jonny just being a boy and doing what boys do.

Big Ken warned Jonny to avoid the rotten douche Darryl, Jonny had no interest in becoming a dropout, but he spent more nights sleeping under his room than in it and wasn't really getting much support otherwise. Aimee knew that Jonny and Brittini were good friends and that they looked after each other, she was oblivious to

Jonny sleeping in her car but knew her daughter would skimp on meals to save some for Jonny. Ken didn't even bother to close the door after relocating Jonny to the porch and then resumed his position in the mouth of Carsey. After a few minutes of Carsey sucking off Ken, his rage was still keeping his heart and fury beating on so he yanked Carsey up off the couch and held her up with one arm while the other removed her pants.

Ken held Carsey up to mount her, her feet barely touching the floor, she felt like a rag doll being tossed around and used up before Ken finished and dropped her to the couch. Jonny rolled the remainder of his body from the weight bench that he was tangled up on, he landed with his back shoulders on the wooden porch and legs on the bench, his clothes tightly gripped in his hands and he tried to protect his head from hitting anything in his way. Jonny knew that fortune dispenses randomly and maybe someday he'll finally catch a break instead of catching beatings by his old man. Jonny was not unfamiliar with being thrown from the house in the buff, he found it a monthly occurrence, and at least this time it wasn't snowing out. Before Jonny got dressed he had to look over his body, his legs, arms, torso and head all hurt, throbbing pain that made his eyes water, Jonny was certain that even though his father was focused on stripping and plunging the girl just inside the door, that if he shed one tear that Ken would wallop his ass again for not being a man. Jonny was reprimanded for not being man enough, and if there was any sign of weakness then Jonny was punished until he no longer wept or flinched, it was a lose-lose shitty situation, or shituation, for Jonny.

Jonny glanced over his red spots that were to be his newest bruises; he had to make sure he wasn't going to bleed through the clothes that he would have to wear for at least a week if not more before he might be able to get back in to swipe more of his clothes. Jonny kept a small Rubbermaid container with a change of clothes under the trailer, he would sometimes have to wash his clothes using a garden hose in any number of neighbor yards after the sun went down and he could sit in his drawers and soak his clothes and ring them back out and hope they dried enough overnight to wear the next day again. Jonny stood with half a hunch to avoid standing up to tall behind the scraggy bushes that lined his front porch, he could see up the street and see everyone crowded around the burn barrel, Theresa, Tammi, Dez'rae, Darryl, Aimee and Tod were the first round of faces

51

that he could see as soon as he stood up after being discarded to the porch like a wet dog. Jonny pulled his pants up and fought to straighten out his *Master of Puppets* shirt before hobbling down the steps and head over to join the party, his wet hair and body gave him the chills and the barrel was piping warm.

Dez'rae and Theresa saw what had happened from up the street; they quickly averted their eyes for the most part to save the distraught teen some sliver of dignity as he walked up. Tammi glanced towards the tattered kid; she took in as much mental imagery as possible, Theresa and Dez'rae had a little more respect for him as they were more aware at how rough his hand had been dealt. Jonny had been beaten down so many times he often assumed that some days he wouldn't wake up, he knew that if there was a god than he was a twisted prick that allowed the sorts of shit he had been through. Jonny sauntered over near the burn barrel and was handed a ripe full Mickey's 40 oz. by Angel. Tod couldn't manage two shits for Jonny most days, the kid was just some little pecker in his hen house but on this occasion he tilted his half consumed bottle towards him in a nod of respect that Jonny took a beating and still got back up, that was the true mark of a man; just getting back up.

The St. Patty's party carried on into the afternoon; after the first case of 40's were cracked and consumed a second case was deflowered for the party and passed around. Tammi begun to feel guilty for having watched Jonny's embarrassing fiasco and wanted to try and cheer him up, she discussed mediocre school events with Theresa and Dez'rae, boys being boys and work being work, when everyone seemed rather pie eyed with their booze and assorted chemicals, Angel hiccupping all afternoon, Tammi nodded to Jonny to follow her to the side, he lit a bummed smoke and headed to see what in the world the snooty bitch wanted with him. Jonny was leary about things, Tammi wasn't one to be trusted and was passed around more than illegal drugs in the *Heights*. Tammi was wearing a pink hoodie with black yoga pants underneath, not ideal pants for someone larger than a size 8, she thought she would proffer up a sympathy hump back behind some neighbors porch, not too far from where Theresa was left wasted last fall. Jonny was still aching and sore, his extremities still throbbed and hadn't eased from the malt liquor in his bottle. Tammi was careful not to kiss at his swollen bottom lip but held him closely and wrapped her arms around him to comfort him.

Jonny was hesitant to touch the older girl, for the life of him he couldn't figure out what the upper class girl wanted with him, he figured it was to poke fun at him much like many of the others' around the heights, Tammi reassured that she held no ill intentions and to prove it she grabbed his free hand and guided it down the front of her pants and suggestively told him she was his to play with. Jonny was trying to wipe away the sweat that was beginning to bead up on his forehead with his hand that held his almost empty bottle, he had heard that Darryl had raw dogged this girl, Curtiss, DJ Wriggle and that she even gave away her coochie for a bottle of Boons and a pack of Newports to the sleazy gas station homo. Tammi opened her stance a bit and told Jonny that she wanted many parts of him in her, she sucked on his neck a bit and struggled to hold him closely with her left arm while she began to work her right hand down his pants, making Jonny further panic and want to hurry back to the safety of the bonfire.

Jonny broke the hold and headed back to the burn barrel, the members around it pretended not to notice his absence but deep down they each knew that Tammi offered him some proven comfort. Angel continued to hiccup, she was growing tired and weary of the diaphragmatic irritation and they often grew so bad that they prohibited her from sleeping. Joey/Lilly reached down into his light blue clutch and hander her a compact makeup container, it wasn't his makeup but it was something that she could use to powder her nose with, he felt guilty enough about what he was putting her through that he himself would exchange *favors* for her cocaine. Joey was once picked up for tricking with some business guy named Oxender from up north, he was some mustache adorned perv and hid his homo tendencies from a wife back home, he paid his fees and bailed but Joey sat over the weekend in a holding cell before having to face a judge. Jonny was worried he'd have to soak his fingers in peroxide to get rid of the rotten fish smell that wafted from between Tammi's legs and was now eating away at the skin on his fingers. Jonny looked around for another brew, he wanted to be cocked enough to go and fall asleep in his stapled together sheets that made a sleeping bag he hid away behind a loose piece of siding under his trailer before Big Ken was finished with Carsey.

As Jonny returned to the burn circle Theresa was standing much closer to Angel, she was trying to be sly in handing a few folded

53

dollars to Angel and doing her best to keep it to themselves as Angel tucked it into her bra strap to prevent anyone from trying to be nosy about the money. Jonny kept his head low when he returned, the whispering increased a bit as all had assumed he got his skin flute played with. Aimee stood close to Tod, his height was noticeable and although her body habitus was more rounded, she felt affluent when she stood with him, it may have just been because of the company. Brittini was back at home, she often kept to herself, reading books like "*Glass Screams*" or "*3rd Hand Ranch*," books about girls with much more inner strength than herself, she was anticipating a set of opposing antagonistic books by the same author in which a cat and mouse relationship between cop and serial killer was to make for a ripping read. Brittini knew he mother was much more afraid of being alone than she was of Tod but Tod was a cancer to society and he ducked almost every form of responsibility for a chance to get twerked up on blow or drinks.

Tod joked with Joey about getting his "*Kany*" tossed, (their slang term for rectum,) Tod played coy that it was fun and kinda tickled sure but it wasn't worth going full on RuPaul for it and maybe Angel could just offer up a finger or strap- on for him for a compromise, Angel just rolled her eyes as to say she had tried everything and then some in order to keep some order in her life, her parents really kept pressure on her to get married and deuce out some grandkids for them, until Joey went and started to become Lilly. Darryl was late to join the St. Patty's barrel as he rolled over on his BMX bike, his main form of transportation. Darryl made mention that his moms was heading home after a long stay away, apparently she was picked up for speeding and forced to stay thirty-days in some county jail for the mix of drugs in her system, and then having a rather unpleasant attitude for the judge, contempt of court is a bitch, especially when you pull your pants down and unkindly suggest the judge eat you out, at least at her age. Darryl quickly cracked a 40 and began to get caught up in the goings on with everyone milling around.

Darryl caught a notion of Angel's makeup compact and was interested in powdering his nose as well; he had a handful of downers like Ketamine but was more interested in some uppers, especially some snow. Darryl stuck his lower jaw out a bit and raised his head to try and persuade Angel to loosen the clamp she held on the small brown case, she did just enough to ease her hiccups but she wasn't about to let the leprechaun sized fool with a stupid looking flat billed Pistons hat on, he'd never even been to Michigan, let alone Detroit but he cried the "D" for some ill earned street cred. Darryl was looking to score an upper so he could have the energy to keep his beer buzz going and also find the energy to clean his trailer, Annabel was always one to dole out an earful of noise and threats if her place wasn't kept clean enough, despite the fact that she was hardly there. Darryl was raised mostly without his mom so of course the lacking created a severe fondness for the idea of a mother, she rode more bikers than bikers rode bikes, she did anything possible to try and live the fantasy biker life that many people imagined being a biker was, except she always snorted any money she made instead of actually put it towards owning a bike of her own.

Annabel was almost caught smuggling Ice half a dozen years ago, she had several baggies tucked inside of her in a few areas, she was slow to wake up one morning after a late party and was caught up in a public bathroom inserting baggies and balloons when their meeting point had been raided, all of her companions had been taken into custody along with a hearty supply of firearms, knives, hammers, chains, and other assorted weapons plus almost one-hundred thousand dollars in cash and almost half as much in drugs after searching each biker member, Annabel was holed up in a bar bathroom across the street because she wanted a few drinks before she began hiding various drugs, plus the bathroom at the meeting house was nasty; what else would you expect in a biker headquarters. Annabel finally walked out after an hour and watched from a bar stool across the street at the DEA supported by other agencies all walked around with semiautomatic guns and one by one strip searched each biker brother of hers and loaded the men into the back of a county sheriff van. Annabel was without any form of transportation or contacts to sell her product, she had a few drinks that she "bartered" from the bartender and then began walking, leaving behind her leather vest that would have pinned her as an associate with the gang.

Annabel sent an envelope of cash back to help out her son, it wasn't much but it went towards a down payment on lot 43 for her son and for her to return to when she made it off the road eventually. Darryl barely ever heard from his mother growing up, she might think to send a postcard but it was usually on the wrong end of the year to be considered for birthday or even a holiday so all he had was the fantasy of a mother that cared, he often sought comfort it sexual dalliances and had no other attainable skills than to pedal low level amounts of drugs or mix the occasional batch of plastic bottle meth. Darryl was excited that his mom was coming home but it also meant that he, Curtiss and Lil B wouldn't have their place to hang out and smoke dope either, Lil B was always super excited to get to hang out with the older crew, he was considered to be one of the boys, the underlying issue was that both older boys want to dip any and all body parts into Lil B's sister Tara, but it also suited them to have a lackey to run errands and do some of the tedious tasks such as pick the small blue crystals from the kitty litter for the meth.

Curtiss was always out walking the neighborhood late each night, he wasn't allowed to be home but for certain hours, his roommate whom paid all of the bills knew better than to trust him, especially being related to Tyrone and all of the trouble he caused with that wonderfully fantastic Zebra Milk concoction that zooted all of its' consumers past the moon. Curtiss had no idea that his belligerent stumbling into Theresa last Halloween had left her in a tough pickle; she had no recollection of him being inside of her or even his pecker having the same consistency as a wet noodle, he still had enough spunk to get her pregnant when he was inside of her, even just briefly. Curtiss thought he was going to have a hip hop album, he wanted Jessica Alba's luscious ass bouncing on his face for his first music video, he thought he was being kept down by the man for being black but it just turns out not all brothers are born with rhythm or the ability to rap, and those that can't rap only catch a record deal 'cause they got shot or something. Curtiss hung out with Darryl because they could sit and get high together, they would strut side by side around the park some days, and others would be Curtiss taking some small packets of pills or powders to sell at school that he got from Darryl. Darryl sometimes rode the bus into the city, he had a handful of dealers in various projects that he bought from, he hated leaving the *Heights* but he had clientele to provide for and by pinching here and there he made his money too.

Curtiss would often make the run to Deal with Gary, he would often offer a pill as a tax that Gary charged in order to get to purchase alcohol underage, Gary knew most of the residents but that was beside the point, he still needed all the interactions he could get among his customers. When Gary would get a few pills of *E* he would suggest that Tammi trade him some skin for his goods, he was near thirty but he always had a chubby for the younger blonde girl. Tammi would take the pill and kill a bottle *Boons* while she waited for the narcotics to kick in before removing her clothes enough to let Gary slip his dick into her and pump away at her, she was always humiliated. Tammi never requested any of her suitors to wear a rubber, she figured if she had to feel any of it she might as well feel most of it and pretend it was pleasurable.

Gary would pull out and shoot his final product onto her mushy backside, once his load left his little pistol it became her problem and after the first time having to use her panties, she became familiar enough with the back store room of the gas station to know where to find the sink and some paper towel. Tammi knew Gary got a few hummers from Theresa, she knew she was the first one to let the older man hump her, then convinced herself that it was desirable to be lusted after by an older man, never mind that he was a fat greasy slime ball with curly black hair and thick rimmed glasses, and his balls smelled of crusty body odor and he needed to "husk the corn" so she wouldn't find his pubes in her creases at night. Tammi let Gary plunge into her snatch and felt sometimes, anytime she felt lonely or was simply out of cigarettes. Tammi lacked the self-worth to keep her legs shut, she desperately needed attention and convinced herself that being wanted, was the same as being lusted after, it was all attention anyhow.

Last summer Tammi and Theresa found it funny to harp down on Tara for being flat chested and still have the hips of a ten year old boy, Tara had some height to her but she also spent a plenty of her own money to have her teeth bleached despite the obvious rot at the base of each tooth, she was pretentious when she was still as straight up and down as a 4x4 post, Tara was hard pressed to struggle for acceptance from the older girls and hated the fact that she was the focus of the harassment. Tara held her good grades until her body began to develop and she could manipulate the weaker willed pussy boys at school to spend their off hours doing her work to carry favor with her. Tara had a moderately attractive body in comparison to the other sophomores but lacked the actual social skills to navigate any success for herself so she was often left with a dumbfounded look on her face, which was genuine.

When Tara's body began to develop she caught attention from Darryl and Curtiss, any form of tits would garner such attention and Tara slowly began to acquire attention from boys and that was all the validation she might ever truly get, she dreamed most nights about becoming a beautician or even running a tanning salon, she wasn't sure she held enough confidence for much more than that in life but it sure beat the sweatshop her cousin Carlos worked in, he spent eighteen hours a day twisting wire for some aged frail ass old lady that ran an "orphanage" but the truth be told it was just an abandoned house that was being squatted in by the old hag that forced the labor and used the state issued labor to make her old wrinkly ass more money.

Tara always strutted like her shit didn't stink, she had fairly tanned skin and respectable posture but her tits weren't all that perky in her bikini top nor her ass all that firm either so her strut wasn't earned but faked, like the color of her teeth. Tod and random members of his crew would joke about abducting her like some Allah chanting terrorists then dropping some roofies down her throat and seeing if there was more fake or real to her taught little body under her clothes, Tuner and Billy were plenty more serious about giving it to her rotisserie style, Tod just sometimes palmed his python watching her walk around the neighborhood in an all-white bikini to gain the attention of anyone with a penis, Tod rarely cared that Brittini may have been in her room within ear shot as he whacked his pud before passing out on the couch in the living room, Brittini often heard the escapades of Tod and Aimee, it wasn't uncommon for Brittini to open her bedroom door to find Tod suspiciously standing right outside her bedroom missing his clothes for some reason.

Brittini ducked and hid away as much as she could when it came to the neighborhood, Tara was strictly superficial and hardly acknowledged anyone besides her brother Lil B, he was often causing some ruckus or swiping her small bras for his older buddies to stroll around with tucked up against their giblets. Brittini could rely on Jonny but he was also shy and doing his best to stay out of the view of his father, he did his best to keep the teachers off his back and to keep them from calling Big Ken and further enrage the cement slinger. Brittini hid away in her room most often, she cried herself to sleep especially on the nights that Tod ran out of enough to drink to pass out before he could get mad about having run out of alcohol, which he took out on Aimee physically, Brittini had no role model to aspire to, she was grateful she wasn't being sold for her girly flesh to perves like Billy or Tuner but she wanted to find an escape route on her own before she ended up getting raped from any number of the neighbors while passed out from any of the holiday burn barrel gatherings or something.

Theresa and Angel mumbled back and forth for a bit longer before Dez'rae overheard the meat of their conversation, Theresa had finally finished paying Angel for an emergent run after the Halloween party, Theresa spent November awaiting a period that didn't come, she picked up a pregnancy test from Gary for a quick hummer because she wanted to save her money to begin saving for an abortion. Theresa was hard up and was able to convince a boy at school to get her an eight ball for her and then convince another boy that she let slip her his dick that he had to fork up fifty for the morning after pill. It had taken Theresa some finagling but she was finally able to come up with the last payment for Angel, whom fronted both the ride and the rest of the money to have the clinic remove the sac of cells that found its self in her. Angel assumed Theresa could find a ride from some non-English speaker but needed a refill on her birth control anyways, Angel was hoping to have some action plus the pill kept her cycle regular so might as well be safe, Joey wasn't spending time in her playground but she hoped someone might so she was headed to the clinic and then fronted Theresa the money to keep some teen from shitting out some kid with an unknown father. After the abortion Theresa made a less frequent appearance around the Heights. Angel still hiccupped around the bonfire as she swelled her cold beer and enjoyed the teeth buzz that came from her coke and the company, they joked and jollied away the Irish occasion.

Towards the end of the afternoon the wood pile wound down but the anxiety to return to their lives ramped up, no one wanted to fall asleep in their bed and wake up themselves again, Tod and Big Ken fed the poser Darryl more alcohol and as his body began to sway in attempts to stay upright, Tod inched over to Joey for an off colored proposition while Big Ken handed Darryl another 40. Joey was unsure why he was being approached, both Tod and Ken were obnoxious to him and he was ready for a fight if necessary.

Once Darryl had finally topped off his tank and could no longer keep his eyelids open, Curtiss was quickly brought in on the plan, "twincest" was a stroke of evil genius in order to dole out the little punk some earned humility. Tod was drunk and bored and asked a large favor from Joey in exchange for some tolerance from Big Ken; Tod was having a rainmaker kind of moment among the barrel visitors. Big Ken and Curtiss half carried Darryl back to his trailer, Tod and Joey parted ways only to reconvene at Darryl's shortly thereafter. Tod headed down to grab a throw away cell phone from Gary at the gas station while Joey headed home to get some supplies. Big Ken and Curtiss helped Darryl to stumble into his living and prep him for his twincest experience. Ken was plenty loosened up after enough alcohol to inebriate a rhino, before he was a good time kind of guy, and messing with the punk Darryl was just the ticket to have a good time to cap off the March holiday.

When Tod and Joey met up at Darryl's it was time for action, Curtiss kept chuckling and talking about how wrong it was but then again, niggas wouldn't be doing other niggas like this. Big Ken and Tod took Darryl's tops off and started dressing him up in some of Joey's girly lacey tops and heaved him up with some socks for fake breasts while Joey slathered on the make-up. Curtiss helped to steady the disposable cell phone and begin snapping pics of Darryl done up as an ugly female version of himself. The makeup done by a tranny was just convincing enough to pass him off as a trailer park princess. The guys cleaned up the wasted Darryl and then for the hell of it took pictures of each of them tea bagging the ghetto wannabe before they left Curtiss to draw black penises on his face with permanent marker, it didn't hurt to add a swastika or two on the eyelids, stuff to make his mother proud when she gets home.

The twincest stint lasted a few weeks, Tod randomly texted Darryl as the female version of Darryl and sent him loving texts, messages of lust and how lovely the night they shared together was. For the following few days Darryl bought into the texts, Tod laid it on slowly to begin with, it is a delicate task to hook a paranoid drug pusher on to a slut he couldn't recall banging...or not. Darryl seemed eager to connect with "Daria" the best the not so bright Tod could come up with for the girls' name. Daria became a deacon's daughter looking for some more fun, she convinced Darryl he was studly and she liked his flat bill, she validated him in his mind, and "she" even had a few pictures to send to him to get him to fall in love with her. Curtiss reported back to Tod and Big Ken and Tod filled in some of the gaps that Darryl failed to mention, like some of his ways he earns some of his drugs, turns out Darryl has a contact in the city he called "Zoofy" some old wrinkled man with a bald head, thick glasses and an assortment of drugs at his disposal. Zoofy doesn't want or need drugs but male companionship and often a warm mouth that swallows, Darryl poured out his heart to "Daria" and "Daria" spilled it all out to Big Ken and Curtiss.

The guys each judged and mocked the unknowing kid, Darryl slept with many girls, he should have a few kids by now because he never covered up but he did have the foresight to spray his inseam team outside of a vagina, he feared being tied down, or the notion of having a kid he couldn't be there for, like his mom wasn't there for him. Tod pried several hidden embarrassing nuggets from Darryl and he and Big Ken each sat around and poked plenty of fun, the little banger wannabe spent most nights biting the pillow or crying each night while he was in county jail. Tod and Ken commented that he wouldn't have had the smallest of balls to even last the initial prison processing, let alone a stint longer than one of those scared straight shows. Daria expressed her father having molested her and needing a change in life, with a few more pictures and several weeks of wooing, Darryl was ready to let "Daria" move in and the two of them start something semi-serious. Tod and Ken planned to really jack Darryl up to teach the little bastard a lesson in fronting; he hadn't earned any credibility and needed to have some swag knocked out of him.

With as much as Darryl fronted that he was hard and a gangster, Tod and Ken just assumed he was a rump pumper and his gangster attitude was overcompensation for his short stature and need to display swagger at all, hell he might have been a rectum repeller just for using the term "swag" as it was. Big Ken was excited to watch the little thug cry like the bitch he was, Ken looked down on most men that weren't as manly as he was, he was convinced that being a fag was a choice and would volunteer to beat the homo out of any that chose to be that way. Big Ken beat on Jonny to make sure he knew what was in store for him if he ever chose to be a fag, and by toughening Jonny up, he was making sure that his own son was going to be too tough to become a sack sucker. "Daria" wanted to meet Darryl at the *Chick Lips* place, conveniently Tod was hitting up

Darryl for a few joints before going to get take out from the very same restaurant, allowing the open door for Darryl to hit him up for a ride, the final culmination for the *twincest* prank. Tod and Big Ken had the last final ball busting aspect of the prank all lined up, Tod dropped Darryl off to head in and await the arrival of Daria while Tod placed his drive thru order for food. As soon as Tod was alone in the cab of his truck he sent his last text, one that was sure to make the short stocky lad drop some fruit in his looms and high tail it back out of the restaurant. Tod texted Darryl from the disposable Daria phone: "I'm pregnant" in time to watch Darryl sit up straight as he sat in the restaurant.

Darryl exited through the doors as Tod did his best to hide his overwhelming smile behind a fresh cigarette as Darryl dropped his lighter twice while trying to light his smoke on his way back to the truck. Darryl climbed in and told Tod to bail, Tod played dumb wondering why Darryl wanted the ride to the restaurant but figured it was to meet a dealer or make a deal after the buses stopped running. Darryl's hands were shaking as he rolled down the passenger window and ashed out of it, he panicked and averted making eye contact or conversation with his driver. Tod knew he had just made Darryl shit himself, the stocky banger forgot his swagger step as he hurried back into the truck and made tracks as fast as possible back to his safe haven within the *Heights*.

As the residents awoke and began to scurry to gather supplies for the Fourth of July party, the adults stockpiled beer and bottles of cheap booze in their fridges, there were kiddie pools laid out to be filled with ice to keep the liquids cold during the hot July day, there were slip and slides lining the grass lots for kids during the hottest hours, the breaking evening afternoons were filled with tables covered in plastic plates filled with different mixes all whipped up by residents and party partakers. The three small streets that joined into the one inlet/outlet road were all that made up the *Heights*, each single wide was propped up on a cement slab, the wheels removed and aluminum siding skirts placed around to hide all of the plumbing underneath, the most basic of housing, the same kind FEMA thought would be acceptable for storm displaced folks further south. Some of the trailers here in the *Heights* may have even come from the cockroach ridden swamps down south, roaches and all.

There were several vacant cement slabs, if a mortgage had lapsed then a company would come in, unplug everything and yank the whole damn trailer from its' perch leaving behind clipped wires and capped PVC pipes. Many of the local kids often moved in chairs for various games such as empty can soccer. In lot 73 someone dragged a portable basketball hoop to the lot for people to have that option until a new single wide makes its' way up from the half trash heap where they were discarded after Katrina. Angel picked up a badminton set from Meijer to set up across the cement slab for people to play across for the days' events.

It was the dead of autumn when Columbus Day gave the partyers another reason to gather around the burn barrel and pass around hearty bottles of Buffalo trace. Darryl had himself a new piece of ass to carry around on his arm, when he was getting tail he was a little more willing to bring blunts to pass rather than hoard his stashes for himself, Darryl had brought some that he laced with oxy, he was gentle with the addition of the powder as he sprinkled it along the green buds. As a few of the residents opened up accepting the generosity, the young girl, Jenny, was giggly and trying to fit in with Angel, Aimee, Brittini and Tara, Tammi and Dez'rae were later to arrive as they had some after school business with Teresa. Jenny wore tight pants which gained admiration of Big Ken and Tod, Joey talked to Jenny about make-up tips and it made almost everyone else uncomfortable, you could tell by his jaw grinding that Darryl had nothing but aggression for Joey but Joey was also an all-state football player in his more manly days of high school so taking a hit from one of his giant catcher's mitt sized hands might decapitate the stocky thug so he kept his silence. Jenny shifted her weight back and forth as she stood in skimpy shoes, you could see her hips move side to side under her hoodie, and Darryl groped her firm ass often to boast up his prowess trying to gain admiration of the older guys that shared his ex-con reputation.

Jenny's tight pants didn't show any panty lines, Darryl had barely been talking to Jenny a week, he strolled his BMX bike past the library now and again trolling for snatch, sure enough with a spliff in his pocket he hooked some game. Jenny had deep dimples and scattered highlights in her hair which was kept back by a pink head band, she inched away from Darryl each time he tried to shove his hands down the back of her pants, exposing some bare ass to the drooling guys nearby. Darryl thought he had an edge with the young enticing body, impressing Tod and Ken should have gotten him some respect around the park, Tod and Ken hit Darryl up every so often for various pills or other required items so he held some worth, Ken enjoyed Dilaudid here and there, it was expensive and required a needle but it was a phenomenal high and he would rather spend his days letting the room swirl around him when he had the opportunity instead of parent and be responsible.

Tod was a much lower class addict, he absolutely loved cocaine and the energy it brought him to roof all day long but for the money, he could binge on meth in the mornings and then assorted benzo's at night to counter the high. Tod mostly leached off of Aimee, she was terrified of being alone and as time carried on she also became terribly petrified of trying to remove him, he had become a tumor that grew into major arteries and would take the life of his host entity if removed. Aimee didn't mind the company most of the time, he hardly brought groceries and always left the gender specific roles to the woman, and most of the man's responsibilities also, Brittini hid away

64

when Aimee had to push the lawnmower back and forth in the hot summer sun in a tank top, her hefty saddle bags would leave sweat dripping down the front of her tank top, Brittini knew that she couldn't be heard over the noise of the lawnmower so she locked herself in her room for privacy when the lawn needed attendance.

Darryl spent half of the afternoon tugging down the top of Jenny's pants to keep exposing a little more and more of her ass, Tod snickered each time he was able to get a little more of a peak at her pale rear end, Aimee knew that once Tod was aroused his attention would turn to her, she felt slightly ashamed that she was sometimes just a warm hole to him and she also knew that for both minutes that he would be trying to skewer her, he would be thinking specifically about Jenny later that night. Big Ken was also anticipating a hearty self-love session later on, Tara was milling around but Lil B and Jonny weren't so Ken didn't even have to pretend he didn't have a chubby for the teen flesh. Brittini was slowly developing, she was still in that awkward phase where she was growing tall but her hips were still narrow and her chest was flat, Tod was pretty certain that in the next year or two when her chest ceased being concave that he would have her trust enough to eyeball her when she walked around in a skimpy tank top, and he would have front seat viewing to her small budding tits, and that was jerk off fodder now and again. Two weeks before the party, the weather had prevented a tar job for him so he lay around on the couch and wolfed down bags of Pork rinds and nursed Old Style's. As his beer buzz kicked in he started feeling the need to "tug his pug", and it excited him that Brittini was in her room and might catch him on the couch of she were to just open her door, besides, Aimee was out and wouldn't stand up to him anyways so it was a mid-afternoon wank session, and poor Brittini was close enough to have heard the *fap fap fap*.

On Martin Luther King Day,(or James Earl Ray Day, named after King's assassin) the Heights residents had a fairly impromptu meeting at one of the open slabs, Tod and Big Ken decided to fire up the burn barrel and spark a few joints, it was a much smaller gathering than most as it was a frozen balls cold day. Tod pondered aloud why it was called Martin Luther King Day when most of the blacks sat around, "should be called Rosa Parks day" leaving Big Ken to chuckle. Aimee had her own curious quip; "how can you honor a man that tried to encourage a nation to educate itself, by giving everyone the day off of school?" the only response was Tuners: "They didn't have to close the banks but did so to keep most of them from getting robbed them days," he tried to contribute more to the circle than a case of Natty Ice. Billy stood nearby and just kept his beanie pulled down to help shield his eyes from the smoke and embers pouring from the top of the rusty barrel. Tuner was often letting his eyes wander towards Aimee's chest, anytime she might have to bend near him at all he was angling to peek down her scrub top as often as possible, her cleavage was pushed up and together but it was still good enough for him. Billy kept his shoulders hiked together enough to give himself a more menacing look, he wasn't all that impressive but he had both of his arms completely covered in dark tattoos, skulls, spirits being raped and tortured, he often referenced them to signify times in his life, some to express his dissatisfaction in the world, others to describe his times of run in with the law, others that it was "the system raping his soul and keeping him from living a life much more congruent with his dreams." Billy was more often silent when the crew was together, a fake "strong silent" front he tried to keep up but he also opened up to Aimee when they found themselves in close proximity.

The cavernous cunt Karen waddled over during the midwinter holiday, she was strangely social, which was a stark contrast to her usual behavior when it came to interacting with other members of the trailer park she was tasked with keeping in line. Karen made small conversation and purposefully turned a blind eye to Tod and Ken passing a thick rolled joint back and forth. Karen had asked Aimee how young Brittini was doing as well as her neighbors; Don and Shelly, people whom Karen had not seen in some time. Karen made everyone nervous when she came looming around, it was hard to determine what the old hag was up to, she and her friends always had an ulterior motive, and there was never a clear outcome until the bitch sprang out her true inner evil and slapped fines in peoples mailboxes for things that she felt she deemed needed be reprimanded.

Big Ken stood up taller and kept his chest puffed up a bit to display his massive girth in an attempt to intimidate Karen. Karen forced her fake smile at each person trying to enjoy themselves around the fire, it was brisk out and the barrel burned warmly, the cold temperature matched Karen's cold heart and disposition, she was limitlessly fake and it exuded from her, her smile was filled with bleached teeth that were still brown at the gum line, giving away her true nature, her freckles weren't reddish with color but brown with melanoma and her stature, even hunched over like a witch. Rumor had it that between Karen and her brood of witch friends, her own daughter kept her distance, despite being a wretched cunt like her mother, maybe one state was too small an area for them both to coexist.

The conversation dulled when Karen rose up from the underworld and joined them, each person was nervous to think about what she may have been up to when she walked up, it was a bipolar opposition to her normal behavior and it made everyone that had ever met her, uncomfortable. Joey proposed a neutral question; "if homosexual is someone sexually attracted to their same gender, and homicide is killing a fellow man, and suicide is killing yourself, shouldn't it be heterocide if you kill someone of the opposite sex?" that level of logic silenced the lot of them until Karen couldn't take the quiet anymore. Karen lived alone and spent most of her days alone but oddly enough, she couldn't handle the silence. Joey perturbed the gathering with his inquisition, most of the people were already nervous around him, most inched away when he came near. No one had an issue with Joey until Lilly became present, once Joey let it out that he no longer wanted to be a male, everyone seemed to look down on him and there was no turning back.

Karen's loneliness may explain her harsh personality but not excuse it, even when she was around people she still made them feel alone. Gelica was her neighbor and loony tunes, the section 8 woman that always boasted about going to the beaches of Jamaica or Costa Rico needed to be medicated, all she ever did was let her bad feet carry her across the street to kick at the sand in the playground and talk to herself, this was what Karen called her closest friend and the two of them hardly interacted on any level that may have existed beyond a pretentious facade. Karen had large gaps between her teeth, she was covered in cat hair and struggled to maintain a significant distance from any of the other *Heights* residents. Aimee had suspicions about Karen, the older woman had some friend in town and Aimee assumed it was more a girlfriend than a gal friend, but Karen didn't wear work boots or any bull dyke apparel to confirm notions. Gelica hardly left the safety of her Mumu and curlers, she often sat on her top step, wedged between the armrests of her wooden rocking chair, her mind spinning all sorts of false social interactions to keep her shallow needs met and her false sense of superiority inflated.

Aimee fought her best to avoid making eye contact with Karen as they all stood around the barrel and faked a pleasant time with Karen in their midst. Big Ken tried to converse with Aimee as Joey made him infinitely uncomfortable, there was no telling how long before a white slip showed up in his mailbox, a fine for god knows what. Karen dispensed white slips as random as Gelica's mind worked, the few residents that knew each other would text one another once in a while and make jokes of what their slip said, either more than six dog shit landmines in the yard, car parked on the sidewalk, trash having been spilled off the porch and into the yard, any random excuses to write up a resident she could find, Karen did. One warning a month was simply a warning, any second warning came with a ten dollar fine attached to the monthly lot rent, and it was more a matter of power than that of principal, and each resident hated Karen and her false notion of power.

Aimee worked as a medical assistant, when she was assisting the mortician before she was let go for siphoning embalming fluid for Tod to smoke. Tod put the embalming fluid in the bottom of his water bong so when he got high he had the added benefit of the fluid, which added a much quieter appeal to the normally edgy man. Karen seemed to strain her ears to listen for any sort of conversation topic being passed around to find something to talk about, which might validate her being there. Karen finally decided to pull the pin and toss the information grenade into the circle of people. "*Chad died*" she broke the silence. Chad was a junkie, he squatted in a trailer the next street over, his father paid most of his bills while he laid around and complained about lower back pain.

Chad made the jump from pain killers to heroin; his trailer had been condemned and almost hauled away last year because of the squalor that it had resorted too. Darryl was one of the only few people to hang out with him once in a while to get high with him, they would shoot up together but once Chad was taken away to some long term rehab facility, Darryl was out of access to his black tar baby and he detoxed himself on other various drugs and sedatives. It had been a while since Darryl had plunged away in Aimee's cooter, she didn't think about it much as she was drugged to the gills and more focused on eluding her miserable life than of his tiny pecker and it invading her pelvis for a bit, the only real aftertaste of Darryl that night was the morning after when she had to scrub off his spunk that was strewn with carpet fibers and cigarette ash.

Darryl was pals with Curtiss but Curtiss was still in high school, Darryl stayed up late trying to stroll along the sidewalks and keep up his thug persona. Darryl spent most of his days hanging out with Chad, at first he merely smoked some of the pain pills and when they ran out between the two of them, they made the transition to heroin, it lasted almost the summer when finally they decided to start shooting it up. Darryl still missed the rush, to watch the bubble form under his skin in his vein, the slight spike of adrenaline as the needled pierced the skin and then when he released the tourniquet, the surge of euphoria that ravished his body. Chad was simply a bum; his father wrote checks but didn't want anything to do with him as long as he kept out of jail. Chad was a painter and had been working up on a ladder high when he took a fall, he had to have some lower vertebrae fused in his lumbar spine but it was a fast addiction to pain killers that had him hooked, most knew he was a pussy and couldn't handle an adult life more than not being able to handle a lower back ache. Karen was partially responsible for the cops coming in and hauling Chad out, she had walked the perimeter and was more than aware of the drug use and his idle nature when she decided to loom a little longer just outside of Chads trailer window. Karen watched Chad leave his shower and jiggle down his hallway back towards the living room, Karen was much more fixated on the needle going into Chads arm than his untrimmed hedges as he shot up a needle into his inner thigh before lying back again and returning back to his lethargically idled state.

Karen was interrupted by Brittini walking the outer sidewalk perimeter that surrounds the trailer park, the footsteps slapped her back out of her fixed gaze and into a slight panic of being caught, not to her awareness but Brittini had caught an eye full of the extremely out of shape Chad laid out on the couch and averted her eyes rather quickly to try and avoid the frightful flashbacks. Karen waited for Brittini to pass in hopes that she hadn't been caught peeping, even if that wasn't the case of what she was doing. Brittini often walked the perimeter sidewalk to clear her mind, not to mention avoid going home, it was tranquil, there was a raised berm topped with privacy evergreens that helped to shield the inner park from the view of the road down the way, walking around the outside gave Brittini an escape as well as a peek that there was something outside of the trees. Brittini enjoyed reading to absorb as much vivid imagery about the world she may never get to experience, Aimee's ideas of a vacation for the two girls was a day at the beach, days spent wrapped in a towel hiding away from pervy old guys that wanted to stare at Brittini's young body or her mom's large chest.

Brittini figured that the loop was almost half a mile around, she could walk inside except that she risked running into any number of guys parked out front of Tara's house making out with her, or anything else Tara gave away for attention, or Darryl strutting around trying to keep up his appearance of toughness. Brittini dreaded growing old in the *Heights*, she loved her mom but also had the wherewithal that she could foresee a drunken loser getting her knocked up if she didn't find a way to get herself out, the only reason Aimee hadn't shat out nine of Tod's half inbred whole redneck babies was the Norplant contraception, one of the few good decisions she had made in the last decade. Brittini often sat and watched most of the residents go about their lives, she made observations based on how their lives had culminated and their actions lead them there, Big Ken let his wife get him involved in making methamphetamines and after having served his prison time, now his wife was incarcerated and he was the sole provider of Jonny, whom had no real outlook on life. Tara would most likely get pregnant or end up working at some salon and spending half of her time trying to keep up her fake looks and shallow life. Darryl would end up dead eventually, probably from getting caught up in a drug deal gone bad while at that Zoofy druggie guys and there was no telling how Joey/Lilly and Angel would turn out, that was a slew of a mess that had no predictions from one day to the next.

Chad was taken to the hospital and then on to rehab for a while, the police had received a phone call from Karen, it was her "concern" for one of her residents and she felt moved enough to dial but the truth is she was a nosy, meddling wench and had no ability to mind her own business, but her snooping and spying finally gave her some small validation for what she was up to, which she deemed "the lords work, and her Christian duty." The police arrived around noon on a Sunday, the residents were mostly home when two squad cars pulled

70

up to Chads home, their intent was initially to do a well check and ensure the safety of the occupant, with a side of DEA enforcement. The police headed around the trailer and up to the door before knocking and waiting for a response, after half a second without an answer they proceeded to let themselves into his home. Chad was curled up on the couch; he had been waiting for his score to arrive so he wasn't actually holding. Other than a few methadone pills, Chads home was a gross mess of over piled trash and wrappers but not enough drugs to detain him in jail for very long. Chad was coming down from his drug of choice and since he was beginning to get ill so they couldn't just leave him there to rot away on his couch.

Chad was taken to a hospital for detoxing, there was a sixty day hospital inpatient admission followed by a ninety day further treatment program that would be judge enforced cleansing to straighten the guy up. The cops sent an inspector to clean through Chads trailer, after hours sifting through the squalor they determined that the black mold content was high enough that the trailer had to be destroyed so a company came in; plastic wrapped the whole single-wide, disconnected everything underneath and hauled it away. Chads father had finally shown up to the treatment facility and gotten a much better understanding of how much of a scum bag Chad had become and had enough with him. Chad had only been detoxing for a few days when he learned that he was being forced to clean up his life, and on his own, as well as his home had been taken away and the few things he called his own, had been compromised and destroyed because he let things go to waste. Chad decided to sharpen his tooth brush on the cement floor to get a sharp enough edge and slit his own throat in the treatment facility. Karen was looking for sympathy, she was needy enough to try and angle herself as a victim, she had the innate ability to seek attention for any reason, and even the tragedy of someone else, and it was pathetic.

Karen explained all of the details of the impending service for Chad; she doled out her ill-gotten information and tried to deliver it in a manner that would allow her to determine that his arrest wasn't on her shoulders... which it was. It took enough beating around the bush for Karen to finally spit out what she had originally come over for, Tod and Aimee had nudged one another when she wasn't paying attention to the couple, the nudge was reassurance that they had finally gotten the reason why she joined them, after long enough they just began to suspect that maybe she was sneaking around but was caught so rather than continue her shady dealings, she walked over to mingle with her trailer neighbors. Jonny and Brittini were hanging out back and Aimee's trailer, Jonny always found it much safer not to be home when Big Ken came home, especially if he had been drinking. Jonny would often sneak in to sleep but Ken was also much more patient when it was cold out, his hatred of the boy was usually at its' cusp in the summer as the long hot work days fueled his rage with his own situation and the days spent listening to the swishing of water overhead in a cement truck left him adequate time to reflect on all of the poor choices he had made in his life.

Karen couldn't find enough sympathy for herself or anyone that cared enough to even raise an eyebrow when she unveiled the news about Chad and his demise. Everything Chad had done was self-inflicted, from day one and no one felt that he was even worth the feelings Karen was seeking, Tod and Big Ken were friends, Curtiss and Darryl, Jonny and Brittini, the rest were essentially acquaintances based on proximity rather than having shared interests, Darryl and Curtiss hung out with Lil B occasionally, especially if they were dealing the ignorant Mexican kid small time drugs like pot to smoke with his friends, or to catch glimpses of Tara when she was around. Tara had manly features to her face but it was her body that the older boys were interested in, she lacked any form of personality and only sucked off boys with nicer cars, she'd randomly flirt with other boys that would buy her things but beyond that, she wasn't of any substance nor interest in milling around the burn barrels drinking beer or liquor with most of the rest of the residents in the *Heights*.

Brittini tried her best to remain hidden away, Tuner and Billy often made that an easy choice when they were around, they would converse with Tod about all of their sexual conquests, biker chicks and loose women that gave themselves away for the sake of not sleeping alone for once. Brittini was subjected to listening to the stories of how the men would request the use of a bathroom if they were roofing a house with an attractive female living in, and they would search through some of the rooms for loose cash, panties, bras, and whatever they could rubs their balls on and titillate themselves to later. Brittini wanted to shower much more than she did from just having to hear them talk.

Karen shoved her hands in her pockets and decided that her time near people had filled some pretend quota for the day and returned back to her afternoon game shows. Karen did an about face and returned back to the direction she originated from, the people gathered around the barrel remained fairly silent until they were sure that she was far from earshot before they began to talk among themselves aloud as to what ever may have driven her over in their direction in the first place. Big Ken joked out loud "in honor of Martin Luther, I'd shoot her just like he got it" referring to Karen, Tod chuckled while Aimee just rolled her eyes. A shadow slinked from around the corner of the light blue trailer near the empty lot they stood in, Curtiss had been lurking to the side, he wasn't on his cousins lease or anything so he kept his head down so the cops weren't called on him for loitering or whatever Karen might concoct to slap him with, he didn't need the hassle. Curtiss nodded to The few standing near the barrel trying to keep warm, Ken pulled boards apart from the pile of pallets with his giant hands, he made the timber snap like he was just pulling apart Lego's, Ken loaded up the barrel enough to pump out heat for everyone and illuminate the area much more so now that the street lights were beginning to kick on and cause shadows to cover most of the partiers.

Curtiss mentioned running into Dez'rae and Tammi up over at the Amaca station, they were filling up on Boons and Newports. "Dez mentioned headin up here y'all, they might be bringing some drinks to share" Curtiss reassured the group. Tod hocked a big snot wad back into his throat before spitting it out, he tossed around the idea of fruity girly ass drinks or walking over to get another case of beer and making sure that scrawny punk Jonny wasn't humping Brittini up on his couch so he tugged up his pants under his large coat and headed back to his place. Tod made it three steps and then turned left enough to be able to whip out his dick and piss just off the edge of the cement, the steam was warming on his hands and he cleared his throat again from the snot that was caused from breathing the cold air half the afternoon. Big Ken pulled another beer from his coat pocket and cracked it open, he was running out but was nowhere near ready to call it a day yet either.

Curtiss lit a smoke and stepped a bit closer to the heat as he stood side by side with Joey. Curtiss had a feeling that Joey was probably good for some blow and turned his head towards the man and sniffled pretty hard trying to signal his intention. Joey didn't turn his face but in the reflection of the fire in his eyes, Joey trained his eyes on kid standing next to him. Joey sniffed back in a return signal so Curtiss knew he was in a good scoring position, now a bit of haggling to get just enough of a sniff to shuck off the cold and get him feeling a little bit better during the chilly afternoon.

Joey licked his upper teeth under his lip, Curtiss was quick to shake off the notion that he was willing to go down on Joey in exchange for a small snort of blow, Curtiss rebutted with scratching his face with his four fingers and Joey accepted the few dollar payment for a small picker upper. As Curtiss and Joey stepped away from the burn barrel for a quick line of cocaine, Tammi and Dez'rae drew closer, passing Tod on his way out. Tammi and Dez'rae were giggling and already finishing off their first bottle of the cheap strawberry wine and reaching into their coat for yet another. Tammi was trying to quickly rinse Gary's taste out of her mouth and was complaining that she is usually the one that has to suck off the obese and stinky gas station attendant and that Dez'rae needs to carry more of her share of the load. Shameeka was heading over to the gathering also, it wasn't much of a happening party but it was a Negro holiday and she be Negro so might as well holiday. Dez'rae handed her mom a pack of Kools and her own bottle of Boons to catch her up with the party as the sun finally set. Tod could hear more voices around the barrel as he stepped further away; his destination was his own trailer and the case of beer in the fridge that his girlfriend bought for the party so the voices faded away. Shameeka looked at the bottle of Boons that her daughter bought for her, she wasn't all that impressed with her taste but the Amaca didn't carry real liquor so it would have to do.

Shameeka walked over to Aimee and asked her how shit had been, Aimee just sighed and forced a smile, Shameeka knew exactly what that expression meant, and it was only a few years ago that Shameeka was balling this blinged out homeboy named Tony. Tony liked to drink and that didn't bother Shameeka, because she was getting hers, except, one night Tony was asked to go back to his peoples house because he was acting a fool up in Shameeka's house and she wasn't having it, Tony thought that she couldn't play a nigga like that and went to swing on the woman. After the police arrested Tony for aggravated assault, the police officer swung by to let

Shameeka know that when she and Dez'rae "defended" themselves against Tony, he ended up with several broken bones in his face, six broken ribs, fractured arm and sprained ankle, he offered a smile and an approving nod that they did the right thing by calling the police when he became aggressive towards the woman and her daughter.

Shameeka wanted her daughter to amount to something, anything, and when Dez'rae didn't back down from Tony but rather help dish out an ass whipping, Shameeka had confidence that her baby girl wasn't about to end up some knocked up hoochie. After the incident with Tony, Shameeka gave her daughter ample respect and treated her like an adult, she had no reserve about Dez'rae drinking as long as there wasn't any legal trouble for her or schooling issues, and Dez'rae respected the boundaries. Curtiss and Joey came back to the group, Curtiss was more relaxed, his shoulders weren't hunched up around his ears to keep him warm, and he was at ease and more social after his small nose powdering session with Joey. Shameeka was considering stepping up her party time, after all it was a negro holiday, She excused herself and made her feet travel in the direction of Darryl, the young white buck with many party supplies, she was thinking maybe he'll get her blew out and then maybe he'll have some Vicodin of a Percocet to magnify her drunk and off she went.

Tammi Mexican zippo'd her smokes, using the butt of her last cigarette to light her next one, she was having an awful need for an oral fix, even after having sucked off Gary the Gas station bum, she wanted to get herself some dick, she was lonely and it was a dangerous feeling for her, even though she had heard from Angel that Joey was hung like a damned donkey, the sex change hormone pills he was on disabled his "pool floaty" so getting skewered like a piece of steak wasn't happening by him. Big Ken had short gray hair and gray facial hair, he was largely overweight and his gut probably hung over his old wrinkly pecker so that wasn't an option, Jonny wasn't anywhere around and last time she tried he had no physical interest in her cooch, even when she wrapped her hand around his junk down the front of his pants, she still couldn't believe that even when she lead his hand down between her thighs and gyrated her pelvis to work his fingers into her, he wouldn't even make eye contact or get a hard on, she felt sad that he was so shy. Shameeka was singing "The Supremes" to herself but loud enough for everyone to hear before she left for whatever reason, so Dez'rae and Tammi were also humming various sections of the chorus, which caused Tammi to tap her hand in rhythm on her thigh as she tried to figure out how she might get humped on this occasion. Aimee and Joey still stood close to one another, Aimee asking if Angel was on her way to join them for the hell of it, he had no idea as they didn't exchange much of their calendars anymore.

A few months ago Aimee had joined Angel for a night of girly drinks at Angels place, Trujillo was nervous to have his house invaded by someone he didn't recognize and needed to be held by his mommy the whole night long. Joey hid away in his room mostly, the two ladies carried and drank on while watching movies and trying to let down their guard from the constant strain from the men that hurt them. Angel constantly had the hiccups from her fentanyl patch she kept on her body for pain, it helped to take the edge off of her circumstances with Joey having not only canceled their engagement, but also the bomb he dropped on her that he wanted to become a woman. After a few drinks Aimee was still distraught that Joey would make such a decision so she yelped for him to come join them, Angel did nothing to stop her; she had been round that conversation millions of times and each time, with no better understanding. Aimee peppered Joey with questions, they all continued through the second box of wine and Angel lamented how much she missed his skin missile, Aimee blurted out that she had heard about the python he carried around, causing Joey to roll his eyes and Angel to sigh in her dismay. Joey shrugged trying to escape the situation, it wasn't very lady like on his behalf to sit and be the center of the turmoil, except he did cause it all.

Aimee told Joey that she wanted to see his junk, Angel joked that she asked him often, even if they just masturbated together, or each other, except there was no soul left in his penis, like a sail without any wind. Sure enough Joey stood up and dropped his gym pants, his member hung like a bent tree limb, Aimee just let her eyes widen while affixed on the appendage, Angel reached out and grabbed hold and looked at Aimee; "see, nothing, not a rise, nor twitch, I could suck this thing purple and it wouldn't have any interest" she informed Aimee about her disappointment. Aimee just sat wide eyed and hadn't realized her mouth had dropped open until Angel reached over and jokingly pushed her head towards his member, which brought Aimee back to consciousness, she was taken aback by the baseball bat sized flesh.

Angel groped at the dangling parts and told Aimee to join her to prove that it wasn't just her that couldn't get a response, Aimee just stood amazed at both the length and girth, especially for a normal guy. Aimee looked up to Joey for approval, he nodded with encouragement, he explained to her that to him, his penis was an unwanted body part, like a mole or gut, except that most woman that saw such a thing, barraged him with questions about it all. Angel held Joeys scrotum in her left hand like skin stress balls and a wine glass in her right hand while Aimee stroked up and down a bit on the flaccid shaft that hung down between his legs. "If only I was still into girls" Joey joked about how he was in the middle of most guys' fantasies except that he held absolutely no interest at all. "Go ahead" suggested Angel, Joey stood firm, almost bored with the goings on, while Angel still held his nut sack and propositioned Aimee to try and go down on him. Aimee put the penis to her lips and then tried to finagle her mouth around the mighty oak, barely able to wrap her lips around the pinkish head of Joey's penis. Letting go of the limp penis it slapped against Angels hand, giving both buzzed women something to laugh about, Angel coupled her laughter with a sad desperation for things to be back to what they once were.

Aimee stood bewildered anytime she was in the presence of Joey, sure she had his dick in her mouth but it wasn't sexual it was for research, her friend had asked her to try and arouse a man that had no interest in women, with a penis that no longer served a purpose for the man. The strange night of trying to arouse a dead penis brought some comfort to Angel that it wasn't something she had done, that it wasn't a matter of Joey just not wanting to be with her any longer but a matter of truly wanting to become Lilly, a fact she was slowly trying to accept. Angel still loved Joey and fought to remain faithful to the idea, despite having the desires and urges of a woman that was still alive and full of zest for life. Joey convinced one of the men he worked with that they should come home with him, and put it to Angel while she played with Joey and hoped that it might bring her some closure. Angel was downright angry when Joey first suggested the tryst, he first bought her a mechanical play toy for her pleasure and hoped that maybe laying there naked for her while she took care of herself might help to satisfy some of her urges, she tried to explain it wasn't a matter of the physical comfort as much as it was the emotional comfort the he was still attracted to her and desired to be her husband, he failed to completely understand on her behalf.

Joey brought a kid named Evan over, an eighteen year old pizza delivery guy that was willing to nail anything not nailed down and didn't care if Joey watched or was present, Joey explained that the whole deal was to pleasure Angel and that was it, and it would be worth fifty bucks for him afterwards and they set the date. After Aimee was up to her elbows in Joey's man parts she purposefully finagled herself some personal alone time to fantasize taking the vaginal beating by the "Joey" club. Aimee walked to her house after the night of drinking, it was only half a block away, as she walked she continued to drift back to the throbbing beast in her hands, she could only imagine how enormous it must have been when it surged with blood and was aroused, she imagined the pounding and how it must have just about filled Angels abdominal cavity when they made love. Aimee took refuge in her car and double checked that no one would walk up to her car in the night, not that she could be seen within her tinted windows at night anyways.

Aimee reclined her driver's seat and pulled her pants down towards her knees, she let her left hand roam and paw at her chest while she let her imagination fill in with what Joey could have done to her if he would have just pumped some spirit into his flesh for her. Aimee licked her lips still trying to taste Joey in her mouth while her right had played in her creases between her thighs. The car windows steamed and fogged on the inside as her breathing grew more and more heavy, intimacy lately was a matter of biting the pillow and hoping that Tod finished quickly, there was very little attention paid to what she needed or wanted when Tod humped away at her, she wanted to be romanced once in a while like a lady, not taken like a stuffed toy and Tod just a dumb humping dog.

Aimee hoped that Angel would show up to the MLK burner, it grew tiring listening to Tod and Big Ken swap black jokes until Shameeka rolled up, Curtiss was a kid and he simply stood there and took the verbal assaults, even if passively mentioned but they still held enough pepper to raise his blood pressure with offense. Dez'rae and Tammi jostled back and forth about different boys at their school, Tammi tried to pretend she was much better than just a warm hole for most of the boys they had classes with, except that she wasn't and

Dez'rae knew it but didn't judge out loud anyways, she also slept with Gary to get to buy booze, the only difference was Dez'rae was a size two rather than a sixteen and didn't pretend she was better than nobody. Theresa was still a bit elusive after the Halloween party, she paid off Angel for the ride to the clinic and for the abortion but out of shame, she hardly showed her face around the *Heights* much, she was still friendly to Dez'rae and Tammi at school and the two girls had no idea what happened to her so they didn't know to suspect much, maybe home problems, but they could have used one more friend with them around the bonfire, except Tammi was glad she didn't have any more competition for trouser meat when she wanted it, Dez'rae was plenty enough competition for attention, she was much prettier and skinnier.

Shameeka made it to Darryl's porch finally, it wasn't all that long of a walk but she drank as she walked and the walking turned into stumbling, which then made her journey longer. With a knock on the door she continued to hum to herself while waiting for him to answer the door, sure enough he pulled the white door open and stood in the opening wondering who wanted what from him. Shameeka followed Darryl's gestures and entered into his house right behind him, fortunately he was alone and not feeling up to going to the gathering for long. Shameeka explained what she was looking for and wanted to join him in smoking a bowl to get her evening closer to her standards, Darryl told her that it would be ten bucks for the weed, and that was just to share since he had primo government shit and the pills were twenty each depending on what she wanted. Problem was, Shameeka only had five on her and she knew that probably wouldn't even be enough to keep her from being escorted out, except she did have one commodity men always had a need for and she asked Darryl if he had a condom. Darryl shook his head but reassured that Jenny, the girl he brought with him to a burner last fall, had just tested clean and he humped her brains out for weeks, according to him. Shameeka told him she'd spread her legs for him if he smoked her out first, hurried up and didn't finish in her or on her and gave her one of each pill, he dropped his pants in agreement and he then took up position behind her. Shameeka spent twenty minutes bent over a counter smoking his supreme herb while the short white boy humped and heaved behind her, he wasn't no brother but at least he was quick and she didn't even lose her beer buzz while he was at it. With pills in hand and pot on the brain, she was good to travel back towards to bur barrel, Darryl knew his line about Jenny being tested was a lie but he wasn't about to pass up ass, ever.

Tod Stepped lightly up into the front stoop and peered in the window to see if he could catch Brittini riding away on top of Jonny, much to his disappointment she was laid out on the couch while he was sprawled out on the floor, and they were watching some rom com together, but at least there was beer. Tod hiked the blue and silver thirty pack up onto his shoulder and grabbed his freshly opened traveler off of the counter and headed back to the barrel, he was in and out without having spoken a word to either living room squatter he passed. The rest of the evening was a series of Tammi and Curtiss volleying eye glances, most men like fit girls, Curtiss didn't have much of a hard on for Tammi, she was too heavy for being white, he was much more attracted to Dez'rae but that was most people who knew the two girls. Curtiss was going to get naked with someone on this holiday, might as well be Tammi. Curtiss nodded to Tammi to hint heading back to his place, she wasn't ready to leave but was already bored and cold from standing around, there wasn't enough going on to keep her limited mental faculties engaged in the crackling of the barrel fire or when Big Ken hulk smashed pallets to feed the into the steel drum, so why not. Tammi made her stop to Dez'rae for the rest of the second bottle of Boons, they purchased a few and it was her mouth that did the work for the night, plus Shameeka was on her way back and would probably share whatever she scored from Darryl so Dez'rae took a large swig and let her friend take the bottle.

As Curtiss dragged his screw partner behind him back to his room where he could work uninterrupted, Tammi figured she had enough smokes and booze to get her through the night and go to school from the local bus stop in the morning, if she bothered to go. Dez'rae did find Curtiss cute, the boy always kept his hair cut close, his clothes didn't hang off of him and of he and Darryl, he was the whiter of the two of them, big dimples and medium tone skin, he was a good looking kid, the problem was that even though he had smart people in his family, like Tyrone, he was caught in the being socially black rather than be his own person, like Tyrone. Tyrone could have been a chemical engineer if only he could have escaped the black mentality of "staying black" which often seems to mean stay on probation or in the legal system somehow and scam unemployment or state assistance in one way or another. Curtiss hung out with Darryl and peddled small amounts of weed to kids at school, he felt he could use his being black and a minority at school to fill some stereotypes and rather than actually work hard and be something, he would follow the cues of rappers and all the other fairly dominant black clichés, just sell drugs and take everything the easy way.

Curtiss dragged Tammi through his living room and into his room; she was trying hard to delude herself with the last of her bottle of piss wine while he worked on taking her pants off. Tammi asked if Curtiss had any weed they could smoke up before getting started, she hated who she was but wasn't about to change anything because as long as men found her attractive, that was enough attention for her, be it Darryl, Gary, Curtiss, DJ Wriggle, Frankie at work or any other of the number of guys she let into her body for whatever reason she had at the time. Curtiss lit up his best cherry blunt for them to share, Tammi removed the rest of her clothes and as she dragged and gagged on the dense chronic, Curtiss was taking off his clothes and pulling back the sheets for them to climb into together.

Tammi struggled to focus on her mind clouding as Curtiss sucked on her tits and man handled various parts of her body, she reached down and gave a weak hand job to him but it was enough to arouse him and get him ready to go. Curtiss thought he was a god in the sack because he thought Tammi's moaning was in response to his prowess, not that he failed at foreplay and she was merely dry and slightly in pain as he thrusted away. Tammi tried to think about the next time she could get high, anything that would mentally take her away from where she currently was, or doing what she currently was. Curtiss had a plump bodied girl in his bed, he tried no to laugh or lose his erection when Tammi moaned, it reminded him of the Kim K sex tape he saw, she could make a cement penis go soft and Curtiss found it funny when he watched the video years back, found it funny that Ray wasn't the biggest pussy in that video. Now Tammi has been through more brothers than a slave auctioneer. Curtis and Tammi fumbled through the rest of their night as drugs and alcohol clouded both of their minds.

Shameeka stumbled back to the group around the barrel, she had saved half of a Percocet for her daughter, she took her pill and half of the next one but felt she owed Dez for the bottle of Boons and for her trouble. Tod was steps behind Shameeka, case still propped up on his shoulder but a few lighter. Tod had just enough to drink to be glad to pass around the cold brewskis, when everyone was drinking and carrying on, it validated all of them standing around and freezing their broke asses off. Joey had grown tired as his coke had begun to wear out, he had been holding for Angel and one of the agreements they had between them is that anything she wanted he was obligated to get, she was still paying a majority of the bills and he was one broke tranny, but he did have his abilities to procure some narcotics for her. Aimee knew of the situation that Joey tried to supplement Angel with, Tommy that is, he brought the eighteen year old boy over for Angel to enjoy, she was at first upset that he thought of her sexual desires like the Tyrannosaurus rex in Jurassic park and Tommy was the goat, she threatened him that he'd be "a Tranny with a sore ass" if he kept his shit up before Joey handed over some powder that would assist things along.

The three adults got good and high as well as liquored and lubed up, Angel let Tommy take care of her from behind while on all fours, she insisted that Joey lay under her so she could nuzzle at his anatomy while he helped to play with herself and him, Aimee was told that Angel had been ravished by Tommy but being eighteen, he hardly had any stamina to speak of. Angel let Tommy get close and then insisted he put a condom on to prevent the mess, she was on contraception but she still didn't want to have to clean up the strangers mess. Tommy was skinny and fairly athletic but he lacked the blessings that Joey was born with and she craved the real meat, Tommy started out without a condom because Angel insisted that if she wanted some rubbery donger inside of her she'd use the one she bought, the warm flesh inside of her was what she craved. Joey laid up under Angel as Tommy thrusted away at her, she still felt deeply saddened that there was nothing she could do to breathe life into the dick she adored, it just laid there with a slight left tilt, there was no mouth to south resuscitation that could work, it wasn't even like Joey was turned on watching either person in the live action skin flick, the hormone drugs simply neutralized most of his feelings and it wore heavy on Angels heart, Aimee on the other hand would have changed places with Angel so quick there wouldn't have been any need for warm up or foreplay.

Aimee wrapped her mouth around Joey that night, she still pictured his boy baton and how her fingers barely even touched when she wrapped her hand around it, she didn't care that it had no effect on him but she wanted half an hour of it just hanging in her face again for personal use, she fought the urge to offer him some money to just let it dangle for her to play with, kind of like a kitten pawing at a butterfly. The fire was warm and the beer was starting to numb Aimee all over, which made parts of her tingle. Dez'rae and Shameeka stood around and helped Tod pass around a few more beers, Neither Tod nor Big Ken had enough disrespect for Shameeka to bust out any racial jokes, she had earned their respect, even if they just saw her as black, black and nigger weren't the same, she held a full time job, a nice car and her own home, had never been on welfare nor probation and the only trouble she's had with law enforcement in the last twenty years has been warnings about a blinker being burned out, she kept her nose out of trouble and a cool demeanor about herself. Any time Tod of Ken would find a joke they thought they could share, Shameeka would listen intently but if they seemed to rant about coloreds or something, she would take all of the wind out of their sails by calmly pointing out that she is not a stereotype and didn't appreciate being roped in with such nonsense. By calmly responding to the two rednecks, she forced them to climb up to a class level above their own and respect her accordingly, if they thought to argue even for a moment, she would remind them of one fact or another about herself that would shoot down any chance of them labeling her as ignorant in anyway, and for that they respected her.

Dez'rae was raised by the much stronger Shameeka, the issue is even though she had a very firm body from athletics, she lacked the self-respect Shameeka had, and did blow Gary a few times for the privilege of buying cigarettes at fourteen and alcohol at sixteen, Gary's minimal age requirements. Tod hardly goes to the Amaca store, even though it was close by and an easy in or out, he had a restraining order against him there and even if Gary isn't working, he isn't allowed to be there. It made things a little hard to deal with but Tod dealt with it much like most other things in his life, he just accepted shit was the way it was and made the extra drive when he found himself in need of smokes or beer.

Dez'rae didn't enjoy blowing Gary, she felt disgusted afterwards and confided in her best friend Tammi about it, Tammi felt it was a chance to one up the much smaller and more attractive girl but that's another point. Dez'rae knew she shouldn't be smoking but it didn't interfere with her dancing or running track and if she didn't it was almost impossible to get Frankie to let her get a state mandated break during her shifts at *Chicklips* when she worked. Tammi often worked four or five nights a week while Dez'rae only work one or two, occasionally during the summer three, she had dance or track to contend with, plus she didn't like how much Frankie hovered around her or "accidentally" brushed his junk against her ass when he had to slide past her when they worked together, he was another horny teen slime ball like Darryl and she didn't want anything to do with it, Tammi on the other hand craved any and all attention she could get, and from anyone.

Six years ago Tod came into Aimee's life, and for the first year it was romance and love, Tod was hot -tarring roofs and working with a small crew of Mexicans, including Tara and Lil B's padre, Salvio. Salvio actually ran it as a small business, paid taxes and did most things legally, despite the amount of jobs he lost to his illegal countrymen because he had standards, things the thickly mustached man didn't seem to pass to his kids. Salvio, Tod and Berman were three roofers that would haul all of their gear up to the top of tall buildings and boil down hot ass tar and spread it around to reseal all of the cracks and what have you, it was grueling but after the time Tod spent working after he got out of jail, he was glad to be off his probation, which he had then transferred back home for the end duration. Berman was a stocky guy, he would often haul most of the bigger supplies to the top of the build so the men could work, they would fire up the tar boiler and toss in large chunks of the solid black goop and wait for it to liquefy, then carry buckets of it across the roof and then mop it flat. The days were hot and Tod would take on an African color to his exposed skin by the end of the summer, Aimee used to laugh that when he removed his wife beater that his skin was so white that it still looked like he had the tank top on.

Brittini was almost nine when she first met Tod, he was tall and wiry but he was a nice guy and he was friendly, she was used to Don and Shelley one or two nights a week when Aimee had gentlemen over but Tod was the first one that Brittini met, things seemed like Aimee had gotten herself together and was finally setting up her life so that she and Brittini might excel and move out from the *Heights*. Towards the end of the first summer Tod and Aimee were together, Salvio had contracted a rather large job for the crew, Salvio had mentioned it was a large enough to put enough scratch in their pockets to give them a good padding through the winter on top of their unemployment, which sounded just fine for Tod as he was going to be off probation before the job was done so he wouldn't have to have a job through the winter. As the job finished up and the men were getting their final pay of the season, Berman suggested the crew go on out to the local "Honker Hub" the titty bar. Salvio was a family man when he could be and passed on going but thanked his crew for their hard work and bid them a good winter and that was that for him.

Berman and Tod went to the hooter hut and enjoyed a few drinks, Tod semi celebrated the release of his probationary binds, he was no longer shackled to the system, no longer required to randomly drug test or remain sober to keep himself out of trouble, it was shots of Jack, Jim, Jose, Captain, Buffalo Trace, whiskey, rum, and bourbon long into the night. Between booze and broads the two racked up almost a four hundred dollar night, with veins running hot with self-disappointment Tod tried to tuck his tail between his legs and leave with any remaining dignity and winter cash he had left, Berman was of a different mentality, he hooted and hollered against such a bill, he groped girls boobs and slapped girls on their asses as the stocky man poured back shots at eight bucks a piece, and tallied up ladies to grind up on his lap over and over again, each girl tallied up at twenty bucks each, the manager even went over the bill with the men but Berman was adamant that he wasn't responsible for all of his actions and that the club was scamming him. Tod was fairly sure that what they had done was self-inflicted and earned. Berman was aggressive and the men were escorted out into the parking lot after they were relieved of the owed money. Berman drove Tod home, all the while still complaining and vehemently against his own part in the night. Tod had Berman stop off and the Amaca on the way home for a pack of smokes, he needed another pack to de-stress once he got home and away from Berman and his drunken shouting and hollering.

Tod walked into the gas station and greeted Bruce, an older man that worked the midnight shift at the station, he was working a crossword puzzle behind the counter, Tod placed a Diet Pepsi on the counter and requested two packs of Marlborough's, Berman yanked the door wide open after Tod had been without the headache inducing boisterous man for almost a minute. Berman had turned his attention to the fact that Tod had half of the tab that they rang up; therefor Tod had half a hand in Berman spending half of his final check. Berman was extremely intoxicated and growing more aggressive. Tod paid for his supplies and tried to coerce the belligerent man back out of the gas station, before Tod could make any headway Bruce had stood up with the noise bellowing from Berman and began speaking loudly and encouraging the Berman take it back outside. Berman wasn't about to back down let alone take orders from a man in his fifties and peppered with gray hair, Tod struggled to convince Berman back out and towards the car, he even suggested Berman just go home since he could walk himself the few blocks back to his place with Aimee.

Bruce let himself out from behind the counter and with spread arms tried to corral the two bickering drunkards outside and to anywhere but in his store, as Bruce drew near, Berman began to push back on Tod whom was trying to get him outside and closer to the car. As Berman began to push back against now two men shoving on him, he grew even more impatient as his blood alcohol level was three times the legal limit. Berman heaved back on the tall lanky Tod, sending him into Bruce and Bruce then into the counter as he fell. Berman continued to shout and raise hell, Tod took a moment to get his bearings enough to rise, but Bruce didn't get up at all. Bruce's brother Steven bought the gas station to retire to, he owned the gas station two years before cardiac arrest cut his retirement, and his life short, Steven left behind a wife named Mary and a son named Gary.

The police had to use Tasers to subdue the out of control Berman, Tod was quick to raise his hands and follow commands and not resist arrest. Tod was eighteen when he first went to prison; he was considered a pretty boy and let some of the older inmates give him shotty jail ink tats to give him a more gruff appearance, the police immediately saw the prison ink and Tod earned himself a night in the local jail. By the time the police were able to breathe after dealing with Berman, and getting Tod secured in the back of the second car, the officers headed inside to speak with Bruce, whom triggered an alarm to summon them before he rounded the counter to act as riot control until the police arrived. Bruce was discovered lying on the floor, he had to have been there almost fifteen minutes by the time all was said and done and the ambulance was called.

Tod sat still on the curb awaiting the second patrol car; Berman had done seven or eight summersaults in the back seat, kicking at anything he could get his feet to. Tod politely requested that he not join Berman in the backseat and the younger officer agreed to keep them separated until the second squad arrived for his transportation. Tod requested the ability to drink his purchased Pepsi and had a suspicion that he request was going to be denied repetitively, so he sat and kept his chin on his knees while keeping his ankles crossed per his instructions. The senior officer was tasked with trying to calm

Berman as his hulk and rage were still cranked to eleven, the junior officer stood guard of Tod to ensure that he wouldn't try and run, he was vigilant of all he could be until backup arrived, Tod did his best to appease the officers and remain on their good side. Tod was proven intoxicated and loaded into the back of the second squad to go in for processing. The officers turned their sights in towards the gas station attendant, whom did not follow the men out, and that was where they found Bruce, with a puddle of blood forming from the left side of his head under his short gray haired crew cut. Bruce was rushed into surgery for a subdural hematoma, which was bleeding on the brain, he survived the surgery but because of the swelling and damage for over half an hour before they could drill a hole to relieve the pressure, Bruce was no longer able to work and help provide for his or his brothers family.

Gary worked some afternoon shifts when his father passed away; he was hardly out of college for graphic design when his father passed away. Mary was so distraught over losing her husband that she grew overly attached to Gary and had a hard time letting him grow into his own man. Gary became a bit of a recluse after his father passed away, he worked the afternoons all week long to help his mother pay bills and keep his father's dream alive, it hindered his ability to try and begin a career or life like he had hoped when he started into community college. Gary, Mary and Bruce's Wife Julie had gotten together to file a lawsuit against both Berman and Tod for their part in Bruce's accident. Aimee was worried when she woke up and Tod hadn't made it home and about the time she was gearing up to head down to the Amaca station for her own cigarettes, Brittini came rushing out of the house flailing her arms to gain her attention for a phone call she was receiving. The officers explained that Tod had been detained for his part in a reckless assault and personal injury and that if she wanted to come see him that she was welcome to during certain hours. Aimee knew Tod had spent time in jail but he had worked pretty hard to climb up in life and she thought she finally met a man that would have helped her raise her daughter and that she could be happy with.

Aimee had so many questions of her own and was filled with the urgency to know what had happened, he never came home and to end up in jail is a whole lot better than the morgue but still inexcusable in her eyes. The county jail was rather modest for the size of the city in

88

served, but it did also transfer many more of its guests to larger facilities further away to help separate them from possible associates in the area. Big Ken always mentioned having served some time with that crooked Detroit mayor but he can never remember which one. Aimee couldn't take in her purse, cell phone or really anything but her driver's license, Brittini preferred to stay in the car, the jail intimidated her and she wasn't havjng it. Aimee's heart sank when they lead Tod out from the holding cell, the guard told her that he had to wait another day before he could see the judge for preliminary sentencing and then from there the judge could decide if he gets out or goes to jail. Tod told Aimee what all had happened, he asked her to also ask for a copy of the security tapes to back up how things went down and that he shouldn't be wrapped up in all of the mess, especially because Berman pushed him into Bruce, if Bruce hadn't been there then everything would have been fine, maybe if Berman would have just stayed the hell in the car, maybe.

Tod kept his head up and his mouth fairly silent, he knew not to ruffle any feathers and wasn't going to let any of the small time punks stare him down either. Tod looked pathetic as the was guided in wearing his shoes without laces (a suicide precaution,) he shuffled his feet to keep his work boots from falling off and his still dirty clothes stank of the alcohol that Tod had sweated out overnight having slept in his clothes. Tod expressed that the worst part of the entire evening was that he didn't even get his Diet Pepsi. Aimee told Tod that she couldn't afford to post bail or even hire a lawyer, she had a hard enough time making ends meet and if she tried anything it might displace her and her daughter, and only having dated him a dozen months that was one hell of a gamble she couldn't risk, he understood and told her he'd be out soon enough. Aimee loaded back up after her twenty-five minute visit, hardly worth the half an hour it took to get to see him but she had some shopping she could get done with Brittini while they were out. Aimee ran through a Meijer for her supplies, Brittini was going to miss Tod but not enough to wish his freedom; she was glad to have her mom back to herself and was grateful.

Aimee stopped at the Amaca station to see who was working and to ask if she could possibly ask for a copy of the security tapes if there were any, the station was closed so her mission had been aborted for the time being. Tod sat and stewed in his small cell for the day, each minute ticked by and his pulse seemed to match the caged clock on the wall, hardly an hour passed since he got to see his girl and he decided that if he was going back to lockup then he wasn't going back out of shape so he began with push-ups, sit-ups and squats to ease himself back into his old prison workout routine, it also helped to pass the time. Tod was told that he would see Judge Vern Smalls, some Jerry Reed looking judge that was already looking up his past, a notion that didn't comfort him to sleep that night.

Aimee and Brittini had finally unloaded their groceries and Aimee did her best not to cry in front of her daughter, she tried to keep the mentality that no man was worth tears, it was a lie but she did her best to stay convinced to keep calm and carrying on. As the afternoon began and Aimee had grown weary of sitting around she left Brittini behind and drove down to the gas station with hopes of finding it open this time. Aimee was in luck, sure enough the station was back open and per usual, it was devoid of patronage, there was a pudgy curly black haired kid inside with thick rimmed glasses and a maroon smock on, it was Gary; Bruce's nephew.

Aimee introduced herself and quickly followed up with the fact that she didn't want any trouble, she apologized sincerely about what had happened to Bruce before delving into her need of a security tape. Gary was stonewalling the needy woman; he was full of angst at what had happened, his jaw remained clenched and tense as Aimee tried her best to persuade the boy to help her out. Gary remained mute about everything; he didn't even mention that his mother and aunt had already convened to press charges against both men in the brawl. Aimee was growing inpatient trying to get a simple copy of a measly ass video tape; she tried another tactic, to use one of her strengths, her chest. Aimee unbuttoned her top once so a little more of her spilled out, Gary raised an eyebrow but his fantasies about being a poker player came to mind and he kept his best poker face and tried to think about baseball. With a second button becoming unsnapped and her lacy white bra strap sliding out a little from under her shirt, she could see a little bit of a response from the pants of Gary and she found her niche.

Gary held out until Aimee had reached her right hand into her top and caressed her breast and asked Gary if he wanted a turn, his lips finally broke and countered her offer; "you need me to go against my family and use one of my tapes and do all the work to run a copy for you for just a little breast play?" Gary was playing his hand well, he found himself in a foreign situation for the first time in his life, and he had power. Aimee asked him if he wanted her to pull her boob out, his pupils dilated and his forehead began perspiring a little, all giveaways that he wasn't aware he was doing but signs Aimee could spot across a football field. Gary began to sit up a bit straighter then realized that he had better not then he hunched a bit more, Aimee brushed the left side of her shirt to the side and let the younger boy see her bra covered breast, it was just a boob but he was a bigger tit and she needed his help. Gary remained strong and then bluffed up a bit more. Aimee offered to show him her pair of Aces, Gary was intrigued but tried to counter with a straight, Aimee knew she had the boy turned on but knew he could always play his own hand and leave her with a flush so she licked her lips and told him she could be his kings queen for a little bit, thinking he was being a joker about all of the bartering. Gary leaned over the counter with his eyes fixated on Aimee's rack and then made an overt gesture at her ass, he propositioned filling her house with his "king", Aimee suggested just her hand to his jack but he wanted all in. Aimee was confident he was bluffing in many ways and maybe if she just had a good enough hand that she might end up calling his bluff and keep some amount of credibility.

Gary told Aimee that he wanted to screw her in the back and then she would get a copy of the tape, Aimee wasn't to mention of any of this and directed her to the back room to take her clothes off. Aimee finished unbuttoning her top, her large chest lead the way into the back room. Gary told Aimee to remove her clothes while he started the tape copying portion of his end of the bargain. Gary stared at Aimee while she undressed, she reached behind her to unsnap her bra, the elastic caused both sides to fling forward as she removed her shirt and bra, setting both on top of a pile of cigarette cartons, she felt a little self-conscience as her heart raced while undressing for this kid almost eight years younger than she was. Gary stared intently, he moved closed and unzipped his pants, Gary bent down a little to stare at the enlarged areolas that capped the ends of Aimee's breasts, her hands shaking as she fought the overwhelming want to shield herself.

Gary unsnapped her pants, his large shit eating grin revealed yellowing crooked teeth, Aimee tried to breathe out of her mouth as she slid her shorts and panties down to her ankles. Gary let his pants fall as he unzipped his smock, Aimee reached forward hoping that between his arousal watching her undress, and his juvenile mentality that maybe if she stroked him a few times, maybe he would explode and save her from having to take him into her body. Amie let Gary reach forward and play with her tits, his exhale was choppy as his pecker hardened even more and thrusted against her hands. Aimee bent forward and began to take him into her mouth, she was pretty sure that she had learned enough in high school that she could suck him off fairly easily. Aimee licked at him a bit and wished she hadn't gotten into such a predicament, she was in hell as she began to bob her head back and forth while Gary grabbed her body.

After one of the longest minutes Aimee could recall, Gary told her that he hoped she was plenty ready for him, Aimee felt enlightened that maybe he was ready to finish, until he put one hand on her shoulder and backed her up from him. Aimee stood up and Gary reached his right hand up to his mouth, he licked his first two fingers, the stringer of spittle stretched from his tongue to his fingertips for almost a foot as he moved his hands towards her downstairs. Gary pushed his left hand on to Aimee's left breast and coaxed her body to lean back against the counter that was behind her, he rammed his fingers back and forth in a crude sawing motion as he made feeble attempts to moisten her up, his uncut finger nails and coarse calluses on his fingers seemed to pull at her sensitive skin and some of the hairs that got in his was. Gary roughly jammed his two still dry fingers inside of her, his lack of experience with woman's genitals was more than obvious, he fumbled and hurried, he only had his computer fantasies to use as a reference as to how to work a woman's erogenous zones, Aimee was bored before he even yanked himself out.

Aimee kept trying to quickly stroke him off, hoping to hurry the inevitable along, she hoped to herself that maybe a little ball handling would give him just enough of a push to cause him to fold. Gary seemed to be trying to shove a beach towel into a garden hose with the motion he was making inside of her, Aimee finally had to grab his hand and give him a break, she encouraged him to stroke himself for a minute while she got herself worked up a little better, she reassured him she was just nervous being in the back of the store and all. Gary slowly pulled on himself, something he surely had adequate practice doing, his rhythm picked up as Aimee leaned back and took care of her already swollen self, she was ever more self-conscious as she wasn't as small as she was in school, she had a belly and it had been some time since she "weed whipped the landscape." Aimee finally felt she was wet enough to accept the grungy bastard, she also whispered to herself that Tod had better appreciate what she was doing and propose to her. Gary stepped up and began to rub the head of his small part against her, she was leaned back at a very strange angle but he was much too focused on her tits to bother to care anyways. Gary pulled Aimee down a bit to give himself a little more trajectory to help compensate for his lacking size, when she felt that he was finally all of the way inside, he had no rhythm and she couldn't tell if he was more than two inches inside of her, she tried not to laugh that she'd come across more satisfying tampons. As Gary became more erratic in his heaving, he grunted and wheezed, Aimee reached her hand down between her legs and used her two fingers to pinch his penis a bit waiting for the bulge in the sides of him to signal he was about to explode so she could stand up and let him hump the air, also she wanted to aim him in a direction that wasn't going to spray liquid nerd onto her clothes on the floor.

Sure enough Aimee jerked at the boy half seizing in her hand as he held a death grip on her right breast with his right and left hand trying to hold him up, his rocking motion made him look like a rock'em sock'em robot right before its head went up. The end result wasn't as much as Aimee had assumed it would be, she assumed he probably spanked his monkey a few times while bored at work, he probably had a bottle of baby lotion and a tug mag tucked behind the counter by his stool. Gary held Aimee captive for another few strange moments, rather than hurry her along and shoo her out, he continued to run his fingers around her nipples, between her sweaty breasts and down to her wet matted pubic hair, she tried to force her eyes closed and imagine it was one of the boys she went to high school with, she tried to pretend she was back to being a cheerleader and one of the footballs players was fondling her, not this pudgy weirdo with a crooked smile filled with even more crooked teeth. Gary let the whole back room take on the wretched smell of his body odor, it was thick and putrid and it began to cause Aimee to gag as the salty smell mixed with hot garbage and onions wafted from his balls and into the air where she could smell it. Gary grabbed a disc off of the counter right behind Aimee right before bending down to pull his pants up, he stood a foot from Aimee and gazed without words, his mouth had a slight lift to the upper right lip as he looked down over his glasses while Aimee redressed.

Aimee looked at the disc, she tucked it into her bra strap as she buttoned her shirt back up and asked if that was the copy she needed, the shiesty bastard already had copies made, it was store policy that in the event to police need to be called that they make half a dozen copies of the security footage so lawyers and whomever each would get copies. Aimee was filled with more rage, her ears felt hot and now she truly began to perspire, Gary took full advantage of her and her trying to help Tod. Aimee explained that Tod was the skinny guy in the incident and she was trying to prove if he had much to do with it all, Gary replied: "mom and the police pointed out that it was the big guy that was responsible for it all and the cops were only really holding Tod because he was so drunk." Mary and Julie had already determined that Tod wasn't involved enough and was actually trying to get Berman out when everything happened. Aimee was extremely pissed off and this dorks spunk was still wet and sticky on her fingers, she stank of this ugly, fat, Jerry Seinfeld looking shit bag and he not only already had a disc burned for her, he also knew enough information for her that she could have avoided all of the unpleasant humping, all three minutes of his pathetic asthma ridden stamina.

"I'm going to tell Tod and he is going to stab you and then have sex with your plump dying body, I will make sure he puts his dick into the bleeding stab wounds as you gasp for your last breath" Aimee furiously threatened the store attendant. Gary swallowed hard and then an eerie calm came over his face and relaxed his eyebrows as he raised his fingers again and dragged them across the outstretched tip of his tongue. Aimee scoffed and made her way back to her car, she had just barely slammed the door behind her before her eyes exploded in tears as she tried to blink rapidly enough to give her that sliver of clarity to see to hold her lighter to light her cigarette that was spotted with tears near the filter line. The first cigarette had been smoked before she even made it out of the parking lot, her nerves were shot and her adrenaline was still giving her the shakes, no matter how hard she tried to puff it away with a second one. As Aimee crept over the speed bumps on her way back to her home, she told herself that Tod was probably having sex with men and that it was OK that she was too, the notion of Gary breathing and sweating on top of her caused her eyebrows to wrinkle again as she pulled into her parking space.

94

Aimee greeted Brittini when she came in through the door, she was sprawled out on their couch with a bowl of Doritos and a bowl of ranch veggie dip, Aimee hardly passed any never mind and headed into her room for clothes before showering. Aimee locked herself in her bathroom and quickly undressed and began to scrub, she figured that even though it might hurt she might have to scrub her coochie with steel wool to get Gary's funk out of her. Aimee scrubbed and scrubbed some more, even past when the water had turned cold, she had flash backs of other less than enjoyable experiences in her sexual past. In high school there was a male gym teacher named Lachu, he was sleeping with a few of the male football players, she tried to approach another teacher Mr. Stahl and tell him but his response wasn't spoken, Stahl told her if she wanted to pass she would have to really step it up in class. Aimee was a little heavier back in high school, the boy she had just started seeing had told her about Lachu and what he was doing with some of the boys and Aimee tried to do the right thing, Stahl raised his leg and his penis plopped out from the leg hole of his short shorts. Stahl rubbed on himself and forced Aimee's hand to touch his prick, he told her if she told anyone then she would fail and get in a whole lot of trouble. Aimee was terrified and cried as she rubbed her hand up and down as the much older teacher pleasured himself to completion.

Aimee spent years trying to block out and drink away what had happened, when she began having sex with boys she replaced the memories most of the time, she enjoyed sex and when she got to have it it meant that the boys she was with liked her back, that's ultimately what she wanted out of high school. Aimee fought and struggled for friends and popularity in high school, it was such a waste of effort, most of the popular girls had all grown fat and married balding men, most of the hot football players like Tod used to be, are like Tod now, marginally employed and had only peaked in high school, only to fall for the rest of their lives. Aimee thought about how she was a little healthy in high school but she was still nice and well liked, most of the mean bitches had their hips spread, their asses sag and their husbands cheat on them, it was a pleasant karma circle but it didn't matter anymore. Aimee was holed up in her room now trying to cry away the feeling of Gary breathing his warm pork rind smelling breath on her bare skin. Aimee cried herself to sleep for the night,

Brittini was nine and old enough to put herself to bed when she got tired, she was an independent girl.

The following morning came with the ringing of a phone, her phone squawked like mad hell, like Gary was in her bed raping a chicken with his twisted smirk and thick glasses, the noise resonated for a moment to intrude into the heavy slumber that Aimee was entwined within. There was a collect call from Tod; he didn't have all that long and at $5.99 per minute, Aimee couldn't afford to bullshit for very long. Tod was scheduled to see the judge around *three p.m.* and he needed Aimee to pick him up afterwards. Shortly after the phone call had awaken her, it sounded like Brittini was clambering up on the counter to get a bowl for cereal so she lit a cigarette and decided to join her daughter for breakfast at the coffee table in the living room. The Judge decided that Tod wasn't responsible for any of the chaos at the store but since there was a blanket request for restraint, Tod was barred from ever returning to the gas station, a cagey last minute addition Gary slid in to protect his fat greasy ass from Tod raping his stab wounds in retaliation to what he did to Aimee.

Since the arrest of Tod and the swindling done by Gary, amends had been attempted between Gary and Aimee, the proximity of the store was a major deciding factor for Aimee to give up such a grudge against the social parasite, anytime she noticed he was talking up some young tart such as Dez'rae, she would remind the girls that he has crabs and watch them squirm and break the conversation on the spot. Aimee still bought her cigarettes for both her and Tod but only if she forgot to get extra packs from the gas station closer to her work. Gary remained propped up every afternoon and late till midnight atop of an aging wood bar stool, he was one of three employees that shared guard over the minimal supplies inside, there was one cooler stocked with skunky beer and he kept the bottom shelf lined with Boons farm booze, he kept it in the front most cooler and on the bottom on purpose, it gave him decent gaze either down the shirts of the girls bending down to reach for it or at their backside, not a bad sleazy idea for a perv. Gary always stared at the bodies of any girl that came into his store, any semi firm ass or bouncy breasts left him wheezy and more excited than his lungs could keep up but he always smirked and used some scumbag term of endearment like "how you doin'

96

babygirl" and things of the like, trying to support his inflated self-delusion.

Aimee lacked the courage to admit to Tod what had happened when she went to get a copy of the security tape, she tried to block out leaning back against the counter while Gary huffed and puffed while thrusting inside of her, she was ashamed that she was tricked but it was just sex, mediocre sex at best and she did her best to put it from her mind, as any girl would. Tammi slept with Gary a few times, she often resorted to sucking him off to get alcohol and then drinking the alcohol in order to forget what she had done with her life, like sleep with Gary. Because of his lust for younger girls Gary was known to sell to minors whom were willing to do more with him than measly flirt with. Tammi knew of several girls from school that would purchase from the Amaca station, for high school girls it was a small price to pay in order to get loaded.

Gary got his rocks off, Aimee knew of most of the transgressions and continued to look down upon the portly kid for what he does, but what could be done? Aimee warned Brittini off from the gas station, it would probably push her to kill herself if she were ever to find out if her daughter was ever another victim taken advantage of by the greasy curly haired round faced man with a slight speech impediment and thick rimmed glasses that constantly slid down to the end of his nose, he even had the same shrill voice that jerry Seinfeld had, just a little less encouraging to commit suicide when you heard it.

Aimee felt mildly responsible about Tod having been dealt the lifetime ban from the gas stations, Gary most likely held the ban in place out of fear that Tod would stab him and have sex with the wound as Aimee had threatened, for the sake of self-preservation the coward kept the restraining order in place and often had the sheriffs on speed dial. Aimee did her best to avoid having to go into the Amaca station and when she had to swallow her pride, she was quick in and out with as little conversation as possible, she still dreaded having had his dick in her, she was grateful she didn't blow him long but having let him hump her was bad enough, she barely felt him at the time but as the years passed she more felt his fingers groping at her, even so much longer later and it made her skin crawl with goose pimples at the horrid memories.

After all of the legal matters with the fight and the disabling of Bruce, Salvio was leery about hiring Tod back but did the following year, which was his last year as the owner before he sold it to take a more reliable job in the AutoLine on the other side of town for the sake of his family. Berman was awarded three to five years for assault resulting in great bodily harm for his part in what he had done to Bruce, his drunken state was a reason but not an excuse for his actions and he stood tall when he was sentenced. Gary and Mary were distraught about what had happened to Bruce, he was Gary's uncle and his almost passing had stirred back up the sorrow of having dealt with his father's death and Gary tried to get his hands down the pants of every girl that entered the gas station. Gary found the ideal ploy when girls were teasingly swaying cleavage in his direction to let him sell them booze and cigarettes, it was right up his alley. Tod struggled to get back onto his working feet after nearly ending back up in prison, his near brush with having lost the progress he made in new Mexico where he worked from a half-way house and finally being freed from the monthly pee testing had finally restored some sense of independence finally into his twenties.

Tod and Berman fell out after the altercation, Berman, like most others, failed at acknowledging his own actions let alone take responsibility and own up to what he had done. Tod wasn't willing to take on any of the sentence in order to reduce Berman's own time to serve. Tod had woken up enough in puddles of puke after nights of steroids and binge drinking with his varsity team back in high school, they would shoot up and hit practice and then take turns stealing half gallons of liquor to ease their twitching muscles in order to relax and sleep each night. Tod and some of the other teammates that would shoot up in the showers before games did so under the blanket cover of steam while the coaches turned a blind eye, anything in order to win their games. Aimee recalled having heard about a girl named Megan that was kind of the team play-thing, she would sometimes take on most of the team in a pack of dogs style sex craze, Aimee was often quick to shy her eyes away from Megan in school but also wondered how she went about letting six of seven horny steroid induced boy hump and screw away at her, sometimes a few at a time from the stories she had heard. Megan had curly reddish hair and legs that were easy to spread, it was a strange combination but putting out makes all girls popular in high school.

It was the summer after Aimee slept with Gary that Gelica Ewts had moved in, she was left on the curb by her hard working husband whom made all of the money while she flaunted around about what she had, except for the fact that he did all of the work while she let herself go. Gelica sat around most days rocking on her small porch with curlers in her hair while she still boasted about having spent time in Jamaica and traveling to world on her husband's money. Gelica rubbed most people wrong as she held her nose up to those around her, even without reason or support for the false sense of self. Gelica was delusional about having been left behind by her husband, she took to befriending Karen, whom was her next door neighbor, but as far as the rest of the residents, Gelica still bragged about going to Jamaica or Costa Rico and relaxing on the beach, which meant she was going to saunter across the street and talk to herself while she kicked at the sand of the park playground; that was her hallucination of the Jamaican beach, sans the ripped guys to stare at. Gelica was considered section 8 because her delusions of grandeur were deemed disabling, she often still spoke about her children as if they were little and still talking to her when in fact they disowned her after she spent a chunk of her husbands' money on some elective surgical procedures, he had intended to use the money to finally retire and purchase another lot to build another trailer park, until he discovered yet another large withdraw from their account to pay for what she wanted, it caused the final straw that broke the camel's back and he then separated from the woman.

After the divorce Gelica was relocated to her trailer, the police had to walk her through moving and escort her out of her large home, several times, she was usually seen sitting on the porch and randomly talking to herself. Gelica was a minimal nuisance most of the time, she would randomly go for a stroll further than just the sandbox across the street, she would glare at people that tried to speak to her, after an evil look she would scowl at people passing her by and sniffle some crude comments about peasants being below her, there was the occasional police call placed when she physically acted out against neighbors. On the morning Gelica had felt it was required to hurl ceramic garden gnomes at Aimee's car, Gelica had been replaying an argument she had with a restraining order server whom was once again explaining that she was no longer allowed at her old home, or around any of her children that had disowned her after an awful plastic surgery botch had changed the way she looked. Gelica had squandered enough of her ex-husbands money to find herself discarded, she had continued to spend more and more money that she hadn't earned to keep up her lavish lifestyle and had done so whilst neglecting her own family and her motherly responsibilities to them, her neurotic mental state had changed who she was. Gelica's spending had taken on ridiculous proportions all to feed her ego and need to attempt to validate herself with trips and spa packages to maintain her social coffee club status.

The park was hardly ever calm with all of the buzzing of life and residents meandering about with different goals and needs in their lives, Gelica sat by and watched most of it go by, her presence was hardly noticed until she became obtuse and a festering sore in the ass of Karen, whom ran the park. Karen hardly spoke to her own bitter daughter and she also struggled to avoid conversing with Gelica about kids, Gelica was in denial that her own children had grown and chose to do so without her, she was also in strict refusal to accept that her life was of her own doing. Angel had crossed paths with Gelica a few years back when she and Joey were still planning to wed, before Joey started becoming Lilly. Gelica was strolling around the sidewalks in a brightly flowered mumu, she was gazing into every trash can she passed and her being nosy had irritated Angel to no end. Angel had no real reason to find herself ready for a physical altercation with Gelica except the fact that she found herself ready for one. Gelica took it upon herself to point out that her girth should exude her affluence and status and then she also voiced to Angel that Angel was so much more below Gelica and that her mere presence to Gelica was deemed offensive. Angel hadn't had the most tolerant of mindsets for Gelica and her snobbling attitude when Gelica began doling out insults and tearing apart the younger Angel.

With a strong left hand to the nose of Gelica, Angel was quick to lay out Gelica whom spent half of the time closing her eyes and pretending that the "lower class" Angel had no rights to touch her, the assault was quickly interrupted by Joey as he knew that Angel didn't need any legal trouble, nor the headache of dealing with the crazy cat lady from down the street. Angel knocked the curlers out of Gelica's auburn hair, there were pink plastic pieces on the beveled sidewalk after the brief skirmish. Angel had skinned knuckled and Gelica a black eye and fat lip after all was said and done. Joey was a large built man, and was to become an even larger built woman once he was able to make enough money to make *him* a *her*. Joey was polite and despite having to listen to Gelica berate him and his fiancé, he still helped the mad woman down the street and back to her home, which he half suspected had padded walls inside. Gelica's neighbor Karen was shorter and just unpleasant in every interaction she had with everyone, Joey just had no notion why she was such a cavernous cunt but all he could do was shrug it off and help Gelica up to her rocking chair on her porch and hoped that her need to wander had been satisfied for the day.

Joey had met Angel when he responded to an ad for help with her parents' horses, she and he hit it off from the get go and even after Angels parents sold their small farm and moved to Florida to retire, Joey and Angle remained in love and continuing to build their relationship. Joey proposed and had all the intent to marry and grow old with Angel. There was no real foreseeing outcome that Joey would eventually want to become Lilly, Joey had strange fantasies of wearing dresses as a younger teen, thoughts that had gotten him ridiculed and would have only gotten worse if he continued to speak about them. Joey struggled through the entire duration of his relationship with Angel about having to come forward and be honest, it was harder to be honest with himself than to Angel, she was caring and understanding and a great friend, and it took a lot of alcohol for many months for him to have to give thorough consideration to his own misunderstandings, long before finding the nerve to talk to Angel. Angel was in love with Joey, he kept his body in shape and his strong jaw made her enjoy kissing on him, he was afraid to hurt her feelings and even further feared losing her, even as a friend. Joey had continued to battle his inner demons all the while trying to juggle a faux hetero life with Angel and slowly she began to suspect something was going on when their sex life had run into flat tires and potholes during their journey.

Joey tried many different tricks in regards to attempting to keep Angel satisfied, most nights he had to find any strange or taboo reason to get himself excited, his blood hardly flowed to his penis, there was no true excitement for him and his libido had lost its' steam. Joey often found himself picturing different people as he had sex, he did his best to perform for Angel and most of the time, he never really finished to the degree in which he enjoyed sex anymore. It had been two or three years of Joey doing his best to fake remaining Joey, some nights Angel went out with friends when Joey would sometimes light a joint and begin drinking Knob Creek whiskey before slipping into some of Angles cute tops to see how they looked on him. Joey had worked very hard on making his body perfect for Angel, he liked the attention and remaining a top physical specimen brought him confidence most of the time. Joey had long lost his sense of purpose, he became lost in keeping up his appearance and making sure that everyone knew he was a man's man. Joey had delved further into drug use to keep himself numb to his feelings, he dreaded hurting Angel if he actually came forward and poured himself out to her, such fear kept him imprisoned within his own mind.

As time crawled on and wedding plans grew more pressing, Joey began to panic more and more until he finally had to jerk the ejection handle and with a heavy chemical presence in his blood, he was finally backed into the corner in which he had to express his inner turmoil, sending Angel into months of deep depression as her world fell apart. Joey tried his best to comfort his ex-fiancé, Angel wanted desperately to understand and was equally baffled as hurt but her need to understand and her underlying hope that things might revert back to their previous engagement had also given her reason to keep Joey living with her. Joey had tried any and every possible strategy he could think of to try to pull Angel out of her dire state, beginning with moderate illegal narcotics until finally finding her some tranquility in fentanyl patches, except for the hiccups it caused. Angel struggled each day to find solace in the way things had turned out, her parents didn't know and she was afraid to admit that her life had taken a swan dive off a cliff and was no longer near what she had pictured in her mind.

Alcohol often helped Angels hiccups, cocaine was even better and Joey felt it was his duty to provide Angel anything she may need, his guilt kept him further chained to her mental well-being, despite that it co-dependently locked him to her for the foreseeable future. Joey delivered pizza for some religiously oppressing company and in doing so he also was able to move small amounts of narcotics to specific high school and college age kids in the city, it was easy to move products as well as run certain "items" from some people to another once in a while, and he did so to save up for his exterior physical change into Lilly. Joey often chased large pills with even larger amounts of alcohol to ease himself into slumber each night as he struggled to accept how his life was playing out. Joey had no long term plan, all he knew was that he was unhappy with the way he was, and without cartel quantities of drugs, he wasn't able to ease enough to relax or be calm. Joey pictured himself becoming Lilly, he began to take up calisthenics to try and reduce his physical size, he was an athletically built male and had the broad shoulders that went along with it, he struggled to come to terms with the fact that he might not end up with the womanly shape he longed to have, the smooth hips, narrow waist and small shoulders that would give him the slender body like Carmen Carrera and be a sensual woman in the eyes of the public.

Joey accepted that he may never be the veiled bride that draws the attention of a large chapel full of friends and family, the country was still rife with intolerant republicans and oppressive dicks that fought to control the lives of others, it was ever more present in the small homes that sat atop of their cement perches around the trailer park. Big Ken was never shy about yelling any number of slurs towards him when he took Trujillo for walks while Angel was out to work. "Fag, Fairy, Meat Gate, penny pony" and many other terms for his trans-gendered state, the irony was that Big Ken had showered with many more people in prison than Joey ever would. Joey was still a top physical specimen, Angel would often ask him to just lay nude with her while she made use of battery operated toys so she had his warm body to assist her in dealing with her life, his flesh had no arousal ability, his testosterone had ceased and even when angry and ready to physically fight Ken and his bigoted rhetoric, the missing male hormone left him without the desire to have any form of physical altercation with anybody. Joey wasn't often one to shy away from a scuffle and he could bet the time that Big Ken could last in a fight was very limited: he was morbidly obese, smoked heavily, drank, probably pre-diabetic and with enough hypertension, he would probably either stroke out his heart would explode in under a minute of heavy exercise.

Joey was raised as a boy, bred as a boy, challenged and grew through school as a boy, it was an abrupt upheaval to his mental faculties easing towards the notion of becoming Lilly, he didn't have years as a teen girl so matching and coordinating was not a niche he had in his bejeweled belt, he tried his best to be less butch, which made Big Ken and Tod even more uncomfortable. There had been many nights spent around the burn barrel and some of the other guys around the trailer park, passing around jugs of hooch or when Curtiss scored some of the taboo zebra milk, now the stasis had been shaken and left everyone whispering and nervous around Joey. Angel sought comfort with her good friend Heather or Aimee, she was heavily drugged most of the time in order to keep from being overrun with emotion or depression, she had been self-medicating with Joey's help and she spent most of her evenings holed up within her trailer watching animal planet hoping that small critters would bring her joy.

Mornings around the *Heights* was a mixture of hustle and tranquility, during the school year you would find Jonny clambering to get moving after Big Ken had already left for a long day of hauling cement. Jonny was pretty self-sufficient and even with minimal scrounging he managed food for himself and often everything else he might need to survive through the school days. Brittini was often one to dress under her covers of half tucked into her closet so her nude body would not be in line to her bedroom door just in case Tod was perched near a crack by the hinges. Brittini could often tell when Tod had left the house for work, his old Chevy truck had rusted holes in the muffler and he was rather inconsiderate when he turned the engine over and mashed the gas pedal to the floor causing unnecessary roaring of the engine early in the mornings. Brittini felt insecure in tank tops around Tod, her petite frame was slender and lanky, she thought herself as having an ideal body that boys would like over the next few years of high school but she was also nervous because many of the males around the trailer park neighborhood were similar to Darryl, just an uncontrollable penis with thrusting urges to hump without having use of a brain, Brittini tried her best to be self-aware when walking around outside, or waiting for the bus.

One morning Lil B was standing at the bus stop with his hands shoved deep into his pockets and a Black and Mild hanging out of his mouth as he dragged heartily onto the stinking cigar. Lil B was obnoxiously arrogant and nodded to greet Brittini as she entered the small wooded school bus stop, Brittini was wearing dark blue jeans, a white tank top under a pink half-zip hoodie, it was still brisk out in the mornings and Jonny was running late. Tara had gotten a ride with some other girls and it had become beneath her to ride the bus a year or so before. Brittini kept her head down as Lil B leaned back against a side wall of the shack, Brittini sat as far as possible from Lil B but he inched closer to try and flatter the quiet girl. B told her how beautiful she was, how he liked her long hair and how his manly urges liked how her legs and butt looked in her pants. Brittini sat in quiet dread as the little Hispanic wannabe tried to pick her up; it was embarrassing to have to sit through his pathetic "game." Jonny came sprinting up as the bus parked and opened its' doors, Brittini was grateful about the timing as Lil B had gotten well into her comfort zone and was puffing thick cigar smoke towards her as he spoke.

Brittini shot up quickly and hurried onto the bus as the driver, an older heavy set man shouted at Lil B to hurry up and put out the nasty cigar before getting on the bus. Lil B reached forward right behind Brittini and poked his finger right into his intended target between her butt cheeks, causing her to hop a bit with the surprise and turn with a raised back hand before stopping herself. Jonny caught up with the two and witnessed his friend Brittini's reaction to the boy, he wasn't sure what had happened but landed a swift smack to the back of Lil B's short cut head, giving Lil B cause to shout obscenities behind him towards Jonny, getting all three of them a stern warning to "hurry up and sit down" by the grisly bus driver. Brittini sat in an open bench and blocked Lil B from joining her, Jonny quickly pushed the smaller boy passed her seat so he could fill the vacancy she left for him, they didn't speak much but they were friends and Jonny stuck up for her and she looked out for him. Lil B sat behind Brittini and continued to whisper into her ear how much he'd pay her to get a picture of her naked body or how much she would love it if they had sex. Brittini tried her best to keep her left ear covered with her left shoulder to keep the young punk from getting to her; he didn't have the guts to speak into her other ear where Jonny might hear it.

As the bus turned a sharp right, Jonny held onto the seat in front of him to keep himself from sliding to the left and into Brittini, Lil B took the opportunity to reach his left hand around the front of the girl sitting in front of him, he slid his entire hand into Brittini's tank up and cupped her breast. Brittini was so wildly shocked that she found herself without the ability to speak for a moment before her brain registered and felt the dirty sticky hands of Lil B rub and pinch roughly at her nipple and breast. Brittini grasped his hand and struggled to remove it from her shirt, the leverage he had from his angle gave him the upper hand in the struggle and he continued to fondle her boob under her shirts. Brittini finally got a breath enough to shout to the kid as his hand roamed and fought against her trying to fend him off. Jonny had recovered from the bus turn and realized what had happened when he heard Brittini gasp, with almost no warning Jonny sprang up and with fist cocked, he flung himself

106

towards Lil B in the bench behind his to pummel the smaller kid that had overstepped his boundaries. Jonny landed one solid *whomp* to Lil B's right eye, the skin to skin hit was met with a hard slap sound, encouraging the boy to finally release his tight grip on Brittini's now tender chest.

The bus driver shouted from his position at the large steering wheel while staring in the large overhead mirror. The driver was adamant that the two boys separate and if they didn't stop immediately than they would both face being expelled from the bus. After a few exchanged punches Jonny climbed off of the smaller boy, whom was shouting and swearing at his attacker, and turned his attention back to his friend. Brittini was sitting with her arms crossed and her right hand on her right collar bone with her chin resting on the back of her hand, she had a bewildered look on her face as she tried to comprehend what had just happened. Jonny shouted a forced apology to the bus driver and sat back beside Brittini, he turned his body to keep Lil B in his peripheral vision as he checked on his friend and how she was. Brittini sniffled a bit with her head down, his grip had hurt her and she kept her shoulders rolled forward to further protect herself, from just behind her Lil B offered to rub her nipple with his tongue, or "massive schlong," whichever she would prefer. Even as his eye began to swell from the reddened fist of Jonny he was still quick with sexually charged comments.

Jonny wrapped his arms around Brittini and sincerely apologized that he didn't protect her any better, she kept her self-hug tight to her own body as she leaned into her friends secure embrace for a safe moment. Jonny stared at Lil B as the boy tried to ease over the seat and take in large breathes of Brittini's hair, Jonny just clenched his jaw and tried to burn the foe alive with his stare as he knew that if he moved to finish what he started, the bus driver would follow through with booting him off of the bus. The bus closed in on the large school, Jonny knew that Lil B would have to disperse to his lower grade portion of the school while he and Brittini would hold to their own. Brittini had a hard time letting her arms uncross from her assaulted chest; she tried her best not to make any movement that might resemble rubbing or caressing her sore body thus preventing any further commentary from Lil B.

Lil B licked the palm of his hand and fingers and crudely commented on his hand "tasting like titty" while Jonny enveloped his

107

arms around her for comfort, she was upset about what had happened and wanted to slap the little bastard. Jonny glared at the Mexican until the bus came to a stop in the long turnaround driveway for their school, Jonny hopped to his feet and blocked all of the other passengers behind him from exiting as he allowed Brittini to head out first. Jonny let a few other students get between him and Brittini to further the distance between Lil B and Brittini to give her a head start away from him. Jonny shuffled off of the bus and hurried to catch up with his seat mate, he laid his left arm across her shoulders and kept an eye over his shoulder behind them to make sure she wasn't going to get groped again, she kept her arms crossed and laid her head against his chest and complained about what an asshole that little spic was. Brittini knew that she and Jonny were friends, there was no sexual tension or eerie weirdness, they were close friends and had a history of sticking up for each other back in the *Heights,* she appreciated his valiant efforts to protect her dignity, she had offered him ample nights to sleep in her mom's car when Ken was drinking and getting physical with him and he also provided an open ear for her when Tod had been rife with crude comments towards her or Aimee.

Early in the school year Jonny was awoken with Big Ken drinking and having a female friend over, some bar skank according to Jonny but he was convinced out of his house in a hurry, he tapped gently on Brittini's window at two in the morning. Brittini opened the window and let the cold boy in; he was only dressed in his boxers and desperately needed a place to sleep before school. Brittini had a few of his hooded sweatshirts that he had lent her over time so he had clothes to wear, Brittini had a few pair of guys mesh shorts to play basketball in as she didn't like the really short girls shorts anyways so Jonny was able to don a hoodie and pair of shorts before climbing into bed next to Brittini. Brittini slept under her blankets while Jonny slept on top but under the comforter, they were friends and considered each other like brother and sister, they were close friends and comfortable with how they behaved, Tod found Jonny weird and often growled in his direction (unless Ken was around) to chase him off.

Brittini stuck up for Jonny at school, he was less than popular and often picked on for sometimes wearing dirty clothing or not having been able to shower daily. Aimee wasn't concerned or threatened by the relationship Brittini and Jonny shared, it wasn't uncommon to come home to find the two of them actually studying, it was sometimes difficult to feed Jonny all that often but Jonny was always quick to do dishes and offer respectful help to clean up after his hosts as often as possible to avoid being a burden. Brittini had no qualms about being around Jonny; he would turn his back to her when she asked of if she was making any motion on changing or undressing near him. Jonny had one true friend and it was Brittini, they were kids together in the *Heights* and having grown up together, they remained close due to their proximity on a social level. After school Brittini had taken a seat at the very back of the bus and once again, saved a seat for Jonny, whom was only a few kids behind her when loading the bus. Lil B was forced to sit nearer the front by the bus driver and the lack of available seats near the back for their duration of the trip home.

Brittini scanned the bus passengers and ensured she had some privacy as she slunk down a bit to show Jonny what Lil B had done, she unzipped her hoodie and eased her hand into her tank top, with a double check for prying eyes Brittini asked for Jonny's attention as she pulled her top down under her right breast. Jonny looked sat up tall to help give Brittini her privacy as he looked down at her chest, her nipple had dark red marks and purple ovals from where Lil B's fingertips dug into her soft skin. Small indentations of purple were sure to turn green in bruise against her pale while skin, her light pink areola was speckled with red marks from his rigid clenching and with her fingertips, Brittini carefully touched sensitive spots around her nipple that were still sore. Jonny felt bad for his friend, that spic had been too rough and near titty twisted her nipple off as the bus turned and he tried to hang on to it. Jonny grew angrier as he thought about how hard he would have had to squeeze her chest in order to leave bruising and marks like he did, Jonny was partially temped to charge forward and pummel the shit out of the younger boy that needed to be knocked smart.

As the bus stopped Jonny clenched his hand and kept a hawks' eye on the boy as he exited down the steps of the bus, Brittini felt Jonny's forearm tighten with his fist and asked him to just let it go. Jonny let Brittini exit right in front of him and followed her down through the aisle of black benches and down the steps towards the wooden bus stop, Lil B was already half way through a cigarette and had a half sneer on his face as he let his eyes roam up and down Brittini, imagining what her naked body would look like under her clothes. Brittini let out a sigh of disgust at the junior slime ball, Darryl had rubbed off on him too much and with a sharp snap to her right she turned to head towards her house. Jonny puffed up his chest in order to show is strength and willingness to stick up for his friend, Lil B didn't even give him any never mind and played with his gold chain on his chin, letting the golden cross bounce off of his chin as he stared at Brittini and her small frame as she walked passed.

Brittini walked briskly to her home and hoped that Jonny was close behind; she knew that Lil B wasn't far as she could still smell the cigarette smoke and his noisy footsteps as his untied Pumas thudded on the sidewalk while he walked. Lil B made another off color comment about Brittini sitting on his face, he told her he wanted to eat her ass and wear her like a hat. Brittini stood up straighter and picked up her pace to get home and to safety. Jonny had finally had enough and again exploded on Lil B, he shoved the boy from the back left side and sent him off the curb. Lil B outstretched his hands to prevent falling onto his white jeans as his cigarette crashed to the ground, sending embers and ash up from the pavement and into his face and hair. Lil B slowly raised himself back up to show how little fear he had for Jonny, Jonny shouted that he needed to watch his mouth and stop talking such shit to Brittini, she didn't do anything to anyone and was his friend, plain and simple. Lil B tried calling out Jonny by trying to say that Jonny wanted to "hit that" and should stop being such a pussy and either tag that hoe or let a brotha tag and release that game. Lil B continued to run his mouth with no hesitation to encourage Jonny to further get riled up and pissed off.

Jonny swung at the smaller boy but this time there was no connect, Lil B had ducked the swinging fist and this time returned a solid undercut punch to the lower ribs of Jonny, knocking the wind out of him, it was at this point Brittini realized that Jonny was no longer behind her and turned back to retrieve her friend and hoped to keep him out of trouble. Jonny fell towards Lil B as he fell short of breath and tumbled off of the curb, Lil B was ready to land another solid blow to Jonny's torso and Jonny desperately trying to grab onto Lil B as he fell. Brittini turned the corner to find herself almost on top of the skirmish; Jonny was hanging onto Lil B as they pushed each other back and forth, exchanging cuss words and insults. Lil B called

Jonny white trash and a loser while Jonny called him a wetback and a beaner that should go back over the border. The two boys jostled for the upper hand in their struggle to establish themselves as the more dominant teen. Brittini shouted "Jonny" and it caused Lil B enough of a distraction for Jonny to shove him again backwards and onto the ground. Jonny knelt on the chest of his dominated adversary and kept his hands clenched into the collar of his shirt to get his point across to leave Brittini alone.

Finally having been bested, Lil B conceded that he would leave the girl alone, he was a kid that was horny for the attractive girl but would have to go back to settling for spying on his older sisters' friends in their bras or panties whenever they stayed over, he even went so far as to try and place a small spy camera in his bathroom to catch any of the girls undressing or even just using the bathroom. Last fall Lil B and Curtiss were bored and wandering around sharing a 40oz when they decided to head over to Darryl's and see if they could catch a peek on him defiling Jenny, sure enough the window was open and the drapes parted just enough to get a glimpse of the fit younger girl and her naked body as Darryl kissed and seduced the girl, right after smoking a large blunt. Curtiss and Lil B wanted to see the light pink nerps of the high school girl, she was toned and flexible so peering in to the window would be spank bank fodder later in the evening for all three of them. Curtiss and Lil B ran around to get a few milk crates to stand on for a better view without having to clamber on unsteady buckets and risk making noise thus getting them caught. With half a dozen plastic milk crates gently stacked just under Darryl's open window allowed for front row seating as Darryl propped Jenny onto all fours and he licked and tongued at her from behind.

Jenny moaned and thrusted as Darryl ate at her from behind, her leg muscles twitched and flexed as she leaned back onto his face as he further dug his mouth further between her ass cheeks, her smaller hanging chest swung back and forth in time with her heaving while her back arched up and down. Darryl had small pudge around his midsection and his untrimmed pubic jungle took away from any impressive stature he might have held in the daylight. Darryl had freckles across his shoulders and a pale body that was hunched over, his position was also on all fours as he plowed his face into the back of Jenny, she managed one arm underneath her to titillate herself while Darryl struggled as best he could to keep himself from culminating too quickly and to keep her satisfied as well. As Darryl sat up a bit to use his fingers to explore Jenny from behind while he caught his breath before returning to his spelunking adventure back into her moist caves. Jenny writhed and wriggled as she got closer to climax, Darryl slowly eased his hands back and forth and slowly eased his face back towards the back of his younger sex partner, as Darryl neared his face back into Jenny's ass out of nowhere came the loudest, wettest, ass ripping fart imaginable, Darryl paused, Jenny shot up straight and they both began to panic and look around, Curtiss looked to his left in shear disbelief as Lil B had his hands braced against his face to create the noise they all had heard, his face was red from laughing and blowing out the air between his mouth and hands.

Curtiss let his eyes widen, his lips became sucked into his mouth and pinched his own mouth shut with his teeth to keep himself from blurting out in uncontrollable laughter as he tried to ease back up to peer into the bedroom, and he wanted to get more mental pictures of the naked girl and hopefully angle at seeing her pussy. Jenny was on the cusp of orgasm when a loud fart came slapping across the room, the noise wasn't from her but it was certainly shocking enough to completely ruin her mood and under the impression that it had come from Darryl, she was quick to jump up and begin getting dressed. As Jenny hurried to gather her clothes Curtiss and Lil B had very close positions to see what Darryl saw as she bent over to grab her clothes off the floor she let her bent bare backside angle towards the window without knowing that either boy had such an intimate view. Darryl was frantically trying not to freak out wondering if her hot naked body was enough to forget that she almost farted in his open mouth and both naked people blamed the farting noise on each other. Darryl assumed that because of her hurry to dress and bail that it was her whom passed gas while Jenny assumed that Darryl had been the culprit of the explosive flatulence. Curtiss and Lil B kept their eyes peeled as Jenny's boobs bounced as she got dressed, she pulled her thong up before following with her Yoga pants, her body was firm and tight, all to be expected from a seventeen year old and being a girl from his school, Curtiss regretted not having taken pictures, Lil B tried to hide his erection under the waist of his shorts.

Darryl was appalled at what had happened, he knew he didn't rip ass and his attention was on fingering Jenny when it happened, he was almost tongue deep into her when it happened and the sound that exuded from her crevice and he tried to shake off the feeling that he was peppered with particles and it was disturbing. Jenny up and left in a hurry while Curtiss and Lil B ducked over the berm that edged the border of the park, they sat on the far side of the small embankment, feet resting on the sidewalk as they finished their shared beer. Days were long and without much excitement or mental stimulation, the room for drug use or alcohol was easily filled and provided a delusional escape for most of the *Heights* residents. Curtiss often resorted back to getting naked with Tammi, he wanted to throw a hard-on into Dez'rae as she was a fit and firm sister, her dancer body called to him and he would pay any price to lick her entire naked body for a night.

Curtiss found himself bored and kicking back with Lil B, the kid that had an empty headed rocking bodied hottie of a sister, Lil B never had anyone over and was hardly home as both parents worked and Tara was mean to him. There were a few occasions that both Curtiss and Darryl propositioned Lil B to swipe one or two of Tara's panties or bras for them to shove down the front of their own underwear to keep themselves aroused at the fantasy of getting to play with her delicates. Tara worked at a tanning salon; she had hopes of managing it one day or perhaps even buying her own. Tara always smelled of vanilla or other stripper scents from tanning lotions and kept herself tan year round. Tara often had some form of body glitter glistening off of her face or chest to attract attention, she disliked wiping down the sticky or slimy tanning beds but most nights after cleaning up the salon she stripped down and spent a few minutes in a standing tanning bed to ward off any tan lines. Curtiss and Darryl both often hit on Tara, both men thought they would be the first to add her to their list of conquests and it was one of the biggest reasons they remained friends with Lil B, he was an annoying little teen and he carried a half rusted kitchen steak knife in his sock trying to front his hard gangster appearance but he was mixed in his attempt, he flagged a "Bloods" red handkerchief in on back pocket while a "Crypts" blue in the back right pocket, all the while wearing as much white clothing as possible to maintain his Mexican association with various Hispanic gangs like he'd seen on TV.

Curtiss hid away a few last remaining fifths of Zebra milk, he had picked up a few bottles for himself to keep in his bedroom if it

113

got the point where he couldn't get any drugs from Darryl or desperately needed to trade narcotics. As Curtiss and Lil B chilled and cashed their first 40 of the afternoon, Lil B tried to hide that fact that he still had a boner from seeing the older more filled out Jenny while Curtiss chuckled a bit at what Lil B had done. Curtiss wondered if long enough had passed that they should wander over to Darryl's and see if he'd smoke them out to better pass the time. Curtiss also wondered if he might slip into the tanning salon Tara worked in to catch her naked, he was feeling a little anxious to fool around, Tammi was always his back up warm hole, she never said no because she was always so desperate for attention but she wasn't always around. Curtiss hardly recalled having laid with Theresa after the fall party but he was only half hard and barely lasted a few pump into her before the drugs further took over and convinced him to get back to the burn barrel. Curtiss had been familiar with Tammi, her body was thicker and her lack of confidence lowered her standards along with her squeezing herself into tighter clothes, refusing to accept that she was more healthy in size than Dez'rae.

Lil B was getting fidgety and was growing restless being half drunk and horny as he could be, he began to rise up to his feet and was intending to head home for a bit to spank one out while he was still freshly filled with the images of Jenny bending over right in front of him. Lil B stood up and brushed his ass off from sitting on the ground, Curtiss was buzzing a little and had very little else required of him so he too stood up and intended to follow his younger cohort across two streets and to his trailer. The two strolled around some of the sidewalk before cutting into an opening in the trees and they then headed towards his light green sided trailer. Lil B kept his left hand tucked in the front of his boxers as he strolled, he kept his chin elevated and stared down his nose and swept his eyes side to side trying to keep up a hard look to display a tough young boy. Curtiss rubbed his right hand across his stomach and thought about finding more beer, he was too sober for his preference and maybe he could find something at B's to get wrecked with, so he continued to follow B.

The younger hood rat unlocked his door and the two stepped in, the house was empty so there was a freedom for Curtiss to rummage through the fridge for a beer. Lil B offered a better alternative, he had a can of starting fluid and a rag for them to huff ether, it was a crude high but it worked well enough. Lil B headed into his bedroom for a moment or privacy to stroke his pud, Curtiss let himself snoop into Tara's room, he searched through her drawers for her boy short panties and lacy bra's. Her walls were adorned with collages of friends; one picture he found was of her in a skimpy enough bikini that he too decided pry the picture from the others and rests it on her pillow. Curtiss knelt in her bed, it smelled of lotions and hair products and it was intensely arousing. Curtiss reached for a pink bra that had been discarded onto the floor and used to catch his load when he finished masturbating, he then proceeded to squat down on her bed where she slept and air lick at the younger girl in a bikini, her cleavage shimmering in the warm sun, her slender hips holding up small tied bows keeping her juicy pussy hidden under the bikini bottom, Curtiss huffed and breathed heavily as he stressed to squeeze tightly on himself while jerking off, as he reached closer to orgasm he used his free hand to squeeze at his testicles and he licked and sniffed the dirty bra he picked up from the floor.

Curtiss finished himself off and left a large sticky load across both cups of the bra, his balls were sweaty and his body seized for a moment. When Curtiss regained control of his arms and legs he brought his knees closer together in order to scoot himself off of the bed, he sat back and used Tara's pillow to wipe away the sweat from under his nut sack and put the pillow back. Curtiss followed up and cleaned after himself a bit by taking the bra he had all but ruined and rubbed it in her top drawer that was full of her panties, he used the bra in hand to mix his semen in with all of her other panties and made sure he mixed it up really good, he found himself getting a chubby while playing with her assorted panties, thongs and hipster shorts and all the wild colors, he pictured her putting on a pair of undies and spending a day sitting in school sitting in a small glob of his goop and it made him laugh. Tara was a stuck up bitch and she deserved to be gang raped in a men's prison, but his escapades will do for now.

Curtiss headed back towards the living room; he dragged his sweaty hand along the wood paneled wall to wipe off the remaining remnants of his man glue on his fingers. Curtiss was still trying to catch his breath when Lil B emerged from his bedroom, he had a brown camo rag in a bag for them to spray with ether and huff in a bag, B already had a slight grin on his face, he had already begun his high while he had been jerking off in his room also with the fresh images of Jenny's hot body in his mind. Curtiss still sat back and began his stolen beer from the fridge to ease his thirst and dry throat, he thought about sniffing all of Tara's dirty panties to get even closer to getting to go down on her, he could easily get another stiffy and he wanted to shove it deep inside of her and watch her squirm to adjust to his size. Lil B sprayed a little more carb cleaner into the bag and onto the rag and held it to his face to take another large inhale as he thudded onto the couch next to Curtiss. Lil B let his eyes roll back into his head as he tried to hand the bag over to Curtiss before passing out. Curtiss held the bag around his mouth and deeply inhaled, he held his breath as he pulled the bag back and sprayed more carb cleaner into the bag and let it refill with room air also before taking his second hit. Curtiss wrapped the bag around his mouth and held it in place as he sucked in air from his stomach, he let his lungs fill within his chest, his chest puffed up and it seemed as if there was no end to the amount of chemical infused air he was taking in, his mind lifted and his eyelids fell creating a blackness.

It had only been a few minute as huffing highs are short but successful when Curtiss shook back to awareness, his beer was still cold and on the coffee table right in front of him, Lil B was spraying a little more of a shot into his baggie before another go around, the kid was a fiend and was intent on proving that he could smoke, drink, or huff just like the bigger kids he hung out with. Curtiss chugged some of his beer before deciding he was going to pass on his next turn to get high, huffing left him with a burning sensation in his throat and slightly dizzy. Curtiss wanted a smoke so he heaved his achy and buzzing body to his feet and headed towards the door to step out and smoke. As Curtiss reached for the door there was a *whomp*, sound, he looked back to see Lil B slump over on the couch and the aerosol can settle after having hit the floor. Curtiss shook his head at the kid that couldn't control his high; he pushed through the screen door and lit up while sitting on the top step for a place to rest. The weather was warm and there were cars coming and going, from B's porch he could see across the playground and over to Gelica's plastic flamingo strewn lawn, she wasn't seated on the top step as normal nor was she sitting with her ham looking feet in the playground sand talking about how much she loved being in Jamaica, "crazy bitch must not have been let out today'" he thought to himself.

Curtiss stared over to Gelica's neighbor next, Karen's trailer. Karen kept her trailer in ideal shape, her grass was cut every five days, watered lightly each night to keep it luscious green and fluffy, her hedges always trimmed and a model of how each of the other residents were expected to keep their lots too. Karen had used to be a paralegal or some legal something or another until she got caught making copies of people's personal information for some bitch friend of hers. Karen had spent so long being a negative nasty bitch that her own wretched bitch daughter hardly had anything to do with her. The fourth of July each year was always the biggest party of the year, being near the first of the month everyone's bridge cards had replenished with food stamps and everyone could contribute. There weren't any real close neighborhoods nearby but many of the citizens would load up on fireworks and all contribute to the pyro show anyways plus being up on a hill you could often see the colored explosions off in the distance miles away. also Karen knew about the parties but the holiday was the once a year her daughter felt she could let the hagged old woman around her kids and her life, Karen wasn't very trustable and even with her own daughter she would mock and judge, always straining the last few charitable chances her daughter Lisa gave her.

Karen would always act like she wasn't planning to go anywhere and frankly, even if she didn't, it wouldn't stop it from being the biggest blow out of the year. Last year the police squad car was absolutely totaled from rocks and bricks, the residents hesitated on setting it on fire after the officers were forced to abandon it and walk back to their department. Karen had taken it upon herself to write out a letter on official letterhead and insert a copy into each and every mailbox stating that the amount of noise was finable and not tolerated. The letter also held her contempt for the destruction of property and that the residents had no right to completely close off the center street for the block party.

This party will be the third straight party that DJ Wriggle will be scratching records. Last year he got some light action and in the midst of the chaos, he felt like a king being able to spin at such a large party. Wriggle had a few small clubs he was allowed to DJ, he hardly brought in large enough crowds to give him a main headline like weekend nights but he did get one or two weeknights at each club over three or four nights a week. The first year Wriggle was a deejay he had brought a self-made system with him, he had a pair of larger fifteen inch stage speakers as well as a fairly basic PA system and lights, all enough to cram into his small Honda but it was the signal repeater that gave him some credit. Wriggle had wired together a small radio tower with a CB antenna, he used an open channel and then pumped his music through all of the radios in all of the homes around park, and everyone tuned in and faced their speakers out windows to further boost his musical reach. Wriggle bumped songs with a hearty bass to them like; "Bombs over Baghdad" but he always started every party with "This is how we do it" old nineties style. Wriggle went to a more privileged school but he was still friends with Curtiss and Darryl, not to mention it was pretty easy to get laid up in the trailer park and he could keep up his practice for when he scored his large club nights and pull high end tail. The first year Wriggle spun for the Heights bash was a big hopping to do, it wasn't topped the following year when a cop car was demolished but it was close.

The first Year Wriggle deejayed he was still a junior, he caught girls attention with his light skin and he definitely caught the eye of one of Angels friends, Nicky, she was a sandy blonde haired girl with green eyes and freckled cheeks. Nicky worked with Angel and was just ending a horrible relationship with a medical student that expected her to pay for everything while he sat back and just did his school work. Nicky was looking to get over the med student with each cocktail she poured down her throat and seeing Wriggle and his chiseled jaw line and stern look as he kept a laser focus on what he was doing under the flashing lights above his head, Nicky thought the man was extremely hot and as she got further into intoxication she succumbed to her urges to walk up the steps to the porch that he was working on. Wriggle let the lights around him be his posse and he felt like a god up on the elevated platform of the wood deck, the card table he set up his gear on was shaky but he still spun the night away and kept the girls dancing. When the independence day parties went on, all of the residents brought friends and families, it wasn't uncommon to find two hundred people crammed in the middle road of the trailer park, people parked cars in ways that everything was safely blocked off from cops driving up and groups of people acted as security. Wriggle was the epicenter of the party, the faster he made the bass boom the faster girls shook their asses, the faster girls gyrated and thrusted their bodies around, the louder the men became

118

while cheering on the music and it was all the strings that Wriggle controlled.

Nicky let the sky grow dark and the lights scatter strobe like flashes around on the crowd as she stepped up closest to be beside the DJ working his equipment, as she stood next to him she tried to talk to him but was too drunk to realize he was dancing while working with headphones on, she introduced herself and his lack of response had left her feeling discarded, Nicky had decided that she was going to turn her back on the DJ and just dance and work her body with the cheers of the crowd down below her. As Nicky raised her arms and rotated her pelvis around, Wriggle took notice of what was going on so he faced the girl and began to seductively dance with her while still scratching records. The crowd cheered and hollered as Wriggle increased his beats and song remixes, Nicky began to get really hot and sweaty from the dancing so she put on enough of a strip tease to remove her shirt down to her bra. Wriggle didn't know who this girl was but as a young man, it was his duty to dance with this freak, He held up one arm and let Nicky grind up and down on him, as she continued to drink and succumb to the cheers of the crowd she decided she was angry enough at her ex-boyfriend to truly put a nail in her relationship coffin, she knelt down under the DJ table and unzipped the DJ's pants.

Wriggle was truly digging the attention and as the attractive girl began to suck his dick, he tried his best to keep focus on the music despite how near impossible she was making it. Wriggle knew from that point on he was meant to be a DJ and that he would forever DJ parties in the Heights. Nicky sucked and jerked from under the flimsy DJ table as the speakers boomed on the ground near her, she was hardly hidden as she worked the dick she sought from the attractive DJ and his mighty hoard of attention. Darryl had witnessed Nicky going down and Wriggle and he knew he wanted some of that action also. Darryl grabbed the girl a bottled fruity drink from one of the plastic kiddie pools loaded down with ice and beers and waited for her to finish up what she was doing; he assumed she'd want to wash down Wriggle's taste. Wriggle spun long into the night, he gripped the table and dropped his head after Nicky spent a few minute jerking and sucking at him, he hardly missed a beat as the girl had gotten him off, she was cute and desperate and he wanted a chance to catch up with her later and go for round two but he was committed to making the other girls dance and give everyone party music.

Nicky pulled on Wriggle's pants to help herself to her feet, Wriggle shouted to her to find him in a bit as he led her off towards the stairs. Wriggle tried to modestly hide behind the table as his dick still hung out from his fly while he tried to slip himself back into his pants and keep spinning sick beats anyways. Darryl outstretched he hand and offered Nicky help down the few dark steps, she was gripping tightly to the handrail trying not to fall because of her heels, once off the steps she resumed her raised arms and danced, this time Darryl was present to stare at her black bra and light eyes in the light shadows. Darryl handed Nicky a drink and because she was so overheated she made quick work to suck it down, like she had done with Wriggle. Darryl complimented her and her sexiness and how erotic her dancing was, she was receptive to his advances, mostly out of her drunken state but also out of anger for her ex-boyfriend, she struggled to listen to the music and avoid crying. Darryl had to invest almost half an hour of freak dancing with her while showing off his Detroit made watch and rubbing his hands on the woman, he would stand behind her so he could grind himself against the back of her and let his free hand roam around her stomach, with the occasional slight shameless grope up and on her chest before she could figure out what he was doing. After he invested time and drinks Darryl finally convinced the girl to step off to the side with him as he wanted to make out with such a pretty girl, she was sincerely flattered and willing to let the charming boy slobber on her tits while she finished her drink to cool off.

Darryl escorted the girl around the side of a trailer down the way, there was barely any privacy but it didn't matter, night was his cover and he pawed at the girl's bra to unleash her boobs. Nicky was slurring her speech, hardly caring that this boy was playing with her tits, she had a full beer and a partial care for anything. Nicky laid back while Darryl raised her jean skirt, he planted his face into her crotch and rubbed her legs and breasts while he feasted between her thighs for a few minutes. Nicky seemed to moan a bit which Darryl took as permission to remove her dark panties and continue on. Darryl was quick to pull down his pants and climb inside of the girl, she was soaking wet with his spit and tried to hold on around his shoulders but her hand kept falling to the ground, she was trashed.

120

Darryl heaved and humped for a few minutes, as he got close he knew he wasn't going to finish inside of her so he grabbed her beer and held it to the tip of his penis to ejaculate into the mouth of her beer bottle. Nicky tried to raise her hand but they continued to fall to her bare body, she had next to no ability to control herself, Darryl was preoccupied with sucking on her small nipples while she remained submissive, nearly incapacitated.

Darryl handed Nicky her beer back with his load of his semen in it and right away she began drinking it without knowing what he had done, he grabbed the bottle he set aside for himself and out of sheer drunken immaturity he used his left hand to hold her legs open and he brought the mouth of his beer bottle to her and rubbed the glass bottle inside of her, he laughed and thought it funny to let her lubrication coat the mouth of his beer bottle and to also pour some of his beer inside of her. Nicky felt the cold air against her private parts as she drank her beer, she suddenly noticed a very cold feeling inside of her private parts and without trying, her bladder decided to void. Darryl had just moved his beer from inside of Nicky but his lap and leg were still in the range to end up with a pissed on leg from the drunk girl. Darryl wasn't sure what had happened for almost two whole seconds until he felt his leg become soaked, Darryl quickly stood up from the urine puddle and with his right hand; he slapped the drunk girl very hard on her labia with his flat hand. Nicky had jerked her legs up close to her chest with the slap to her pussy; her underwear was still around her ankles but so what. Nicky had laid on the ground for half an hour after Darryl had penetrated and discarded her, Angel was curious where she had gone until she came stumbling back out topless with her bra in hand.

After Wriggle had wrapped up long session he let his shuffler play for half an hour on random so he could hook up with Nicky when she made it back near his table. Nicky was still pretty drunk but Wriggle was a young man still and her simply sucking him off wasn't enough for his evening, he wanted to rifle the slender girl. Wriggle bent Nicky over the porch railing next to his equipment table, he lifted the wet skirt and pulled down her soaking panties, Wriggle assumed she had been sweating but it was late and the few people left were much more drunk than he was and he wanted to hump this hot drunk girl. Wriggle sure enough removed his pecker and rubbed it against Nicky for a second before roughly entering her, Angel and

Joey were close enough to see what was going on and frankly, "good for them." Nicky was rather drunk but it was a turn on for both Joey and Angel to watch Angel's friend get pounded. Angel decided to let her half-drunk voyeuristic side out with her fiancé Joey, she placed her hands on the edge of the porch just a few steps from where Nicky was taking it like a pro and pulled down her jeans for Joey to do the same thing. Wriggle watched the much larger Joey mount up behind Angel and watch as he stepped up behind Angel, it was hard to see as he slid in and out of Nicky but her tight body felt great in his hands and the angle of her pubic bone on the underside of his shaft due to her bent over angle was phenomenal. Joey watched Angel watch Nicky get railed, it was also arousing to watch Nicky sway back and forth as Wriggle humped her from behind also, he kept one hand on her waist and the other on one of her swaying breasts. Joey and Angel watched Wriggle get off for the second time of the evening, he shook his head and nodded a little bit as he almost didn't make it to pull out and let himself slide forward between her legs, aiming his load in front of both of them.

Once Wriggle got off, Angel and Joey figured it was more than time to take Nicky back to their place and to help her get into bed. Nicky had taken a seat on the deck after Wriggle was done with her, her skin was covered in all sorts of sweat, semen, beer, urine and heavens knew what else, Angel tasked Joey with hiking her up onto his shoulders to fireman carry her to the next block. After Nicky had been slurring and groaning because of her perch. Angel tried her best to follow behind her and reassure her that she was OK and headed home with then so she could go to bed. As Joey walked and her head bounced, Nicky was feeling the urge to vomit come stronger and stronger, Angel held Nicky's hand and tried to comfort her as best as she could until Nicky let her lower jaw fall open and let all of her mixed stomach contest rocket out of her. Angel tried to raise her friends head as she began to hurl, it was a failed attempt to try and keep her from vomiting all over Joes back while he carried her, Angel also ended up getting splashed on her arms and chest from the violent expulsion, Joey stopped walking for a moment and turned to lock eyes with Angel, his level of discontent had reached an all new high and Angel was overcome with a shear look of dread about what had happened. After a few steps Joey's shoe had begun to squish as liquid had run down his left leg and fill in his shoe, he dropped his head and

The next morning following that Fourth of July party was an especially crude one for most that had attended the jumping party. Nicky awoke with her lower private area intensely hurting, it was hard for her to keep from doubling over as she struggled to make sense of why she was only covered in a sheet and missing most of her clothes. Angel tied her hair up into a ponytail and headed out to the living room where Joey had left her to sleep on the couch. Angel spun a story about Nicky having been separated from she and Joey and that when they found her she had been half naked and soaking wet until she yakked all over them when Joey carried her, Angel neglected to tell her that she and Joey had used her unconscious body for a sex toy, it may have been best to not bring that up anyways. Angel told her she washed her up and laundered her clothes, Nicky let down her guard enough to believe the story being told to her by her friend. Nicky was still in a lot of pain and her head throbbed, and the taste in her mouth tasted what you'd expect hot garbage to taste like and she had a sense of urgency to get half a bottle of aspirin into her followed by half a gallon of Gatorade and then into bed for a week. Nicky gathered her things and thanked Angel for looking out for her and letting her crash for the night after the party and then she left.

Aimee and Tod woke up after that party also hungover as hell, Tod partook in the hair of the dog technique and lit a cigarette while cracking open a beer before packing a bowl of pot to smoke away his headache. Aimee had danced half of the night with Tod and her legs were absolutely killing her, she didn't wear heals all that often but wanted to be cute to entice Tod all night, her thighs were swollen and she had to hobble from their bed towards the living room, slowly. Brittini and Jonny were sitting on the love seat finishing off a box of Cap 'n' Crunch from one large bowl, Aimee greeted them and couldn't tell if Jonny stayed the night or just arrived for breakfast. Tod and Tuner stood near each other through half of the party while Billy and Karl had brought dates to dance and then take home afterwards. Billy, Karl and their dates were the ones that also took on the responsibility of firing off the dozens of mortars for the crowds to enjoy; they shot them off from the farthest street to avoid the crowds but also to have some privacy to practice their erotic debauchery with their ladies under the romantic lights of exploding fireworks. Brittini tried her best to avoid Tod's workmates, they were a shady bunch like he was but with less self-control about letting their eyes wander towards her.

Jonny and Brittini had spent a large portion of the night researching Jonny's idea, he wanted to create a small unit that was a webcam and small monitor in which someone could Skype into with their cell phone to this unit in their home to interact with their pets to help reduce separation anxiety and also lock or unlock a doggy door. Jonny called it "pooch time" but it would allow someone to notify their dog that it was time to let them out with one such signal, and have a similar signal on the outside of the door so the person that was logged in could make sure that if their dog was going back in, did so alone to prevent unwanted creatures or even people from doing so while you were at work. Brittini thought the idea was genius and that Jonny should patent it and try and sell the idea. Jonny knew he had a lot of research to do in order to finagle a locking doggy door plus the sound alert whistles and also the whole remote log in stuff in order to log in from your cell phone or computer while you're at work and can check in with your pets. Jonny had no real working knowledge of computers outside of the rudimentary practice at school to research some nonsense topics or papers so Brittini wanted to encourage his use and help if she could, plus it was a loud party with a lot of drunks that didn't interest her in being around.

Carsey had only lived in the heights for a few months when she attended the party that left a squad car destroyed, her trailer was close enough to see what had happened but she was closer to the center of the party when things went airborne. Carsey was extremely bi-polar and wrought with manic depression, which she mostly controlled with medications. Carsey was on section 8 state disability so any additional income she made would count against the money the state paid her. No one was sure who actually owned the trailer she was in but it didn't matter, section 8 people can't own property but they were getting a fairly regular paycheck from the state for her rent and she also got her bridge card topped up each month, she was set to just sit around at home on her dead ass and moan about some made up headache or something. Carsey sometimes would have dates come home with her so she could supplement her income, when she knew she was going to bring home a John or two she would hire Brittini to watch over Brodan, there have been a few occasions in the past where Angel or Brittini had found Brodan wandering around in the playground without his mother. Angel and Carsey got to know each other over the previous year. Brodan was still a small tyke yet and fell in love with Trujillo one day when Angel was walking him near the playground; Brodan scooted and bounced on his diapered butt when he saw the small dog so Angel walked over to introduce them.

Brodan was a small boy with dark black hair, he seemed pretty happy which was a sign that his mother cared for him, he played with a few matchbox cars in the sand while Carsey enjoyed a cigarette and played games on her cell phone as Angel walked up. Brodan made a strange deer bleat like squeak when he got excited, as Trujillo neared, Brodan was definitely excited, Trujillo was nervous about going near the child but the kid probably smelled of food so Trujillo got past his hesitation and licked Brodan's face clean. Carsey hardly looked up from her phone when making Angels acquaintance, she spoke momentarily without even raising her head. Angel smiled at Brodan as he ate handfuls sand without his mother bothering to stop him. Angel felt a profound sadness that things were going south between her and Joey at the time and that was why she got Trujillo, because she sensed she may never get to have children and the small dog was a wonderful substitute while she went back to square one with her life and tried to figure out what was going to happen or what she was going to do with her future.

Joey had gotten Angel loving the constant numbing effect fentanyl had on her senses, she kept a new one on most of the time and even though they always caused hiccupping, it glazed her over enough to not bother to care. When Angel was enjoying the wavy vision associated with her patch she hardly bothered to care that the man she so deeply loved had decided to become a transvestite, or trans-parasite as she often referred to him, he knew she was emotionally hurting and prone to lashing out which was why he also helped by keeping her plenty stocked with illegal narcotics to cope. Angel tried to forget what all had happened between them and having him still live with her seemed to feed the delusion she fought to hold on to. First thing in the mornings there was that sleep laden half dream half reality that she especially liked,he'd be in the bathroom shaving and she would be able to go in and run her hands over his rippled body, she would awake to hearing his electric razor buzzing from the bathroom and she would smile that things were better and she had just awoken from a bad dream. Angel would rise out of bed and let her feet carry her dreary body towards her fiancé in the bathroom, as she would turn the corner to see Joey with a leg propped up on the toilet using his electric razor to finish shaving his balls before starting at the bottom of the other leg, that was when reality truly hit her, to see him "Captain Morgan" standing with one foot up on the toilet with one clean shaven leg and one stubbly waiting for him to finish shaving his genitals, that was the reason Angel stayed so heavily medicated, she didn't want to face what was going on, she had so many long term things planned out and now "it" was shaving its' balls getting scrotal hairs on her floor.

Joey was raised in your average blue collar fashion; both of his parents worked and committed their lives to Jesus, and all of the hypocritical bullshit that that entailed. Joey was shunned by his "love thy neighbor" parents when he finally admitted to himself and them how he truly felt. Joey's father Korum was a hard pressed church going and preached as frequently as possible, the bible was the word of god and any naysayers were to repent and be baptized in the brimstone or risk an eternity in hell, Joey loved to ask him if the bible was the word of god than why king James had written it without any reference to the actual bible. Korum had zero tolerance for blasphemy and it had already strained the relationship he shared with Joey when Joey began to exercise logic over blind faith and obedience. Joey hated himself and struggled with anorexia in high school, no one knew because he was a well-built jock and played sports but he spent most of his time trying to be everything he could to honor and impress his father, and his desire to please left him endlessly unhappy. Pleasing Korum was unattainable and exhausting, Joey constantly felt like a failure and because that wore so heavy on him he was often depressed and dealing with the internal hatred for himself for never getting approval. Joey considered suicide several times but worse than not getting his own fathers' approval, was the thought of really letting him down, if he killed himself then Korum would preach at his own son's funeral that his own son was a sinner and burn in hell for eternity. Joey had slowly began to accept that maybe he was to burn in hell for being gay, or at least a transvestite, he did often question that if god made everyone then god made him, and if god made him maybe he made him the way he was, and if that was the case then why didn't his own father accept him instead of promote his own bigotries while hiding behind a book of psychological delusions and fairytales?

Joey tried his best to be a good person; he held no ill will towards any man even though many seemed to have the wrath of god towards him just for existing. Joey was wise that it was pure ignorance that caused so many Wal-Mart shoppers to hate someone just by shear appearance. Joey often found himself at the verbal attack of some dirty scrubby drunkard or young kids, he hardly crossed paths with anyone with enough balls to step to his large frame and actually talk their rhetoric bullshit but it was still oppressing nonetheless. Joey sometimes prayed that if there was a god, to send him a signal that he was a loved child along with all of the other children of his around him. Joey wondered in silence, he had to remain steadfast in his decision and no longer waver under the social expectations of others, this was his only life and he had to start living it the way he wanted to, not buckle and be what everyone else expected, even Angel. One night of heavy drinking he and Angle had slowly inched towards a shared peace between them, he understood she was hurt and that she may never understand nor support him any longer but he couldn't let that fear imprison him any longer, the two had talked like friends, like they used to. Angel posed the idea that maybe god made him in such a fashion not to suffer whom he was but to use his large size and strengths to be like the Samson from the bible, maybe he might stand after all of the trials and tribulations and emerge that much stronger and maybe inspire others' that might be questioning themselves also? Angel had a good point and it came when she put her emotional self to the side and let the rational portion emerge.

Carsey loved being a mother, she struggled many days to even get out of bed, and she kept many of her pills near her bed and tried to remain structured to keep to her routines. Carsey was in her early twenties and had been slightly bipolar her entire life, it didn't show through until her teen years when getting mad left her kicking holes in walls and excessively flying off the handle over losing a bobby pin or hair tie. Carsey kept a collage of pictures next to her bed and it was full of pictures of walls, windows, doors, burned clothes and assaulted people, all things she had been responsible of when she had decided to stop taking her meds because they made her feel funny. Carsey had a few small slips when it came to her young son Brodan. Carsey had an older brother Chris whom was a Marine, he loved being a Marine and everything he did, was for the Marines. Chris had enlisted right out of high school, he wanted to sign on much longer that the initial four years except he promised their father that he would start with four and re-sign later if his lust for the military was still surging through his blood. Chris was three years older than Carsey and they were pretty close. One Christmas leave after Chris' first tour in the godless desert, he brought a pal home with him for the holiday as the friend's family wasn't able to host him or something. Chris brought a fellow brother in green, the other Marine's name was Kevin, he was a sharp man with sharp snapped salutes and impeccable posture, even when relaxing on the floor with the family Kevin still sat up straight as Kevin and Chris filled in the listeners with some of their missions clearing shit huts in the sand.

Carsey had only spent a few days with Kevin but knew she liked him, he had auburn hair and green eyes, his teeth were clean and straight, his temples bulged when he ate and none of his socks had holes in them, he was well kept and spoke intelligently. Carsey had

130

exchanged smiles with Kevin over the holiday break and that was the first time they met. Carsey was slow to like people as she was afraid to open up to strangers and risk getting hurt if they got to know her, she was heavily guarded because of being bipolar and unsure of herself. Chris brought Kevin back later that summer for her high school graduation and from that point, they wrote each other frequently. Kevin sought Chris' permission to write to his friends' sister, Chris was reluctant simply because it was his sister but also having shared sand and blood with Kevin, he knew there was no one he would rather protect his sister and be there for her. After two long years of correspondence and another tour over into the shit heaped litter box, Carsey and Kevin exchanged vows, Carsey was slowly trying to put herself through community college for social work while holding a fulltime job, Kevin still had many years of his second sign up to go but was saving most of what he earned and looked forward to the two of them purchasing a home together.

Kevin and Chris remained each other's shadows in the service; they were assigned one more mission as the summer drew to an end. The boys were granted a three week leave to spend with family before a one year deployment for military support. Kevin and Carsey had spent the entire three weeks in a hotel, finally having a proper honeymoon, there wasn't enough time earlier. The couple hardly wore any clothes during their time in a ratty hotel, they intimately explored each other and ordered room service the entire time, they behaved while dating and spent their quality time truly getting to emotionally know each other, and they knew they had the rest of their lives to intimately explore each other. Life was coming together for Carsey, she had her meds dialed in, her husband knew every shameful detail about her and still made her feel accepted and unconditionally loved. She was gearing up for her final year of school before she could graduate and begin to try and help young girls with emotional issues like she's dealt with, her whole life puzzle was filling in and the grand picture she was staring at was beginning to look like a masterpiece.

Kevin and Chris both shipped out in early September, they both promised her and her parents that they would each bring the other home. Carsey cried and knew she would miss her husband but he promised that after this tour he would apply for a stateside job, but first he had to make sure all of his brothers could come home safely and he wouldn't be able to sleep with a clear conscience if he didn't.

Carsey was preparing for her final year and with Kevin being out of the country, she was still working her ass off to try and look at potential homes for them when he returned. Kevin and Chris had been in some unpronounceable village for a month when they had been overrun by camel jockeying pissed off terrorists.

According to the high ranking general and the letter he wrote to Carsey and her parents, the two men held off the opposition throughout the night after taking heavy fire and sustaining multiple injuries before finally being overrun by the enemy. Carsey had begun to pen a letter to her husband that she found out that she was pregnant with their first child together when her parents had knocked and let themselves into her room. Carsey hardly looked up from her letter as she wanted her husband to be the first to get the good news, she wanted to tell him over the phone but the calls had been scarce and she also wanted to cement the memory of finding out he was to be a father, in his mind with the letter. Carsey had only known for a few hours when god smited her. With father and mother looking distraught, Carsey blacked out and saw white spots as her father began to speak. When the letter had been read aloud it took a few days for Carsey to be able to piece together each sentence, she could only read a few words before her eyes welled up and tears streamed down her face rendering her ability to read, useless.

Carsey found it harder and harder to get out of bed, her new embryo was already an orphan and she a widow. Chris and Kevin died fighting, as any proud Marine would, they died as brothers and defending the rights for democracy that they upheld belief in. Carsey hardly held anything together, when she had to join her family to retrieve the bodies of their loved ones, Carsey was an absolute disaster. Carsey struggled with depression but luckily the depression inhibited her from being very bipolar and it coincided with her trying to be pregnant with very little medication. Carsey struggled her best but occasionally partook in Xanax to be able to fake function when it came to burying her husband and brother. The day of the dual burial was a blur of shots from the twenty-one gun salutes and Taps, Carsey cried through most of her pregnancy until Brodan Kevin Christopher was born. Carsey bore all of her burdens; she fought almost every day to keep from spinning out of control. Brodan was her reason not to fidget on little imperfections she noticed about her face, she fought with herself not to pick over and over at zits or fixate on things that

132

Brodan might be up to until her medications kicked in each day. Carsey had figured out that if she woke up at 4 a.m. for her main medication that it would ensure that it was in effect when she woke up and lasted the day until she fell asleep again. Carsey struggled with the glazed over numb feeling each and every day and some days she wanted to forgo her meds in exchange for a rail of cocaine or handful of uppers to blast some alive feeling into her brain and let her heart feel alive for a day, but she knew that her urge to break free was better off neglected for the sake of raising her husband's legacy with clear and vivid memories of a docile and adoring mother.

Carsey felt like she was wrapped in a wet blanket each day, her footsteps felt like she was trudging through waist deep mud each day with her medicated mental state, it was a daily fight, Carsey felt mere seconds of her true self before taking her 4a.m. pill, she occasionally felt like she should drink an ice cold beer or skip the medication for a day and go out and join some friends for a drink or a night out at the club, she wanted to dance and feel free and alive. Carsey set three reminders to hit on her cell phone to nag herself to take her pills so she wouldn't easily give in and just skip a day. Each day was a constant struggle for Carsey and there was a day or two a year her inner trapped girl would win and she would forgo her daily pills, each day ended a gamble and even though some days ended on the positive without her medications, the nights that ended in a violent rage without wasn't worth it. Carsey would make plans one or two nights a year in which she would make arrangements for her parents to keep Brodan and she would spend a day with less responsibility and not take her meds. Carsey knew she only had a few paroled days a year when she didn't have to don the cloak of meds and she would aimlessly wander the mall or outside and let the warming rays of the sun freckle her face.

Carsey had a hard time with the fact that even though she was a wife for several months, she was only a bride for a few weeks, she still kept the flag strewn military pictures of her beloved Kevin, his soft smile and easy eyes still lifted her heart, she still found herself getting lost staring at him, she sometimes tried to pretend that he was just still over on deployment and that maybe he might be calling soon. Carsey tried her best not to get caught up dating or liking people, it was on rare occasions that she found herself craving the physical attention of a man and gave in to let herself be taken. Once or twice a month Carsey had to make ends meet and would take a small financial bribe and with a small tryst set up, she could close her eyes and pretend that the man lying with her was still her husband. One of the perks to being drug addled all day every day was that it numbed her senses to the extremes of her emotions, especially when it came to the hurt of losing Kevin or the fact that she's cheated on her deceased husband with strangers for money.

Carsey just looked at her life as if she was floating in the ocean, not even treading water in a feeble attempt to get anywhere, just floating in order to keep from drowning. Carsey tried her best to stay hunkered down in order to get her son raised to become a man and from that point on and it hardly mattered what happened to her. Brodan was naive to the minute to minute struggles of his mommy; he spent most of his days with a red Kool-Aid stain mustache and playing with his hot wheels cars. Carsey packed the ends of her cigarettes with just a small amount of marijuana, it wasn't enough to get her high but with a small piece of bud in the end of each smoke gave her meds the small edge twenty times a day that she could ease her anxieties without having to get a prescription of Ritalin which would further make her feel medicated and sedated. With a small hit of pot with each cigarette Carsey was also more confident in her parenting, with the slight easement of pot in her she was much more relaxed, she watched cartoons with her son and was much more likely to crawl on the floor with him to play and draw with crayons, and it kept her from being robbed of all control.

When Carsey first moved into her trailer she was rather unnerved about uprooting from her parents' home, she had been planning such a move but it was supposed to be with her husband. Not just herself and small baby. Carsey held out pretty well against all of her inner demons through her pregnancy, her parents were truly impressed at her strength to carry on for her sons' sake. Once Brodan was born they were able to relax much better and trust that she was much more in control of her meds and destiny. Carsey kept a few cartons of Newports on her nightstand so she wasn't on the verge of running out, she also kept half an ounce of pot tucked away to stuff into her cigarettes to prolong her self-control. When Carsey moved in she enjoyed the proximity of the Amaca station, she enjoyed the walk with Brodan in a stroller and the fresh air was good for him. Carsey bought her cartons from Gary, she first went down and introduced herself, and he was as usual, hunched over onto his elbows and locked eyes with her chest when she entered his store.

Gary stuttered through pickup lines each time Carsey came in, she smoked a pack a day and bought a carton every other week, Gary always knew when to expect Carsey and ogled at the body of the young twenty something gal with baby in tow. One midafternoon Gary had encouraged Carsey to open up to him and tell him how her week was, she thought he was being friendly as usual but he was always angling to find a way to get his pecker played with, or to even just get a good view down any girls shirt. Carsey explained the hardship she struggled with, she was on a limited budget from her disability and Brogans social security was also strict and she often had to balance co-pays for her medications alongside with feeding her son, it was stressful to find a medium in which she and her son could eat and she could stay in control of her mental well-being. Gary suggested that there were things that she could do for money and explained that as an attractive lady she held all of the right anatomy to make an easy twenty or thirty bucks rather often, he followed up with an offer of twenty dollars off a carton of her cigarettes for a blowjob.

Carsey was ever so hesitant to go down on Gary behind the counter, she tried to convince him to give her the discount of she showed him her breasts, he played coy and rebutted with only if her breasts were really worth it, she was still nursing occasionally so her breasts were still full and firm, she raised her shirt to expose her chest still in a bra and Gary didn't feel moved enough to give the discount. Carsey really wanted to get her cartons at almost half off, she figure two blowjobs a month for the portly man was worth the forty bucks to help feed herself and her son. Carsey felt terrible as she rounded the counter and kept an eye on her sleeping baby just a few steps behind her, Gary leaned back on the counter and spread his legs enough to let Carsey unzip his pants. Gary was smart in that if he pulled his dick out then he might be liable for her trying to charge him but if he just let her than she was willing and it was consensual. Carsey ran her shaking hands up Gary's thighs and towards his crotch, she tried to keep her fingers from shaking enough to pull his fly down, her eyes clenched in despair and she struggled to fend off tears. Carsey leaned forward as she pulled Gary's semi hard rod from trousers, he was sweaty and smelled like raw onions and it made her gag reflex act up, she tried to picture that it was Kevin's penis and she trembled as she leaned her mouth towards him.

Carsey took Gary into her mouth, Kevin had plenty of length left over even as the head of his penis used her uvula as a speed boxing bag, and Gary on the other hand hardly surpassed her teeth. Carsey tightly closed her eyes and stroked as fast as she could, she tried to mentally escape from where she currently was and back to her honeymoon with Kevin. Carsey pictured Kevin and his military body, his throbbing penis thrusting in her hand and then exploding in her mouth. Carsey tried to imagine the salty goo was her husbands and not that of the body odor laden momma's boy gasping for breath as he tried to last more than a minute in the girl's mouth. Carsey was grateful that it ended quickly, she had sweaty breasts and a sore jaw, Gary wasn't impressive in anyway and she wondered if his pudgy belly maybe retracted his penis a bit, Kevin was ripped and toned and his jut out from his washboard stomach like the top mast of a sail boat, just tall straight and true, Gary's had a small weird twist at the end and it curved to the left a little, Carsey was grateful that the endeavor was quickly over. Carsey saved the extra money each month by taking Gary's load and she put that money towards groceries or pot to help keep her mind from overtaking her and causing her to lose her shit.

Carsey was strolling back with her new carton of cigarettes when she crossed paths with Angel, whom was entering the gas station for her own pack after returning from having taken Theresa to the free clinic shortly after the Halloween party. Gary was still leaning back against the counter and wiping sweat from his brow after having finished with Carsey, Angel was greatly stressed and needing a nicotine fix, Gary was rife with pit sweat running down his sides from being more excited than his body could keep up with, he was panting and gasping for breath when Angel barked her order to the meek man. Theresa was still sitting in the front seat, lying back with a cool wet cloth across her forehead; she was only hours after her abortion and feeling like a pile of lawn mowed dog shit. Angel agreed to help nurse Theresa back to herself for the day after her surgery that Friday morning. Angel knew she was struggling for friends when she agreed to take Theresa to the clinic two weeks prior but it was mostly out of the idea that she needed more birth control anyways and she assumed that Theresa was due for a refill also, she wasn't ready for the high school girl to step out with her head hung low and weeping.

During the car ride back from the initial clinic appointment Angel had sat quietly while her passenger sobbed and blubbered, Theresa didn't know how she ended up pregnant as she only remembered the blowjob after the Halloween party until the effects from her drugs kicked in. Theresa had barely missed her period when she decided to get tested; she didn't recall anything that night when it came to Tammi finding her with her pants down around her calves, and her bare snatch steaming in the cool air. Theresa had no ability to recall that evening or its' events but now that her pregnancy test had come up positive, she was certainly terrified of what she had only imagined originally. Angel felt obligated once she had Theresa sobbing and snotting on her neck; she saw the bigger picture and knew the girl couldn't handle being a mother.

Theresa was a junior in high school, she didn't want to be another underage pregnant teen statistic, the same girls she and her friends poked fun at for being reckless sluts, the problem that made it all worse was she got pregnant and had no recollection of how, or by whom. Missing her period started her concern and wanting to get on the pill at the clinic was her initial motive to go, except that the bitch nurse Helen made her take a pee stick to double check her pregnancy potential. Theresa was panicked that she might be met by some toothless picketers holding up signs that abortion was murder and ignorant shit like that, they weren't the assholes that had to get an abortion and the status of it all was pretty easy to understand for those who aren't products of inbreeding, if you don't like abortions then don't have one. Theresa hated the world, she was mad that one blurry night left her in such a desolate situation.

Theresa was thankful for Angel having really having been there for her, she knew she would have to pay her back for fronting the abortion cost but this wasn't something that she could have trusted Dez'rae or Tammi with, and god forbid anyone at her school find out, she would be ruined and shunned. Theresa had her wad of uninvited cells removed; it was hardly bigger than a pen tip so it was minimally invasive to perform and her recovery was a short stint in a post anesthesia bed and then walked out to Angel's car. Theresa lay back in Angels reclined passenger seat, her head pounded from the anesthetic and her girl parts were sore from the rooting instruments.

Theresa was just passed a chemical ejection for the tumor so they had to go in directly and administer a hormone that caused her body to abort the cells. Angel padded the forehead of the girl as she fought off a fever and chills as she slept heartily on Angels couch for the remainder of the afternoon.

Angel waited on the younger girl hand and foot, she kept the forehead cloth cool and damp, it suddenly entered her mind that Gary had been huffing and puffing when she went in to buy smokes, the overweight Seinfeld looking scumbag was probably jerking off behind the counter as Carsey was leaving and maybe she almost walked in on him, *Gross!*. Trujillo laid with Theresa on the couch as she sobbed and cried about what she had been through. Theresa was the one that had to make the decision to do what she had done and anyone that thought they had any privilege to say a god damned thing about her or what she had to do, then they should be god damned to hell. Theresa thought long and hard about what she had to do, there was absolutely no way she was physically or emotionally equipped for a baby, let alone financially, she was a high school student and there was still a long life of hers ahead of her that wouldn't warrant being a young single mother, especially not knowing who got her pregnant or how, well she suspected the biological how, just questioned the circumstantial how.

After the abortion Theresa was riddled with self-doubt and her mental stability wavered, she avoided any further situation that left her pregnant in the first place, she didn't party anymore or even partake in drugs or drinks and had turned a page to get her life onto the path she felt she was meant to take. Once December hit Tammi and Dez'rae often questioned why she distanced herself so much and why she didn't come around the *Heights* anymore, she had become a ghost in the hallways and deactivated her MyFace account, she hid herself away from many large social gatherings and focused on her studies, she wanted to get back on track to get into college, this close call was the one and only thing that she would need in order to realign her future. Theresa withdrew from her friends; Tammi and Dez'rae missed hanging out with Theresa and began to call her a bitch for having closed herself off from them.

Aimee tried to warn Brittini off from ending up like Tammi, she didn't want her daughter to spend most of her life with her legs spread open like Tammi did. Aimee remembered what it was like to be in high school, the social pressure to fit in was overwhelming, she remembered the girl Megan whom was the cum dumpster for the entire varsity football team, the girl was ridden with acne but it was always assumed the acne was caused from all of the facial shots of jizz, she took more shots to the face that Mohamed Ali. Aimee and Tod frequently spoke back and forth about high school, Aimee had such a crush on Tod that some nights she would end up having to get herself off because she was too riled up to sleep over her lusting for his athletic build and football pants, he was an upper classman and didn't even really notice her before his arrest.

Tod was an avid gym rat in high school, he worked out in the mornings before school because after school he had hardcore football practice and by the end of the night he was too tired to even lift his arms. Tod came a across an older guy named Lenny, Lenny was in his forties but still benched three bills, he was always at the gym each morning and Tod saw him as friendly competition when working out, Lenny waited a few weeks to bait Tod and traded some workout tips with the younger man. Tod worked out with Lenny and mid-season of his junior year, Tod was running slow and sore from his rugged training schedules, and Lenny had just the right thing to get him performing at his peak.

Lenny met Tod back in the locker room the next morning, he gave Tod a very small amount of a brownish liquid, and he injected it into the thick muscle at the back of his hip. Instantly Tod felt his batteries reach top strength, his muscles no longer ached from his training or weight lifting, that morning Tod added twenty pounds to his bench press and eighty to his squats. Tod felt enormous as his muscle pump surged and pulsated through him with strength, he was hooked right away. Lenny gave Tod one needle and a small vile for one hundred bucks, he warned Tod to keep his doses small so his superior performance edge wasn't obvious to his coaches or even teammates. It had only taken a week when Lenny was approached by Tod and a fresh hundred dollar bill in the locker room again. Tod had kept his use small but he wanted to take his varsity team to the state level and with his six closest teammates he knew would join him in his beastly performance in the games.

Tod had initiated his suggestion to an already muscle bound kid named Jeremy, Jeremy had a pizza faced complexion and short reddish curly hair. Adding Scott, Rob, Jake, Joey B and Brad all on his list of extremely close friends to share in his vile of frowned upon enhancement. The seven of them shared one needle because getting a new one was hard to come by, Joey B suggested the running back Jarcel should join in but most of the guys didn't want any black blood mixed in with their steroids. The team lost the state game in their junior year and Tod's purchases to Lenny quadrupled over the next year to keep up with the demands of the entire team, he was also making a few hundred bucks a month for his troubles. Tod became the go to guy for roids; he even lined up his teammates under the cover of the shower steam to inject them one at a time before games to better ensure their victory in the grueling games under the night lights for friends and families in attendance. Tod was at the peak of his physical stature, his strength was intimidating, his sexual prowess lasted for hours and even if he couldn't find a new piece of ass each week, he would still dial up Megan and plow into her for a large portion of the afternoon without tiring, she would often leave walking with a limp and complain about the massive amounts of goo running down her legs from her crotch after each team mate had their turn with her.

Megan was a popular girl, she was on the pill so there was no need to worry about pregnancy and she had the attention of the entire team. Megan liked each boy she slept with, she had a different boy each night and some days after school she would meet with an additional to give them her attention also. Megan was passed around the locker room like a muscle rub, she had seven or eight guys she humped pretty regularly and sex gave them better focus for the season, she had no problems spending special time with each player and on the weekends she would meet up with some of the second string players, she loved being lusted after, she loved being shared and all of the attention, she felt a little dirty letting most of the guys just cream inside of her but the warm moist rush of them finishing, got her off also.

Tod spoke highly about having been the king of high school, he had ass when he wanted it, he was ripped to shit and his muscles ached and bulged in his t-shirts, and that was what Aimee couldn't keep her eyes off of. Tod was making a weekly purchase from Lenny, he didn't divulge his hook up for his roids but his teammates came to him anyways. Tod was selling his teammates monthly doses and marking it up twenty bucks, as well as siphoning off his daily doses;

he was getting his daily doses as well as was making money for his efforts. Tod smirked at thinking back to how many younger girls he got to nail as a big shot football god at school, he felt he could walk up to any girl from his school and whip his dick out and have the girl of his choosing use it as her pogo stick, he didn't feel like he'd ever be told no for nothing. Aimee asked a few times why Tod hadn't noticed her, except for being flat chested and a freshmen, he just repeated every time that he was distracted by tits and ass but she had him now, which reassured Aimee that she won over all of the blonde haired perky cheerleader types that had all become fat desperate housewives with cellulite and highlights.

When Tod got busted it was in early January, the football season was over and there was hardly any warning, officers had walked the school hallways once in a while looking for some of the stoners to have weed on them, which most people knew not to keep in their cars, the high school was run by a bunch of homo Nazi's and felt that if you parked your personal vehicle on their parking lot that they had the rights to subject your car to a paint scratching drug dog. As the second to the last bell rung in school, two officers and a janitor were opening lockers and picking through peoples coats and backpacks looking for who knows what at the time. Tod turned a corner to see his locker pried open and one officer staring into it, Tod spoke about how he suddenly felt the urge to drop some fruit in his looms and run, except that a large hand landed on his right shoulder from behind. "Son, are you Tod?" a large godlike booming voice echoed in his ears, silencing the entire busy hallway between classes. Tod shuddered and after the split second of blank mind, Tod shrugged off the strange hand and turned to shove the large mustached officer, he had just turned eighteen and had no idea how to braid hair, he was terrified of going to jail.

Tod turned his whole body and with his hulk like strength he heaved the burly cop against the wall to his left, all of his years of football practice and drills running through dummies had prepared him for what had instinctually set in, he tucked his arms under his ribcage and began barreling through underclassmen. Tod used his long legs to put distance between him the meaty hand of the law, Tod must have shouldered through twenty smaller girls and boys knocking them to the ground in his attempt to flee. Some short statured office bitch named Carol had stepped out from behind the office door that

141

Tod was running full blast towards, she widened her stance and smirked as she tucked her arms underneath Tod's ribs and without budging, she was able to stand her ground and knock the boy to the ground, flat on his ass.

Carol stood over the winded Tod and smiled when she asked him in a soft voice to please refrain from running in her hallways. Carol straightened her blouse sleeves and turned herself back through the office door as the officers closed in on Tod while he laid there trying to catch his breath. To this day Tod couldn't figure out how the small lady had bowled his ass over when having been knocked by man sized football players couldn't deviate him from his running course during a game, bitch must have had pain in the ass kids or something. Tod spent a week in the county jail before his processing went through, they were trying to further follow the trail of roids, Tod had a hard time keeping his mental focus, worked out as much as he could in his cell, there was ample time and after two or three days of push-ups and squats, his prison style workouts, he felt himself grow less and less strong in his workouts, he could feel his body deflate as the steroids left his muscles. Tod served time in prison for distribution of a controlled substance, and that was when Tod shit for sure.

Tod didn't even get to finish high school, he missed all of the perky titties and tight bodies of the teen girls he had his way with, he now had to share a stainless steel toilet with another man, and being the younger cellmate, his attempts to try and pretend everything went away was hard to ignore, especially when his older heavier set cellmate decided to crank one out at night. Tod was viewed as being a very fresh fish, his December birthday had delivered him into adulthood and he was charged as such. Tod spent most of his days working out to stave off any potential attempts at his virgin ass; the attempts never came like in the movies and the constant state of stress and high blood pressure from having to always watch his back gave him intense acne and bags under his eyes. Tod had watched American History X and Shawshank Redemption a bunch and was pretty sure that prison rape was a daily occurrence and it took almost a month of not sleeping and hardly eating that he grew understandable of his surroundings. Tod slid from a built one-ninety running back frame to under one-sixty, his roid filled body had shed most of the chemical procured weight and not he was just a skinny six foot two.

142

Tod was never warned of the hemorrhoids that often accompanied steroid use, Megan once tried to tongue punch his ass and all but threw up when she made the discovery. Tod had been on top of life in high school, he was one of the most popular guys there had been and like most athletes, his grades were fairly padded with teachers having been bribed by his varsity position on the team and his coaches encouraging his propagation. Tod had the reading level of a seventh grader at best, he struggled to read or write and hardly any of his teachers tried to find any help for him, they simply passed him rather than bother. Tod was proficient at getting by, he could fill out the essential portions of some job applications but he preferred cash jobs to avoid dealing with taxes or the government having a hand in his pocket. Aimee stepped up for most of his reading and writing needs, as well as having most of the bills in her name

Aimee often questioned why she was the one that shouldered most of Tod's responsibilities; he was like a big fifth grader that likes drugs, tits, and booze. Tod was often out and working so when he and she had time together it was spent drinking beer in the evening and often times in amorous activities before going to bed and repeating the next day. Tod reacted differently to each drug he put into his body, with Methamphetamines he wanted to have sex or jerk off for days on end, Aimee was often the recipient of harsh handling and collected bruises over those days, they would often start at her wrists when he would hold her down, he would bite at the backs of her arms or underarms as he thrusted at her from behind. The rough intercourse progressed into anal, and slapping, Aimee didn't tolerate many sessions of the violent interludes despite his moderate stamina that she found enjoyable for a majority of the time, until he got out of control. Tod would pull hair, explore her body with his hands, tongue, self, feet and just about anything else he could insert in different areas of her body.

The last time Tod had gotten ripped on some Ice he fractured four of Aimee's ribs, his humping, heaving, and thrusting had gone from him slapping her on her ass to onto her side and from slapping to hammer pounding his fist into her back, Aimee had been crying and fighting to crawl away from him after his third overhead dropping of his hardened fist into her back right side, leaving her in such agony and struggling for breath that all she could do was try and kick him off of her, he found the struggle that much more erotic that he fought

143

back and continued to hang on her like a mating male frog. Aimee spent two weeks after Tod's meth binge in pain trying to breathe, he had come off of his three day party and cleaned up after he realized what he had done, he often got past the point that he injured Aimee and then felt terrible enough to try and nurse her back to health, an action Aimee used to reassure herself that he truly cared for her, plus the sex was amazing even though she sometimes ended up hurt. Aimee liked the attention, she was terrified to be alone and Tod was often lusting for her enough to fulfill her needs to be desired, she was no longer a fit bodied teen and she realized that sex was a major bartering tool in gaining attention anymore. Aimee focused on her life day to day, she lived check to check for herself and Brittini, Tod helped financially some of the time, even though it hardly covered his own expenses but it was nice to have the company both during the evening as well as during each night.

Aimee sometimes wondered what it would take to improve her life, she had dreamed that getting her Associates degree to be a medical assistant would be her ticket out of the trailer park, except that she had Don and Shelley to help her get through it, they watched Brittini and gave her the ability to get a college degree. Aimee had all of her friends living in close proximity to her, she could text Angel and go have some drinks or have her over, she had established herself in the area and was comforted knowing that she had Darryl on speed dial for a Xanax or Ambien once in a while when she was getting edgy about wanting to mentally escape, she had a reliable world for Brittini to grow up in and in the overall picture of her life, ensuring Brittini had anything she might need in order to progress in her own life, was the main biological goal of Aimee. Brittini had her mom to provide for her and Jonny to stand up for her, she was insecure about her small body, her chest had hardly begun to develop and one breast had swollen to almost twice the size of the other when Lil B had clung on like he was falling for his life, she showed Jonny her bruised and reddened skin, he felt terrible for her and caused him to reach his boiling point and attack Lil B.

Aimee deluded herself daily with various drugs or sex, Tod had moved in only a few dates after they had met, she felt that she was easy but they had mostly lasted several years so she felt that her gamble to sleep with him early in their relationship was worth it. Aimee had a few trysts behind Tod's back, Gary and Darryl and both times flashed in her mind once in a while, especially while on Dilaudid and under Tod a few times. Aimee tried to ignore when she was leaning back and Gary sweating and humping away at her wet snatch in the back of his gas station or Darryl tonging at her between her thighs like a bloodhound lapping up water. Aimee had a slew of poor decisions when it came to sexual partners but she focused on her next time getting drunk or dealing with work long enough to get passed the day, she struggled to erase many of her memories from her mind. Brittini was growing older and many of the goals Aimee had set for herself had simply failed, she wanted a better job, she wanted to get out from under her student loans and ten years later she was close but it was like quicksand and once the loan companies squatted over your mouth, you were forced to swallow whatever came out. Some nights after Tod had used her to pleasure himself until he passed out she would cry, Aimee often felt that crying was at most all that she could do sometimes, Tod often left his sticky goo for Aimee to clean up when he was done, he would finish and quickly fall asleep while Aimee had to often do the awkward thigh clasped walk to the bathroom to scoop out the mess from her crotch so it didn't harden and dry overnight.

Amie often sat on the toilet and buried her face in her hands, most times Aimee would get the bathroom door shut before her eyes would well up, some nights she would take her battery operated toy into the bathroom to bring herself to orgasm because Tod often did not, but the end results were the same, tears at the end of a brief moment of pleasure. There was no way out, she was trapped with the boy she once found hot and had all of her attention, now he was covered in shoddy tattoos and a crooked smile on his slender body. Tod wasn't going to back down from anybody, he was willing to fight to prove himself, he wasn't going to be proven a punk in jail and there wasn't going to be anyone that was going to stare him down on the outside either. Tod had a close call when Berman had gotten them ripped up on Buffalo Trace at the nipple nook and then gotten into a shoving match with Bruce. Tod hadn't been off probation a few days when he was instantly found back in a holding cell, luckily for him the booking procedure hadn't actually occurred as it was just a fingerprint scan to prove he was who he was as the investigators were still piecing together everything that had happened. Aimee didn't tell Tod that she had let Gary into her body, it was her body anyways but she was doing to try and help Tod at the time, but she was grateful that she had gotten Norplant birth control right after Brittini was born and she was vigilant about making sure she'd never get pregnant again, Brittini was financially hard enough to take care of, she wasn't about to dip further into poverty with yet another child she couldn't afford.

Aimee often made her purchases from Darryl without Tod present, he would often snipe in on her purchase and obligate her to share her own awards, Aimee liked Xanax and it really did make her feel good and relaxed in her life, she would also enjoy when she convinced Tod to take one with her, she would feed him a few beers and let the goodtime Friday nights rip and roar. Tod was usually docile and complacent when he had a few tall PBR's and a Xanax nestled in his belly, Aimee would feel pretty relaxed and with Tod willing to go along with whatever she might want to try. One night Aimee pegged Tod with her toy, being able to have the dominant hand in their relationship had filled her with excitement and her orgasm that night had been immense, she found herself ravaged with excitement and being able to fondle the near passed out Tod. Aimee didn't mind going down on Tod and found that it turned her on being able to pleasure him with her mouth, she would shake him trying to bring blood back to it after he had passed out, she would often imagine what it might be like to be a guy, her drug haze would float her along playing with his testicles or wave his penis around in her hands out of sheer boredom or just curiosity. One night Aimee had squeezed behind Tod's nuts to rub on her face and play with coarsely, it had left him in pain the next morning, she had drunkenly flicked at his balls and the head of his penis while squeezing his shaft, she hardly remembered what she had done but quickly explained to him the next morning that he had roughly handled himself in the height of his erection when they were playing together, she was afraid he'd unleash his bad temper on her and he was often quick to get pissed off.

In high school there was a boy named Bob C, he was a fat sumbitch and with lawyers for parents, he was spoiled beyond belief. One night in high school he was pulled over with Vick's inhalers wedged into his large nostrils and a baggy full of pills in his lap, not wearing pants and with a small shriveled penis covered in icy-hot. Mommy and daddy got Bob out of jail and tried to make sure the

146

charges went away. Most people called Bod "Blob" and he decided to get his tongue pierced and brag about how many women had taken to the tongue stud. Tod told Blob that "girls that get their tongues pierced will suck your dick, and guys who get their tongues pierced with also suck your dick," Blob shoved Tod over the aggravating quip and in a flash of an instance; Tod swung and connected with one of Blobs chins. Blob fell back against the lockers before sliding to the floor where Tod watched his eyes cross and the fat kid begin to cry. To prove his dominance Tod unzipped his pants and pulled out his dick and urinated all over Blobs reddened and sobbing face right in the hallway with a surrounding hoard of fellow students. Tod had skated through the punishment for what he had done to Blob, the teachers were persuaded to look the other way by Tod's football coach but Blobs parents were unhinged about everything and how it was handled. Blob hid the rest of the day away in the office, he stank of piss and was unable to refrain from crying uncontrollably in both shame and embarrassment, his parents tried to levy legal matters against the school and Tod but even their inflated egos weren't enough to support such matters and it wasn't viable in the court of law.

Tod had a long history of aggressive reactions, he found himself in the throes of anger more than most other reactions he felt, Shooting up with the other guys in the locker room before football games gave him an adrenaline rush, sharing the needle with most of the other jocks would cement their bonds as teammates and they stuck together both on the field and off. When Tod had been arrested for selling the vials of wonder workout drug he refused to narc on any of the other teammates, or his hook up at the gym. Tod went down hard for his actions, he was raging with hormones and even though his skin was brazen with acne, his muscles bulged and twitched and it was a fair trade. Tod was offered a chance to rat out his connections as well as anyone else he knew did the drugs in exchange for a reduced sentence but he was going to prove his toughness to the world and he remained silent about everything instead of be a punk bitch. Tod remained silent about many aspects of his life, Aimee often tried to question him as he let drugs set in and drop his guard late at nights. Tod hated prison but he let it further harden him, he got over having to shower with endless other guys and tried to just look at it as if it was after football practice and focused each day on surviving through that one day.

Tod had run into one other inmate halfway through his sentence, his name was Jake Vermont; he was a ripped to shit man. He kept a short military style haircut and something about him gave Tod the impression he was possibly the one inmate that shouldn't be screwed with. Tod told Aimee that Jake was a dirty blond haired guy with a rigid facial expression and a propensity to quickly scan all of his surroundings. Jake hardly spoke to anyone but Tod sat next to him a few times during the mess hall routines, Tod learned to scan his environment and search for certain physical clues or ticks that other inmates might be up to something, if in inmates has his fists clenched than there was a fight brewing, if a jaw was clenched it might let on that they were stashing a razorblade in their mouth, or even yet, if someone was walking with a slight hobble, than it was a hint that they either received an unwelcomed shower surprise, or were transporting something in their rectum and to watch out for a shank. Tod learned a lot when on the inside and even kept up some of the paranoid and skeptical habits of looking around and eyeballing strangers to prevent getting jumped.

Jonny was a slim kid, he wore his hair shortly buzzed so it was harder to pull or be pulled by, Big Ken had a short temper when the temperatures were high, in the winter he treated Jonny like a pal at best, they often got along with minimal interaction, Jonny tried to mostly hang out in his room, he kept his head buried within his headphones, Ken would cook hamburger helper and Jonny would sometimes get to join him and eat in the living room, Jonny was always "yes sire, no sir" when it came to his father and he struggled to maintain decent grades to keep his father from being bothered by the school. Jonny often forged his father's signatures when it came to report cards or field trips. Jonny was really self-sufficient in his own life and did his best to avoid Ken's rage. Ken would relax and not growl at Jonny when he had a few drinks, this was always the hour or two after dinner, Jonny always took this time to wash not only his laundry, but his fathers, their understanding was that Jonny would keep up the chores so Big Ken wasn't bothered by such, in addition to having to work and pay the bills.

Jonny never bothered Ken once he had fallen asleep for the night, some mornings Ken would bark and his boy for allowing him to fall asleep in his chair as he would wake up endlessly sore, other mornings Big Ken wouldn't say a word as Jonny would hand his father a cup of coffee and hide away in the kitchen to stay out of sight until his father had left for work in order to sneak through a shower and get himself to school. During the summers Jonny avoided being caught in the house, Jonny learned last summer that even though school was out, it was dangerous to be at home during hours when school should have been in session, during a rain day Big Ken had been canceled for a job so he decided to come home early, to find Jonny sitting on the couch watching TV, running up Big Ken's electricity bill, Big Ken snapped his fingers and swung his sternly pointed finger from Jonny to out the door, signaling Jonny had better move his ass and not be at home. Jonny hopped up like a bunny and ran is ass out the door, he had no idea what to do during the wet ass day so he spent half the day hanging out with Brittini after that ordeal.

The next time Jonny was able to spend time around the house while Big Ken was out, Jonny had found a lose panel in the skirting under his own room, Jonny spent half a day under the trailer padding and setting up draped plastic sheeting to create a small hiding place in which he could hide out and stay warm or dry in cases such as the rainy day again. Jonny had managed a small extension cord through the floor board in the corner of his bedroom closet, with a small plug in work light Jonny had light and there was also a clock down there, Jonny didn't dare an alarm but with a spare backpack to hide away some clothing he had a secondary room established for the school year if he needed a bunker

Most of the time Jonny spent spare time with Brittini, he knew that Tod and his dad Big Ken got along but also that they weren't good enough friends to chatter about Jonny spending many days at his house rather than at Kens. Aimee knew Jonny wasn't a threat, his beta male insubordinate attitude kept him from making much eye contact and he was always willing to help clean or tidy up so he was a welcomed visitor. Jonny and Brittini were close friends, Jonny was a quiet and shy brother like person to her daughter and Aimee was most clear about strict limits between the two of them. Jonny respected Aimee for allowing him refuge on Kens more temperamental days and above all he and Brittini were like siblings and there was nothing that would encourage him to violate that. On several occasions Jonny had spent the night at Aimee's, he often slept on the couch until Tod had come in obliterated out of his mind on both pills and fentanyl laced pot, Aimee awoke to Tod berating the "weird fag kid" and Jonny tried his best to brace himself to be assaulted at three a.m. by a much taller and older pissed off man. Aimee had to physically heave Tod into their room to get his attention off of the boy trying to sleep on her couch. Aimee had gotten irate at Tod for thinking that he had a say about Jonny, she paid the bills and she'd be damned if she was going to let him take charge and threaten her daughters best friend.

At the height of Tod's shouting Brittini had awaken Aimee, Brittini was in tears that Tod was being such a douche and had dared to threaten her guest, Aimee told Brittini to let Jonny go back to sleep back in her bed but they had better behave, resulting in a dreadful look from Brittini. Aimee apologized for Tod's actions and had taken Tod back to their room, Aimee had a hard time wrangling Tod back to their room but as she removed her shirt his argument changed

150

tones. Brittini cried at Tod's outburst, he had already been making her feel estranged in her own life and his coworkers ogled at her awkwardly growing body whenever they were around, Brittini cried herself to sleep and all Jonny could do was spoon behind her and rub her shoulder in the most platonic way as she fell back to sleep. Jonny tried his best not to disturb anyone or their lives, he always felt out of place no matter where he was and living in a constant state of tension, often left him exhausted. Anytime Jonny found himself in a place that he felt even the slightest bit of safety, he was able to close his eyes and fall asleep in an instant, Aimee could always tell that Jonny was heavily burdened by his constant biting at his lips or inner cheeks, his jaw ever stopped grinding at his teeth and his lips were always chapped and scabbed from constantly gnawing at them and the bags under his eyes were always puffy and darkened against his pale complexion.

Jonny had become used to sleeping in the back of Aimee's car, it was hot under the trailer and miserable to sleep in, at least in the car he could crack a window for the night air and hide away behind the dark tinted glass and tall front seats. In early May the electric company began rewiring some of the underground bundles that traced from each individual lot to the main branch just past the outer perimeter embankment. Jonny was trapped out and was left with no other choice but to have to sleep in Aimee's car because there was a muddy mess keeping him out of his makeshift bunker for well over a month before the Fourth of July party, he had been sleeping in Aimee's car for almost a month, in the warmer temperatures he tiptoed around Big Ken when he was home and didn't dare to try and go to sleep in his own bed at nights after Ken had worked a long day in the heat, soaking and sweating through his tight wife beater before his ten A.M Diet Pepsi had been finished. Big Ken trudged through his days, he spent most of his time driving a cement truck and pouring it out to groups of illegals willing to work for cash smoothing out driveways and sidewalks, he hated every damn cement slapping illegal that didn't speak English, he wanted to throttle each and every throat he could wrap his large hands around until they stopped their "Speedy Gonzalez talking" and he could get back to his beer.

After having spent several years behind bars for the actions he and his wife had partaken in in order to pay for their drugs and quasi provide for their son. Jonny was about two when the feds kicked in their door, because there was no other family Big Ken served his time while Jonny continued to be raised by his mother and then when Big Ken came out, with more tattoos and body weight, it was his mothers' turn for her twelve years in some woman's correctional facility up in Pennsylvania, Jonny certainly missed his mother, she spent nine months getting clean by court order in a facility that he was able to join her in, she had weekly piss testing to ensure she remained clean as well as weekly counseling. Jonny hardly remembers the three years of therapy and counseling but he remembered how much better of a parent she was than his father. Big Ken only had to piss test for drugs every other week for a few years and then once a month for another five of his probation.

Big Ken had to rehab and come clean while incarcerated, there was no detox or medical professionals, there was just a cot and twenty four hour watch for three months until the cold sweats and suicidal urges were over with. Big Ken just had to curl into a ball and rage on and on, he wanted to rip the toilet out of the wall, scream and shout, and get bloody ripped to the gills on anything he could drink or snort or smoke. Big Ken had risked additional assault charges when he was in for his second day, his sickness from with drawls had overtaken him and he refused to calm down. Big Ken had torn the thick canvas anti-suicide blanket he was given, his large meaty hands and irate strength of ferocity and when three officers entered his small cell to subdue the screaming man, he was ready for battle. Two of the three officers ended up in the infirmary as a result of the large crazed Ken going on a rampage in his cell. The judge was lenient in adding additional time onto Ken's sentence; he was gracious only because of the stress of being newly admitted as well as detoxing from a long list of narcotics.

Big Ken spent his days laboring and grumbling about all of the immigrants taking American jobs; he hated having to pay his large monthly bill to the courts just to have to go in and piss in a cup and keep being "gainfully employed." Each day Ken spent listening to the swashing water above his head enraged him with a fury like no other, the water swishing made him have to take a leak every ten minutes, he pissed more often than a small girl and dealing with the frequent lower back pain from sitting and also having to constantly piss, kept him agitated. Ken spent his days pissed off and legally unable to snap someone's throat, he couldn't risk the legal trouble to drink during the last few runs to deliver cement so he just grew more angry each day as his long shifts drew near and all he wanted to do was get home and drink himself into a stupor. Ken relaxed after two or three beers and that was when he didn't see Jonny as a burden, an unwanted expense or even as a nuisance, this was the safe zone that Jonny could step with ease around his pops and it was often too small of a window, and that window always closed with the morning alarm and started all over again.

Big Ken hardly interacted with Jonny, he expected his son to figure out life on his own, do the chores he was expected to and to earn his keep. Ken didn't necessarily expect Jonny to fork over rent but keep the house clean, keep his grades up and to keep his teachers and such off his back. Ken couldn't afford to spend time away from work for parent teacher conferences, worry about social services showing up or causing him grief in anyway so Jonny did his best to be invisible. Big Ken noticed Carsey last spring, she had a decent little body and a fairly perk rack hoisted up in her tank top as she was walking Brodan in his stroller near the park, she was wearing firm fitting pants and Big Ken had to slow down extra slow to gaze at her ass muscles flexing in her pants as she pushed her stroller, Big Ken found a different fix to feed his neglected addiction center in his soul. Big Ken decided that afternoon that he should go for a walk, that the fresh air might be good for him and if he so happened to get a good gaze at the young titties he passed on his way in, well then he had fodder to spank one out too. Ken put on his small bowler hat and a short sleeved camp shirt with cards and flames on it, it didn't button around his barrel chest but it didn't have to, then he headed out.

Halfway around the block Big Ken had realized he was out of shape, his lungs burned from being winded, his knees hurt under his weight as he sauntered. Big Ken lit his third cigarette since leaving his home, it was a long walk when the young Carsey came into view, she had light highlights in her hair and her bosom heaved up and down lightly as she stepped, the seams in her bra shown through her tank top and her cleavage bounced to Ken's delight. Big Ken slowed his pace to try and catch his breath to hide his wheezing and act composed. Ken stood up tall and tried to smile behind his cigarette as Carsey drew near, she made eye contact to be polite and as she stepped through his exhaled cloud of smoke, her nostrils flared and the nicotine stopped her in her tracks.

153

Carsey asked Big Ken if he had one to spare and that sparked their first conversation. Ken and Carsey stood and shared smokes for a few minutes and chatted, they spoke about how long they had each lived in the *Heights* and how they hadn't seen each other before. Carsey had small dimples near the corners of her mouth when she smiled, Ken could feel his heart still beating from his labored walk but he fought his best to speak without sounding winded as he flirted aimlessly with the girl, Brodan asleep in his stroller, giving them plenty of time to talk. Big Ken steered the conversation towards his end goal, to flatter the girl with compliments and test her reception to his advances. Carsey was grateful for the compliments, it was nice to be noticed and because she spent most of her days alone with Brodan and Big Bird, it was nice to have another adult to talk to. Carsey had expressed her own slight struggles as she fought to make ends meet, fought to retain her composure each and every day and how some days she could just use an extra fifty buck and a hard humping, and an accord was reached.

The first time Big Ken came through with fifty bucks and an hour in his schedule they made their way to Kens. Brodan was left to sleep in his crib. Big Ken kicked Jonny out and quickly picked up his room a bit, they didn't even make it that far. Carsey was nervous but finishing her joint as she walked up the steps to be greeted by Ken, his nervous energy caused his hands to shake as he held the screen door open. Carsey was enjoying the oncoming pot buzz and as her mind clouded over, Big Ken began to kiss along her neck in an almost sensitive and romantic sort. Big Ken enjoyed the rush, his much younger plaything had a young firm body, she had a few deep colored stretch marks along her love handles and her butt sank a bit without the support of her blue panties. Ken felt like a schoolboy un-wrapping a Christmas gift as he could almost touch his hands completely around her small waist; he removed her shirt and began to kiss and suck on her chest jamming his tongue down inside the bra cup, lapping at her nipples while she ran her fingers through his wiry hair. Carsey didn't mind the graying hair, the stubble gave away its color as it protruded from the shaven scalp, she focused on how his mouth felt on her skin, his fingers to her flesh and tried her best to hide her mind behind her buzz until all was over and she had fifty dollars of grocery money in her pocket.

Big Ken struggled to unhook the bra clasps, his fingers were too large around and lacked the dexterity after years of building up calluses steering cement mixers. Carsey reached back to unhook her bra while still holding his head into her breasts, his slobbering was cold on her chest and the large size of his fingers ravaged her delicate parts, it was almost painful until her natural lubrication eased the skin pulling a bit. Big ken paused and removed his wife beater, it was already soaked from armpits to the waist of his jeans and his gray chest hair was matted down from the sweat. Carsey breathed through her mouth after getting a whiff of the onion smelling body odor hidden under the tank top. Big Ken thrusted into the fully nude Carsey, she kept a small triangle of pubic hair to help hide her C-section scar but Ken wasn't the least concerned with anything but the small target between her thighs. Carsey heaved back and forth as the large man pawed at her and roughly handled her body; she was mentally going back to being taken by her husband and ignored the significant physical difference between Big Ken and her late husband, whom she missed so deeply.

Carsey often lost herself in her sexual desires, being taken to the cusp of orgasm and pleasured by the girth of Big Ken's fingers, his crude attempts at intimacy came up shy of Carsey's requirements for romance but a down and dirty body sweat swapping session of animalistic body slapping distracted everyone well enough from the mundane routine of their lives. Carsey fought her best to remain deluded from her having to have buried her husband, her brother and her future. Every day was a self-struggle against her own brain, she sometimes wanted to overdose on anything she could take in excess, pills or smoke or powder if she could get ahold of them, but sex was the closest accommodation she could come up with and not have to risk leaving behind her son. Carsey found herself completely exhausted from her struggles each and every night, the ease to pass out was never far but then followed the early morning rising to take her meds, sometimes a self-induced orgasm gave a rise in her hormones enough to get through a tough morning before another long day. Carsey dragged herself outdoors with Brodan as much as possible, she realized the benefit to being out and in the view of potential neighbors that might encourage her to behave herself, she shook and dragged heavily on each slowly smoked cigarette, the hot cherry grew long before the ash coating caught up and fell off, Carsey knew smoking wasn't the most healthy thing to do in the long run but with as many suicidal thoughts that flashed across her mind, doing it in such a slow manner was the least of her concerns. Carsey had one goal in life now, to live it long enough to see her son Brodan into adulthood, after he graduated high school then she would be without the burden of struggling to stay alive or sane.

Big Ken was still legally married, his wife was still committed to a penitentiary for several more years, they had been apart for almost all of Jonny's life, she was simply a memory and a distant one. Big Ken had no remorse about how he was living his life, it was his life and he was a grown ass man whom did what he wanted, he didn't set out to hurt anyone and if he wanted to drink than he was having a drink. Big Ken still had to piss in a cup occasionally and it was still random so it kept him from being able to enjoy a high here and there but when Tyrone first brought his chemically concocted mixture of undetectable tincture, everyone around was raving. Big Ken was nervous about pissing dirty after sipping some of the Milk, your vision became a swirling vortex of dreams with a sprinkle of nightmare all to become a flying carpet for the users to fly through the galaxy on, it filled every void and desire to get annihilated when it arose

The average Zebra milk high was sedative, it brought on slight visions and tracers and the occasional snake head could be seen in the dark corners of rooms, the shadows would sometimes tease the sight of an awaiting wolf to strike and as your goose bumps stood on the surface of your skin and your eyes raced to focus on the delusion, you were brought the rush of relief when it wasn't true. Zebra Milk encompassed all sorts of highs, it eased anxieties like Xanax and relaxed your muscles with the alcohol, it also induced a numb that you couldn't stop smiling with that you can find with morphine or even heroin. The most dangerous part of Zebra Milk is in its making, it's not as bad as making methamphetamines per say, there was no risk of explosion but getting bit by a snake was still a risk, and then there was ensuring that the concoction sat in high proof alcohol for over three months to slowly denature and chemically change or whatever. Tyrone figure it all out, he aced the hell out of all of chemistry classes, he was near genius in school but having nothing but thugs and ghetto role models, his ambitions were simply to defy "the man" and not do anything long term with his intelligence. When

Tyrone finally got bit and passed away, he was stark naked with a young girl on his bed and had plenty of Zebra Milk in his body. Most of the residents that took up position near the burn barrel for drinks and assorted other party favors, but everyone thoroughly enjoyed the mild blend of the Zebra Milk, Tyrone met up with Curtiss and they brought a few gallon jugs, Tyrone charged five bucks for a double shot worth of milk in a red plastic cup, he made a wad of cash from each gallon jug and was one of the more popular attendees at parties.

When Tyrone first brought over his Milk, a few of the first partakers were leery about sipping on it, the smell was strange and it had a light milky white tinge to it, hence the reason it was called "Milk." Tammi and Shameeka were the first ones to willingly take a course shot from a cup and as the evening progressed they loosened up and giggled away. As Tammi twirled and let her hands swirl in the air for her amusement, she looked longingly into the night, the stars aligned and then dispersed, demanding all of the girls' attention. During the first night Tyrone easily convinced Tammi to join him in his old Buick, he convinced her to earn another shot of his custom drink, he eased the girl out of her top for light petting and suckling while she sipped at her second cup. Tammi was often easily persuaded out of her clothing and to let any number of takers into her cooter, anyone who ever met her knew she'd give away her snatch or a quick blowjob for a cigarette or even just to pass the time, Tyrone didn't care to spend a little hooch for some action.

After the official product release of Zebra Milk everyone realized and enjoyed that the high was wild and the come down was slept off. The morning after wasn't even half as bad as a hangover, the amount of actual alcohol was a small amount but it was enjoyed with the trace amounts of venom and its' neurotoxin properties. A few parties later Tyrone was called up by Curtis again to bring some liquid fun, he was making the milk in five gallon buckets and had acquired a pretty decent bankroll to purchase bins to house snakes rather than have to continue to trudge through the woods or swamps looking for fresh ones to milk. Keeping copperheads in storage totes made them easier to wrangle but there was constant feeding them and keeping them warm under heat lamps and so on. Tyrone kept his room pretty well stocked with snakes and breeding feeder mice while he hauled the settling liquor in buckets up and down from his basement in his mother's house. Tyrone was purchasing cheap concentrates to add sugar and yeast to ferment before distilling and then adding the venom too. The chemistry came easily to Tyrone; he enjoyed the tinkering of chemicals and being in charge when making it all come together. Tyrone kept fist full of cash hidden in various cubby holes in his room and often had a wad in his pocket, he was a baller and knew it, all from easily working nature itself and not having to risk getting shorted or shot at running powders or illegal drugs, as far as anyone was concerned he was simply brewing moonshine, not jail able but possibly fineable.

Tyrone had something big for Dez'rae and he sure wanted to give it to her, she had a tight dancer's body and legs that ran halfway up her body, her light skin and sharp cheek bones made her the idle of everyone's sexual desires and Tyrone wanted to sample her honeypot. Dez'rae enjoyed having everyman's attention, she held her head up high and kept her small firm chest raised up in the air, she was slow to even consider letting any man play around with her downstairs but a few well maneuvered blowjobs and she had many of the right players willing to bend some rules for her, such as Gary. Tyrone always fronted like he was the hardest and baddest nigga around, he was still in high school but with his IQ and ability to put it to use, he had a lot of potential. Tyrone slung endearing comments like "sup baby girl, how you doin, and you aright?" whenever he saw Dez'rae, the epitome of all of his wet dreams, in hopes of convincing her to let him into her panties.

Tyrone got a chance to get close in with Dez'rae on one occasion, Shameeka was milling around the burn barrel, she was giggling on with the sharp minded sixteen years old, Tyrone liked the attention and wanted to get with Dez'rae, even at fourteen she at the time she was tall, slender, had just enough butt to make it pop a but no upper thigh jiggle, everything on her young body was firm and he wanted to have her. Shameeka knew her daughter was going to be a fine young woman, it was important for her to push the awareness that she needed to keep her daughter in dance classes, after school programs like track or volleyball, really anything to keep the girl in shape and out of trouble in her young life. Shameeka worked her ass off raising her daughter, she wanted to see her girl out of jail or bad relationships and get into college after graduating, she had seen enough of her people slathered all over the news or TV, broke, busted, and making fools of themselves. Shameeka didn't want her daughter to become

158

another statistic of black crime or teen pregnancy, just to be safe she got her daughter Norplant for a fourteenth birthday, it was good for five years and would at least get the teen girl through high school.

Shameeka found herself giggling and carrying on with Tyrone, Curtiss was still a punk but his slightly older cousin had charisma, and good posture, and a drink that called to her bones. After most of the burn barrel partyers had dispersed to wherever they were to end up for the night Shameeka was feeling Tyrone. Tyrone had been smooth all night as he complimented each girl near the fire trying to secure any game or action possible. Shameeka ignored the twenty year age difference, he had the necessary equipment she needed to scratch an itch she was having after some drinks, and so they hit it off. Tyrone was looking to get Dez'rae naked but her momma would do, both people had plenty of drinks in them and they headed on over to Shameeka's place to enjoy each other's' company. Tyrone poured Shameeka and Dez'rae some heavy drinks as the three headed back to the trailer, Dez'rae found it strange that her mother was angling to bed a boy only a little older than she was but she had no interest in him so who cared.

Tyrone hung on around Shameeka's neck as he watched Dez'rae's ass flex and bounce with each step, the small firm ass of Dez'rae was what was getting his engine running. Shameeka was too drunk to worry about why Tyrone was turned on, all she knew what that he was down to throw down and get wild in the sheets, she wanted to get hers as the sista hadn't had her none in a while and Tyrone was young and virile. Shameeka figured Tyrone was poorly skilled and would need training but young guys tried hard and could go a few times so it was a fair trade, sure beat so old worn down brother that got his, then got out. Dez'rae was halfcocked and stumbled her way to bed as Tyrone poured himself and Shameeka another drink as they headed back to her bedroom also, his gallon jug with a handle was almost gone and carrying it around grew old and tiring.

Tyrone was cocky and arrogant as all hell landing an older woman, it was dark in the bedroom and he tried to imagine he was rubbing up on Dez'rae as he caressed and fondled at Shameeka, her breasts were flatter and her stomach not nearly as flat but he had himself a naked lady to play with anyways, so to hell with the world. Shameeka let the boy poke and play away with her as her mind spun from the drug, it was all ecstasy and each touch felt like orgasm, her body writhed as he climbed into her and thrusted away at her with himself. Tyrone almost came as he entered the already warm and wet snatch, she moaned and began to breathe heavily and the initial penetration had him already at the edge of cumming. As the couple fondled and grabbed at each other they brought each other closer to orgasm, Tyrone thrusted faster and harder at her pelvis and as she grabbed his upper arms with her gripping hands. Tyrone finally unleashed his load deep inside, it felt wonderful to gush inside of the warm wet cooch and the cleanup was her problem to deal with. Tyrone had no intention to leave and finally lay beside Shameeka, she was struggling to remain awake after the physical exertion and her ability to speak coherent sentences had given way to mumbling and drunken stutter as she let her inebriated state take hold.

Tyrone poked and fingered Shameeka to arouse himself again, she was out cold and her body could become his plaything again, he still dripped from her and she was still wet and ready to receive him, all he had to do was move her a bit to roll her over and he was ready for round two. Tyrone pushed at Shameeka again, she was out cold so he decided that he might try and sneak into the girl's room right next door. Shameeka was a seasoned drinker and was passed out, Dez'rae should be equally tranquilized and unresponsive, and his! Tyrone eased the first door open, he scanned the hallway and stepped past the doorway, reaching out towards Dez'rae's doorknob, he was inhibited by a locked door, it was all but enough to keep him from tasting the young fit girl, and the slice of heaven he had masturbated to for some time. Tyrone stepped back to his pants, his cock still thick with blood and unwilling to let him just go to bed, pulling out a CVS card from his wallet was enough to jimmy the locked door open, sure enough there she was, in the shadows of the street lights streaming in through holes in the blinds, Tyrone could make out the silhouette of Dez'rae. Dez'rae was asleep under a sheet; Tyrone whispered her name to ensure that she was unconscious; his heart beat like a set of stage speakers at a concert, his pulse raced through his fingers as he reached out his hand to pull back her white bed sheet.

Tyrone felt the sweat seep from his forehead, his nerves were unraveling but his lust for the young pussy was at the most forward part of his brain and he wanted to caress the young firm body of the sleeping girl. Dez'rae didn't budge as Tyrone pulled the sheet back, Dez'rae was wearing dark colored bra and panties, the curve of her

Tyrone raised Dez'rae's right leg and raised up her backside into the air, her knees up near her collar bones, Tyrone stood over her and put himself into her again, he jackhammered up and down and watched her body sweat in the specks of light that evaded the slats of the blinds in the window. Dez'rae had a slender face and high cheekbones, her face remained expressionless as Tyrone had his way with the girl as much as could physically muster. Tyrone found himself stopping from cumming again and let the girls legs back down onto the bed, he turned her over to lay her flat on her stomach and he reached up between her legs and inserted his first two fingers to play within her again, his forehead still profusely perspired, his lungs burned from the physical exertion coupled with his raging nerves and parched mouth, his body tensed and throbbed as the alcohol evaporated his sweat and he grew increasingly dehydrated.

Tyrone laid his penis between the supple butt cheeks of his unknowing victim, her firm ass pushed back against him just as hard as he pushed into her, her back was tone and the valleys between her back muscles looked like a black river flowing from her neck to her lower back in the dark, her skin was soft and smelled of vanilla, the random wafts of her body lotion further enticed Tyrone as he guided himself into her again. Tyrone struggled to place his hands under Dez'rae to continue to grope at her chest, Dez'rae let out a small uncomfortable moan as she stirred a little underneath his thrusting, and her closed legs were cool to the touch and felt wonderful against his bumping nuts. Tyrone couldn't contain himself any further and finally exploded his seminal fluids into Dez'rae, his neck muscles strained and his jaw clenched as he struggled through his orgasm. As Tyrone let his goop leak deep into Dez'rae, his legs tensed, his arms shook and the girl underneath him stirred a little, she flexed muscles inside herself which teased at the still orgasming intruder, her squeezing around his shaft caused involuntary pelvic thrusts into her, his eyes began to water from such strain.

Tyrone climbed off of Dez'rae and gazed upon the firm supple body that lay half covered in his sweat, her youth was half of her toxic beauty, her long slender body lay strewn out on her bed, her right arm half hanging off the bed, her right leg with a slight bend at the knee and an even darker shadow laying over the sweet spot Tyrone where left his spooge inside of her. Tyrone patted at the floor beneath his feet with his right foot searching for his phone again, with luck as he felt for his shirt he also found his phone and leaned in again to take even more candid photos of her soft delicates between her legs, the flash from the camera illuminated the toom, the magnificent light reflected off of her skin and glistened off of her moist body parts.

Tyrone was still seeing spots against the dark background from the camera flash as he fumbled up his pants, once his pants were up he sat to put his socks and shoes on, as his Milk buzz began to wear off he got a strong whiff of his own socks and determined her was long overdue to change them. As Tyrone sat and struggled to make his fingers work to tie the laces on his white K-Swiss shoes, he glanced to his right to see the balled up pair of shorty panties he removed from Dez'rae, he reached out and grabbed the pair, he wanted a souvenir to remember this night by, he could smell the panties and look through all of his ill-gotten pictures anytime he wanted, he felt the blood rush back to himself a little as he thought about maybe one day even flashing her a picture of her own crotch without telling her to whom it belonged, a teasing notion that would help him to relive what he had done, she probably wouldn't recognize herself nor believe it had even happened anyways, be it would be a turn on to tease her about it.

Tyrone put the panties in his mouth to hold onto until he rose back to his feet, his legs were stiff and hard to move, his thighs still ached from having plowed and spunked into both Dez'rae and Shameeka! Hitting a mother daughter combo reassured him that he was the shit, the man, and now a true player. Having now demolished both pussies within a few hours of each other there wasn't much more he could think of he wanted out of life, and having the sweet, young, tight cooch of Dez'rae, he wanted more and more just like it. Tyrone found his feet and had to touch Dez'rae one last time before finally fleeing the house in the wee hours of the morning. Dez'rae was still warm and moist as he reached between her legs for another lasting memory of touch; he forced three fingers inside of her and roughly jarred her up and down by her privates. Tyrone coarsely rubbed his fingers up and down within her crease a few times and as she began to stir more and more, she shivered from being uncovered and wet, Tyrone found it was his time to leave. Tyrone let himself out of the trailer and didn't bother to care if the door slammed loudly behind him, he was exhausted and ready to get to his car and go home.

164

The next morning Shameeka knew how she felt, slightly hung over and relieved from having been drunkenly humped to sleep, she felt refreshed and ready for the new day. Dez'rae awoke crying, she had no recollection as to why she was nude, why she was in such pain in her privates or to why she was so filthy and sweaty, she could only assume that she sweat out everything and was simply needing a shower after her night of drinking, she didn't have much drinking experience and every inch of her ached and hurt. Dez'rae eased herself onto all fours, her private area was red and swollen, and she had experienced an infection once or twice as well as irritation when she began using pads after the onset of menstruation so she attributed her problems with some form of infection or what have you, and she headed into the shower. Shameeka was in the kitchen pouring cereal as Dez'rae made her way into the shower, her body felt sensitive to the robe that covered her and her head throbbed as each loud sound echoed within her ears.

Dez'rae let her pink robe fall to the floor, she had red marks on her hips bones, her slim slender legs were covered in dark dirty black marks from where sweat had gathered and dried on her skin. Dez'rae noticed the asymmetrical redness of her nipples and they were sore to her touch, there were red marks all over her chest and sides and long red marks on her neck, she couldn't recall what had happened during the previous night so maybe she got caught up in her sheets and it was like a rug burn, but it all hurt. Dez'rae was extremely careful when she got to the point where she had to wash her tender "tutu," it hurt and as she cleaned, she felt a strange sliminess within her as well as dried and crusted funk all around her down there. Dez'rae needed a Gatorade and some aspirin before she broke down into tears from the pain. Dez'rae was concerned she was coming down with a girly based infection and even putting panties back on, hurt.

After carefully applying an ointment to her swollen red girl parts, Dez'rae put her clothes on, she continued to look at herself in the mirror and find more and more red marks on her back, her butt and her thighs, she was baffled as to their origin and couldn't struggle hard enough to come to a conclusion as to how she ended up so battered. Dez'rae joined her mother for breakfast and began to pepper her with questions about the prior evening. Shameeka could only really recall that the girl was still an inexperienced drunk and stumbled a bunch, including into a few shrubs and maybe in her clumsy state maybe she tumbled into any number of obstacles, Shameeka herself had holes in her memory from the prior evening, she remembered having herself some young meat for dessert and he was long gone before she woke up. The Zebra milk had an Ambien like effect in which everything was a faint memory of an illusion, almost as if things were a dream of a dream, as if there was any real recall of events having happened anyways. Shameeka found plenty of evidence of Tyrone having been with her, she assumed the brotha "hit it and quit it" and bounced in the early morning hours.

Shameeka had dragged herself out of her disheveled bed and straight to the coffee maker, she iced her first cup of coffee to mainline it in the shower to bring herself back to life, her body ached and her head slightly clouded from exhaustion but not heeded from hangover. Shameeka was in her mid-thirties, she no longer healed like she did when she was twenty but she partied like it, she wasn't going to let her looming fortieth birthday in a few years keep her from having a good time. Shameeka did her best to avoid most of the harsher drugs like coke just in case she got popped with a piss test, the Zebra Milk on the other hand, melded most of the best highs and so far, there had been no tests that could detect its' use, it was a bitter drink but it accompanied any and most other drugs without taking things over the top, but overall, it was a sensational high on its' own and hardly needed a booster. The Zebra Milk was on the verge of becoming one of the best street drugs, even better than "Black Death" which is Heroin mixed with a zip of Fentanyl, or anything else for that matter.

Shameeka worked her ass off for herself and Dez'rae, she put her daughter through dance schools and extra tutoring for school, she often worked a second job once Dez'rae was ten and could fend for herself at home. Shameeka had seen enough thugs and news stories of young black kids ending up in trouble and she sure as hell wasn't going to let her baby girl become a statistic, she had her daughter on birth control in her early teen years and educated the young girl as best she could to avoid boys and drugs, but with close supervision she would smoke a bit now and then or enjoy some booze at a few of the burn barrels. Dez'rae was seen as stuck up and being light-skinned, it was conflicting in her social life. Shameeka had an older sister, Riqa. Riqa was real ghetto and it often boggled Shameeka how her sister could purposefully embrace such ignorance, she had four abortions before the end of high school, and the fourth one left her sterile so rather than have to excel in life for any potential children later on, she let herself become a drop out and just exist. Riqa had deluded herself for almost twenty years now; she had been hiding from the truth about her, inability to have children, so she took to all day smoking and drinking instead. Riqa helped to raise Dez'rae to some degree, mostly when Shameeka was held up working long shifts. Shameeka was always hesitant in letting Riqa watch Dez'rae to long without her own supervision, she woke up with a forty and ended most nights with handfuls of pills or pot, there was hardly anything Riqa wouldn't do, even if she was babysitting.

Dez'rae heard plenty of her mother's warnings, and complaints about Riqa, so she was fairly judgmental from the get go but she also held a small place in her heart for her aunt. When Dez'rae had extra time after cheer practice she would walk to the closest bus route and take a liner to Riqa's apartment complex, she had a few friends from there and despite the stern warnings about not being around there after dark, and Dez'rae still hung around the complex anyways. Riqa lived in dirt cheap apartments, it was a shady ass area, most cars in the neighborhood had expensive as rims, the iron gate around the complex has various spray painted colors on the black bars but the cars inside were immaculate. Riqa held a busy night life and when she and most of her neighbors were chilling on the back patios, everyone kept a watchful eye on their cars nearby. Kids in the complex knew they risked getting shot at if they messed with any of the shiny cars or their rims; there was a safe five foot distance to keep from each car if there was to be life after passing by one of the flashy cars. Most of the apartment complex neighbors had themselves bridge cards and when it came time for refills, there was always bartering going on, most of the users hung out at supermarkets offering fifty cents on the dollar to purchase a customer's groceries on the bridge card in exchange for cash.

Life in the complex was just that, complex, residents mostly hung around their apartments, once in a while there was some random foot traffic and lives going on, but mostly it was calm but filled with bass bumping systems and shouting. Last summer Dez'rae was leaving Riqa's after she met up with some friends in the complex, they shared a few joints with Riqa and some of the friends were tight neighbors with Riqa anyways so they were in close proximity.

167

Dez'rae was leaving the complex when one of the local dealers named Terrell was waiting for a delivery and let the small fine girl catch his eyes. Dez'rae was full well aware she was lusted after, she kept her pants tight and her shoes loose, her white K-Swiss shoes glowed in the orange hue of the street lights as she walked, she had hoped Terrell hadn't seen her, but she knew she was out of luck when he did. Terrell sauntered over with one hand free to sway across the front of him while the other hand grasped onto the front of his pants to keep them from falling down as he made a direct line towards the young girl astray at night.

"Guurlll you looking tasty" Terrell murmured when he got close to Dez'rae, he had seen the girl a few times and like all other girls he had seen around the neighborhood, he felt owed to bed her down. Terrell was as dark as they came, brother could bring midnight at noon, he had his gold grill always holding up his pink lips and wore a permanent sneer on his face and a watch cap down over his eyebrows, his tight braids shot out in every direction from under his hat. Terrell was a larger man, over two hundred fifty pounds and stood well over six-three, he dwarfed the petite Dez'rae when he stood near and every word out of his mouth was meant to flatter, but it made her skin crawl. Terrell stood close enough to block out the streetlights as they spoke, Dez'rae tightened her leg muscles to fill them with blood just in case she had to make a run for things, she felt her heart beat in her ears and her hands begin to shake as she waited to see the bus angling towards the small glass structure. Terrell reached his giant hand towards her and began to play with the neck of her shirt and crack jokes about how filled with prowess he was, and of course how much she'd enjoy it if she just let him make love to her.

Terrell eased his hand down the front of her shirt and let his outstretched finger run down the front of her right breast over her shirt, her skin covered with goose bumps and she let out a whole body shiver as he traced her shirt down towards her waist. Terrell slipped his large index finger inside the waist of her pants, he tugged left and right while still mumbling and trying to sell the girl on all of the reasons she should let him into her, all the while she was fighting to find her focus. Dez'rae was blank, her mind had shut off and she was frozen as he worked his finger further into her waist, Terrell took her silence as permission to continue to allow him to do as he pleased, and he couldn't focus on anything other than getting his rocks off.

Terrell flaunted about all of the conquests he'd had, they were all hood rats but pussy was pussy and he had plenty of it. Terrell did his best to sell his dick to the girl, waiting to hear her comply at any minute or to even drop to her knees and take him into her mouth for a blowjob right there in his parking lot, the petite girl was frozen with fear.

Terrell was easing Dez'rae's waist on her pants down slightly as he tugged back and forth, he had gotten them down just enough to find the elastic band on her panties and he began to slip his large finger inside of them as well, he wasn't being deterred by hair stubble as he felt the course pubic hair nubs just below her panties, he wanted to feel her warm snatch and being almost triple her weight, and age, he wasn't going to be told "NO." Dez'rae was still frozen, she didn't know what to do and the whole time all she heard Shameeka's voice in her mind berating her over and over not to have been out at the complex after dark, and this time she was about to get raped for disrespecting it. Dez'rae snapped back to reality when she felt the large finger rub at her most intimate private parts through her pants, it startled her and she felt traumatized that the whole ordeal wasn't over, she was scared to death that she might actually have to be conscious through the rape, and she felt her left eye begin to well up. The corners of her sight were still orange and blurry and she could feel her pupils widen to take in more light as she stood in the shadow of Terrell, his mass towered over her like a skyscraper, his shadow cloaked the girl in night and all she could do was stand frozen with fear. Terrell rubbed against the girl and continued to spit skewed compliments at her, his ghetto tactics worked on young girls that were already high or wanted to sample whatever he was holding but Dez'rae had the promise of a high school diploma in her future and she was elusive with her private parts, careful to exercise extreme care with her honeypot.

Dez'rae shook off her fear, she could hardly hear anything past her own heartbeat pounding in her ears, and the bass in Terrell's voice seemed to echo off of the solemn parking lot around them, the bass reverberating in Dez'rae's ears made her eardrums tickle, she let out another shiver and this time complete awareness hit her. Terrell had two fingers tugging at the waist of her pants, she could feel the cool air on the exposed skin of her hips and belly. Dez'rae fought off the urge to panic, her whole body tensed up and filled with adrenaline as she let her eyes jet back and forth looking for the easiest and most successful exit route in order to get away. Terrell shifted his weight and let the front of his pants sag a little more, he reached out and grabbed the scared girls hand and lead it towards his own waistline, his boxers were covered by mesh shorts tucked into his pants, and he eased his white jailhouse boxers down enough to allow Dez'rae access to himself. Terrell coaxed the girls hand into his waist belt, his standing close wasn't conducive to her good fortune but the problem at hand was a large man with a raging hard-on for the girl, she was as good as raped as he licked across his gold coated teeth in anticipation of her getting ready to go down on him, he was going to plow this little girl like a corn field.

Terrell wanted to get his thing on, he wanted the little girl buck naked and pinned against a car hood, and for him to be the one to do the pinning. Terrell paused for a moment as Dez'rae cupped him, her hands were cold and he could feel the blood rushing to his pecker in her hand and it was inching out of the top of his waistband as he guided and coerced her hands. Dez'rae was frantically trying to figure out what she was going to do, she didn't want the grubby smelly prick anywhere near her and she was already breathing through her mouth to stave off the smell of rank stagnant cigarette film that filled his clothes. Terrell stunk of the onion like body odor of unwashed scrotum, the putrid smell filled her nose, and she fought the overwhelming notion to vomit. Terrell put his large free hand on her shoulder and began to let the weight push her down, he shimmied a bit to let his pants drop as his hard-on rose up from below his white boxers. The black snake that rose from under the clothes looked like a turd, it wasn't even circumcised and the smell from it further made the young girl need to gag, her body heaved as he coerced her head closer to him, her eyes watered and tears began to stream from her eyes and down her face. As the girl opened her mouth she moved her hand down his shaft, the foreskin pulled back and crusty bits of white gunk fell from underneath, the smell resembled hot garbage and then the urge to hurl finally overtook her.

Dez'rae squeezed onto the shaft of Terrell as the rest of the muscles in her body spasmed, her stomach emptied itself onto the bare crotch of Terrell as he was expecting to feel the warm wet mouth of the girl kneeling before him. It took a brief moment of shock to set in as he began to feel the warm and wet, it was the further warm and

170

wet feeling begin to run down his inner thighs and the splashing of vomit in his shorts that alerted him to a problem. Terrell opened his eyes and looked down to see the girl still tight fisted on his penis and violently vomiting all over his midsection. Terrell lifted his hands to get a better perspective on what the hell was happening and as soon as Dez'rae could feel the weight of his hand lift, and the easing of her uncontrollable muscle seizing, she saw her moment of opportunity. Dez'rae looked up and didn't see the yellowed whites of Terrell's eyes upon her; she released her grip on the penis and cocked back her arm to deliver a solid fisted punch to his hanging bean bag. His crotch was dark and it wasn't easy to find her precise target but she delivered a mighty uppercut to his scrote and grundle anyways, the punch splatted in the vomit and caused the giant dark Shrek shaped man to fall to the ground, letting out a painful bellowing howl all the way to the ground, ending with a hard "thud"

Dez'rae ran until her young lungs felt like they were going to explode, her panties had wedged so far up her backside as she ran that they thought she was going to be split in two as she ran for the farther bus stop, cutting through a vacant lot of tall grass and broken glass. Dogs barked in the distance and the ground crunched beneath her feet as she ran in large strides to cover more ground faster, while she ran she fought the urge to look behind her. Dez'rae couldn't hear anything but her own hard packing steps as she ran, she was frightened that Terrell would be close behind her and she feared that he would certainly rape her this time, maybe even strangle her for puking all over his nuts. Dez'rae caught her bus and she didn't even notice her pants hung under her ass and her panties yanked up over her butt until she sat on the bus seat, the cold plastic was a jolt to her system and her lungs burned to catch her breath as she heaved in and out.

Riqa had heard that not long after Terrell had been dropped to the ground, a local competing dealer had found him on the ground and with the help of a few boys then pummeled the shit out of that giant; he spent several days in intensive care at the hospital and then spent several weeks hobbling around with a cane. He spent the first day searching around the parking lot thinking that his gold grill had just fallen out, it was his pride and joy, he finally realized that it must have been taken and melted down for someone else's' mouth. Riqa missed chilling with her niece and had heard from her neighbors that schooled with Dez about what had happened, Terrell wasn't telling no

171

one that he got his ass whooped like a little bitch by some little teeny girl he was trying to make it with. Dez'rae had never been so scared in her life and as she sat on the cold hard bus bench, the noisy rumbling of the bus droned in her ears as her adrenaline still raced through her body, her hands shook as she tried to pat herself down trying to put herself back together.

As the day ramped up closer to the party, people awoke and began moving more and more, Don and Shelley had dreaded this party a bit, the noise sucked and over the last few years more and more of their belongings had been destroyed during out of control parties. Last Labor Day their Ford Taurus had been damaged horribly. The chaos started out with Big Ken fighting some lowlife that had arrived to the party and began getting handsy with Carsey. As the evening progressed and the drinks continued to flow, the speakers bumped Dre and Luda to keep the girls jiggling and guys amused. Some pudgy douche with a popped collar and short hair named Justin, took a liking to Carsey. Turns out Justin was just some overweight and out of shape tubbo that had knocked up some fat girl named Shantel, he was out looking to have some fun while his overweight wife was nursing their first child. Justin was groping and grabbing at Carsey, he had an affinity for wanting to sniff girls panties or some weird shit. As Big Ken delivered huge hammer blows to the stranger, it turned out he was even wearing a girls thong, his wife must have been huge for his girth to have fit into her undies, then again maybe they didn't start as thongs until he heaved himself into them and the fabric sucked into his ass.

Big Ken shoved Justin from behind as he wrestled with Carsey, she was frantic and trying to fend off the fat hands of Justin. Justin continued to control the girl as he pushed Carsey closer to a small gap between trailers, he had no intention of taking no for an answer when he continued to grope and shove her. When the music silenced for the break in the music and the chorus of the entire group of partiers shouting "SMOKE WEED EVERYDAY" in unison, Big Ken heard is gal pal (and monthly arrangement) cry out "NOOO" as she tried to push back against the adamant asshole. Justin kept his hair close cropped, almost buzzed; he fought to hide his being overweight doughy body under baggy shirts and a gapped tooth smile. Big Ken sent Justin stumbling to the ground after a shove, his body rippled and jiggled as he crashed to the ground. Justin came back with a cocked fist until he locked eyes with Big Ken, whom stood as calm as a

Buddhist statue, there was nothing anyone could do to rock Ken from his post, he stood with a shoulder width offset stance and braced to square off. Justin had landed a hard fist to the side of Big Ken and as his chin wiggled slightly, his eyes shook to realign his vision, Justin had a look of dread on his face as he was on the verge of crying before he returned a blow to Ken.

Ken turned his head back to the front to lock eyes with Justin again, the punch to the face had hardly fazed the brute and as the music began bumping again, Big Ken reached forward and grabbed the shirt of Justin and delivered an almighty hand of god blow to Justin, a blow that shook him down to wetting his jeans. Justin took the "whomp" to the thick skull and double chin, his body all but went limp after the first hit, Justin began to sob and blubber as Ken delivered another hay maker to the falling adversary. Justin began to weep as he sputtered past his snot covered lips, he hated his over-sized wife and was tired of listening to her whining and nagging, he lusted after so many girls he worked around as a janitor at a middle school and he loved trying to guess what types of panties the little girls were wearing. Justin laid in a puddle of his own piss with Ken standing over him, Justin had delivered his best punch and Ken wasn't even moved from his stance, he lorded over the submissive male with Alpha dominance and he felt invigorated with the slight whiff of battle before him, now he had been woken up with the slight brawl and now wanted to drink like crazy and carry on with his rough and forceful mindset.

Justin's body had dented the hood as he rolled off of it after Big Ken had walloped him, he fell against the hood and near caved it in and that was just the beginning. After Ken had his blood brought to life with the power of a bolt of lightning, it raced through him and he was ready to relive his twenties all night. "House of Pain" took over the airwaves; Ken grabbed his half gallon jug of beer and wrapped his thick arm around Carsey to bring her in close. Carsey was grateful and enthralled with Big Ken having saved her from the pants pissing Justin and she was beyond thankful. Ken had stepped in in time to keep her from being manhandled any further and with just enough Zebra Milk in her system; she was more than willing to receive Ken for his heroics. Carsey hiked her skirt up and began to rub on Ken, he was quickly aroused after his blood had already been lit afire from the brawl, Carsey was more than excited after having been rescued and now at the cusp of voyeuristic excursions, with a fun buzz... Carsey was ready for the humping of her life.

Ken plowed into Carsey as she sat on the trunk of the Taurus, the back of the car buckled under their weight, Ken was rough and forceful as he thrusted into Carsey, her moaning caused him to push harder and harder until the back window shattered under their weight, the crowd cheering them on. Once the sound of breaking glass hit the crowd, a ravenous anger took over, the music in the background fueled the rage and people began to kick and hit at the car, there wasn't much anyone could do except stay out of the way. Ken hoisted Carsey up so they could continue their tryst, he thrusted away while still standing and leaned her against Don and Shelley's home, his rocking caused the trailer to rock and awoke them to problems outside. Don and Shelley had hidden themselves away from the noise and commotion inside of coconut headphones to drown out most outside noise; it wasn't until the home started rocking that they became aware of any problems outside. When Don made it to the side door to set eyes on his car, the mob had gained so much momentum that they couldn't be quelled until the car had been tipped on its side.

Don hurried out the door and grabbed his garden hose, he frantically yelled and sprayed the crowd and the car, there were teen boys jumping on the car from on top while it was flipped onto its side, Don was irate and wanted to kill every piece of shit he could find and as he sprayed the crowd to try and calm them down, they only changed gears and began to wallow in the mud of the yard next them. Don started spraying and it wasn't but a minute when another hose had come to life from next door, it began to create an even larger mud puddle in the yard as well as set the makings for a wet t-shirt contest for the willing ladies. Shelley had to wrestle Don back inside to keep him from hurting someone, he was so filled with rage and fury that he had to drop to a knee with chest pain. Shelley was consumed with fear, she was worried about the car and with a massive party going on outside, her car having been destroyed, she was a prisoner in her own home. Shelley texted Brittini and told her she needed help A.S.A.P. Shelley called 911 from Don's phone and arranged to have an ambulance meet them at the park entrance, she knew the wouldn't come any further.

Brittini and Jonny came rushing out of Aimee's and towards Don and Shelley's next door, Jonny tried his best to block out the sight of

Big Ken heaving against Carsey with her pinned up against the side of Don and Shelley's trailer. Jonny and Brittini helped to escort Don out to the waiting ambulance while Shelley gathered their belongings and tried to help hurry them all along, she was frightened for her husband and had a hard time communicating with the group over the loud music in the background from the party. Don struggled with each step; his arms almost choked Brittini and Jonny as he tried to hang on them and also clench his tightened chest. Jonny fought to keep them all standing upright while Brittini fought her best to ward off tears from being terrified. Jonny and Brittini acted heroically under the pressure, Brittini was almost too scared to think with Shelley crying and Jonny shouting instructions to keep Don moving. Don struggled to keep his knees from buckling underneath him, his strength waned and his chest became tighter. The ambulance was waiting with two weary paramedics sitting on the back bumper, the heavier set blonde lady with wavy permed hair was snubbing out a cigarette as the middle aged man stood and shouted, asking if the hobbling man being held up by the two younger teens was "Don," as soon as Shelley could gasp a large enough breath between sobs she shouted " YES" in a terror filled shrill, she was frightened and trying to keep her composure without spilling her purse or wits.

The paramedics helped to ease Don into the back of the ambulance and onto the awaiting stretcher, as the heavier set blonde strapped him down and began running wires and lines to his chest, the man slammed the back doors shut and scurried around to the front and drove off with the sirens blaring and lights flashing. Brittini was shaking in her Nike's and once Don was locked into the back she felt some relief, Don was her biological uncle and only other family she had besides Aimee, and of course Jonny, her self-assigned brother. Brittini worried about Don the rest of the night and she and Jonny tried to help clean up some of the glass that was shattered all over their small paved parking space, where their Taurus sat before it was flipped up by a mob of liquored up out of control partiers being fueled by DJ Wriggle and several rave bumping songs. Jonny suggested that they sit vigilantly on Don and Shelley's porch until the party wound down and keep an eye on their property to prevent any further issues.

Once at the hospital Don and Shelley were greeted and taken great care of by an ER nurse Crandall, she was thorough and diligent in replacing the heart monitor leads on his chest. Don was less than happy to have patches shaved into his chest for the stickers, his heart raged like an explosion with each beat and he kept his eyes locked closed with the pain. Nurse Crandall forced him to chew down a few baby aspirin while they waited for the EKG readout, Shelley twisted the leather strap on her purse as she was drowning with anxiety, the nurse was in control of her patient and of her duties but she went the extra step and kept a watchful eye on Shelley as well. Nurse Crandall was concerned Shelley might blister her hands twisting the leather strap so she offered her a glass of water, holding it would give her hand something to do for a moment until the EKG was over and she could hold her husband's hand again.

Don winced in agony as each heart beat was forceful and wrought with pain. Shelley watched each and every move the soft spoken nurse made, she jotted down things on the clipboard and watched the noisy beeping monitor above them, and the beeping was sporadic and added to the confusion of the emergency room. A tall surgeon named Osama walked up to the side of Don, he had conflicting news, it was good over all but needed about forty-five minutes of Don't time to perform a quick heart catheterization to fix a slight blockage causing a murmur and "Bingo."

Shelley heard "heart" and began to feel her windpipe begin to swell shut. Osama was a kind hearted guy, in his mid-twenties and to keep from standing over her, he took a seat on the ground beside her to help put her at ease about the situation. The young resident explained to both Don and Shelly what the plan of action was, they were going in through a vein in his thigh and were going to snake a wire up to his heart and use a balloon to open a slightly clogged artery, the EKG showed a slight agitation in the beating and should be an easy fix, in and out and all set with a one night room reservation upstairs for the night. Osama explained the procedure; he knew that with the stress that Shelley may not have caught each and every word so he repeated himself tactfully to reiterate his point without belittling the terrified patients. Osama was enjoying his rotation and enjoyed the intricacies of surgery and the heart catheterization was a largely beneficial and minimally invasive procedure.

Osama and Nurse Crandall spoke briefly and passed a small fist bump back and forth, Shelley was leery about the strange interaction between the nurse and Resident, Crandall had been a nurse for almost twenty years, she still kept a large smile on her face after all the stuff

177

she had seen, she enjoyed her job. Osama was a tall slender man with an immaculate syntax for grammar when he spoke and wove together the hard earned knowledge he gained from years of college. Osama used the proper language for his patients, young or old, to understand. Nurse Crandall leaned on the side of Dons bed and warned Don that he needed to be "prepped" for his procedure and that meant he was about to get a "swirly circus straw crammed into his pee hole" right after they shave his nether region, she chuckled a bit trying to make light of the situation. Shelley smirked a bit while Don just laid back and focused on his breathing.

The nurse put an injection into the IV for Don to begin blood thinners, she told Shelley that the resident had a plan to request a private post-op room with two beds so both Don and Shelley could each have a bed, the nurse and resident came to an accord and that was the reason behind the fist bump. The nurse introduced herself as "Gloria" and let a younger nurse wheel Don to the third floor for his procedure and she escorted Shelley to a waiting room, Gloria had to juggle a cellphone that didn't seem to stop ringing from her belt, she apologized to Shelley each time she had to answer it but she was in charge and even taking a break, she was still choked with phone calls. Shelley was astounded with the personal care Gloria took in personally taking her to drop her things to her room while they prepped Don. Shelley and Gloria made a quick stop for familiarity and then headed down so Gloria could drop Shelley off to meet up with Don before his quick procedure. Gloria and Shelley shook hands, Shelley hadn't eased up much but at least the tears of worry had ceased as Gloria clasped her hands and bowed her head goodbye and walked briefly back to her charge role in the ER.

By the time Shelley found Don she had only been apart for fifteen minutes or so, he was already in a flowery hospital gown and his face no longer tense with pain, the corners of his mouth had lifted a tad and whatever the doctors had given was beginning to set in. As Shelley neared her husband he smiled seeing her, he lifted his down to show his wife what a cute little nurse had done, he flashed his wife his shaved man parts, his wooshing of his gown sent a large air bubble up towards his face and as he lowered his gown back down he had a smile on his face, which had carried over to Shelley, she was ever so relieved that he was feeling better and to catch a glimpse of his man-scaped parts was not what she was expecting as she neared him. Don was often a serious man, he played with Brittini as if she was his own child when she was younger, his brother Roger was Brittini's real father but he was a douche and flaked out, it caused a falling out between them long ago and they have yet to speak. Don never regretted shunning his sibling, if a person is a shit-ass than being family is no excuse to leave yourself open to more of their abusive ways, and Don meant it. Don worked hard and did his best to always ensure that Brittini was looked after, Shelley was slightly jealous at times that Don always made time for her even when Shelley had asked or wanted it first. Don was a stand-up guy and carried a world of burden on his shoulders, he and Shelley hadn't had any children but took in Brittini as a replacement, he was often rigid but always had a place for her to make him smile.

Shelley was tickled that Don was goofy and playful with her before his procedure, they hardly played anymore and she worried that maybe they had just settled into their ways and that maybe he just never had fun anymore. Don may have been doped to the gills but his inner playful child was peeking out and it was still in there, and in love with his wife. Don joked about the car really having "taken it like a porn-star tonight," the comment made Shelley open her eyes widely and giggle at the notion. Don admitted maybe it was time to get a new car and luckily the insurance hadn't lapsed yet so maybe things might turn out. Osama rounded the corner in a blue hairnet looking thing and surgical scrubs on and asked if Don was ready, Shelley felt her chest get tight worrying Don. Osama did his best to reassure the patient and his wife, Don hadn't a care in the world but Shelley more than made up for it. Osama himself unlocked the wheels of the bed rather than leave the scut work to a lower level resident, they headed towards the back of the pre-op ward and Shelley was escorted to a waiting room.

Shelley paced in the waiting room, a younger girl with a pink streak of hair tucked behind her ear was sitting behind the desk playing with long fake nails and clicking a tongue ring against her teeth. Shelley couldn't hear anything besides that tongue ring and she was disgusted that a large hospital would allow this hair dyed girl to represent them as a worker. As Shelley nervously paced and struggled to keep watch on the TV on the wall rather than the clock frozen in time, she was distracted each time she heard the metal click against the girls teeth, she wanted to walk up to the younger girl and reach in her mouth and yank that damn tongue stud out and pull the girl over the desk by it. Shelley found herself stomping her feet with each step, her anger replaced her concern and she felt her own fingernails digging into her clenched hands.

As the weather radar turned from blue to green on the TV screen Osama entered the room. The clicking stopped and the young girl turned to eye the young resident lustfully as he walked over to Shelley. Shelley's heart stopped, his face was still as he took his first step into the room after locating the wife of his patient. Each step Osama took seemed to bellow in Shelley's ear, by the third step she was beginning to see spots and feel light headed, she honed in on his mouth awaiting for his lips to part, his slight stubble gave the hint that he had shaved in the morning but had been through a long day, his thin lips didn't budge.

Shelley began to black out as she strained to keep watch on the lips that were moving towards her, suddenly the corners lifted and the two skin folds parted, "everything went splendid ma'am" the polite resident neared and shared the news. Osama noticed the pale color washing over Shelley and he reached forward to grasp her hand and help her to take a seat in the blue fabric chairs behind her. After a few moments of seeing white Shelley began to see her blue and red striped Zubaz workout pants next to the grayish blue scrub pants of Osama, he was lounged back sitting beside her, his arms were outstretched behind his head as he rolled to his left to ask again; "you OK?" Shelley was trying to gather her surroundings as Osama continued to explain: "you seemed pretty determined to have a seat so I helped you to sit and I thought I'd chill here and watch the weather with you until you were ready to finish talking," Shelley explained that she felt faint and asked how long she was woozy. "you were out for about ten minutes, the weather was about to come back around again but I wasn't leaving you, you sure you're alright?" Osama inquired once more.

Shelley nodded to comply and rubbed the palms of her hands on her eyes to try and shake off the weary feeling, she was gracious that the busy resident took the time to help her keep some dignity about her actions, despite the fact that she was wearing striped workout pants and a hoodie sweatshirt, almost too embarrassed to be out except it was an emergency. Osama crooked his arm like a true gentleman and escorted her down a long hallway to the post-op ward, he wanted to ensure that she was well enough to walk on her own, he warned her that Don was already up and doing his finest "Tim Curry" impressions, of course "Pennywise" being his best and favorite, Shelley could only shake her head and snort a bit. Osama lead Shelley to the bedside and made sure she had a seat while he skirted off to snag the woozy woman a small orange juice on his way out. The post procedure nurses shared the info that all was well and in the morning they were free to go, Shelley waited till they got back to their private room before texting Aimee that they would need a ride home in the morning, hoping that Brittini told her mother what had happened.

Jonny and Brittini swept up most of the glass shards, they spent most of the rest of the night hanging out on the small stoop in front of Don and Shelley's place to help ensure that nothing further would happen to their property, after the party Brittini slept on their couch while Jonny headed home, or to wherever after the party died down. Aimee had no idea about what had happened to Don during the party, she was drinking heavily with Tod while the car was being overturned, she had no idea that Don was in trouble or that Brittini and Jonny sprang into action to lend a hand. She was on hand with Tod as they cheered on Big Ken and his romp with Carsey on the car, she almost thought about feeling bad when Justin wet his pants and cried about his wife having a blown out snatch and giant thighs. Aimee was focused on Tod wearing her out once they got pretty lit up and climbed into bed together, he was getting turned on looking at all the young fit girls shaking their bodies to the music, then getting to see Carsey's tits as they bounced and jiggled as she laid back against the rear window of the car as Ken thrusted into her before the window shattered.

Aimee wasn't all that hot and bothered having seen pants-less Ken, his back had rolls in it and random body hair sticking out everywhere, with his pants down he had no ass, just a crack between paper white cheeks. Aimee and Tod got back to the party after the car was toppled, the crowd dispersed with more hoses and some of the younger girls took to a picnic table or two as a stage for a wet t-shirt contest, which got out of control quickly as the booze flowed. Wriggle aimed some of his lights towards the dancing girls and continued to pump out the booty shaking songs to keep the girls dancing and popping. Theresa has been standing on top of the picnic table with Tammi and a few other girls, all of them writhing in the

181

water and lights being sprayed down on them, their bodies like moving disco balls, reflecting the colored lights off of the beads of water and their exposed bodies, their hair whipping about. Wriggle had a great perch and with his headset on he shouted instructions for the girls to keep shaking what they had and flaunt their bodies and for all of the partiers to cheer them on.

Jonny watched the party move like waves in a pool, up and down and side to side, Brittini just watched all of the people do different things while the girls clambered all over one another on top of the tables; desperate for attention. Brittini watched as the dancing girls gyrated and bounced their asses back and forth, Tammi let her stomach jiggle as she groped at her chest, Theresa kept her bra on but kept pulling the cups down to let her nipples reflect bits of strobe light as she spun around. Brittini found the girls on the picnic tables beautiful as their bodies flowed in the lights, the music making them dance like marionettes, beauty wasn't about caked on makeup, it wasn't about what they wore, or by this point what they weren't wearing, Tammi was considered "healthy" as she was thicker and that encouraged her to be promiscuous but Theresa was in better shape and fairly pretty. One of the other girls dancing on the table was a girl Curtiss brought, she was light skinned and tall, her hair stayed in a ponytail as she removed her shirt and her chest remained firm as she wiggled. The fourth girl was another stranger but quick to hop up onto a table and earn her portion of cheers and hollers.

Brittini just stared and watched the girls dance into the night; the music seemed to slow with the rhythm of their swaying bodies, hips butting left and right, bare bellies showing off various curves, Tammi wasn't ashamed of her love handles pouring over the waist of her tighter pants, her thong ridden half way up her back. Brittini couldn't figure out what drove Tammi to be such a slut, her need for attention was more than a desire, it was like a dick addiction, she was like a cat in heat for attention. Jonny shared his advice to Brittini what true beauty was; confidence1 faces can wrinkle, stomachs stretch and young teen asses sag in your twenties, but being confident in yourself and knowing that you don't spread your legs for any wagging dick then you should stand tall and hold your head up when you walk. Jonny and Brittini sat side by side as the party wore down, they both contemplated the weirdness of watching a bunch of girls show off their boobs and butts to a bunch of horned up guys in the party crowd next to one another on tables.

Wriggle played some of the latest hip-hop records and took as many requests as he could late into the evening. Brittini discovered an up and coming country artist a while back named Pauline Jayne and let her music hide her away from the world she was trapped in. Hip-hop seemed to propagate ass shaking and sleeping around. Brittini looked upon her small world from a third person point of view once in a while and tried to navigate how her life was going to go, she wasn't going to let some low life drag her down and piss all over her future. Brittini was going to take up art or acting in college, something beautiful that she could create on her own and share with the world, and that was why she liked Paulina. Jonny had no ambition, he had spoken about maybe taking some welding classes in high school or some other trade, Jesse James was a self-proclaimed "glorified welder" but yet he made sick ass choppers and had a TV series for a bit. James was loaded and famous and was able to dress well when he wanted to and attend the biggest events, not try and avoid the meth peddlers two streets over or have to sleep under his own trailer to avoid getting the hell whipped out of him by his drunk and pissed off father. Jonny wanted to get out of the *Heights* on the first bus leaving and wasn't going to look back, but he didn't know how.

Aimee found the text from Shelley in the early morning hours during a restroom run, she was getting ready to finally go to bed after climbing off of Tod post party style, she was still half drunk and fumbling to set her alarm as she sat on the toilet and concentrated her attention to her fingers. It was ten in the morning before Aimee was with her mind enough to piece things together, she searched for her daughter but not until after pulling the sheet over the nude and sprawled out Tod. Aimee was sore in certain places, assuring her that he must have gotten carried away with her. Tod was still passed out and would probably be that way for several more hours, she covered him and gathered clothing as she texted Brittini to check on her whereabouts. Brittini responded that she was cleaning for Don and Shelley while waiting for their return. Aimee headed next door to get the whole scoop from her daughter about what had happened during the party. Aimee passed Jonny out front standing near the overturned car, he was trying to climb in and out of the shattered window gathering their personal effects into a box to save them the trouble later on, green coolant pooled on the cement as Jonny wedged in and out of the back window.

Brittini was on her hands and knees hand scrubbing the kitchen linoleum, the house looked impeccable and Aimee was impressed, she asked why it wasn't like that at home, Brittini replied; "Tod can't even not piss all over the toilet seat, why should I join you in being his maid too?" her reply made Aimee exhale exasperatedly, she closed her eyes to shake off what she had heard. Aimee knew Brittini was right but it didn't mean she wanted to hear it; she was already trying to process what had happened to Don overnight and figure out what else had happened during the party. The yards were trashed with plastic cups and beer cans, some of the shrubs had been trampled and there were random articles of clothing strewn about, the trailer yards were a mess and looked like a tornado had passed through. Brittini told Aimee about having to help hold Don up, how scared she was and how much Jonny had helped her uncle keep moving and how nice it would be for them to return to a clean home. Aimee stepped out and searched her pockets for her car keys, Jonny stood up with the last of Don and Shelley's belongings from the inside of the overturned car, he was grimy and had flecks of blood all over his forearms from crawling on the pieces of glass, Aimee had nodded towards her place looking at Jonny and unlocked her car door, suggesting he go in and shower.

Aimee texted Shelley as she drove through the yellow speed bumps, sure enough even in the pre-noon hours Gelica was sitting and scowling on her stoop. The blue and pink flowered Mumu and pink curlers gave a false cheery impression to the bitter old hag, Gelica, she stared into Aimee's car, Aimee just waved to be pretentious, it was too early and she was beginning to nurse a hangover, she had to force a smile too the miserable wench, whom would succumb to hypertension soon enough. Aimee found her way to the hospital and waited for her passengers near the entrance, Don was looking in rough shape, but grateful to get out. As soon as they left the parking lot he and Shelley were both quick to flick a Bic and light a smoke, the wait had been long and miserable, and off they were.

Tod woke up to an empty bed, the sheets were cold, telling him he had been alone for some time, he was still sticking to the sheets in places. Tod had to pry his right eye open a bit to find his Marlboro's on the table next to him, his lips stuck together, he felt so parched his eyelids stuck to his eyeballs, his balls had dried crusted to his leg and the sheets stuck wedged in his ass crack, as he sat up he felt out of sorts, he had to take a deep drag on his cigarette to push enough blood back into his brain to recall being pegged by Aimee, it had been a wild night and even his silver fillings in his mouth, hurt. A deep guttural hacking wasn't enough to bring up any spit to moisten his mouth. The crackling of the tobacco gave way to the sounds of the shower, with a sore backside and aching bones, Tod dragged himself to his feet, he had half a chub and rather than waste it, he headed towards the shower, hoping to "accidentally" walk in on Brittini.

Tod turned the handle to the bathroom, his member hung half full of blood and ready to get back to work after the nights' work it had, it was leading him towards the shower, half smoked cigarette dangling from his lips and all. The silhouette on the other side of the shower curtain was too slender to be Aimee, she was heavier but was often a wild ride in bed. Tod's penis surged with blood at the anticipation of pulling the curtain back and finding Brittini, her young slender body had begun to develop and he certainly noticed her form under her pajamas, no bra or awareness that she might be needing one most of the time, he often tried to angle to get a better view down her shirt or would stare through the sides of his eyes to peak at her other areas as she lounged around the house. Tod reached his right hand up to the shower curtain, the tattoo of a Fleur De Lis on the webbing between thumb and first finger was looking like a black blob against his scarred and rough hand, he got that specific tattoo in jail and the ink was still black, but the lines were blurring and losing detail all of these years later.

The shower curtain pulled back to reveal a pale white ass with black hair lining the crack, Tod lifted his left foot to begin to step into the wet shower as he followed his eyes up the ass of "JONNY" he shouted with surprise. The startle sent the rugged tattooed Tod stumbling backwards and crashing into the wall and sink behind him. Jonny heard Tod shriek right behind him and startled him to the point of flailing around to attempt to defend himself against the older man, he had no idea what to think, at first he was worried that Tod was there to make him his bitch. Tod berated Jonny for being there; he didn't understand why the kid was in *HIS* shower, let alone when he was already expecting to discover a soapy sudsy Brittini. Tod was

185

furious and his slight head throb had become a full blown migraine, Jonny got the verbal assault of the year for that. Tod didn't stop shouting while he stood over the toilet to piss while lighting another cigarette, toilet seat down of course.

Tod shouted and called Jonny all sorts of demeaning names through two full cigarettes, he didn't even bother to put clothes on as he called the young boy a "*FAG*" in various forms over and over, even though he was the one that tried to climb into the shower with another male; it was still Jonny's fault. Tod rubbed his temples as he tried to remove the mental images of Jonny's bare ass from his mind, Tod was irate and his blood pressure had peaked, and it wasn't even noon yet. Tod pulled on a pair of mesh shorts and headed to the front porch to smoke a joint to put some ease into his day. Tod knew Aimee didn't like him smoking pot in the house so he stepped out onto the porch; he slid on sunglasses to keep his migraine from making him physically ill while he fumbled to get his lighter to ignite a joint. Across the way he caught a glimpse of Big Ken sitting back on a lawn chair in the shade on the empty cement slab where the neighbors' trailer used to sit, his feet propped up on some railroad ties that used to line a small flowerbed. Ken was heaved into a white wife-beater and blue basketball shorts as well. Big Ken raised a red plastic cup to salute the 'Hair of the Dog' ritual they were both partaking in. Tod could still hear the sounds of Jonny inside and picked himself up off the top of the porch and headed over to sit with Ken.

Tod let himself fall into a plastic patio chair next to Big Ken, the two men looked around and pointed to random articles of clothes that they could spy, the overturned Taurus was one of the more strange sights, it even topped the rock and brick smashed cop car, this one belonged to Don and they felt bad that their neighbor had gotten screwed over, Ken didn't even acknowledge his hand in it. Tod kept his head firmly placed in the palm of his hand in disbelief as he and Big Ken shared a drink to ward off the morning pains, he didn't want to bring up almost having soaped up with Ken's damn kid Jonny. Tod could feel the slight breeze blow into one leg of his shorts and around his giblets and back out the other leg, the cool feeling aired him out as he was already sweating and his nuts gathering even more funk and sticky residue. Ken leaned back and out of Tod's exhaled smoke, he couldn't risk the pot being found in his urine since he was still on papers to drug test randomly. The two men sat in disbelief of the previous night; they avoided any responsibility, especially Ken for having ignited the fury by breaking some glass.

Their night was wild and both men fared poorly the next early afternoon, Tod wasn't about to disclose having let Aimee peg him as their bedroom antics sometimes got out of control when there was flowing booze and lust for younger bodies to stimulate them both. Tod attempted to rub his temples in cadence with the throbbing veins, "you look like a used condom" Ken piped up, Tod responded calmly and in his raspy voice; "I was born like this" leaving both men to chuckle lightly. Tod rubbed away his headache with the assistance of his weed, there were so many discarded plastic cups, the yards and shrubs around them seemed decorated like Christmas trees with all of the green covered in red spots. Ken and Tod sat silently for a bit, Jonny exited Brittini and Aimee's home and kept his eyes locked onto the ground at his feet as he stepped out, he had caught a glimpse of his father and Tod sitting across the way and shuttered at the thought of making eye contact. "Hey boy, why don't you get up that girl and help pick up round there" Ken shouted over to Jonny, Jonny didn't raise his head but he began nodding to ensure that the message had been clearly received.

Aimee pulled in with Don and Shelley in tow to find Brittini and Jonny gathering garbage to fill their third of fourth bag of trash at this point. Jonny was becoming pink on his cheeks from so much time in the sun and Aimee recommended sunscreen or even a break as she climbed out of her seat, leading the way for her passengers. Don was slow to rise and was given strict orders to take it slow and easy for the following several weeks. Brittini scurried over to greet her uncle in great relief to see him improved, he too was relieved. Brittini and Shelley went back to their day, Aimee had her own list of chores within her domicile and the day began to get hot. Tod and Ken remained tucked away into the shaded nook they perched in earlier, the day was warm but not enough to motivate them from their seats, Don was tasked with trying to lay calm but as a busy body, he had a hard time remaining still on the couch. Don wandered out to join his neighbors, pitcher of lemonade in hand and a heavy head. Tod and Big Ken nodded to Don as he crossed the street to join them, Tod moved to a different chair to offer the more sturdy white plastic one to Don as he slowly made his way to join them. Don pulled his cell phone from his pocket as he sat, he looked over at his upended car and muttered; "what a bitch huh?" Ken and Tod both nodded in agreement. Don made the painstaking call for an insurance adjuster to come out and assess the damages; the whole series of events gave him stress and grief. Tod and Ken observed Curtiss heading back to his place on the next street over, he was missing one shoe and his shirt thrown over his shoulder and as he unevenly walked, he struggled to keep his pants hanging below his skinny ass.

Tod rolled his head over to Ken and posed the question of "is it "Once you go black you won't go back" or a matter of not being wanted back? Look at that skinny nigger; sickening." Ken snorted as he finished filling his emptied beer can from the pitcher Don brought over. The three men discussed the prior nights' events as well as Dons ordeal within the hospital, the three men sat for half of the afternoon, the sun peaked at noon but it was when the temperature peaked an hour or two after that finally encouraged them to retreat to their couches and places in front of fans. Shelley doted on her husband and ensured that he had most everything he needed. Jonny didn't speak to Tod or of the awkward meeting they shared within the shower; he didn't even share such news with Brittini, despite her being his best friend and confidant. Don and Shelley had fared quite well when the insurance was all squared away, they had purchased a much newer car and put some repairs into their home, it was a long and difficult process to get the police report made out and everything situated to finally collect the payment for their trashed vehicle but it resulted in a tainted bit of fortune.

As the fourth of July party prep gotten underway, Don had parked his newer car he had gotten last year near the gas station with Gary's permission, he wasn't going to further gamble another car to a party that was certain to rage like a wild fire, nor was he willing to leave his home behind and unguarded for the night either, especially with the fact that most of the block parties were full of undesirables like Darryl, Curtiss, Tod and all of the other hood rats that come out of the city sewers to binge on Boons Farm and cheap jungle juice and bounce ass and tits to a DJ's music. Don worked hard to provide for himself and his wife of seventeen years, he often thought of leaving behind the trailer park in prospect of a better neighborhood and lower risk of getting his property trashed or stolen, but they had what they needed and wanted to help look out for Brittini, she had enough of the

188

world out against her. Don gave Brittini a book titled "3ʳᵈ Hand Ranch" over the spring and she fell in love with the furry critter within its' pages, she daydreamed about leaving her trailer park behind and spending a year working with horses and being around teen girls her age that wouldn't sleep with any guy she knew, or try to stab her in the back. Don didn't understand the mindset of teen girls but Shelley helped to bridge the gap a bit, she was a thicker teen girl and most girls can simply be bitches, Brittini was thin and lanky which put her at the whim of ridicule.

Brittini and Jonny remained close friends despite puberty and their hard living environment; they had to learn everything the hard way and from their surroundings. Jonny wasn't warned of the maturing stages until the short and poorly informing school video, he still had to learn what was going on first hand, he didn't hang out with older boys like Curtiss or Darryl, they picked on him and harassed him to no end when was younger for the slightest speech impediment and inability to throw a football in the most masculine of ways. Brittini had her mother and aunt to confide in when it came time to need Maxi-pads, a horrifying moment in most young girls' lives, but they understood. Brittini always felt Tara glare at her anytime they passed one another, she couldn't figure out what it was they had rubbed Tara so wrong, it was probably that Tara had cellulite at the top of her thighs and Brittini had almost no body fat, this was the most observed difference by Aimee and Tod in an attempt to console the insecure girl, Tod just followed up that Tara was a "superficial bitch," a more comforting quip from him at the time.

Don and Shelley pulled out their small plastic kiddie pool to fill with beer and drinks and then to top off with ice. The Fourth of July kicked off in midafternoon with a cinder block barbecue of bridge card purchased hot dogs, the smaller gathering was for the community residents to eat and drink before the music began to pump out after eight and the fireworks kick off at ten. The party always started slowly and gained momentum as the evening progressed, last year left a cop car smashed but also a hefty fight between Angle and Joey, his coming out was still fresh and Angel was still really sensitive to the matter. Angel and Aimee cried together half of the evening, Aimee was in shock and it was such a waste for the large man whom was well blessed in body and looks, to want to change everything he worked for and change genders. Tod was scraggly and covered in

189

tattoo's, he had a low body fat content but also lacked much body mass as all, it wasn't hard to think about Joey taking her from behind and pulling her hair instead of Tod, she often let her imagination assist Tod in pleasing her when they were intimate. Last Fourth of July Angel and Aimee sat in close proximity of Don't kiddie pool for a while, it was relaxing to pull down their shoulder straps of their shirts in the waning sun to blur out tan lines and dip their feet in the drink pool to cool off while laying back in lawn chairs.

Don often did the grilling, he set up an easy to use cinder block rectangle and metal grates to cover in hot dogs, he didn't particularly condone the parties but his home was near the center of the action and if he offered up his services then he would stay in the good graces of his neighbors and hopefully keep his affects in order. Don dragged the cement blocks over towards the end of his small lot, the fire always killed the grass until he set a layer of sideways blocks underneath which helped to insulate the grass from the fire and made the lawn much easier to salvage afterwards. The bricks were placed on the insides and filling the center of the pit with charcoal made for ample cooking surface, he would light one side and let the heat from the ignited charcoal on one end slowly inch across the pit to prolong the amount of cooking surface to ensure that the hundreds of hot dogs got their burn before being served on a folding table on the sidewalk. Don called a coworker named Colon to the party, Colon was a mixed guy, he had light skin and eyes as green as Irish grass, his demeanor was always calm and willing to lend a hand, he and Don were close work buddies and often enjoyed an intelligent conversation, something that couldn't happen in the *Heights*. Colon held a degree in engineering and made major cash, he dressed really well but always kept a sleeveless shirt and pair of jeans on standby for an impromptu dirty work session, he stayed clean at work and also enjoyed working outdoors. Colon stepped up a fair amount to help Don after his heart ordeal, Don could mow the lawn at most because he had a small lot but as far as sliding under the car to wrench an oil change or change tires, Colon was always willing to help.

Colon was married to a girl named Terry, she was also mixed and together they had two of the most adorable children you'd ever seen. Colon had Don and Shelly over often but Terry wouldn't allow herself or her children to even talk openly about going to the *Heights*. Terry and Colon had a white collar house in a gated community but

Don and Colon were close and class didn't bear much weight on it. Colon agreed to come help stand guard with Don, Terry had taken their young children to other families for the holiday so he was free to camp out and help play crowd control in regards to Don's property. Colon helped drag out cinder blocks and pour charcoal to get ready for the party, the work wasn't overbearing and there was plenty of time to get it all done so they paced themselves and kept the raspberry lemonade flowing. Don hadn't drank since his heart episode, he wasn't a large drinker as it were so having to give it up wasn't a challenge, Colon forwent drinking in support of his friend, they conversed about retirement options and IRA's, not a subject of much substance around the area, Shelley set up the card tables for food and the large patio umbrellas over the food and the yard.

Everyone had their rituals to set up for the party. Each trailer tried to contribute, either a case of beer or package of hotdogs and buns. The three streets of the trailer park came together for the party; each connecting road surged with people, during the party people flowed from one side to another like water in a bowl. Shelley worried for Don, she knew he was a man of integrity and wasn't someone to just let others do the work that he could do himself; he was still learning how to let others lend him a hand. Aimee knew that all the hot young bodies riled Tod up and she spent a little extra time preparing for the party and for him afterwards.

Curtiss and Darryl spent the first half of the day finishing up their batch of methamphetamines, the night before they had enlisted Lil B to gather his usual list of supplies, the three of them sat out behind Darryl's place and made two two-liter bottles of the bubbling reaction while smoking blunts and wondering if "homo's shared underwear" a topic that Darryl felt he needed an answer about. Darryl had intentions to sell plenty of his product to some of the attending partiers from further in the city, he also intended to make a run to his old and wrinkled dealer for larger quantities of most other narcotics, if he could acquire enough merchandise then Darryl planned to sell enough during the party to make several thousand dollars in one night and add it to his stash. Curtiss hadn't sold anything more than pot but he had invited several of his old classmates and also intended to make some sales as well as get some girlies high enough to get them naked, pills were a tempting and easy sale. Everyone was gearing up for their roles during the party, each trailer had their support roles, most had

191

their radios turned towards the windows, DJ Wriggle had a small transistor and put out his music to several hundred yards and let all of the other speakers play his chosen beats, it helped to boost his play radius and reach farther than his own stage set up could.

Wriggle had a full size pick up; he had two large subs in the bed and could be heard from two blocks away. Wriggle had a hardcover over the bed of his truck to protect most of his deejay equipment, his tables, speakers, lights and everything else, he was good at what he did and booked several nights a week at different bars and clubs, despite being under twenty-one. Wriggle had a large following and tons of potential to become a large player, he had an eclectic collection of mixes and remixes from three decades of tunes, any of the girls that danced to his music often found music from their high school days to dance to, no matter if they were born in the eighties or nineties and also enjoyed current beats to dance to. Wriggle had flashing lights, lasers, dual fog machines, bubble blower and everything else that might further fuel a good time at any club or rave he spun at. Curtiss helped Wriggle to set up, Big Ken sat on his porch and just watched most of the day unfold, he leaned against the weight bench that sat on his front porch that stayed half hidden under a few plastic bags of empty cans and bottles, he had to save his energy for later in the night.

Karen was gone, the cavernous bitch had taken off the day before and now there were no parental controls over the park. Karen's lap dog Gelica hardly ever left her Mumu, let alone the porch so no one was worried about her tattling; she still sat and stewed in her delusions. Gelica was married to a trucker whom built the trailer park she still resided in, he discovered she and her selfish ways had almost bankrupted their entire family, he divorced her in order to protect their children. Gelica still had a hard time admitting her role in everything that had happened to her, she denied that her life was as it were, she still convinced herself that her trips to the sandbox over in the playground were really to Jamaica or Florida, somewhere sunny and rife with tanned bodies and fruity drinks, she hid herself away from the reality around her. Karen ruled at the trailer park like a communist, she often fought for her self-imposed power, citing fees for dog poop or grass that was too long; she would often alert the police to some of the younger kids out after curfew as well. Anytime Karen saw Lil B out after dark she was quick on the dial 911, same

192

went with Jonny or Brittini, despite that they were two of the better behaved individuals in the area, she just wanted to keep everyone on their tiptoes.

Tod had already ensured that his coworkers had plans to make it to the cookout and firework show, they hadn't missed many and they needed to blow off some steam together from the constant hard work days of roofing. Aimee didn't like Tod to hit the hooter hut, it wasn't that she was insecure that he'd get a raging hard-on at some young naked body, but last time he was there is was with Berman and the potential for disaster was a whole lot to gamble with. Curtiss and Wriggle pulled his truck into the parking space across from Aimee's lot, he customized two light stands to sit in the holes of the truck sides, he now had a small workspace standing right in the bed of his truck ,it was up off the ground and kept him secluded from masses of people on the ground around him. Wriggle had acquired his skills through diligent work, his lights, speakers, and hardware with funds he earned, he didn't mind the occasional joint or even a drink or three but he left the harder drugs to the partiers that writhed and danced to his music, because he made them "Wriggle," that's what he did and how he chose his stage name.

When Wriggle first started out, it was the *Heights* that gave Wriggle a chance, they simply needed something a bit better than an MP3 player wired into a loud guitar amp, he had a small PA system and a handful of tunes that he remixed on a borrowed laptop, he was nervous during his initial performance, it was a meager set up on a porch with his small system and some cheap party lights for support. Wriggle stood on the porch and played for twenty or so people, it was an embarrassing bust but he still found his love for performing. Wriggle caught the fever to perform, he had to spend long days practicing scratching, mixing, and making sure he jumped through every hoop the club owners threw at him before they would allow him to perform, on Tuesdays. Wriggle chewed at the chains that kept him down, he lived in a more privileged neighborhood growing up but that merely taught him to stick to it and not cheat out and take the short road for things. Wriggle often now booked and filled clubs. Wriggle gave priority to the *Heights* from which started him out, he only ever deejayed holidays at his starting point and showed his love, although when he spread the word that he was playing, he could easily add another hundred or so bodies to any party he worked.

193

Wriggle had a well off enough background that if anyone attempted to cause a stink for him that he wouldn't have to fall back on some public defender that had less of an education than he did. Wriggle was parked up in his stage spot, his truck about ready to go when the sun goes down and the lights go up. Wriggle knew he had dinner provided; Don was grilling up bridge card burgers and hot-dogs for the park so he was taken care of there.

Brittini and Jonny weren't bothered by the party, they were shunned from partaking in illegal substances and that was even if they had any urge to delude themselves. Jonny hid out with Brittini in her room, they were searching through the newer Pauline Jayne videos and discussing what they might have to do to stay out of the way while their homes were surrounded by drunkards and pukers. Aimee and Tod were strewn out on the couches; they were discussing North Koreans and tiny penises. Brittini and Jonny would often pause to listen intently to what the adults in the other room might have said, then giggle about it. Brittini and Jonny couldn't figure out why such atrocities could be handed out by the only fat kid in North Korea the one that was running the country, a privilege that was doled down from a lunatic father, and abused for three generations of sadistic aphallic nullos. Tod couldn't fathom what any of those terms might mean, aphallic being lacking a penis and nullo meaning no penis or testicles, terms that fit Kimmy Un to a T. Brittini knew that one day she would be out of the *Heights*, she wanted to get into a community college and maybe even someday a four year school, Jonny wanted to learn a trade, he had thought about learning welding later on in high school and hoping that maybe he could find a job up on the east-coast, maybe at some big factory and possibly change his life for the better. Jonny and Brittini had their own plans; they saw the lines of trailers as the links of the chains that kept them shackled in poverty.

Aimee and Tod had once discussed getting married, Aimee always dreamed of exchanging vows and before Tod had become abusive, she wanted to with him. Tod had spoken about marrying Aimee, doing it the right way and taking her down to a court and signing the papers, they could get all dressed up nice and having Brittini wait for them at the door and throwing rice on them as they emerged newlyweds. Aimee almost let her guard down and risked dreaming about having a larger family, sometimes but Tod wasn't an ideal husband, but in the beginning things were good, and after a few

194

months of being canoodled and doted on by Tod, she let herself dream about maybe having a child with him. Things were good, he and Brittini got along, it was when he began to use drugs again and party harder and harder with his fellow roofers that everything went to shit; now she was half afraid to try to get out from under him, except sometimes it was nice to just not be alone. Aimee feared when Brittini would grow up, what would become of Aimee when Brittini moved on and became alone?

Aimee and Brittini used to enjoy watching the "Little Rascals" movie together, it was recently that Tod had ruined it for them, he would make crude comments about how Darla grew up to be a smoking hot piece of ass and Buckwheat looks like the rowdy negro in "The Condemned" and as they tried to reminisce back to watching the movie with the little girl on her mothers' lap, each fabled attempt was spit on by Tod and his ludicrous comments. Tod spent most of his nights sipping back beers and keeping his eyes and lust locked onto Aimee, he sometimes let his eyes wander over Brittini's forming hips and rounding ass, he timed most of his perverted peeks to eye down her shirt as her chest began to fill out, he had met her when she was eight but she wasn't his daughter, and at fourteen almost fifteen, he almost had a front row seat to her blooming body.

Tod was looking very forward to partying for the fourth of July, the last few parties had been off the chain and he was looking to get wrecked with drink and drugs and naked with whomever, it was looking like the night was full of potential and he wasn't willing to miss any of it. The history of wet t-shirt contests, beer pong events, kiddie pools of jungle juice, the masses of joints and inhalants going around, the nitrous crackers going off like firecrackers filling balloons for whippits, and the laughter of deep voices bellowing in the background as everyone continued to boost the positive energy level of the neighborhood while Wriggle kept bumping out the beats, it was a good time for all and each holiday party added memories good stories. The temperatures continued to climb as more picnic tables lined the streets, card tables filled in the sidewalks and umbrellas shaded small pools filled with ice and drinks.

The Fourth of July was always the biggest party, Bridge cards refilled at the first of the month as *Bone Thugs N Harmony* sang about, each resident was tasked with picking up supplies and when a few dozen people contribute, the stone soup fills up and everyone gets their fill.

Colon and Don were laid back on Don's picnic table, the cinder block barbecue pit already assembled in the grass and ready for a struck match to kick things off. Colon placed the picnic table towards the sidewalk to barricade off the hot cooking pit as well as keep people out of Don's shed and home, and especially away from anything else that might get destroyed. Don's lot was at the bend and it as often a cut through for most travelers like Angel and Joey, whom lived further down around the corner. Joey had become fairly scarce as he continued to progress towards becoming "Lilly," the gender change wasn't being taken all too easily with some of his further *Heights* associates. Big Ken suddenly wanted to kick this "faggots" ass when previously they shared plenty of boozing nights passing around a number of bottles of Buffalo Trace or Jameson, the changing of his ways, as a guy, didn't sit well with Ken.

Ken and Tod took to harping on Lilly, he/she would walk that little rat dog he and Angel shared, he would flaunt real short shorts and a large sweatshirt with smooth shaved legs. Lilly stood tall and tried to find security with herself and whom she was becoming, but it was harder for the more closed minded to deal with the situation. Aimee and Angel were friends, Angel relied more heavily to mentally unload on Aimee when Joey had let her down, and she had no one to turn to so it fell on Aimee. Angel still had a hard time dealing with Joey and what was happening, she also compensated with more and more cocaine and her parents were threatening to send her to rehab, flexing their muscles from Florida.

Angel trusted Aimee to explain to Tod to leave Joey alone, the harassment only made things worse and when Aimee threatened to cut him off from the pussy, he growled and lamented to back off, even a little but for the sake of poon, he subsided a little when Aimee was around. Tod and Big Ken still kept their prison attitude about themselves and kept their chests puffed up and be badder than any MMA fighter that could ever existed. Angel was still at odds about Joey, she still loved the man she fell in love with except he was no longer him, and he was becoming a she that she didn't know, nor cared to know. Angel's ability to comprehend was shrouded in cocaine and pills, her hiccups came heavily with her drugs and she was losing control of her life. Angel was stuck, her parents threatening to send her to rehab and stop paying her trailer rent, Joey was gone and she was stuck with Lilly, a very ugly Lilly at that, her powder and drink were her closest companions and she couldn't think of what to do from day to day.

There is an unspoken law in the *Heights*, you don't steal from your neighbors, don't mess with their shit and be respectful to them, even if y'all don't get along. In the past, each person was themselves, one can only be themselves and that was understood. Thieves are thieves but where one does their thieving was the matter at hand and it wasn't to take place at the *Heights,* period. Two years ago after a summer raver, Big Ken caught some young kid trying to boost cans of starter fluid from his small metal shed, the kid had to have been fifteen or sixteen, some little bastard in a TapOut shirt, and even when confronted, the kid denied having done anything, he turned rabid and then tried to lunge at Ken. Big Ken caught the scrawny kid by the throat and stopped him in his tracks; it was when the kid brought his right hand around and swung a can towards Big Ken's head in the dark shed that gave Big Ken the surge of rage to hospitalize the youth. Big Ken hoisted the kid off the ground and as he turned to hurl the aggressive kid to the ground, the kid hit his head on the top of the metal doorway, knocking the kid on conscious. The kids' limp body slammed to the ground, there was neither moan nor sound beyond the thud of the skin bag plopping to the ground. Big Ken delivered a hearty kick to the ribcage of the kid before he realized the kid didn't fight back or even defend himself against the kick.

Big Ken had to enlist the help of Darryl, and even his cohort, Curtiss "the coon," to take the kid down near the Amaca station and alert the cops. The kid was laid up in the hospital for almost a month according to the newspaper. Big Ken hadn't bothered to spare a second thought about his actions, the kid had crossed the line and if his life had been snuffed out, so be it. Big Ken let the kid bleed on the grass next to the shed as he hobbled on his bad knees to find Darryl. Ken knew he could trust Darryl, he knew Darryl's secrets and that was powerful leverage, but more than that, he knew he could trust his neighbor because they both had a firm understanding of how things were. "Errbody needs to steer clear of Big K yo" was the only response Curtiss could come up with when he grabbed the bleeding kids' legs.

Curtiss and Darryl hauled the kid by his baggy white pants, change falling from his pockets and clanking on the pavement. Darryl and Curtiss worked together to get the body near the front of the gas station, Darryl dialed 911 and told the operator about the injured man and how to find him, Curtiss rifled through the kids pockets, scavenging lighters, cigarettes and an empty Velcro wallet that contained an expired condom. Darryl slammed the phone down, alerting Curtiss that it was time to bail, and they hiked their asses back to the party. Once back the boys let Big Ken know that his errand was done, and with that he was in their favor for the time being.

Rumor spread real fast that Big Ken had almost killed someone again; a word that gained familiar association with Big Ken, the large handed man used his hands like sledgehammers when he slammed them into other people, their bodies jolted with each "*THUDDD*" when his fists connected with people. When Big Ken whipped the crap out of that wannabe gang banger Justin, the one with the wife that had giant thighs, the man began sobbing after the second blow connected with his misshapen his head. A crowd gathered when Justin was beaten to tears, he took hold of Carsey's arm and began rubbing against her body against her will, prompting Big Ken to come charging like an enraged bull.
When Big Ken snatched up the pilfering kid in his shed, the kids' life depended on Big Ken recalling self-constraint and not letting his mind go white hot with fury.

The shed was a small confined space and when Ken hoisted the kid by his throat, his head collided with doorframe and sent him from intoxicated and high looking for more to huff, to unconscious and headed for the hospital with blood gushing from his head. Other than the slight concern of going back to prison, there was no remorse for what Ken had done, boundaries had been crossed and the punk deserved what he got, Ken returned to his partying after getting Darryl to agree to run the body to the gas station. When the kid was picked up by the medics, an assaulted kid brought the cops around and all Gary the attendant could answer is that he didn't see anyone or anything, leaving Big Ken and Darryl in the clear from the law.

200

The residents in the heights knew to leave one another alone, Darryl had a large favor from Big Ken and with that favor known, he also had a safe little barricade protecting his small methamphetamine production set up in a dug out cubby in a dirt mound just outside of his trailer. Darryl had the absenteeism of his mother Annabel, he was free to screw, smoke and sell without any reprisal. Darryl had a reasonable set up going on, he got his little tally-whacker tugged and kept his brain coated with weed smoke, and he hadn't a care in the world. Curtiss was often right by his side unless he was mounting some flake, in which Curtiss and Lil B spent their time on his couch smoked up and laughing to themselves while Darryl grunted and groaned from his bedroom.

Angel and Joey knew plenty of what went on during the parties, despite the severe disagreement about Joey's change in lifestyle, they still had a history and stood by each other out of habit, they had several long years together and instinctively stood up for one another. Joey took to pedaling coke for Angel, it supported her habit and also his hormone replacements, it was expensive to shift from a "he" to a "she" in addition to the mental toll. Joey struggled to adapt, Tod and Ken had turned their backs on him and other than Angel, and he was alone in his life. Aimee had just enough leverage between her legs to keep Tod from verbalizing his disgust or acting on his aggression towards Joey, which brought Joey a sliver of peace in his own neighborhood. Joey visited a few clubs now and then to associate with more open minded people, people more willing to accept him for *herself.*

Angel was lost, she had been powdered over for a while and it numbed her to how her future had disintegrated, it blew away like a pile of fall leaves in a tornado. Angel had nothing left except her trailer, which her parents paid for, and the memories of the man she used to lay with, whom now slept as a large woman in the next room. Angel was being threatened by her parents to either clean up or lose her trailer and get sent to rehab for a year to straighten out, somewhere on the east coast where she'd have to start from scratch, a suggestion that sounded better and better as the days progressed and June passed. Angel still cried herself to sleep, her patches helped to keep her numb enough to rest at the end of each day, only to start the next day all over again. Joey was still a few years of hormone therapy and several thousand dollars away from his final metamorphosis, he had his augmentation lined up for later in the summer and still many more steps to go afterwards. Joey still spent a majority of his nights watching "Chuck and Larry" while cursing Betty Crocker for discontinuing the frosting with the rainbow chips.

The fourth of July party was inching closer to kick off, when Don fired up the grill and the meat hit the coals; that was when Wriggle started his music at a level of 1, and then eased it up a notch every half an hour till the bass was all you could hear after nine p.m. The local residents wandered towards the grub and milled around making acquaintances until many more people showed up from further in the city. Conversations often ranged from: Tod and Ken discussing old Guns'n'Roses, back when it was Axl's hair, not labia, that blew in the wind, back when Traci Guns was included instead of Axl's maxi-pads, to having witnessed the delivery man rip a hernia hauling Karen's big box of vibrators up to her porch for use with Gelica, even including that Nine-Eleven was a set up by the government to get public support for the stuttering "Dubya" to get the big bad man his father couldn't. Jonny and Brittini were dreading the party, it was often a loud late night and even with it being summer, it was nauseating to deal with the extra crowd of people roaming their streets. Brittini hated being out while so many other people were drinking, she was often groped and grabbed at by so many of the drunkards, her legs and butt often ended up bruised and she despised each event.

Aimee worked hard during the weeks, even when she moonlighted at the funeral home until she was let go for lifting jugs of embalming fluid for Tod and his cohorts to free base with. Aimee tried to let go and relax during the weekends, her days at the small doctor's office were busy and each afternoon she still walked on eggshells to avoid whatever mood Tod might be in. Tod preferred being high, and as long as Aimee kept several beers poured down his throat he wasn't such a testy bastard, and as long as he had his pot, he lacked the ambition to get aggressive or physically assertive with her. Aimee was very talented with her abilities to cover over bruises, Tod was known to lay his hands on her and leave a split lip or black eye as a reminder that she needs to remember her place and watch her mouth. Aimee felt ashamed, she worried that Brittini watching her let a man slap her around might trickle down and then she would have to watch her daughter succumb to the exact same abuses, and there was nothing she could do.

Brittini often found it hard to even look her own mother in the eyes, especially when Tod was around, she was appalled at her mothers' choices and didn't understand why she bailed Tod out of jail a few years ago or even let him keep coming back around, it was her mothers' house and she needed to just say enough was enough and hurl his mongrel ass out and lock the door. Aimee was afraid of being alone but Brittini was also there so she wouldn't be alone, she just lacked the courage to stand up for herself. Tod had taken so much of Aimee's personality, courage, strength and sense of self from her, he took his time to demean her, to rob her of her self-worth and remind her often that she couldn't do any better than him so it wasn't worth trying, he had her under his heel and he was plenty aware of it.

Brittini regretted many of the choices her mother had made, letting Tod into their lives, keeping them in the *Heights* and leaving her a target for ridicule for wearing knockoff brand shoes and often having greasy hair, she fought her best to hide the poverty line that she dressed by, but the snooty bitches could smell fake anything, and it embarrassed the teen. Jonny had grown up near Brittini and oppressed by the same poverty line, he understood her and she him, and they stood up for each other in every way possible. Jonny and Brittini struggled in their home lives, Big Ken had no use for the kid and had seen him as more of a burden than a son and it made for a neurotic and anxiety ridden boy, but Brittini accepted that.

Brittini could hide out in her mother's car or cry on her own where no one in the living room could hear and become intrusive. Jonny and Brittini often hid out in the backseat of the car, behind the tinted windows and talking in private about anything and everything: from the new front man for Queen rocking shit out to what brought them to their weakest points. Two months ago Brittini was at the end of her rope, and damn near ready to hang herself with the end of that rope, she was having one of the worst times of her young life and she was ready to overdose on pills and finally escape her life, Jonny talked her down from her ledge, he convinced her to not take a razor to her wrists.

Brittini was conflicted, she was afraid to leave Jonny behind and that was the only real reason she didn't take her own life, he already had a hard enough time getting by and without her, he would end up in a gutter real fast. Brittini didn't know what to do with her life anymore, she couldn't wait to get out of high school and move the hell away, she struggled to eat most days, and only did when Aimee noticed that she hadn't been. The days grew hot each time the sun rose as summer progressed, Brittini was nearing the age that she could begin looking for a small job, perhaps at an ice cream shop or stocking pharmacy shelves, anything to begin saving with the intent to move away as soon as possible, even if it were just into the city. Jonny had a hard time thinking about looking for a job, he had applied to dry off cars at a carwash and the money would be enough to feed him, he was waiting to hear if he got the job or not. Brittini thought about the idea of Jonny and her renting a room somewhere in the city, it would be cheap enough for them to afford and be able to still finish out high school, they both desperately needed a drastic change and to be uprooted from the trailer park they were trapped in, they could also share a room together without it being weird.

Aimee had wandered out with bags of Better Made chips and stacks of paper plates to pile on the picnic table at the end of her small grass plot. The two tables closest to Don's fire pit held the supplies, the rest were for sitting and conversing among neighbors while they ate. Don and Colon were halfway through their pitcher of pink lemonade when Don checked his watch and stood tall to stretch, he shifted his head left and right to check any foot traffic headed his way before pulling a book of matches from his pocket and step towards his cinder block fire pit. Don did enjoy grilling, he was able to participate in the party and without much hassle, it was after the grilling was done that he excused himself and no longer partook.

Aimee caught notice that Don was up, it meant the kickoff was upon them and her smile reassured her she was in for one hell of a night. Aimee headed back inside to snatch the big plastic bin of flatware and to let Tod know that the fire was lit; a promising signal that the party was ready to go. Tod was stretched out on the microfiber couch, one brown throw pillow under his knees and the other under his head as he watched the History Channel, he hardly budged when Aimee informed him that Don struck the match and that meat was on standby. Tod was sweaty and angled to let the small rotating fan blow right down into his shorts, Aimee rolled her eyes at the thought of her house smelling like his rank nuts, she just shook her head. The day was in the upper eighties and even though the sun had peaked and begun to set, the temperature wasn't backing down.

Tod had sweated through his wife-beater by noon; his pit stains were dark yellow because his heavy smoking made him sweat tobacco resin, his teeth stained from poor hygiene and his tattoo ink looked fresh as the black moistened up with the sweat, despite being blurred from age. Aimee spent half of her time wondering how things had gotten to the point that they had, half of her income went towards supporting the couch troll while his money went to keeping him tranquilized and high with his boys. Tod let the sweat stream down from his forehead, when the fan circulated in his direction he let the breeze flow down his right leg while his left remained planted on the floor, he was hard to budge and with a cold beer in hand already, he had no reason to leave his perch. "*THIS IS HOW WE DOOOO IIITTT*" came blaring out of the silence, the official party anthem of the *Heights* had resonated from the large speakers propped up from the bed of Wriggles truck, it wasn't Friday night like the lyrics suggested but when all of the neighbors heard the calling, they came out of their homes to come take up position at picnic tables with armloads of Bridge Card groceries. Slamming screen doors could be heard from all over the neighborhood as people swarmed to the grub. Aimee was looking to let loose for the evening and maybe get frisky with Tod when he had been turned on enough by the young teen bodies that come out to grind up on each other and dance. Aimee wasn't insecure that her man got all riled up overlooking the other tight young bodies as long as his body didn't wander as much as his eyes did, it also saved her some of the hassle getting him hot and riled up sometimes.

Aimee let Tod have his affinity for the fine bodies, she had Tyrese (when Tod wasn't "tuning in the right stations" anyways) so it was all fair, an even give and take in that portion of the relationship, she just wished she hadn't compromised herself to the point of suffering under the work boot heels of the verbally and sometimes physically abusive roofer. Brittini found it ironic most of the people dancing to "*California Love*" couldn't find Compton on a map but it didn't keep them from shaking their asses to the beat, she felt the vibes tingle in her and she too wanted to gyrate her hips and dance with the other girls except she didn't want some strange mans' hands all over her as she tried to enjoy herself. Brittini had a much larger

205

personal space than other girls, she presumed. Brittini was hesitant to leave her room as she and Jonny were ducked away from Tod still sprawled out on the couch and filling the living room with evaporating nut sweat. The bass from the back of the parked mobile deejay station made most of the nearby windows rattle along with the music, Young PaperBoyz' song "*Party People*" kept the upbeat tunes pumping out and introduced some of the gathering residents to the Nigerian R&B group as they waited for Colon and Don to finish up the hot dogs for dinner. Brittini stood up to ensure that her window was all the way open, she was wearing short shorts and a tank top to try and keep cool under the revolving ceiling fan, she could feel her sheets sticking to her moist skin as she rolled out of bed, Jonny was reluctant to move over to give her room to step on the floor, he too was hot and sweaty and had cleared away enough of her dirty clothes to give himself an outline on the floor, a hard fought battle for a place to lay, especially in the heat of the summer.

Aimee decided that because Tod was being a couch herpe that she would sit over and converse with Don, Shelley was doing well and Don was still holding his own. Aimee was glad that Don was still healthy and that his heart issue hadn't become a larger problem for him, and he was also fortunate to have Colon by his side to lend a hand. Aimee leaned back on her elbows as she sat on the picnic table, watching Don line up dozens of hot dogs on the grill grates was one of those summer tasks that reminded her of summers when she was a little girl, it was an insignificant gesture but it brought back memories of her father and how she always wanted a stand-up guy that also grilled out in the warm weather. Aimee convinced herself that Tod didn't do any of it because he already spent many hot days out roofing or whatever, but deep down she knew it was because he wasn't that kind of guy, nor the right guy for her, luckily with a few drinks, those notions went to the wayside. The sun burned heavily on her hair and the warmth of the grill could be felt against her right forearm, encouraging Aimee to move her elbows further apart to let a slight breeze into her perspiring armpits, the wind was calm and her sleeveless blouse was wet with sweat halfway down to her waist already but her red plaid button up shirt went with her white shorts in a country outfit so she wasn't going to change her clothes due to sweat. Aimee just unfastened one more button from the top allowing her sweaty cleavage to breathe a little better.

206

Brittini glanced out to see half a dozen bodies milling around outside of her house, she rolled her shirt further up her stomach for air as she turned back towards her bed, Jonny didn't budge the tablet he was holding over his face as he attempted to finagle some game level achievement. Tod could be heard squeaking on the couch springs as he jostled to air out better in the blowing fan, Brittini could just roll her eyes as he was being a disgusting person, she had walked into the living room plenty of times to catch him tugging at his crotch to adjust his boxers or quell an itch, he had no shame and she could often feel his eyes on her as she did her best to avoid even looking in his direction as he worked out whatever problem he was having, he made her skin crawl most of the time, she thought he was a putrid choice and even having spent the latter half of her life with him in it, he still gave her the creeps. Brittini and Jonny resumed their laid out positions, they were able to confide in each other and comfortable enough to discuss any of the questions that may come from their tainted youth and exposure to life. It wasn't long ago when Brittini was finally urged enough to ask her friend; "are balls all that itchy? (She asked because she always noticed how often men were itching theirs.) How weird is it to have things dangling right there, especially while walking?" Jonny passed a raised eyebrow at the spontaneity of the question. Jonny explained that when nuts sweat they'll stick to your leg, he then proposed the idea that after enough years and gravity, like probably in Big Ken's case, they might stick to your knee by that point in life, but mostly to the upper inner thigh. Jonny explained that an often skin tug removed the adhered skin and often they were too sensitive to itch hard but often rolling the skin a bit satisfied itches. Brittini shuttered at the mental image of Big Kens balls sticking to his knee.

Jonny and Brittini were familiar with each other, it was more to quench curiosity and not in a sexual way, she had ample questions about the body and genitals of the opposite gender and didn't have any female friends to help answer questions so she asked Jonny. At one point in her mother's car she asked him to let her see his parts first hand, another time they were alone at home and in her room and the topic had come up again, Jonny was hesitant to comply but he then dropped his pants and took a few steps to show how walking really wasn't such an assault on his giblets as body mechanics might suggest. Brittini repaid the incident, by showing her curious friend how some of the other parts worked, there was no sexual nature behind their questions but a matter of young curiosity about the opposite sex. Aimee used her knowledge of medical terminology to explain menses and the upcoming life changes that all women experience, but there were still many questions left unanswered but Brittini got all of her answers when that change came to her. Brittini was grateful she had Jonny to stick up for her and confide in, she couldn't bring her problems to her mother, especially about Tod and the poor choice in a mate Aimee made. Brittini spent a large portion of her home life tucked away in her room, Aimee accounted the withdrawn antics of her daughter to just being a teen and hardly gave it a second thought.

Aimee enjoyed the smell of the charcoal; so many memories rode the scents of summer. There was once a summer that her dad had loaded up food on the grill and as he bumped it, the rusted leg had finally given away and of course on an afternoon cookout that the whole family was waiting to eat. The grill leg had failed and poured the meat, veggies and charcoal all over the ground, ruining everything. Aimee's father was distraught, watching the grill tip over happened in slow motion for all of those that witnessed the tragedy, that instance lead to her mother having to extinguish the burning grass with the hose and ruining dinner. After the upset, the whole family, granny and all, headed to the buffet. Towards the end of the quickly recovered family meal, gran-momma was stopped and harassed by a waitress for filling her handbag with biscuits for later. Gran-momma was quick to raise her voice and shout for the manager to fire the young girl for making such accusations of the elder woman. The manager had to ask the entire family to finish their meal and excuse themselves once Aimee's father stood up and began to defend his old mother, whom did in fact have a purse full of food for a later meal. Aimee chuckled to herself as she remained lost in stare towards the grass while recalling such cherished memories.

The picnic table shifted and jolted Aimee back to the present as Angel sat down, Aimee apologized for not having seen the gal walk up. Angel offered her a cigarette as she dug into her own pack for one and the two ladies shared a smoke while waiting for the food to finish cooking. Angel cracked open a beer as she wiped her wrist across her forehead to keep sweat from running into her eyes, the crackle of the burning tobacco at the end of her cigarette was muffled by the music

208

playing a few feet behind them and they spoke with an elevated volume to be able to converse between themselves, Angel wondered why Tod wasn't by her side and explained the latest issues between her and Joey. The girls both hung their heads when they discussed their male problems; Tod was still self-centered and only cared for his booze and getting laid occasionally. Angel sighed heavily at the length of time that had passed since her female buttons had been pushed, she longed for male touch and even with the fentanyl cloud she wore for months; she could still feel her human desires to be touched, bubbling just beneath the surface.

The topic had become dismal and Angel pulled out a small metal chapstick container from her pocket, she wasn't going to waste a party night being depressed. With a dip of her pinky nail into a small bit of white powder, Angel had lifted up her mood. Aimee knew exactly what the heavy snort meant, and to shuck off her own foggy feeling, she looked longingly out of the corner of her eye until Angel offered a hit to be polite. Aimee rotated on the wooden seat to face Angel and dipped a fingernail into the covered metal container as well. As both girls leaned their heads back a notch to let the mood change, Don spoke up loud enough to be heard; "knock it off you two." Angel tucked the holder back into her pocket and let the corners of her mouth lift with her spirit, it was a night to party and damn it, she was going to party. Don carried a large aluminum tray loaded down with hot-dogs over to the table where the ladies sat. Aimee kept her eyes closed while her pulse picked up, each drag on her cigarette filled her lungs with menthol and it made her skin tingle and muscles twitch.

Don stuck his left finger and thumb in between his perched lips and let out an ear piercing whistle to let others know that the first round of food was ready to eat. Angel grabbed a paper plate and slapped two hot-dogs in buns and then mac and cheese across the top, her head began to sway a bit to the music that was increasing in volume behind her, she had a hearty sniffle every few minutes to clear her head. Aimee followed suit and loaded up a few hot-dogs, Brittini was sure to hear the whistle and know where to find food; she was old enough to fend for herself anyways. Aimee needed a night to not be a mother or a maid, screw doing dishes or even cooking in such hot weather.

Angel and Joey had been arguing once again over his intent to become *Lilly* permanently and she was still bewildered over how the man she adored, had become such a stranger before her eyes. Angel had watched Joey struggle, toss and turn for countless nights and break down over and over about his conflictions, she supported the man she loved, even if that man had ceased to exist anymore. I was hard for Angel to let go and as long as she continued to put fine lines of cocaine up her nose, then she could avoid the harsh reality of having to move on. Angel became stagnant in her life; she still quasi lived with Joey except it had all morphed into some pathetic reality show without any fat assed whales whining about mundane shit. In mid argument about Joey wearing and stretching out Angels favorite shorty-short panties and how she was sick and tired of having to buy ladies clothes for the both of them, both Angel and Joey were on the verge of another domestic violence disturbance when the party initiating theme song of Montell Jordan came ringing in the windows, putting a ceasefire to their argument.

Angel said to hell with Joey once again as she headed over to the party, there was no concern to whether or not he was close on her heels, he had to trade a half used Lowe's gift card and a shady pair of socks for an extra bit of blow for Angel to keep her happy for the night of the party. Angel had a much shorter fuse, the Fentynal patches caused never ending hiccups and though alcohol helped to relax her muscles enough that the hiccups all but went away, it still stuttered her sleep and increased her irritability day to day. Angel had shaved her nether region with her women' razor, after one-third of a hack job it appeared that she had done so with a barbed wire wrapped shards of broken glass. Once splotchy blood divots littered her personal landscape, it set in that Joey had used *her* razor to shave *his* toes again, and that was the final straw, setting off another nuclear argument. Angel had to deal with her underwear pulling at small scabs as she walked to the party, each step agitated her and with the heat and humidity climbing, the sweat didn't lubricate her thighs enough as they rubbed against themselves. Angel was pleased to run directly into Aimee, she was about the only person she was comfortable enough to hang out with and not shy away to snort some coke during the whole party.

Big Ken was kicked back in his recliner, sitting solely in county jail style plain white cotton boxers, trying his best not to sweat so profusely that the chair cushions might need to be rung out. Ken's chest hair had matted down the center and even with a fan directed

210

right at him, his stomach hair still glistened in sweat as he watched "Any Given Sunday" while debating palming his python to a Shania music video. Big Ken was hesitant to put pants on to join the crowd around the hot grill, the half bottle of Zignum Mezcal on the lamp table next to him had already been calling his name, it was too hot to drink it from the bottle, on the rocks was much more fitting. The scent of the grill had been wafting in Ken's windows, his rotund stomach had been gurgling for part of the afternoon but being empty, made the alcohol much more efficient, and was just as draining of his motivation as the heat was. Ken had planned to make it with Carsey also, he was too heavily guarded to admit he liked the much younger girl, his wife Michelle was still in jail for a few more years and it was with her that he was busted and sent to prison, he fought the urge to contemplate how he really felt about everything, it was easier to remain numb and keep with the momentum of staying hardened and fighting the notion to take a good look into his life.

Lil B was thumbing through porno sites on his small tablet computer in his room, he was expecting to get to grope up on ladies at the party. B missed the wet t-shirt contest and had heard so much about it from Curtiss and Darryl, but he was determined to get pictures of real titties. Lil B had been stashing away some weed and hoped to get Tammi or one of the other sluts to smoke out with him and whip their honkers out for him. Lil Bonito hid away several times a day to jerk off and it was becoming more of a habit than a hobby to pass the time, his ten angst was in full control and it was the main focus of most of his days. The young teen kept his cross close around his neck, it was the lord that would keep him protected and soon his prayers for titties would be answered. Lil B had religious parents and all of their candles, chanting and other strange rituals never amounted to much but they attributed many good things to the lord so Lil B was certain that he'd be getting some pussy for sure.

Tara was in the adjacent room, her radio playing some hot list of newest tunes and standing around in skimpy underwear deciding what she intended to wear. If she wore too skimpy of a top or shorts then surely she was going to get groped, an ass grab was flattering but if a guy gets too aggressive, she didn't want a strange finger slipped inside of her. Tara decided to go with her jean shorts with a bikini bottom underneath, she decided to keep her shorts unbuttoned and use her hips to keep them up, her tummy was firm and she certainly wanted

211

to show off her abs. Tara pulled a sparkly tank top out of her closet, it had an open back so it offered an airy breeze to keep her from sweating too heavily. To keep her hair off of the back of her neck, Tara used a hair tie to tie the back of her hair up but loose enough to fan the back of her neck as she walked and bounced. Tara planned to spend almost an hour doing her makeup, she had a few skin pits to cover over but she wanted to do some smoky eye traces with black light neon yellow outlines for both her eyes and lips for later when the lights were down and the black lights came out.

Darryl and Curtiss were waiting for their backyard chemistry plastic bottle to finish bubbling out their batch of meth; they leaned back on the plastic chairs that crowded the back stoop of Darryl's trailer. Darryl's trailer backed up to the outer perimeter, the chairs gave the boys a good view of the small cavity dug into the embankment which was their place to hide drugs. On the opposite side of the embankment was the sidewalk that surrounded the entire trailer park, some of the residents walked around that sidewalk, it became dimly lit and eerie to walk after sundown but it made for a more enticing view to walk out past the trees rather than inside the trailer park, with streets filled with potholes and mounds of dog crap all over the place.

Brittini often ducked away with her headphones on her ears to walk off a lot of her anxiety, she often felt uncomfortable in her own skin as a budding teenager, Jonny sometimes walked quietly with her, also trying to figure out life. Darryl grew suspicious when he had drugs in his cubby hole, he was nervous to get robbed or for someone to discover his backyard chemistry lab, he dealt a little bit with an old wrinkly guy named Barry, the old schlub always tried to get some downstairs action from the much younger boy but he also had ample pills to trade as well as a large stash of marijuana to sell or trade for meth. Darryl always hated being propositioned for sex by the old guy, he was a lonely old stoner; he was deaf as hell and blared death metal, despite his stature resembling an old cold penis.

Annabel was always gone and left Darryl to do whatever it was he felt like doing, he paid all of the bills so his house was entirely his, just titled under his mother's name. Darryl had Curtiss over most of the time, they spent most of their afternoons smoking blunts and talking about sleeping with any number of random bitches when it came time to dole out some pills, hoping get girls to loosen up and improve the party. Darryl had given thought to buying a piece off of Barry, the old man had access to a few handguns that weren't traceable and as his cash pile continued to grow, so did his paranoia and want to protect what was his. Darryl held the favor over Ken for a short while, he tried to barter a small hand gun from Big Ken with that favor, and Ken just laughed off such an idea. Darryl and Curtiss had their secrets from everyone, including each other, Curtiss had a slew of people coming, he already intended to sell most of them weed, before Darryl had a chance to swoop in and get more of their cash, Three blunts into the afternoon while getting ready to filter out the chunks from the backyard made meth and the beckoning call of "This is how we do it" could be heard from down the street.

Jonny and Brittini had been exhausted from the heat, he lay on the floor in his baggy jean shorts and wife beater tank top, he had a black t-shirt shoved into the back pocket of his shorts and it gave him a slight twist. Brittini tugged at the bottom of her shorts to keep them from creeping further into her as she sweated and tried to remain cool, she was unsure of what she was really up for the evening but the smell of the food was beginning to make her stomach growl. Jonny blurted out "why do you suppose women check out more women than men do, yet women get all bent about it when a guy does?" Brittini let her right eye blink at twice the rate of the left eye and tongue stick out while she gave brief thought to what she might have been hearing. The length of time spent laying on her bed smelling burning charcoal had been long enough, Brittini rolled to her left to remove herself from her comforter, her hunger had given her enough ambition to get up and put more clothes on to head outside.

Brittini told Jonny to face his right as she stepped over him as she headed to her dresser to change into a more conservative pair shorts, he rolled his head to face her bed, away from her as she changed, his eyes didn't shy from the tablet he was playing with anyways. Wriggle's upbeat remix of "Poison" filled the windows causing Jonny to spring up and scare Brittini as she was pulling her khaki capris to her waist, his spontaneous spazz out caused her to flail her arms to swat at him and then have to catch her breath for a second from the startle. Brittini shoved Jonny away from her with a chuckle and as he fell towards the bed. Brittini knew she had to watch Brodan and that loomed in the back of her mind, but she wanted to eat first.

Brittini removed her tank top and kept an eye over her left shoulder to make sure he didn't come back after her and snap her bra strap while she changed her shirt. Brittini was still smirking about Jonny having improved the hot and humid afternoon; Jonny was excited about eating and filling up on sodas before carloads of strangers rolled in and took over their streets. Brittini pulled her bedroom door open, she and Jonny followed Bel Biv Divoe through the hallway and past Tod still sprawled out on the couch. After the shower encounter with Tod, Jonny still couldn't face the neck tattooed guy laying out on the couch and constantly angling to get the fan to blow down the leg of his Dickie shorts to cool off his "engine compartment."

Jonny followed Brittini closely towards the front door, she hardly looked behind her to let Tod know food was ready; Jonny made the mistake of looking for acknowledgment and caught Tod glaring at Brittini's backside as he jostled at his groin and licked at his yellow stained teeth. The air was more humid once out the door but the slight breeze helped to compensate for it and the twosome both stood up a bit more straight and took stock of the homes around them beginning to come to life. Brittini whipped her head to her left and let the wind blow her long hair towards Jonny's face, as he braced his two hands on her lower back and then began to lift her a bit to push her towards the food table. Brittini tried to wiggle his hands off of her as she rose up onto her tippy toes to walk strangely towards the picnic table her mother and Angel were seated. Wriggle was across the street standing in the bed of his truck that seconded as his stage for the evening, Angel walked over a plate and a few beers for him as Brittini arrived. Don and Colon were taking turns pacing back and forth along the grill pit as well as the tables, their pitcher of lemonade sat on a small table with an umbrella sitting over top near his front door. The neighborhood smelled like grilled meat, Jonny was impatient from his hunger and trying to hurry Brittini up.

Down the street Curtiss and Darryl were finishing prepping, Darryl wanted to look his best for the ladies that might arrive and if he could get the chance to bed any one of them, he wasn't going to pass up the opportunity. Curtiss already had on his bleached white jeans with cotton tee; he felt it made him look like Usher, especially when wearing his white K-Swiss sneakers. Darryl opted for his baggy black jeans with a plain t-shirt under a white basketball jersey; he felt

214

fresh to death and was sure to get some pussy tonight. The two guys were all but ready to head out, just as soon as the new batch of meth was hardened and ready to go, Darryl even added a dose or two of Dramamine to it to help with any spins or side effects. Tod got a call from Tuner, one of his boys, they were on their way to join yet another epic bash and they were loaded down with booze and antsy to get started, he had Billy and Karl with him and the three had a trunk full of 40's and were already blazing a joint on their drive over.

As Brittini and Jonny neared the food table, Aimee was sniffling heartily and using her index finger to wipe away anything near her nostrils and starting to smile while loving life, "*HEEEYYYYY* ......*WHAZZUUUUPPP*" spilled from Aimee's lips to greet her gorgeous daughter and her friend. "You two are such a cuuute couple, but wait, we aren't supposed to talk about it" Aimee followed up with a tease in her voice, Brittini blushed a bit but rebutted quickly with "how many have you had already?" Aimee answered her daughter with a stern but informative; "one, the first of many tonight, I was just saying you two are cute together and Jonny has always been very polite and I respect that." Jonny had his eyes fixed on the growing mountain of hot-dogs but cocked his head enough to convince Aimee he was paying attention when he thanked her for the compliment while reaching out for a plate. Brittini reminded her mother that she was to watch Brodan for Carsey so she could enjoy the evening for a few hours. Brittini turned to look for Jonny to see if he was interested in helping her watch the energetic toddler or if he had any intrigue to mill around the party, where his father might be. Brittini had spun around almost twice before realizing that Jonny wasn't by her side but rather seated next to Angel and tight fisted around a hot dog and root beer. Jonny looked like a hairless hamster as both of his cheeks were so full of food he could hardly close his mouth, Brittini let out a snort as his appearance wasn't expected and caught her off guard, "Well?" she asked as she gave a piercing look over to her friend, "MURRR" he replied with a mouth full of food. Aimee was smiling in awe at her young daughter being so grown up, she encouraged her to eat dinner and to let her know if she needed anything for the evening, Jonny swallowed half of his cheeked food and piped up; "money for beer and porno" causing Angel to blush a bit before turning and delivering a playful slap on the back of his head.

Down the street Curtiss' cousin Monte was also gearing up for the party, he hardly saw his younger cousin as he worked long shifts and Curtiss was often out with Darryl for a majority of the time. Monte tried to help look out for his cousin and it was a responsibility to look after his people but his younger cousin was becoming more of a burden than an adult. Monte wanted Curtiss to get a trade like him and work, not spend his time chasing ass or running the streets, he saw enough young black men fall into the ways of the streets and end up in some manner of the legal system, and to hang out with Darryl; whom already had two stints in the county jail, it wasn't looking good. Monte was a clean cut man, he wasn't the most educated but he took the time to browse news apps on his phone to stay up to date, it wasn't like reading the newspaper but it wasn't wasting time on hip-hop channels or some shit. Monte had begun seeing a young girl named Claire, she was mixed and had green eyes and really deep dimples, and she was the most adorable girl he had ever met. Monte had told Claire all about Curtiss and what he was trying to do, and she admired him for it, but Monte was still nervous that Curtiss might screw things up for himself, which might spill over and become a mess for Monte. Monte couldn't decide which collared shirt to wear to impress Claire on his date; he had big plans and had really hoped that he could show the girl a good time under the romantic setting of the overhead fireworks.

Monte heard the music kick up on the next street over, he started out wearing a bright green polo shirt but between the heat and his nerves, it didn't take very long to sweat through his first choice in shirts. Monte was eager to wait for Claire, she was an assistant manager at the company he worked for, but she worked in the office portion, she had a four year degree and for some reason, she saw something in the hard worker. Monte knew that Claire was the kind of girl that would give him a reason to keep working hard, the kind of girl that was smart enough to avoid thugs and troublesome guys, the kind of girl that didn't put up with bullshit. Monte was expecting his date anytime and as the time ticked closer and closer, the music grew louder and his evening was getting ready to commence as well.

Carsey was in her trailer when she heard the official party song of the trailer park; she had her radio set on 104.3, which was static until the song bellowed across. Carsey was trying to convince her small boy Brodan to keep his blue dinosaur shirt on because it matched his blue shorts, he was insistent that it was too hot for a shirt. Carsey had shorts and a bra on and each time she neared the brief second it would take to retrieve her shirt and slip into it, Brodan was screeching or causing some interrupting commotion. Barney had been Brodan's favorite DVD and it had a few crackles on the screen from constantly being on repeat during his waking hours. Carsey knew that Brittini wasn't very far behind in coming to watch Brodan, and when she was away from her son, then she could have her mental break from her reality for the evening. Carsey was proud that she held her wits together, her struggles to remain calm and ignore her bipolar itches were a real challenge most of the time and on occasion she would leave her son in his jumper and step out for a calming cigarette, she felt guilty having to put herself first once in a while but she also had plenty of reminder sticky notes all over her house that no matter what, she needed to take her meds and stay the course, she owed it to her late husband and brother. Once Brodan was distracted enough with Barney and a string cheese, Carsey was rewarded with time to lotion her skin and finally finish getting dressed.

Carsey stretched in the doorway of her dining room, her body ached and was tired from spending a majority of her time playing on the floor with her son, she yearned for the days when her energy level was at its' prime, not suppressed by her medications. Carsey ran her hands down her sides under her shirt, her stomach muscles were tight and it felt good to stretch. Carsey let her fingers run up and down the stretch marks that lined her sides, she acquired the darker colored stretch marks when she was pregnant and for the most part, she was embarrassed by her body. Carsey's husband truly loved her and with him she felt confident, safe, and loved, now she viewed herself as an out of shape mental case with a kid and a deep seeded urge to just run crazy. Carsey felt ashamed about the frequent hook ups with Big Ken for money, he was much older than she was and there was no way she was going to let herself fall in love, and in that she felt some security. Big Ken paid her for her time, she knew that the man would pay her for sex, it was a sort of sideways compliment and to her it meant he liked her enough to be willing to pay, and besides, with his size, age, and poor health habits, he was hardly able to maintain a decent erection most of the time and even after huffing and puffing for a bit, he was easy to finish with her mouth. Carsey felt her mind was often clouded over with her meds, her body hardly resembled the one it did five years ago, in shape and put together but there wasn't much she could do about it anymore.

Brodan bounced in his bouncer that was suspended from the living room ceiling, the music bumped from her own radio but the bass carried in from the window, the subtle thumps were off time from the music. Carsey grabbed a cigarette from her pack and stepped out onto the front porch, the slight breeze coupled with the sun rays on her squinting cheeks, brought a slight relief to her as she lit her small break. Carsey lowered her head down onto her forearm as she sat perched on her front step, she was close enough to hear Brodan if there was a problem, she knew it was a matter of time before young Brittini strolled around the corner, the weight of her life seemed to affect her posture, she let out a deep breath full of exasperation and with a sliver of clarity, she felt the urge to cry for a moment. Carsey brought her smoke under her arm and took a drag, the smoke from the lit end of her cigarette burned in her eyes and she raised her head back to her original seated position, then lifted her head even higher up to exhale high into the air. As Carsey opened her eyes once again, to her right she caught a movement that startled her as she was enjoying the solidarity. Carsey was expecting Brittini to come from the left, this wasn't Brittini, it was Gelica, for some reason she was out and fumbling around, normally the lady was porch bound and talking to herself, but his time she seemed to be addressing Carsey.

"How-do young lady? "Gelica had her hair in her curlers but rather than a trademark flowery mumu, she was wearing jeans and a rather pleasant looking blouse. Carsey was rather surprised to interact with the woman, she was often known for running her toes through the playground sand (which was rife with cat shit) and convincing herself that she was off on some vacation in Jamaica or other foreign islands. Deep down Carsey felt bad for Gelica, her husband was originally a trucker whom partnered up with a contractor, his company built the trailer park while he hauled all of the trailers in and together, the business partners made a fortune. Gelica's husband Jimmy had worked his whole life to support the woman, only to learn of her obsession with the finer life. Gelica had not only almost bankrupted the family with her splurging, but also almost gambled away the college savings of their kids, she was dangerously reckless. Jimmy bought her a trailer during the divorce and her income was as minimal as the impact on her, she was growing ever more so delusional, her grasp on reality faded.

Carsey was hesitant to respond but her interactions weren't all that bad so she responded back in kind. Gelica proceeded to tell Carsey about her old dog, which had cost her thousands of dollars and how it was specially bred, except that it died, and then the focus of the conversation turned to the loud bumping in the air. "The helicopters are hovering" Gelica had warned Carsey, suggesting ducking away indoors so the government couldn't track her from the sky. Carsey tried her best to inform the woman that the bumping was just the bass from speakers and there was nothing to be concerned about. Mid-sentence Gelica shuttered, her shoulders rolled forward and her back hunched, she resembled a frightened cat. "Run misses, it's them" Gelica began stepping lightly as she turned back from where she came, her arms spread out as if suddenly blinded and feeling her way home. Carsey asked the spooked lady if all was alright; "This is why it is always safer in Jamaica, the Feds can't fly their silent helicopters that far and the sand has healing crystals in it, I must go now, my plane is leaving."

Carsey shook her shirt to air out her body as she dragged on her cigarette, wondering how far gone her neighbor really was. The interaction made Carsey tensed, her muscles twitched as she dreaded the notion of looking so foolish, if she strayed too far from her daily course of medications or strict regimen that kept her balanced. Everyone snickered and sneered when Gelica sat at the playground, talking to herself and kicking at cat turd lumps. Carsey felt badly deep down for her part in joining in when it came to passing judgment onto Gelica. Gelica had small moments of clarity, a shimmer along the horizon was what it was called, until things ceased making logical sense, that small tick when shadows dance a little more or voices seem to echo.

Carsey knew how easily it was to get fed up with the haze of medication, it was like a wet blanket of the mind, she also knew how much more dangerous it was to her son if she let go of all that she had worked for. Carsey missed her husband and her brother, and all that she had left were fading pictures and memories to rely on as she struggled to see her son into manhood. Carsey felt the skin on her face tighten from her time on the sun, it was warming and calming, Barney was playing just inside her front door and the smoke from her cigarette whirled in her nostrils, each slow breath was clouded and made her lungs ache with desperation for air, but it slowed her mind enough to help her find her realignment.

Carsey rolled her burning cigarette between her bright red painted fingernails, each one was only a few minutes of time for herself but each one seemed to be a much needed and an earned break from the confines of motherhood. Carsey could feel her backside begin to numb as the hot coal of her smoke reached the lines near the filter, signaling time to get back to her boy, the bass continued to echo and as she reached for her rail to pull herself up by. As she rose she could see the petite young girl in the distance heading towards her. Carsey could already feel her body begin to jitter, she wanted to dance and smoke and leave her life behind for the evening, maybe get lost in the dirty flirting's of some strange guy that would enter her and take her to wildly erotic highs. Brittini was still digesting dinner as she made her way over to relieve Carsey, her thin shoes slapped on the pavement as she walked. Brittini felt warm in her capris' and her shirt wasn't as airy as she would have liked, she was glad she chose longer shorts when she babysat, last time she found mushed graham crackers near her rear and crotch as Brodan slapped his hands together and flung squishy goo into the leg holes in her shorts. Brodan was a funny young boy but a young boy nonetheless, and they were a messy bunch, Brittini took caution to prevent strange things ending up in her pants from that point on.

From the center of the street the closely lined trailers seemed like adequate homes, each one had its' own flaws, dings and dents, missing siding or half rotten stairs leading up to bent doors, things seemed pleasant if you didn't look too closely. Brittini couldn't wait to escape the social shackles that seemed to keep her walking around the glass littered streets, used condoms weren't a rare sighting in the shrubs, red plastic cups or a dead cat were also often within view from anywhere you stood. Some nights the "pop pop pop" could be heard around the trailer park, the snaps of an air rifle or two taking out one of the many stray cats in the trailer park, rabid with mange. The rotting stench of dead animals sometimes wafted from behind the wood lattice adorned porches, behind the west dirt berm was littered with brownish white bones, whenever some stray dog impregnates a bitch, or a litter of kittens were discovered under a porch, often times the babies were tossed to the woods to be picked at by the birds or raccoon's. Brittini walked or jogged around the outer sidewalk as often as she could, she always felt saddened when she caught glimpse of rotting flesh in the woods, she felt saddened that puppies or kittens were just thrown to the woods and quickly forgotten. Sidewalks were often stained from any number of ill fluids, semen, vomit, blood, whatever may have leaked from trashcans or people as they sat on the curb awaiting trash pickup, Brittini preferred to walk in the road rather than have to walk around the cars parked up on the walkway.

Jonny heaped several spoonfuls of potato salad into his plate as Angel and Aimee chuckled and jawed, Brittini ate and then excused herself to head to relieve Carsey. Jonny hadn't looked up from his plate when she left, he was too heavily distracted by a plate of food to be bothered with anything else around him. Aimee had asked Angel if Joey was around, they chuckled as they spoke, the powder had lightened up their mood while Don and Colon continued to cook and avoid getting caught up in whatever topic the two ladies had in mind. Aimee and Angel ignored the perspiration that welled up on their foreheads, their conversation had bounced around and many inside jokes passed between them, at one point Angel looked behind her at Jonny near face down in his plate, Angel glanced back at Aimee and raised a seductive eyebrow at the slurping sounds of Jonny as he ate.

Angel had been lonely, she was so torn between wanting Joey and also her inability to move on, Aimee too was trapped, Tod was abusive when he wasn't getting his way but he was a half decent lay and it kept her from being lonely. Aimee kept herself and Tod eased with booze, Angle had her Fentanyl and cocaine to make life easier to deal with, but together the two ladies made due. Jonny ceased eating for a moment when he thought he was being spoken about, his bigger concern was to fill his belly and go back to being invisible before his father came around. Angel and Aimee knew that Jonny lived an anxiety filled life on eggshells, except there was nothing they could do.

Aimee scooted in closer to Angel as Angel pulled out her small metal container for another quick snort of bliss; Aimee glanced back at Jonny as he stood up and headed off. Once out of ear shot, Angel asked if Aimee thought Brittini and Jonny had "played doctor?" Aimee continued smiling and prompted that she hadn't even caught any notion of such things. Angel came back with how she wondered if he were hung or if he even had anything worth her time down there, she was only half curious but at fifteen, most boys would lay with any girl willing to let them, and she might be willing to let him if Brittini wouldn't find out, she was just craving a man's company.

Carsey was finishing getting ready for her night, through the front window she could make out Brittini turning the corner up towards her stairs, the knock was loud enough to be heard and despite being anticipated, it was still startling enough to make her eyes pop open wider. Brodan turned to watch Brittini enter, he twisted and with an outstretched hand he grasped for his babysitter as his mother let her in. Carsey hugged Brittini and gave an appreciative kiss on her cheek before barreling out the door. Carsey was free for the evening and the walls of her small home had been closing in long enough. Carsey knew she could trust Brittini and she leaped off the middle step on her way to the pavement, she found herself winded quickly and slowed her pace before she even reached the road. Down to the left Monte could be seen exiting his home, the man was often in sooty work clothes but this time he was looking sharp and pressed in plaid shorts and bright white shoes, he had a bit of a dance to his walk and even from the distance, his bright smile could be seen. Over her right shoulder Carsey could see a few cars pulling in, unfamiliar vehicles that were probably arriving for the festivities, not much of a concern to her for the time being, she headed towards the same direction as Monte.

Darryl was ready to get his night on, a car full of people had pulled up out front and it quickly spurred his curiosity, Curtiss jumped up from the recliner he was perched in, the car contained some people that Curtiss had invited, he knew the driver was looking to make a solid contact to buy from. The drivers name was Farkam, an Arabic kid that kept his hair moussed up and his clothes baggy, he wanted to prove to the other Arabs he hung out with that he was gangster and tough. Farkam stepped out of his Charger, he was cocky and arrogant because his father had some money, the kid never broke a sweat but you wouldn't be surprised. Farkam had some of his crew with him, two more guys and two girls, they all seemed to hang on him and look up to him, he was tall and thin while Ashm was shorter and stocky, also with the same ridiculous spiked up hair. No matter how much they straighten or mousse up their curly hair, or tanned to look like they were from the Jersey Shore, there was no hiding the smell of them, too much cologne and body odor. On Ashm's arm hung a short girl, her head wrapped and covered, she was silent and kept her head bowed to the ground. Another thin kid climbed out of the backseat, the two older boys chuckled and spoke in strange tongues, the younger boy and two girls laughed with them. Darryl suggested Curtiss have them move their car, the driver had a lazy eye and he was certain it was the mark of dis-honest shit bags. Curtiss bolted out the door and asked Farkam to move the car up a bit, he used the excuse that Darryl was waiting for more visitors and guests and leaving their car would be rude. Farkam mumbled something that couldn't be understood anyways, and then tossed his car keys to Ashm and let him move the car up, the younger Arab and the two girls stood huddled near one another while Farkam and Curtiss shook hands in greeting.

Darryl retreated back to his room to secure that all of his loose money and such were safely hidden away, an Arab with a lazy eye was the most shiesty of all scumbag ass people, he grew leary having the shady people even know where he lived. Darryl shot Curtiss a stern eye as he locked up his front door and joined the small group, Farkam was already cracking a cigar to roll a blunt with a small bag of what he had just purchased from Curtiss, the girl with the white head wrap thing pulled out a lighter from her pocket and offered it up to Farkam after he finished licking the blunt closed, Curtiss was impressed at his ability to walk and roll. Darryl was nervous around the foreigners and kept a close eye on their hands, the group headed towards the burning fires and picnic tables in the center of the park. Farkam and Ashm spoke back and forth in Arabic and took turns bargaining with Curtiss on what prices were for what drugs, Darryl knew that the Arabs were good at barraging people, bullying their way to get what they want all while underhandedly speaking in their mush mouth crap to do it. The two girls remained silent, they followed slowly in the back as the guys walked forward, and the younger boy was only a year or two behind in age but still walked ahead of the girls. Curtiss offered a hit off of the blunt to the girls out of respect, Farkam snatched it up before it got close to them, Farkam piped up that "women weren't worth decent pot, or even of hearing them, just good for warm holes."

Darryl shook his head at the barbaric mentality of the animals; he was disgusted at the lot of them and kept his hands clenched as he walked towards the party. Ashm had his tight white shirt on, it was a thin material and showed that he spent ample amount of time in the gym, probably in the showers by how pretty he was. As the group walked the girl in the black head wrap packed a small bowl for her and the girl in the white head dress to smoke. While Curtiss walked with Ashm and Farkam and discussed business, Darryl fell back and shared a joint with the younger smaller boy that walked ahead of the girls, he asked what was the point of dragging the girls around like dogs, the boy just piped up that the girls were less than people, any man would trade a girl for a pack of cigarettes, he explained that the men were the strength and smarts, as well as the cock and balls, Darryl listened intently and tried to fight his inner growing rage.

When Darryl and the Arabs strolled up near the deejay working his magic, Aimee and Angel had already seen them coming, Angel was leery about the entire group, none of them were trustable, and each one would put it in your ass when bent over near them, male or female. Carsey rounded the corner and passed joining the party, her intent was to arouse Big Ken, she eyed the swelling crowd for him and didn't locate him; she knew that he would protect her and give her the sense of security she needed in order to participate in the party without the overwhelming dread of anxiety. The crowd continued to swell, more and more people arrived and walked towards the main stage, the pickup truck near the fire pit. Stepping up the white painted stairs, Carsey kicked her shoes off on the top step and reached out towards the rusted handle to let herself in, she could already hear the TV through the screen in the door. Carsey stepped in to the sight of Big Ken, faded tattoos strewn across his large sweaty body as he laid out on a recliner, fan blowing sweat beads across his body.

Big Ken had almost already sweat through his plain white boxers, the fly was bent open but not offering any route of blowing air from the fan. Big Ken rolled his head to his left to watch Carsey step in the door; she was sweaty from her walk and tugging at her shirt to air out her body. Big Ken cracked a smile, seeing her come with her hair tied up and smelling of sweet lotion, he reached down to scratch at himself, letting Carsey look into the opening of his boxers. Carsey was too hot and sweaty to acknowledge his feeble attempts to put her in the mood to get even sweatier. Big Ken heaved his body as he struggled with his weight to sit up, he was out of breath as the chair sat up and he was on his feet. Ken reached out for Carsey's hand and smiled grandly to express his happiness to see her. Ken pulled Carsey to him, he was already in the mood and he thrusted his waist against hers, the sweat from his body joined hers on her shirt as he spun her around and began to toy with her through her shorts. Carsey looked over to her left to see a group of people milling around just down the street, she wasn't sure if being taken in the doorway was an appropriate move for her but it was mildly enticing. It was hot, Big Ken lost his breath just getting out of the chair, Carsey wasn in no mood to get even hotter or any more sweaty but he was half hard and untucking himself from his boxers. Ken reached around Carsey and unbuttoned her shorts, she was without panties and she enjoyed the slight breeze between her thighs for a moment as the shorts fell to the floor, Big Ken reached up under her shirt as he took up position behind her and rubbed himself against her.

Carsey stared ahead at the wood paneling on the wall, splinters exposed the cheap undercoating of wallpaper, she fought the urge to cry. Big Ken placed himself inside of her, she felt disgusted, his sweat already ran down the back of her legs, she could feel his hands sweat as he pawed at her chest, his course hands were unappealing to the touch and his large hands enveloped her breasts as he thrusted into her. Carsey felt the pains of him as he penetrated her, he hadn't taken adequate time to warm her up to him before entering her, he didn't care enough to wait, he was ready for her instantly. Big Ken had a long list of bad things he'd done in his life, demons he ran from and even more things he had paid for, he felt as if he was justified in many of the things he had ever done and didn't let much enter his mind. Kens' drinking numbed his conscious and being able to still saddle up behind a naked young twat, meant to him that all was just. Carsey clinched her eyes, thought about her husband and the voyeuristic ways that she made love with her husband as a young bride, the smell of Old Spice that filled the living room made it hard to relive the smell of her late husband, she trained her ears to listen to the music down the street instead of the heavy breathing by the man pleasing himself between her legs, she tried to focus on the post coital payment that always occured.

After a few minutes Big Ken shuttered and jerked as he completed what he set out to do, Carsey had pulled her shirt up over her shoulders to keep from sweating through it, she was in a hurry to clean her crotch a bit and get to partying, Big Ken sauntered towards the bathroom to take a washrag to his body, Carsey carried her shorts with her to the kitchen, using a wet paper towel she roughly cleaned her crotch and armpits but the activity made her sweat even more. Carsey looked at some of the postcards and papers on the yellowed fridge as she cleaned up; some of the papers were court documents, parole requirements and custody hearing orders. Carsey found it strange that Big Ken held the custody papers on the fridge for easy location but he hardly ever spoke of the child, or was even ever seen

226

with the boy. Jonny tiptoed around his father, became a ghost in his own home, and even less than a shadow when Ken was home. Carsey didn't let herself be bothered with concerns for a son that wasn't hers. Feeding and caring for Brodan and herself were her only priorities, she took a vow to her husband and even though he passed, his death wasn't going to part her heart from him, she was going to raise up her son in his fathers' memory and get the chance to cry at his graduation, his wedding, and at the birth of his own children, she put a great distance between her end results and what she had to do to get there, Big Ken was just one of those things. Brodan was what mattered to Carsey.

Angel wasn't all that serious at first when she joked about jumping Jonny's bones, he was a young boy and as often as they were inexperienced and clumsy in bed but their youth gave them the stamina to go again and again and often they were more than eager to please. Angel put the notion of bedding Jonny in the back of her mind, her teeth buzzed and her nose tickled from her poweder, her mind raced as fast as her heart, the bass from the speakers consumed her and made her wet down below. Aimee was laid back on her elbows, no matter how hard of a drag she took, each menthol cigarette came and went without satisfying her urge for it. Angel let her hips sway with the beats, she swayed side to side and Wriggle raised his cold drink to her already starting the night out by dancing alone to his music. Aimee heaved herself up from her wooden plank, she had a request for Wriggle to play, she was feeling her pulse race and wanted some feel good tunes to bring her aging body to life.

Aimee requested Wriggle to download and spin up some Paulina Jayne, a young country girl that Brittini liked, she wished her daughter would never grow old, never get any more independent or one day leave, it was all she could do to keep her mind for her daughter, there was never enough time in the day or money in her paycheck. Aimee knew she had a good thing going at the funeral home, it was off hours and good pay, the problem, like so many others, was that Tod screwed it up. Aimee deeply regretted letting Tod stay as long as he did, he had become a festering sore and now is unable to be removed from her life. "Pass the moonshine" was a familiar song, it was laid over with plenty of extra bass and a faster beat, Aimee recognized the lyrics one moment after they began, the upbeat tempo was catchy and with a bit of a techno tweak added to it made it a club worthy raver, and Aimee let her pulse run like wild stallions through her veins. Aimee joined Angel in dancing, their bodies absorbed the energy from the music, their minds were not of their own but belonged to the chaos of life, but suddenly free from their heavy burdens and responsibilities.

After the music climbed several more notches and snuffed out the ability to converse, Tod finally peeled himself from his well-worn imprint on the couch. Tod had only had a few cold beers, not enough to cool him off but enough to perpetuate his want to join the party and keep drinking; there kiddie pools full of icy brews and trays of food to feast on. He slipped his sweaty feet into his work boots, there was no use lacing them as he wasn't wearing socks anyways, he just wanted to protect his feet from the shit and glass on the ground. Looking out through the screen he could see Curtiss leading a pack of middle easterners, they strutted and walked with an arrogant sway to them, thinking their sand filled shit didn't stink, and it began to piss him off. Tod slammed the measly screen door open, the hinges near ripped out of the door frame with his rage. The breeze felt cool to Tods skin as he could feel his blood begin to boil while watching the two taller Arabs chuckle and point at Aimee and Angel twist and twirl in the street. Lines gathered to make their way past the picnic tables covered in food, parents brought younger kids out for hot-dogs and pop while they cracked and raised beers among themselves, the crowd swelled with random faces, neighbors whom rarely waved in passing were exchanging pleasantries and chit chatting beside one another.

Tod walked with a brisk pace towards the center of the forming crowd, he wanted to make his presence known and made it painfully obvious that Arabs were scum and that he despised them, all. Aimee was busy twirling with Angel to notice Tod walking sternly; it wasn't until he walked right into Farkam and almost knocking him over on purpose, which caused his shorter companion Ashm to turn with a clenched fist, ready to brawl. Ashm began to swing his arm as the younger boy placed his hand on his chest, at the same time Curtiss stepped between them, telling Ashm to chill, and looking at Tod and telling him "chill down homie" while offering up a joint to calm down with. Tod took the rolled joint from Curtiss and also reached forward and took the remainder of the joint still perched between the lips of Farkam, with a glaring look and cheek muscles bulging under his thin skin, Tod despised the darker skinned group, and with an airborne bit

228

of spittle, Tod sealed a promise of ill feelings and gave the less than ideal guests of Curtiss and Darryl a reason to curse him in Arabic, which Tod scoffed at and grabbed himself a paper plate to eat.

Very little could be heard over the volume of the speakers but with the stark commotion, all eyes were on Tod and Farkam. Aimee ceased her dancing when Tod bumped into Farkam, she was enjoying her cocaine buzz but also knew that she couldn't let there be problems so early on in the evening. Aimee joined Tod's side as he heaped mac'n'cheese onto his plate, his forearm muscles remained tense as Aimee placed her hand upon his left arm in comfort, he failed to look her in the eyes to show how unhappy he was. Aimee told Tod: "go Frozen, *Let it GOOOOO*" and handed him a beer. Tod shucked his elbow to remove her hand, and with a growling tone to his voice he reluctantly agreed as he headed towards the food tables. Angel leaned in to whisper and giggle into Aimee's ear; "Uh Oh, is he mad that the Arab kids are prettier than he is?" Aimee let her lips part into a large smile and whipped her head back around to return to her dancing. Ashm continued to speak in an angry manner to Farkam, he wanted to deck the older tattooed white trash, Curtiss was trying to quell the heated temper while Farkam returned equally harsh words back to Ashm.

Carsey was pulling herself back together and working her shorts back up over her sweaty legs, she hadn't been able to find any form of breeze near the open window where she used a handful of moist paper towel to wash herself off while waiting for Big Ken to finish his quick rinse of a shower. Carsey dragged the wet paper towel up her inner thighs to clean the sweat off of her, with the sound of the shower running in the background her fingers began to wander by themselves. Carsey was enticed looking out the kitchen window and seeing many people begin to gather, none of them had a single clue what she was doing and that made her blood rush back to her delicate area, Big Ken didn't push the right buttons anyway. Carey continued to take care of her needs, the sky was easing into the setting crown as she felt her pulse race, her climax was met with the ceasing of the shower, the surge of panic struck Carsey and her entire body writhed on her fingertips. Carsey zipped her shorts closed and ran her hand under the cool water of the kitchen sink, as she heard Ken exit the bathroom whistling, she splashed water on her face and was ready for a much better night of hanging out with other adults; sans Barney.

Big Ken was stretching a wife-beater over his meaty frame as he made his way back out of the hallway towards his waiting date for the evening. Carsey had a cigarette hanging out of her mouth and was lighting one for Ken as he stepped near to retrieve his cigarette and put on some body spray to help conceal his sweating. Ken was already out of breath from hustling, he just wanted to pour another glass of ta'killya and chunk his ass back down on his chair, except Carsey was ready to go and Tod was expecting him. Big Ken stood tall to wedge a fresh pack of smokes deep into his front pocket and his chained wallet into his back pocket after he laced on his shoes and headed outward. Big Ken took a hefty look at the swelling crowd and was instantly irritated with all of the people; Carsey slapped Ken on the back to push him to get moving.

Wriggle sent Nelly out through the speakers as Ken and Carsey crossed the littered road and joined up near Tod, he was ripping bites from his hot dog like tearing at a carcass, Big Ken stood next to him as he sat and thrusted his weight into him, nearly knocking him to the ground. Tod hadn't had the chance to recognize the face of who was messing with him. Tod scurried to his feet and lunged at Big Ken. Tod had his hand clenched and ready to deliver a haymaker into the face of who had become his aggressor. Big Ken caught Tod in midair and by the look on his face, was absolutely surprised at Tod's reaction. Tod expressed his concern that there were some "shady ass sand monkeys up over yonder, ones even got a lazy eye so you know you can't trust 'em" Big Ken set his friend down and immediately reached behind him to ensure that his wallet was still where he placed it moments before.

Carsey pranced off to investigate all of the bodies that were milling about, she could see down the walk way that Tara was strolling towards the crowd with some girlfriends in tow, all of them in overly large sunglasses and skimpy tops. One girl was shorter than she, had long blonde hair and short jean shorts on, her shirt was a plain white t-shirt with a small black emblem over her left breast, the four of them were bubbly and cheerful as they were young and ignorant to life outside of their small circle. Carsey remembered being so young and naive, when your body didn't jiggle with each step, when you had all of the young hot boys chasing your still tight ass, back before old divorced dead beat dads were the only ones left turning their eyes to look at her longingly. Carsey turned back to loop around the back side of the party, two doors down from Aimee's trailer was where Carsey found herself glancing to the next street where Brittini was entertaining her son Brodan, whom she missed already.

The gaggle of teens brushed past Carsey, Tara had lived across from her and wasn't ever very silent in her judging, she often snickered and sneered as she passed. Carsey tensed the muscles in her neck and jaw as she felt her anxiety come up on her, she didn't like the young swarm of girls so close, they hardly parted as they surrounded her and passed. Tara lead the way with her large sunglasses, a smaller framed girl with pink bits of hair woven in behind her ears was snapping her bubble gum as she walked; she had no hesitation to brush against Carsey as Tara had instructed the group to just ignore the "skank" as they walked. Carsey held her ground but felt herself get bounced between bodies as they passes, she had no idea why the young hoard were being such bitches, she felt her blood pressure continue to spike and there was a small itch in her that made her want to rub a finger in her ass and then smear the results in the teeth of the leader bitch that instigated the rough passing. Carsey looked even harder at her home, the siding needed a power washing, not something you'd notice from up close but from afar, the dirt could be made out from where she was standing. Brodan was the only reason Carsey held her head together, he was her reason to live and he would also be the only reason she doesn't assault a skint bitch on such a beautiful day.

The bass bumped, Carsey felt the itch deep inside of her want to break out of her routine and run wild, her overview of her son and the example she wanted to be for him was normally her chains, she tried to put it all from her mind for small moments, hoping that each small break would be enough to keep from coming unwired. Carsey could hear the small group of uptight twats still giggling and carrying on, she hung her head for a moment and just accepted that maybe she was just jealous. Carsey was jealous because of how much time was ahead of the girls to figure out life, and make their own mistakes, time she no longer had. Brodan was still a young and an impressionable boy, he had big set of dimples and a wide eyed look, Carsey knew she was blessed to have him; it was her choice to keep him as her sole responsibility. Carsey let her eyes sink from her small trailer the next street over and down to the cracked sidewalk, the ants near her feet carried on with whatever tasks they had to do, they didn't pay any never mind to the woman staring down at them. Carsey was jealous of so many other lives and their happiness; she quickly wiped the tear from her eye and headed back to the crowd of people.

Big Ken milled around with Tod, the ethnicity of the crowd was getting darker during the waning daylight hours, and Tod held contempt for the Arabs while Ken wasn't fond of the blacks. Big Ken defaulted to his idea that the only reason blacks are so athletic was because they were bred for the hard work as slaves, and how much of a shame it was that they weren't still in chains. Tod found no purpose in half of the dicks standing around him, the food was warm, the bodies young and he could keep the cold drinks in hand before retiring to bed with Aimee for some belly slapping when the party was all done. Farkam and Ashm kept a nervous eye over on Tod, Ashm chewed on the notion that the skinny white guy with faded tattoos on his arms and torso had snubbed him; he didn't take disrespect very easily. Tod knew that the pair of sand munching shit bags with the popped collars were eye balling him, Big Ken laughed it off; "they probably want to suck your dick" Ken suggested to Tod as they both lit a cigarette in unison, Tod nodded in agreement.

"Alright People, it's time to kick up the volume and the party, everyone grab a drink and here we go" Wriggle piped up over his microphone, he flicked on a few more lights that swirled and strobed around the crowd, the girls hooted and hollered while the men all raised their beers. Farkam and Ashm didn't turn their backs to Tod, the sight of Big Ken was menacing and his sheer size was a threat, and they didn't trust the old felon. The two hijab wearing girls that were with the Arab boys swayed their hips, they danced together with very little regards to the taller boys they had ridden with, the smaller framed boy with middle eastern olive drab skin danced with the girls. Farkam and Ashm continued to smoke pot and pass a joint back and forth but kept their mouths pointed to their suitors, Darryl and Curtiss. Darryl and Curtiss were budding entrepreneurs, they were using the loud music to mask their conversations, and the party was the excuse to have a bunch of clientele come to help with arrangements, and the Arabs were the first of a list of potential to buyers.

Curtiss stood close with Farkam and Ashm while Darryl walked a bit and surveyed the area. Curtiss had a few more people meant to arrive, Darryl was the main vein for types of drugs that they were looking for, the Arabs wanted pot, plain and simple, but in true Arab form, they wanted it cheaper that anyone was willing to sell it for, they wanted to haggle and barter the prices well below the originally agreed upon price. Another car of brothers arrived; it was an old rusted Toyota full of cornrowed thugs looking to strike a deal with Curtiss over some pills and more pot to pedal further back at the apartment complex that Dez're's aunt lived at. Darryl knew he already had buyers for his meth; the old wrinkled guy named Barry, Barry was just as bumbling and useless as any member of the Bush family, the same family that fumbled the shit out of the country. Darryl kept his Shinola watch shiny and his K-Swiss shoes bright white, he had a very small reputation but with Curtiss helping to run product to kids back near school he was setting himself up to bring his game up a level when it came to selling dope. The Toyota had three large brothers in it; they melded into the crowd and added more bodies to the wave of bodies flowing from one side to the other.

Carsey caught up with Aimee and Angel, they were still near the heart of the dancing crowd, and they knew a little about Carsey, Aimee's daughter Brittini did in fact babysit her young son Brodan. Tod liked that Carsey was a decade younger than Aimee and her tits still defied gravity plenty and he always waited around to see them, especially after getting to smack her when they were both nude. Tuner, Billy and Karl strolled up; each had a few cases of beer in tow and was ready to put all of the cans into the kiddie pools with the lights reflecting off of the ice inside. Karl chewed on a plastic tipped cigar as he eyed the scene, he was wearing a white polo shirt with tainted yellow armpit stains, it was still hot out and there weren't cold enough drinks to keep him from sweating profusely. Tuner hadn't bothered to wear anything more than an old Bud Light sleeveless t-shirt, his jean shorts were ratty and splattered with paint from his last side job. Tuner twitched his eyes to all of the bodies that were nearby, he spotted the girls walking with Tara real quickly, his lower jaw opened and pushed forward as he licked the back of his lower lip staring at the young girls. Karl had his sunglasses propped up on top of his head, his eyes squinted and he walked with a wide stance as he carried his share of the beer, his forearms were strained and flexed and setting the beer down was a much needed relief.

Karl said his greetings and quickly headed towards the group of younger girls, he was convinced that with a few drinks, he was bedding one of them girls before the end of the night. Aimee was distracted by the music, she felt truly enlightened and the night air was beginning to cool, though the sight of all of the sweaty bodies would beg to differ. Karl danced his way over to Aimee, she was oblivious to his presence as he writhed up against her, what he had been wanting for a very long time. Karl still brought up the Tod coerced blowjob, it hadn't quenched his hard-on for her but rather fueled it even more, he held the mother-daughter fantasy at the most forward part of his brain every time he saw either Aimee or Brittini. Watching her sway in rhythm to the beat, her shirt hugged her curves and Karl wanted to see her body in its natural bare state for himself.

Aimee and Angel laughed and giggled, whenever they caught any of the strange guests staring in their direction, they would give one another a quick peck on the lips for the attention and laugh when the gawker would drop their jaw and proffer up a large smile or even money to take things further. Karl caught a kiss shared between Aimee and Angel, the small stringer of spittle glistened in the reflection of the party lights beaming from the DJ stand, Karl wanted to taste the juicy spit and it overtook him. Karl was a slave to his dick, his mind blanked and shut off when it had a chance to get played with.

Big Ken nodded Tod over to take a gander at his girl, arms in the air and hips rubbing against Angel, Karl eased his hands onto Aimee's hips, he inched his way closer under her cocaine hazed radar, by the time Tod caught the glimpse of his girl being closely embraced by his cohort Karl. Tod didn't care that Karl was going to try to rub up on Aimee, he had an eye on any number of younger bodies that were close by, the trailers left plenty of space to duck behind if there were any takers to his own prowess. Tod knew Big Ken had dibs on Carsey, she was an attractive younger girl but no one crossed Ken, he's put enough people in the hospital. Tod rose up from his seat on the wooden bench; he snubbed out his cigarette and began to glance back over the crowd. The music blared; the younger girls that arrived with the snobby Tara all kept near one another, their young minds were free from the heavy burdens of smarts or of concerns for the future. Darryl broke away from his Arabian buyers; they were busy

234

ignoring the girls that were with them and staring longingly into each other's eyes.

Darryl pulled a cigarette box out of his pocket as he approached the gaggle of girls with Tara, the taller blonde girl hardly turned enough to see the shorter stocky man before she huffed loud enough for him to hear, "muddy cunt" Darryl shouted, which stopped the bitch's nagging before it even began, she turned a wide eye back to the incoming guy. Tara snorted pretty loud at Darryl's interruption, Darryl flipped open the cigarette pack to offer Tara a joint, he had a whole pack of them ready to go and he was looking to contribute party favors to up the ante of the party. Tara reached forward to grab a joint, but was stopped as Darryl recalled the offered pack. Darryl raised his right eyebrow and glanced at her chest and cracked a smile. Tara put her hand across her chest and shuttered, Darryl spoke up and told the rest of the girls the offer was fair, "a joint for a good look at some tits."

The shorter sandy blonde hair girls hardly waited a moment; she reached her left hand towards the bottom of her gray shirt, and her right hand towards the pack in Darryl's hand. Darryl locked his eyes on the chest of the girl willing to take his deal, as the shirt revealed the girls pair of breasts, more eyes locked on the bare skin being exposed. A brunette girl reached her hands over and cupped the breasts as they fell from under the rising shirt. Darryl let his glassy eyes sink a bit as the strange hands covered over the breasts that were about to let his eyes have a peek. The girl swung her chest free from her friend and Darryl quickly went back to being pleased and let the girl take the joint she had earned, the brunette reached to take a hit from the joint but was quickly denied by the girl that earned it. Darryl made one last sweeping offer to trade pot for skin, the other girls lamented accepting so he strolled away, leaving the other girls to paw for the joint but also to ridicule the girl that was brazen enough to flash her fun bags.

Angel danced with Aimee, she eyed one of the black guys that arrived in the Toyota, not either of the dreadlocked thugs but the buffed man with a large smile and short faded hair, his dark complexion added a bit of mystery to him so they exchanged flirting eyes back and forth. Angel danced and swayed, the other end of her eye contact was a man named Lamarc, and he was the driver of the Toyota. Lamarc was only at the party to spend the night out, it was his two passengers that were there to make a deal with Darryl. Lamarc gave Angel large smiles, he was tall and had a dark complexion, he was dressed much nicer than the other two he arrived with, he held a job and hardly dabbled in any drugs, he didn't like the smell of pot smoke but he liked his Cognac, he had class and taste, a stark contrast to his compadres. Karl continued to grind at the back of Aimee; she hardly noticed with the cocaine throbbing through her veins, the alcohol in her brain and music in her ears, she was dull to his small stimuli. Angel grew more and more enticed as Wriggle ran through his play list, he had 80's hits mixed with club beats and some techno, most of the party attendees hooted and hollered recognizing tracks like Linda Carlisle with a Reggae beat woven in, Wriggle had talent like that.

Lil B piled in with a small posse of his own, he had a blunt hanging out of his mouth that he was passing between six or seven other little twerps, two other boys with thick gold chains and four girls to hang on them, little tarts that dressed ten years older than they were, and stank of gallons of perfume. Lil B spoke much more black than anyone in the park, including Curtiss, an actual black kid. B slung his scrambled phrases trying to impress the girls that hung on him, and gladly shared his weed with. Lil B kept his group near the sidewalk in front of Aimee's trailer; he kept an eye towards the trailer behind him hoping to get a vision of Brittini, unaware that she wasn't even home. Lil B had a tiny hard-on for the slender girl; he was always pining for her and would jump on any opportunity to jump her bones if it arose, with or without her consent.

Jonny stopped by and ensured that Brittini was having an easy time with Brodan; the music could still be heard clearly though the windows, Jonny stood idly by the party and reported the usual goings on back to his friend. On the way back to the party Jonny ran into Lil B, the thorn in Brittini's side, and Jonny was the thorn in B's side, except this time Lil B had two more friends than Jonny did. Lil B pushed the out-casted Jonny as he rounded a corner. Lil B had a payback ass kicking on his mind; Jonny was unaware of Lil B's intent until the two smaller boys had stepped closer to Jonny, giving him an uneasy feeling, fast. Jonny felt his stomach sink, he kept his eyes locked on the shorter leader, B. Jonny took the first punch from his right side, the smaller fist landed on his temple, causing Jonny to get real dizzy real fast, Jonny connected an upper cut to B before he was able to curl his arms in to begin defending himself, the kid to his left kicked a hard blow to Jonny's left leg, which caused him to drop to his knee. Jonny tried to fall forward, trying to take down any of his muggers, Jonny grasped onto the thick chain that Lil B wore around his neck, almost dragging him to the ground. The girls laughed and giggled as Jonny took kicks at random from the three boys, the girls let it go on for a few minutes before finally getting bored enough with it and want to return to dancing, they nagged at the boys that were getting even sweatier as they kicked at Jonny. Lil B succumbed to give the order that they should head back to the party and be done with the bleeding kid on the ground.

Jonny remained curled into a ball after the assault was over with, the kicks weren't even in cadence with the bass; getting his ass kicked to some DMX was not his first choice. Jonny felt most of his ribs ache, sending sharp pains through his back and into his neck, making it hard to breathe. The small fight caused enough commotion that it drew the attention of half of the crowd, the teen girls that arrived with Tara all turned towards the fight, Darryl and Curtiss headed towards the stomping and rooted for their younger pal as he and his two friends kicked at the defenseless Jonny. Darryl had crossed with Jonny a few times, there was hardly much between them except he knew that Jonny was the one to stick up for Brittini. Aimee wouldn't allow her daughter to sleep with anyone like Darryl but that was hardly of any concern for Darryl, he just wanted to get with the hot little girl. Darryl was glad to see a fight, a bumping party should always have at least one good fight, and he was satisfied.

Jonny was no stranger to bruises, he was left with plenty from his own father, plus much worse. Jonny picked himself up from the pavement, the taste of blood filled his mouth, the metallic taste was common but he also knew that swallowing enough of it would make him sick. Jonny wrapped his arms around his ribs to ease some of the pain from breathing; he headed over to Carsey's to get some help cleaning up his wounds. The commotion from the scuffle had disrupted the flow of the party, after Jonny had been laughed up from the ground and off into the distance, things quickly returned to a party. Jonny made his way over to see Brittini; she often bandaged him anyways so he trusted her to do it again. Jonny knocked on the door, Brittini often knew better than to let anyone in but Jonny was the exception. Brittini searched for what she could find to help patch him up but was lacking a large sports wrap for his ribs. Brittini left Brodan to watch Barney with Jonny as she walked quickly down to the Amaca station. The music carried out into the distance as she walked, it was getting dark and there was a lot on her mind. Brittini had been chewing on many things lately and even though Jonny could tell that she was troubled, he didn't want to intrude. Brittini loved walking, she often walked around the outer perimeter of the trailer park, it was fenced with a mound of grass and lined with trees, it wasn't enough to obscure the park itself, but she walked and looked at the pavement enough to make it all disappear.

Jonny helped Brodan crunch up his graham crackers, he also continued to wipe blood away from his lips and eyebrow while he waited for his friend to return. Brittini wasn't missing much of the party, the music was fun to dance to but she didn't have any friends from school to laugh and have a good time with, she had Jonny and Jonny was bleeding. Cars continued to pour in through the entrance, cars parked along the side as parking choked shut. People filled in as the sun let out of the sky, the light blue turned to oranges and reds and now the purple was leading in the black of night. Brittini let her flip flops flap against her feet, she kept a hurried pace to get to the Amaca station, she had ten dollars in her pocket and only one or two needs so she could get back to her friend that was bleeding and in need of her help. The parking lot at the gas station was covered in gravel, there were reflections of broken glass littered about. Brittini was worried about getting glass in her foot as gravel already stuck between her sandal and her foot, she limped into the store while shaking out the sharp rocks. Gary greeted the young girl, he was leaning forward on his forearms on the counter playing video games on the security monitor, "hell of a party huh?" he remarked.

Brittini nodded to Gary to acknowledge him out of respect, she was raised to be polite. The nearest wall had a small half rack of aspirin and Band-Aids, Brittini stood and stared at the aging inventory, she was trying to find what she was looking for and wasn't having any luck. Brittini walked over to Gary and asked if he had any sports wraps that she could purchase, Gary said that it was a pretty big order and that he might have one in the back room, if he looked. Brittini crossed her arms and sternly asked that he would look, and that it was important, Gary simply shifted his weight as he looked the petite girl up and down; "what's in it for me?" he asked. Brittini told

Gary that her business was what he was in business for; he was not amused at her naive response. Gary asked again, this time he was eyeing her up and down, as well as licking his teeth as he spoke to her, laying on the innuendo hoping that this time the girl would take a hint. Brittini stared at the man and once again expressed her urgency in her interest in the sports wrap, Gary told the girl that she would have to be pretty convincing in order to motivate him to leave his post behind the counter and then to rummage through all of the boxes of inventory in the back room for just a measly few cents in profit, hardly a venture worth his while.

Brittini was young and unaware of the clerk's intentions; she asked him what it would take in order to convince him that she desperately needed the sport wrap for a friend that was really hurt after he was beaten up. Gary told the girl that he wanted to see her firm young chest or for her to unbutton her pants and let him see if her bare ass had any tan lines. Brittini let her jaw drop; she was appalled at such a request. Gary stared at the girl's chest, she was protecting herself with crossed arms but it didn't prohibit Gary from picturing what was underneath anyways. Brittini huffed and asked "Are you freakin serious?" and with a much more stern voice, Gary raised his eyebrows to reassure the girl that he meant business. Gary tried to assure the girl that no one would have to know, nobody would judge and that it was just them in the store, he just wanted to see her "sweet supple body" and that he had longed to see it for quite some time now. Brittini tightened her crossed arms, the man behind the counter was a gross pig and she could hardly see past the spots in her eyes as her fury raged. Gary un-paused his game and resumed whatever he was playing, no longer giving any attention to the girl or her needs.

"My friend really needs the bandage, if you don't have it then whatever but if you do he needs it!" Brittini insistently told Gary, to which his response was; "no skin, no chance sugar ass, your call." "My choice?" Brittini questioned Gary's request again, she was out of her comfort zone at the sheer notion of dropping her pants and showing the man her bare ass, or even worse, lifting her shirt and exposing her chest to the obese Seinfeld looking slob. Brittini felt her eyes well up, she was concerned about Jonny and even worse that she ditched her post back at Carsey's, she was supposed to be watching Brodan rather than be cleaning up Jonny, but he stuck up for her

239

fight back tears, here she was with her pants down trying to help her friend and then the fat greasy slime ball rubs his hands and penis on her bare ass. While the tears flowed Gary continued to fondle himself, he told Brittini that her body was ever so much better than when he had his go at her mother, it was then that Brittini realized why Aimee had often persuaded Brittini against going to the gas station no matter what.

Gary headed into the backroom, leaving Brittini to fidget and fumble with her pants, the poor girls hands shook so bad that all of her attempts to rebutton her pants failed, over and over again. Gary didn't worry about the girl standing near the counter; she was much to shaken up to be of any concern for the time being, he could also use her pictures as blackmail to keep her silent. Brittini shook her hands and tried to refocus herself, she stared at the stubborn button that hadn't been cooperating and then followed into the backroom. Brittini felt her adrenaline surge through her, her pulse pumped in her ears like the bass from the speakers back at the party. Brittini turned into the small back room to find the heavy set man leaning over a small counter, breathing heavier than she was, and appearing to be doing something to himself that was foul. Brittini screeched "EWWWW," but Gary didn't stop mid-stroke, he turned to see the girl walk into the room just behind him. Gary turned to look at the young girl, he stood straight up and turned to face the girl in time to finish what he had started, Brittini had to take a large step back to avoid getting any "Gary" on her. The large man shuttered and shook as he came down from his peak, Brittini looked around the back room really fast, there was nothing more than cases of soda and beer as well as cartons of cigarettes, no sign of the sports wrap she was originally after.

Brittini began to see white with fury, Gary continued to stroke himself while staring at the smaller girl, Brittini was disgusted, appalled, and beginning to rage with fury, she stepped closer and took one last quick look around the back room, Gary reached forward and locked his free hand onto her chest and smiled, his lips parted and his crooked teeth revealed brown coffee stains. Brittini paused, time suddenly stood still for the girl, her heartbeat ceased, Gary held his hand in place on her chest, leaving her motionless for a moment. In a flash something clicked in Brittini, rage and clarity clashed. With Gary's hand on her chest Brittini rolled her shoulders to the side to charge at the larger man, she shoved both of her hands in the large mushy chest and pushed with all of her might. Gary was unstable on his feet after having finished masturbating and he began to topple backwards. Gary held onto the girls chest as he tumbled, almost taking her down with him. Brittini swatted at Gary's hand trying to keep him from ripping her shirt off before he hit the ground. Brittini began to panic as Gary thudded to the ground; she reached to her right and grabbed two cartons of cigarettes from the counter top and backed out the door.

Gary groaned from the fall as Brittini turned to leave, her eyes were flooded with tears; her vision blurred and obscured her ability to see straight. Brittini turned and bumped into the chip shelf. The metal was cold and unforgiving, her senses were numb but she still felt the blunt feeling of the rack on her shoulder, further aggravating the girl. Brittini dropped the cigarettes to the floor, she placed both of her hands on the shelf and let herself weep for a moment, her tears turned to rage again, she let her weight sink to the floor. Brittini's small bit of might pushed her feet into the tile on the floor and she began to push. Her frantic mind was dull to the noises around her, with her eyes clenched tight the tears flooded down her face. The shelf began to tilt, chips fell from the far side of the shelf and began to spill onto the floor and the rest of the shelf crashed to the shelf on the other side of the aisle. The sharp piercing noise of the metal clanging together brought Brittini's eyes open to see the disaster she caused. "Hey you bitch" Gary shouted from the floor, he tussled and inched on the floor while trying to get up right behind her, Brittini let her vision focus in and then back out to take in all of what just happened. Gary's voice made her shiver for a moment, which made her realize the shit that just happened, and give her the notion that it was time to run.

Brittini began walking towards the door with a brisk pace, from back over her right shoulder Gary could be heard "You bitch, why couldn't you get naked like your mother," Brittini heard her mother mentioned and turned to see Gary struggling through the doorway with his wrinkled penis still hanging out of his zipper and his forehead glistening from sweat. Brittini waved the two cartons of cigarettes in the air as a shove off gesture before she hurried through the door and out into the poorly paved parking lot. Gary stood and looked over the wrecked shelf and expired produce all over the floor. Gary put his hands up on his head trying to contemplate what had happened, there was such a mess and Gary felt he had really gotten himself into a whole lot of trouble this time. Brittini hurried through the parking lot and back towards Carsey's home.

Tara and her friends continued to hassle the girl that willingly exposed herself, they were secretly jealous of her brazen self-confidence but they masked their insecurities with mean tainted razzing and shallow names like "slut and penny-pony." The girls danced to the music and continued to drink to enjoy their night, the temperatures were still very warm and they sweat out just as quickly as they could drink, all the while shaking their shirts out for a slight breeze on their bodies. Darryl kept an eye on the hot young bodies, Tara had a firm shape and her friends were all comparable as well. Darryl had hopes for a chance at any of the girls from the group, healthy young bodies in scant clothing and plenty of skin showing was just his type, most men's' types. Angel and Aimee carried on, Aimee knew Tara was a snotty little prissy bitch; she grew up in the trailer park but fought all that she could to keep up her front that she was much higher end than her family income would support. Tara often shook her ass in tight pants and lightly jogged in a sports bra and short shorts, she dated many jocks in school to get the chances to be driven around in cars that costs more than she could make in two years.

Curtiss spoke with his boys as they stood around and eyed all of the arriving visitors and hot little bodies, they discussed what sorts of shipments that Curtiss would be helping to run and what sorts of money they were going to be making. Curtiss and Darryl had a small corner on some pills and pot, and of course making meth, but that was a secret until further down the road. Wriggle watched over the girls out in front of him, the bodies jiggled squirmed against one another and his beats kept them dancing and having a great time. Angel continued to make curly smiles towards Lamarc, he was well dressed and unlike many of the other men nearby, he had good posture. Carsey danced lightly next to Big Ken, he was reluctant to join in but he liked having the younger girl grinding on his leg nonetheless, his free hand caressing over her body. Big Ken kept a cold beer in his hand, he and Tod struggled to keep themselves cool with drinks, the kiddie pools were filled with drinks and ice but the ice was melting quickly and the drinks sweating on the outside.

Dez'rae and Tammi walked around the party, they knew Tara but also knew that the uppity little bitch was too busy holding her nose in

243

the air and looking down on everyone else in the trailer park to bother with them. The bases of Tara's falsely whitened teeth were still stained and rotten, just like her personality. Tara kept up her fake tan, and with her bare back and short shorts there weren't any tan lines that could be seen, supporting the fake baked bitch in her struggle to hide away her trailer park upbringing. Dez'rae was aware that her mom struggled; she could tell that it wasn't easy but she appreciated what she had, she knew Tammi was insecure about her being overweight and homely but she tried to be her friend, she knew that she wanted to work hard in school and try to improve her life once she was older. Tammi liked the attention that she got from the boys; she knew that sex would always get any boy to look in her direction, even if they were thinking about Dez'rae. Tammi didn't think that she would ever amount to much; she dressed as sexy as she could and even when her friend was trying to suggest maybe dressing more conservatively and hide her thick love handles, she still heaved herself into her clothes.

Lil B walked around with his friends, he kept a lit cigarette in mouth as he walked around with the two little girls that seemed to hang on his words as well as the two other boys that helped him to jump Jonny. A small girl named Lizzy looked starry eyed at Lil B, she ran her fingers up and down his arms and wanted to be his girlfriend, he thought of himself as a player and didn't want to be tied down with one girl when he could have several. Lil B would still take every advantage of Brittini he could get, even a pair of short shorts that he could slid his hand into. Lizzy wanted to be the girl whom had Lil B first, she hadn't even bled yet but she was talking about how much she was in love with the little wannabe kid and she'd do anything to make him hers. Lil B sat at a picnic table in front of Aimee's trailer, an ideal location if Brittini came around, and a place where he can let Lizzy rub his shoulders and have his two friends near him to show that he had his own crew, not just belonged to Darryl's.

Darryl walked the sidewalk, there were plenty of people swaying and standing around drinking, he walked to look around, he walked to clear his mind, and he walked look for new potential buyers, and especially for new ass. Darryl hadn't seen Brittini in a while, she darted off to the next street earlier in the afternoon and he was hoping to find her for a good time later. Between Dez'rae and Brittini, Darryl had been looking for any chance he could get to hook up with either of the young girls, and it was getting to be a real hassle that neither of them were willing to drop their panties for him. Darryl passed Dez'rae, she was looking extremely sexy in yoga pants and a silver club top, she had neon makeup that caught the last bit of light and seemed to glow on its' own. Dez'rae was heading to catch back up with Tammi when she was stopped by Darryl; he was looking really well dressed and as usual, he was more than willing to help her have a better night. Darryl offered the girl her choice of any pill she might want; he removed a breath mint tin and flipped the lid open for her to choose what might help her to have a better party.

Dez'rae snagged a small pill that Darryl insisted was a Xanax, not enough to make her lose control but enough to quell her nerves and give her the courage to go and flirt with the sexy spinning dj she couldn't take her eyes off of. Darryl flirted and complemented her body, her cleavage was supple and her ass barely jiggled in her pants as she walked. Darryl wasn't shy to show that he was looking and he felt he was owed for the cost of the pill. Darryl leaned in to kiss the girl on her lips, she turned her head a little to let him kiss her on the cheek while she kept her eyes locked on the dj as he worked. Darryl took a hearty whiff of the girls perfume and took the opportunity to taste, he licked her from her collar bone and up behind her ear, the wet kiss left her with a shiver and feel of disgust. Darryl offered the girl a swig of his beer to wash down her fun pill; she accepted and used the condensation of the can to dissolve the saliva on her neck before she swallowed down the small pill. Darryl leaned in a little closer for last hug before she headed back towards the party; Darryl let himself place a firm hand on the ass as it walked away, he held on firmly for the moment.

Brittini finished jogging back to Carsey's, it was difficult to keep her chest in her stretched out shirt, her eyes continued to leak down her face. Brittini hurried in through the front door where Jonny was still sitting on the couch, arms wrapped around himself over his sore ribs. The first sight of Brittini worried Jonny, her shirt was slightly ripped down the front and her clothing hardly covering what it did when she left. Jonny raised his eyebrows at the sight of the cigarettes, he didn't smoke consistently and she didn't smoke at all, her face was red and puffy from crying. Jonny leaned forward with concern, he was ready to head out and get back to fighting with Lil B, whom he was sure had manhandled his friend. Brittini was trying to calm herself down enough to tell Jonny what had happened. Jonny was slow to stand up to try and comfort his friend, her hands were shaking as Jonny reached to take the cartons from her. Brittini was frantic and crying, Jonny packed and opened a pack of smokes, and pulled two of them out to light.

Brittini snatched a lit cigarette from Jonny's mouth and took a deep inhale for herself; she hacked and coughed a bit but began to calm down as Jonny hugged her as best as he could. Brittini looked around for Brodan but Jonny reassured her that he put him down for the night and she was free to talk. They decided to step out on the front porch to smoke and talk to avoid waking up the sleeping little guy. Jonny helped her to put her shirt back on right and tried to help put her at ease as he rubbed her back and tried to let her talk. Jonny grew furious, the night already went to shit after Lil B and his two boyfriends jumped him, his body hurt and poor Brittini was put in a situation Jonny was trying to keep her from, he felt at fault. Jonny and Brittini continued to smoke on the porch, the air was still warm but the breeze helped to relieve some of the discomfort, Darryl stepped up from out of nowhere and greeted the pair sitting on the stoop, he was cheerful to see Brittini but dropped the tone in his voice when he said Jonny's name.

Darryl could tell that Brittini was having a bad night, her shirt was stretched enough to offer an extended view down her shirt, Darryl stood close and kept this eyes locked on her sternum, hoping that her movements would reveal more soft skin. Jonny suggested to Darryl that he move on, he suggested to Darryl that Lil B was a bastard and deserved an ass beating when he got the chance. Darryl apologized that his little cohort did what he did and offered to talk to him, Jonny was clearly agitated and Darryl was receptive to the attitude. To help make peace Darryl pulled out his small metal container, her offered an open hand with two small white pills, he suggested they each take one and explained how much it would take the sting out of their night. Jonny reached out and took the pills, careful to keep his free hand wrapped around his sides, he winced as he moved. Jonny put one pill in Brittini's mouth and one in his own, Darryl offered over his open beer for the younger teens to use to swallow the drugs. Brittini was still shaking, her hands jittered as she raised Darryl's beer to her mouth, it was a hard swallow but it helped to rinse the cigarette film from her throat. Darryl angled all that he could to try and line up the side lights from the living room and her chest but his attempts were unsuccessful so he decided to move along back to the party.

Brittini wasn't sure of what she took but Jonny suggested it, he placed his arm back around her shoulders trying to comfort her as she went back to crying. Jonny felt terrible for Brittini, it was his fault that she was victimized; she was just trying to help him out by getting bandages for him. The young couple headed inside once Brittini was calmed down enough to be able to control the volume of her voice. Jonny thought he was being funny to keep raising a finger and poking Brittini in her butt cheek as they walked, she swatted at him a few times before she finally broke a smile at his escapades, it also caused her to turn with the intent slap him, she stopped herself just as she caught a glimpse of his already beaten face.

Darryl rounded the corner in front of Monte's place, almost around the corner where Big Ken lived when he thought he caught a sight of skin. Darryl quickly discarded his cigarette and began to creep, he could see a tall shirtless guy and what appeared was a shirtless girl underneath, no man passes up an opportunity to see some titties. Darryl crept in closer and closer to see whoever the girl might be, if it was one of the skanks that Tara brought then a firm pair of teen breasts were more than enough to persuade Darryl to creep down and go on stealth mode to get in nice and close. The guy on top was just at the edge of the shadow, the muscles on his back flexed and as he made out with the girl underneath, they were wild in their passion, the guy on top was chaotic with his hands, Darryl was getting turned on watching the pair go wild with each other, it was better than porn, real life humping was often what Darryl got out of bed for, but hardly in.

Darryl watched on as what looked like Farkam in a passionate session with a girl, maybe even one of the girls he brought with him, it didn't matter, any minute there were going to be boobs! Farkam rolled over the top of his lady friend, they were growing more passionate with each other and Darryl was as close as he could possibly be without getting any slobber on his Detroit made watch. Farkam turned and began revealing some of the skin underneath him, his build and height confirmed that it was him, but the face was hidden in the shadow. Darryl Looked to his left across the street to make sure he wasn't going to be busted peeping, but then again if you're going to get freaky in public, then you are willing to let the onlookers get their fill.

Farkam rolled off of to his right, exposing Ashm underneath, Darryl jumped to his feet with overwhelming surprise, "Holy Shit Balls" Darryl shouted as loud as possible, the two men turned to locate the source of the noise. Darryl ran hooting and hollering to find Tod and Big Ken, the two Arab men had begun to put their shirts back on as they tried to follow the shorter guy running from them. Darryl turned the corner back into the party lights to almost blow over the two girls that had come with Farkam and Ashm, almost knocking one of them to the ground. The younger boy that came with the others, tried to put his hand out on Darryl's chest to stop him, Darryl slung his left hand around and slapped the boy to get him out of his way. The girl in the black hijab introduced herself as Nahiel and told Darryl that it wasn't all that strange, it was a cultural thing and that most men didn't like girls other than for reproducing, the girls were all supposed to stay pure so the boys practiced "Hisham" which meant two boys settling each other's' desires together. Darryl sided the talking girl and sought out Tod to share his new found news. Tod was standing near a picnic table with Big Ken, Darryl was struggling to keep his pants up as he hustled, he was short on breath as he spat out his findings, Tod was overly curious to hear all about it.

As Darryl spilled his guts like a pathetic high school girl, Tod was smiling as he rose to his feet, he lit a cigarette and began heading towards the guys he hadn't liked since they arrived at the party. Carsey turned her head to listen to what Darryl was hollering to Ken and Tod about. Carsey was just as interested as they were. Carsey hung onto Kens arm as he headed toward the far side of Don's trailer, where Tod was charging with rage. Darryl put his two fingers under his tongue and let out an ear piercing whistle in the direction of his little protege, who was seated between the legs of Lizzy on a picnic table in front of Aimee's place, with the two other preteen boys that helped him to jump Jonny. Lil B nudged his crew to hop up and follow him to back up Darryl; Lil B's main drug supplier and idol. Lil B rushed to catch up with Darryl, as they walked together with a scurry in their steps, Darryl shouted to B as they jogged to back off the Jonny kid, just to make peace for the time being. Darryl and his prepubescent posse caught up in time to see Ashm and Tod exchanging punches and grappling. Big Ken was making light work of Farkam and his younger whatever he was.

The girl in the white head wrap tried to size up with Carsey, who was squaring up with her. The girl told Carsey they just wanted to get their friends and leave, Carsey delivered one square punch to her nose, sending her stumbling backwards to the ground. The girl named Nahiel stood up to Carsey, she put her hands up palms forward and pleaded; "I'm a black belt, please don't do this" Carsey tried to send another solid fist towards the shorter girl. Nahiel hunkered her weight down in a crouch and used a side stance to deflect one fist and to try and catch the enraged Carsey to ease her to the ground. Carsey couldn't get her feet underneath her as she fell, Nahiel grabbed the back of her shirt trying to keep her from falling to hard, a sign of her desire to remain peaceful, she ended up with a handful of Carsey's shirt and not much else. Nahiel continued to explain that boys satisfying other boys was just called "Hisham" and that it wasn't a big deal, she asked Carsey to listen to her and to help her to just separate the brawling boys.

Nahiel shouted to "Ja-lal," the smaller boy that came with them, he was picking himself up from the ground after Big Ken had bitch slapped him, she shouted something in their foreign llama tongue, he then put his palms outward to express his interest in not getting hit again, his face swollen and red. Carsey kept to her word and eased up to Big Ken, her standing in a bra caught his attention rather quickly, she asked him to just let them go so they could get out of the neighborhood. Lil B's boys had taken a few measly hits and retreated, Lil B was a little more persistent in trying to help Tod and Darryl against the much more built Ashm, he was trying to prove how tough he was for Lizzy and any of the other girls that were watching.

Tod and Ashm remained tussling on the ground, Tod was winded and exhausted but he wasn't going to lose a fight to some towel headed terrorist fag that was sucking face and who knows what else with his fag terrorist sex toy. Tod took to head butting the muscly Arab on the ground below him, he had learned plenty in jail as a young man and you take any advantage to win a fight as it takes. Ashm went limp after the third head but, his legs went straight and his arms that were trying to choke Tod, fell flat to the ground. Tod was full of hatred, his life of poor choices flooded into him and came out as white hot fury, he didn't even notice Carsey standing in short shorts and bra to his right.

Tod wrestled himself free from the entangled mess that was Ashm; he stood up tall and looked at the pile of blood he caused. Tod stood up and ran his forearm across his nose to keep some of the blood flowing from it off of his clothes. Tod dropped his hands down to his zipper and began to unzip his fly. The crowd around him was split, some chanted "fight" while the rest just milled around to watch the brawl. Tod pulled himself out of his pants and offered; "let me wash some of the sand out of your mouth" he told the unconscious kid, as his stream of urine began to flow. The two girls that came with Farkam turned away, "aww shit man" was shouted from him as Tod made sure he pissed plenty onto the face of the guy that rubbed him the wrong way from the get-go. Tod looked around at the crowd with a smile on his bruised face, he took a few hits but he still came out on top, he was feeling real alpha male about everything.

Darryl had his eyes locked on Carsey's tits, during the half way mark of the fight Darryl realized that she was standing in a skimpy bra and his eyes were trained on them as she stood and watched the remainder of the fight. The three younger Arabs tried to wake up their larger friend, it took some work and as they all sat around and discussed the shame that being pissed on had brought Ashm. Once their friend had awoken after his face had been smashed in, it took a few moments of recovery before they moved along. Tara and her girls hadn't gotten too closely to the fight, the girls were visiting one of the kiddie pools filled with beer and fruity drinks, helping themselves to

251

further intoxication. The fight circle began to disperse and Wriggle changed the music after fight that he could see from his platform, his choice was a metal mix with a rage undertone to propagate the fighting, now he returned back to booty bouncing club beats. The girls returned to the ass shaking as he played "Bombs over Baghdad," a club favorite for the girls. Tara and her friends all danced together, there weren't enough boys of their caliber or interest, but they played well together, grabbing one another's asses or chests, sometimes even trying to assist each other in flashing random strangers by sneaking up behind each other and pulling their tops down or to the side, their drunken stupor was furthering childish behavior.

Darryl hung close to Tara and her friends, the random breasts were a large perk and he was willing to continue to keep supplying assorted narcotics to make sure everyone was having a good time, his generosity was out of place. Tammi broke away from Dez'rae and made her way over to the kiddie pool of beers closest to Darryl, she found herself conversing with him on purpose. Tammi was too close to reality for her own comfort, she knew Darryl was always holding drugs and she wanted her share also. Tammi tried to rub on Darryl's leg, she thought maybe a little physical contact would get him to proffer up a few pills like he did to Dez'rae, but he knew she was always willing to offer up her gash for drugs, or attention for that matter. Darryl winked and smiled at the girl, he tapped the metal container in his pocket with a lighter as he began to light his smoke. Tammi agreed to drop her panties for a few pills; and to the shadows they headed. Tammi grabbed two pills from the metal box Darryl flipped open for her, she took a blue and a white pill and chugged an almost full beer to wash them down. Darryl groped and grabbed up on Tammi as they neared a dark corner behind Aimee's home. Tammi worked her shorts down, it was a bit of a struggle to remove them over her thick sweaty thighs, and Darryl was quick to help her remove her shirt.

Between the tipsy Darryl and Tammi quickly losing grasp on reality; the couple worked their way to the ground. Darryl eased himself out from his clothes and with Tammi's help, he was in her and beginning to work. Darryl let Tammi mumble and blurb her words together as the drugs kicked in, Darryl suckled at her chest and thrusted in between her legs, the music gave him some rhythm to work with but his stamina wasn't of note. Aimee headed back into the party to dance with Angel, she was still making "hump me" eyes with Lamarc and keeping her mood up with a few sniffs of her nose candy. Tod headed towards his home to wash his face off, the kiddie pool in his front yard was a nice cold place to rinse the blood off his face, and grab a cold beer. Tod neared the pool and knelt down to get a handful of icy water to wash his face off. As the water splashed back into the pool, the water tainted red with his blood and after a hearty nose clearing, a clot shot out of his left nostril, the water rippled and as it went silent in the reflections of the lights, then Tod heard something.

Tod decided to peer around the corner, sure enough there was Darryl's pale white ass thrusting up and down in the air, it was hard to tell who was buck naked and lying underneath of him was but it was worth checking out. Tod ducked back around the front of his home and cut through to the back, he eased the back door open carefully; he didn't want to alert Darryl or his little tart that he was two feet away watching. Tod stepped lightly, his heart still beat like a blacksmiths hammer, after the fight he was already feeling his body wearing out, but he wasn't worn out in his groin. Darryl humped his way through Rihanna but not much longer, by the time he was done Tammi was incoherent, she hardly mumbled and a mix of Darryl's spit and hers gargled in her throat. Darryl seized and jerked as he shot his first round off and lay on top of her for a few minutes, still slowly moving in and out while still groping at her before finally climbing off.

Tod made the recognition of Tammi's face, she was a young teen girl and had caught his eye once in a while, a loose girl will always catch a man's eye, and Tammi flaunted enough of her ass to catch everyman's eyes, including Tods'. Tod watched Darryl pull his pants up and turn back towards the party. Once Darryl turned the corner and was out of site, Tod was climbing up and over the chain-link fence while Tammi was still rolling her head but unable to verbalize even the simplest words. Tammi laid on the ground with her shirt up around her neck, her bra shoved up under her shirt and her chest giving in to gravity to either side of her. With her shorts and panties tangled around her left leg, she was hardly conscious but that didn't bother Tod, he whispered her name to see if she was aware of it enough to fend him off. Her body wasn't ideal nor even close to in shape but she was already wet and ready to receive him.

Tod rubbed his hands up her thighs; sure enough she was wet, she even glistened a little in the shadows. Tod helped himself into

Tammi, her body laid still enough for Tod to enjoy himself, Tammi was nowhere near tight or pure, she had been plowed more than a cornfields it was just his turn. Tammi's body jiggled as Tod heaved away at her, she was less than half his age and still in high school, she wasn't perfect but it was new pussy. With some light rolling and turning Tod finished up, as he was ready to climax he pulled out and climbed up to her mouth to finish off with. Tammi choked and gargled a little as she swallowed down Tod's load. The music continued to blast in the distance and from what it was looking like was that Karl, Billy, and Tuner were beginning to shoot off fireworks overhead, in the colors exploding in the air lit up Tammi's body as she lay there on the ground, her eyes glazed and struggling to remain open for the view.

The party continued to wind down, the fireworks blew up overhead and rained shards of paper and burned bits down, the clinking could he heard pelting the roofs and vinyl siding all around the party. Aimee held near Tod to watch the light show above, no idea that he had ducked into Tammi for a brief hump, Big Ken stood with Carsey, she was always sentimental about this holiday, her late husband and brother both gave their lives for their country, she missed them both with all of her heart and her eyes welled up as she stared through the galaxies above. Angel was leading Lamarc back to her place; she was ready to move on from Joey, she was on enough cocaine to be sure she was making a bad decision she was going to enjoy. As the fireworks began to kick off Brittini and Jonny were laying with each other on Carsey's couch, the Ecstasy Darryl gave them was kicking in, neither youngster had ever felt so relaxed in their lives, the explosions overhead hardly phased them.

Jonny spent his entire life on edge, his anxiety was the only thing that was constant, the drugs suddenly gave him a reason to smile, he often enjoyed being friends with Brittini and together they had laughed enough to keep themselves sane. Together they dealt with abusive parents, drug addled neighbors, bullies at school and the rigors of life, they clung together through it all. Brittini began to cry, she was frightened that she was so relaxed, she hated being at home and there was so much she had to tell her mother, so much that she trusted Jonny with but there was still something else that she was struggling with. Jonny kissed Brittini on the forehead, she had such a long day and he wished he could take it all from her, he didn't have anything in his life but her, he didn't have anything to give but his friendship and it was all for her. Brittini raised her chin; her lips lingered for a moment and then met Jonny's.

Jonny was still sore from his beating but he hugged her tightly, Brittini kissed Jonny on his neck slowly, he clenched his eyes and rolled his head. Brittini rolled off of the couch and began to unbutton her capris, she was shaky and nervous but she was ready to be with him, she kept her eyes locked on Jonny as she slid her pants down, next her shirt came off and hit the floor. Brittini straddled Jonny, she unfastened his shorts and pulled them down under her, he kept his eyes closed and she felt for his bulge a bit. Brittini led Jonny's hands to her chest as she eased her panties to one side to be able to rub him on her. Brittini liked the feeling of him on her, she moved her hips back and forth. Brittini and Jonny had watched some porn once together to see what it was all about, they giggled a little watching the people on the screen do what they were doing, absurd groans and noises and the whole show, she was trying to emulate some of what she had seen, she tried to focus on what she was doing, even though she felt uncoordinated and unsure.

The crowds thinned, the hours grew late and more and more bodies passed out along the roadsides. Some of the spoiled rich kids that couldn't handle their booze could be heard puking over on the outsides off of the party. Big Ken was tired and stumbling drunk, Carsey struggled to keep him on his feet as they made their way towards his home. Big Ken kept one hand on Carsey's butt and the other pulling at her bra, it was hard for her to swat his hands to keep him from ripping her bra off. It was all the covering she had left after the scuffle she had been in earlier and Ken kept pulling it down. Carsey was uncomfortable in her own skin, it came with being a girl, every girl everywhere was a little insecure and she tried to shy away with her arms crossed or cuddling up beside Big Ken. Carsey caught a lot of eyes on her chest, her stomach wasn't tight or as firm as it was when she was a young teen like Tara or her friends, it had been a long few years, she felt like her body wasn't the biggest concern, it was her mind she was mostly afraid of. Carsey was haunted by her own brain, she had urges to flee, urges to take back her young twenties, to leave and travel to see the world, acquire stories of lavish trips, or even to spend secluded time alone and without any form of responsibilities,

255

but she kept reminding herself that what Brodan needed was so much more important, no matter what.

Big Ken continued to flip Carsey's bra cups down, letting alternating breasts out into the night air; she found his behavior mildly irritating as he was drunk but his inner childish actions of him playing with her tits was slightly comical. Carsey liked the attention, she wished she could find a good man like the one she had, except she still missed the one she had, she wasn't sure if she could ever let go, just take small moments to stop remembering. Carsey had to struggle to help Big Ken up the stairs, his weight and size made it hard to help him up, his large arms weighed her down, he was more than twice her size and the only thing she really had to hold onto, was his waist band. Ken continued to mumble what he wanted to do to her once they got back to his place, he spoke about using her lady parts like a moth guard, he thought he was still twenty and had the ability to fire off more than one round in a few hours, he wanted her to slather all over him and to go at her once again. Big Ken seemed stable enough to stand on his own as Carsey dug into his pockets for his keys to unlock his door, as she turned towards the door and began to work the key into the lock; Big Ken began to fall backwards and out of her reach.

A large thud alerted Carsey that Ken had taken a step backwards and tried to fall to a seated position on the weight bench on his porch, the crash startled Carsey and she nearly snapped the key off in the handle. Ken slid onto and quickly off of the bench and landed solidly onto the deck, once Carsey's pulse hit its' top limit she spun wildly around to make sure that he was still OK, he jawed on about the pristine view of her ass and that she should drop her shorts and just back up onto his face. Carsey laughed off his feeble attempts to woo her; suddenly another loud bang rang out, causing Carsey to jump again. The loud thud was the barbell loaded with weights that Big Ken occasionally lifted had fallen to the ground, near breaking the boards underneath. "That was my dick hitting the ground" Ken informed Carsey about what the noise was. Carsey scoffed about the idea and heaved the gorilla sized man up off the ground, his weight was cemented to the ground and Carsey couldn't get enough leverage to haul him up. Big Ken fondled at Carsey's hanging chest as she leaned over him trying to lift, he wasn't making any effort but being poked and pinched a few times finally encouraged the large man to crawl into his home.

Carsey jokingly straddled Ken as he crawled, she hooted a little acting like a cowgirl, delivering a slap to his backside as he crawled. Ken mumbled about wanting intimate parts of her rubbed on various parts of him, the weirdest she thought was her snatch on his head, he wanted to rub his balding head between her legs, he wondered if it would restore his thicker hair from his youth, the hair that mostly fell out during his incarceration. Carsey found no joy in her life, it was pleasant to have Ken dote on her a little but she really just needed the money to make ends meet for herself and her son, her medicated haze blocked out all other types of pleasure. Ken swayed side to side as he crawled, his bumping into the door frame jarred into his sides as he passed. Carsey tried to find the smallest sparks of happiness to hold onto, most days she spent living were merely existing, waiting for her son to mature and become independent so she was no longer responsible for keeping it all together.

Big Ken crashed past his screen door and plowed his way into the living room. Carsey tried to encourage him to his bedroom but he was adamant that he was lying out on the ground, telling Carsey to squat on down on top of him, he was certain he wanted a romp again. Carsey stared down at Ken as he smiled, smirked, and said rather filthy things to her from the floor. Carsey questioned if he could even get it up for another go round, he wriggled back and forth like a walrus on an ice berg as he fought to heave his pants down below his man compartment. Carsey couldn't help but laugh, the sight of his rotund torso swayed back and forth, it almost tilted past its' balance point and near tipping him over, he grunted and strained to move on the floor. Ken yanked and tugged at himself trying to bring life back to himself, Carsey tried to explain to him that things were looking more like a hold up than a stick up, they'd have to play bank robber another time. Big Ken argued that he just need a minute to get the blood flowing again, he suggested that Carsey remove her top and let him play with her tits, Carsey laughed off his proposal once again. Ken tried to convince to perform a little CPR on his man hood, Carsey lifted her foot up to his wrinkly bean bag, she twitched her toes in his groin, he couldn't see over his belly but from what he could barely tell, she was going down on him.

Dez'rae had noticed that Tammi hadn't rejoined the party for quite some time, she was more focused on DJ Wriggle and his magic fingers anyways, she watched him scratch a few records to add club beats to songs that not many would think about turning to hip hop, and she was in awe. Wriggle was a good looking older boy, he had himself a private school education and good breeding, and he was extremely cute. Dez'rae was letting her practice of sound judgments give way to the heightened effects of the Xanax she took; she was also no longer shy about making eye contact with the cute boy. Wriggle knew how hot Dez'rae was, there were plenty of rumors about how fine her body really was but she was often conservative enough not to wear shape revealing layers, but tonight she was in tight pants and a skimpy top, her cleavage glistening with sweat in the party lights as she looked up to him in the bed of his truck.

Towards the end of the party Dez'rae worked her way into the bed of the truck with Wriggle, he was enveloped around her and using her hands to spin records, they were flirting heavily and exchanging turns grinding on each other, she liked the guy and he was rock hard for her. With a curtain of lights between them, Wriggle slid a less busy left hand down the front of Dez'rae's pants for the enjoyment of both of them, she was often reserved but the Xanax relaxed her and despite the public setting, it was an intimate delight to both of them. With a hand down her pants and his crotch grinding against the girl with the dancers body, Wriggle was enjoying the party immensely, it was often very worth his while to haul his gear and work late into the night while everyone else partied hard. With his headset microphone he could easily direct wet t-shirt contests, he'd take bribes of girls flashing themselves, he had a higher vantage point to see every fight or people having sex, this was the job he loved, and now he had an attractive girl grinding up on him and hanging on his every move, while he was finger deep inside of her.

Aimee and Tod decided to retire for the night, once they watched Carsey wrangle Big Ken in and through his door, Aimee knew it wasn't long before Carsey made it back to her home and released Brittini back to hers. Tod and Aimee finished a few more drinks; Aimee was feeling particularly frisky after a few rails of coke and plenty of dancing while watching plenty of sleek buffed men dancing with their women. Aimee was removed enough from reality to neglect the smell of another girl on Tod, she wanted him up and ready for fooling around and that was all she could focus on, especially before Brittini got home and she had to be quiet. Tod was tipsy and sparking another joint, he did his best and with Aimee's help, he was able enough to let her climb on top and do what she wanted to with him. Aimee straddled over onto Tod, she slid a hand underneath for her benefit and let her free hand roam her chest, Tod tried not to lose the hot ember off the end of his weed.

Curtiss had left with the two brothers with cornrows, Lamarc on the other hand, was dragged by the hand by Angel back to her place, she was certain she was ready to get over Joey, by getting under him. Angel was tired of her life, tired of struggling each and every day, she was exhausted from her routine. Caffeine and Fentanyl to start her day, and enough of the two to mask her pain, cocaine to kick in when the caffeine wore off and any other assorted narcotics like pot or Ambien to finish out each night. Angel suffered hiccups from the stress and Fentanyl, it was exhausting and taking more and more work to keep going each day, there was only so much that someone could do to continue to hide from what was really going on, Angel was nearing that point of failure.

Darryl climbed off of Tammi and left her sprawled out naked on the grass between trailers, where Tod found her and then carried on with what he had been wanting to do to her for quite some time. Darryl was still looking to party after he spent his short time in Tammi, the girl spread her leg plenty and it often didn't matter who it was. On his way out from Tammi Darryl passed Karl, the man that lusted after Aimee, Karl wasn't satisfied enough with the blow job he got from Aimee at the encouragement from Tod. Karl stared at Aimee and Brittini and wasn't discrete when he adjusted his crotch when they were around, he was willing to wait for Brittini in a dark shadow in order to get his chance at the girl, but he also wanted more consensual time with Aimee, just the two of them. Darryl apologized to Karl when they bumped into each other, they only interacted once in a while when he needed to buy pot or meth from Darryl, and Karl was one of Tod's boys so there was minimal interaction on purpose. Darryl shared his intel about some pussy; Karl of course was all ears.

It wasn't long after Tod taking his turn with the barely conscious Tammi when Karl texted Billy and Tuner about his discovery, he snuck around the corner as Tod was kneeling over her face and finishing his business. Karl didn't mind waiting his turn, this girl was young and ripe and conveniently pre-moistened and already naked for him, most of his work was done. Tod was done and Karl stepped up to begin to warm the girl up, he thought of himself as a bit more of a romantic, he laid down next to the girl and caressed her body, his fingers running up and down her ripples, the contours of her bodies left plenty of room for him to let his fingers wander. Tammi slurred as she tried to piece together whole words, with Karl working his hand between her thighs she writhed her pelvis awaiting him. Karl was insistent that the young girl tell him what she wanted, it was his idea of consent and he also wanted to hear the girl ask him to get into her, she was lonely and with a body full of drugs, she was that much more lonely. Karl let the girl easily convince him that she wanted him, her thighs were soaked and ready for him and he wasn't going to be shy with her.

Karl spent quality time with Tammi, he turned her and rolled her around in the grass, he even treaded where he though no man had, there wasn't much struggle for Karl to make his way in between her ass cheeks, Tammi continued to moan as she shook underneath of Karl, her body hardly struggled, all of her muscles were like jelly and Karl had no problems coercing her body to contort to his likings, leg propped up or shoulders turned so he could grab at her chest as he thrusted away. Tuner left Billy to finish firing off the mortars so he could hurry over and get his turn with Tammi. Tuner wanted Brittini much more than Karl did, he was terrible at gawking at her ass muscles flexing when she walked, he tried every angle to peer down her shirt and he awaited the day when Aimee let her guard down and he could sneak into Brittini's room and lick her panties. Tuner thought about Brittini when Aimee was going down on him, Tod stood by and enforced Aimee to perform on each of his men, he laughed at how funny it was when he held her head down, her eyeliner ran as she choked and gagged.

Tuner took his time with Tammi, the finale was going on over head as he climbed into the girl. There was no clue that he was just the latest in a string of suitors but ass was ass, and she was a young girl, much to his liking. Tuner followed suit and had his way with Tammi, he performed each depraved notion he could have thought of and the unconscious girl didn't complain or object. Billy caught up with Tuner and Tammi and saddled up for his turn, his actions weren't as vile as Tuners' but the girl remained barely conscious as he made

260

use of her warm body. Carsey wandered up the middle street after she left Big Ken to breathe heavily on his floor, slipping away to sleep. Carsey felt the breeze on her skin, she was in shorts and a bra, she wasn't sure where the handfuls of her shirt ended up, she considered running back home to get another shirt but she didn't want to miss any of the party, or go back home so soon, even if only for a moment. After a few moments of feeling insecure standing in a bra, she began to enjoy the added attention and took the notion that it was because she was being lusted after. The streets were mostly quiet; Wriggle turned off the music and wasn't standing in the bed of his truck any more. During the night it wasn't much to see Wriggle piss off the side of his truck; he didn't leave his equipment out of sight for anything so he was probably close, perhaps loading his gear. The streetlights were giving off a dull orange glow and the shadows engulfed most of the homes that lined the littered streets. Aimee's trailer could be seen rocking; her weight riding on top of Tod was causing the home to rock a little.

Passing the back of Wriggles' truck Carsey could see the dj standing near the passenger side of his truck, his pants down around his ankles. There was a darker body bent over the passenger seat of his truck, skimpy panties could be seen hanging about knee height and she was being mounted by the dj. Sure enough Wriggle had gotten the much lusted after Dez'rae loaded up enough to be willing to let him hump her, he wasn't hesitant to pull her panties down and slide into her, he had been toying with her up on his platform ensuring she was plenty wet for him. Wriggle made her feel like the entire crowd was worshiping her, his hands roamed her body for her excitement for over an hour and with the Xanax in her body, it was like nirvana running through her veins. Carsey watched for a moment as Wriggle pumped and thrusted into the backside of Dez'rae, the girl sounded like she was enjoying the dj after the party and his grunts and groans proved that he was also.

The air was brisk long after the sun set and the temperature of the pavement was beginning to cool, Carsey was sticky from sweating and the cool night air felt good under her armpits as she walked. Brittini ran charging out of Carsey's place, she was only wearing a bra and her underwear as she ran full speed away. Brittini ignored the sharp stones from the cracked asphalt on her bare feet, the distance back to her home and the safety of her mother's arms was real close,

and she was barreling towards it. Carsey could hear the slamming
door from several doors down, it wasn't easy to pinpoint where the
noise came from but it echoed through the trailers. Carsey didn't
notice Tammi sprawled out in the grass next to Aimee's trailer but
two more doors down Lil B was rolling around with his little bright
eyed girl Lizzy, she was younger than he was and even more naive,
she just knew that she wanted to be with the kid that could get her
weed and her friends looked to her to be the experienced girl.

Tara and the two remaining friends that kept by her side left her
bedroom to step out back for a cigarette, they giggled and laughed
from their alcohol as they sat on the back steps, they thought about
hopping the fence to sit on the swings of the play set except the rusty
chains left marks on your clothes from rubbing against you. Melissa
was a shorter brunette that came with Tara to the party, she hid away
when Darryl offered them a trade of skin for smoke but with enough
drinks she was popping up behind Tara and the other girls and was
prying their shirts open to flash their boobs to the cheering crowds.
Melissa was still AWOL, she had decided she was going to take
Darryl up on his offer, and she found him as the music began to wear
down. Melissa often grew tired of Tara, the girl was tall and tan but
her tits sagged and her bleached white teeth were still brown near the
roots, she didn't know how to chew with her mouth shut or even
converse about much more than makeup, but the boys liked her and
that made her mildly popular, which got Melissa and the other girls to
befriend her and put up with her narcissistic berating.

As the three girls jawed and finished their smokes they heard the
screen door slam across the street, they each stopped their chattering
for a moment, just long enough to hear the high pitched moaning of a
girl, Tara didn't want to bother investigating, she sighed and laid back
on the porch to stare up into the sky, and finish her beer. The other
two girls worried that it might be Melissa so they crossed the back
yard. Nearing the chain-link fence the two girls couldn't believe what
they found, Lil Bonito. The two girls couldn't help but burst out
laughing when they caught Lizzy calling her new boyfriend, "El Jefe"
which meant "chief," which he was anything but. The two girls
laughed so loud that Tara came running, hoping to catch Melissa in an
embarrassing and very compromising situation that she could use
against her for the rest of her life. Much better than Melissa bent over
with Darryl reaching to her lungs from behind was Lizzy, rolling over

262

the top of her baby brother and she was wincing with as they fumbled together trying to attempt to do adult things together, Lizzy was whispering about pain and how much he was hurting her as he squirmed around.

Tara and her friends heckled Lil B, Lizzy began to cry that she was caught without her clothes, the three girls poked fun at her for having the body of a ten year old boy, the girl cried as Lil B joined in on the laughing, she was quick to remove herself from the boy and frantically search for some of her clothing before fleeing off into the night. The three girls stared and laughed at Bonito, mocking him with the "El Jefe" nickname. Bonito tried to stand proud and act as if none of it bothered him, he couldn't seem to find his pants fast enough. Bonito stepped near the fence to offer up his naked body for the girls to use for their pleasure, sans his sister. The taller blonde reached out as he passed through the fence, she acted interested and he wasn't able to tell if she was serious of joking but he lunged forward and almost dropped himself into her outstretched hand; the other girls shrieked that she almost gave the younger boy an accidental hand-job.

Bonito thought for half a second he was about to get punked but he also tried to hit the girls hand with his pecker. The girl retracted her hand as the other had shrieked, she was just simply playing but there was a tinge of curiosity behind it. The girls still looked up trying to find the source of the slamming door, it was hard to determine he direction as the sound echoed in the air. Tara grew inpatient that Melissa hadn't returned, she felt snubbed by the friend and that wasn't an insult she was going to take lightly. Tara mumbled that Melissa was probably sucking off Darryl, the two friends had considered such an exchange for his higher quality drugs. Tara's friend Laura had flashed her tits for dope, it was a small price to pay and if the offer had come back around a little later, she might have been willing to further barter.

Brittini burst into her home, the slamming the door wide open as she spilled through. Aimee heard Brittini sobbing and crying in the living room, she stopped mid stride on Tod and flung herself off and towards her upset daughter. Tod was still up for more loving after haven taken a dick pill for another go round, a common requirement to handling Aimee. Aimee pinballed down the hallways trying to get a shirt on over her body as she entered near her panicking little girl in the livingroom. Aimee yanked the shirt from over her eyes, the sight of Brittini standing in her underwear made her heart stop. Brittini was crying and antsy, unable to stand still or keep her lower jaw from quivering enough to tell her mother what happened. "Gary, he t-t-t-touched me" Brittini stuttered out as she tried to start from the beginning of the whole ordeal. Aimee fought to piece together her frantic daughter in her panties stuttering on about Gary, her seized heart brought on a sobering adrenaline surge through her. Aimee was enjoying the remains of her line of coke and some fun time when Brittini came home and disrupted everything, now panic was in control. Aimee yelled to Tod to get dressed and in a hurry.

Tod was weary from his afternoon and the hour was late but with Brittini screeching in the living room and Aimee shouting at him, there was zero chance of getting to sleep. Tod came into the living room to see Brittini, wearing very little, she was still crying and Aimee was trying to stroke her hair and calm her down. Tod tried to get his eyeful of Brittini and her young body while she frantically cried. Aimee instructed Tod to haul ass down to the Amaca station and deal with Gary. Tod resisted the notion to leave two naked girls behind to go and deal with a fat grease ball and his pit-stains. Aimee got furious when Tod grabbed a beer from the fridge while keeping his eyes locked on Brittini. Aimee decided to tell Tod about what happened several years ago when he got locked up, about trying to get Gary and his family to drop the charges and how it turned to Gary taking advantage of her and then blackmailing her with it.

As soon as Tod realized that Aimee he had given it up to Gary, the fat gas station clerk, he paused for a moment, his heart began to pump in his chest, sure Gary tagged her while he was locked up but he considered Aimee his property. Tod grabbed two more beers from the fridge and stepped into his work boots. Tod scrambled into Aimee's car, he was in an enraged hurry and squealed the tires leaving the trailer park. Tod he was overcome with a white hot rage, he realized that the lifetime ban was to keep him from finding out that Gary was in Aimee, more than it was to protect himself. Aimee wept with Brittini, she apologized for not warning her daughter about how truly terrible Gary was, she never meant for her daughter to fall prey to the pervert also. Brittini struggled to calm her nerves down, she reached for Aimee's pack of cigarettes, lighting two then giving her mother one. Aimee was surprised that she didn't know her daughter smoked, she wrapped Brittini in a blanket to cover herself with and let

264

her take a deep breath. Brittini told Aimee that it wasn't all Gary that had her upset and that Tod shouldn't go and deal with Gary, Aimee shushed her daughter and told her that Gary had it coming no matter what.

Carsey stepped into her home to find Jonny sitting on her couch smoking a cigarette. Before Carsey had the gut reaction to get upset he stood to greet her and apologized sincerely. Carsey asked where Brittini was, Jonny explained that she suddenly got upset and only left a few minutes previous to her showing up. Carsey tried to figure out why she was upset but with a fast look around the small pile of her clothing on the floor, questions were quickly answered. Carsey told Jonny to look at her, she stepped closely and removed his cigarette and put it in her mouth. Jonny began fidget uncomfortably, his eyes darted everywhere but towards her. Carsey had a weird tinge strike inside of mind, she took a deep breath in order to heave her chest in his face as he tried to explain what happened. When Jonny averted his eyes Carsey worked her right hand down the front of his shorts and used her left to pull her bra down. Jonny blushed and turned his head, with a tight grip on his genitals he couldn't run. Carsey stared into the sides of Jonny's eyes, "You're gay" she purposed, Jonny opened his eyes wide and he began to deny the wild accusation with everything he could do

Carsey straightened up her chest and suggested that he listen, they heard squealing tires outside and it gave them a reason to pause for a moment. Carsey smirked, she had a good grip on his bean bag and there wasn't a change in his pulse, no activity in his engine room and that was all telltale to Carsey. Carsey heaved her bosom up and down while waiting for the corners of his mouth to smirk or any muscle twitches of his, in her hands. Carsey fondled the boy for another moment, waiting to see if there was any sort of interest before releasing her grip. Jonny lit another cigarette, he pushed the cartons to her and told her what had happened to Brittini, and explained that they were a gift.

Carsey continued to pry and try to better understand everything that had happened, Jonny explained that Brittini attempted to seduce him, she was upset and after Darryl gave them some party drugs, she was relaxed and opening up. Jonny hung his head and apologized for everything as Carsey returned her bra to her body where it belonged. Brittini didn't want Jonny to be gay, she used to think he simply didn't

265

have any feelings for her but after having hung out as much as they had, she continued to hope that he would develop those feelings. As Brittini tried to kiss on Jonny, she really wanted to thank him for being such a good friend, she also wanted to try tell him what had been bothering her for a few weeks now, but she got upset at his rejection and left, without her clothes. Brittini wasn't as clear headed as she should have been when she fled, she was upset and also besides herself from drugs.

Carsey and Jonny spoke for a little while, Carsey explained how hard she struggled, how much it meant to be able to find comfort in the arms of someone else, how physical intimacy means so much in times of need and that's probably what she was in need of. Jonny's hands shook as he took a puff out of his cigarette, Carsey knew first-hand how trapped he felt, she too felt trapped. Jonny wanted to go and catch up with Brittini and apologize immensely, he explained how terrible he felt and how destroyed she seemed as she bolted through the door and ran through the streets going home, she must have been panicked out of her mind in order for the quiet shy girl to have left her clothes behind, and it was all Jonny's fault. Carsey continued to suggest that Jonny go home, get some sleep, he needed to sleep off the drugs so he'd be better equipped to apologize and talk to his friend in the morning. Jonny begged that Carsey not say anything, if Big Ken found out then surely Tod would find out and then he would go through the same hell that Joey had been going through(except not wanting to jump genders).

Carsey tried her best to fend off a constant barrage of yawns, it was extremely late and it had been a painfully long day, Carsey escorted Jonny to her front door, the boy looked weary as his feet scuffled and his head hung low. Carsey felt awful bad for the day he had as well but she had to keep her son at the forefront of her mind. Jonny bumped against the hand rail as he eased himself down each step, it was extremely quiet without the music blaring from the next street, his head throbbed and his ribs burned, he lit another cigarette as he headed down the street to make his way back to get some sleep. Jonny tried to keep his head turning, he wished he had eyes in the back of his head, he knew it wasn't long before Lil B popped up and then he either had his friends jump back on him like a pack of dogs. Jonny waited for the day he'd have his chance to pummel the bastard kid, which was long overdue.

Tod squealed his tires into the gas station parking lot, he wasn't sure what he planned to do but Gary had to pay for slipping it into Aimee and almost putting him back in prison. Tod locked up the brakes and had the car in park before it had even come to a complete stop, he then jumped out and tore the gas station door open. Gary popped up from behind the farthest shelf, he still looked sweaty from working, he looked up to lock eyes with Tod, and his heart dropped into his scrotum. Tod tried to nod and headed towards the beer fridge, he tried to play off his arrival as just a beer run, his hurried pace wasn't as convincing as he had hoped it would be. Gary tried to keep a few shelves between himself and Tod, it had been years since they had seen each other, Gary wouldn't forget the tattoos and gapped toothed sneer.

Gary began to quake, he hoped that Tod hadn't come because of Brittini, he couldn't help himself when it came to the young girl and when she pulled her pants down, her supple rear overtook him and he just had to play with it. Tod yanked the handle on the nearest cooler and reached in for a forty ounce bottle of King Cobra, the unsnapping of the cap seemed to echo in the store. Gary shuttered a bit at the slamming of the cooler door, he was on edge and trying to make his way up the middle aisle and close to the police button. Gary tried to play calm; he focused on his breathing and took large steps to get back to his post behind the counter. Tod broke in Gary's direction, Gary only let him make two steps before he let out a squeal and a crow hop towards the red panic button mounted under the counter top. Gary felt relieved that he had the safety of his button, tapping his fingers on the countertop just above the button. Tod stepped up to Gary and asked for a tin of dip and set his bottle on the counter. Gary let out a big sigh of relief and turned to reach for a plastic container of dip for the customer.

Gary turned back around to meet Tod, who was swinging the half full bottle and connecting with the side of his head. Glass and beer foam went flying into the air, the large window behind Gary reflected glass in every direction, beer splattered all over the two men and the floor. Gary felt his face burn, his eyes were blurred with beer and he could feel glass trickle down his shirt. Gary tried to fumble to trip the police alarm, his fingers couldn't the button under the counter and he was beginning to weep from the pain. Tod turned to his left and rounded the corner of the counter to drag Gary out by his fat rolls.

Gary's fingers found the button with the divot in it; Gary pushed the button frantically and cried out as soon as Tod slapped his hands on Gary's chest to drag him out by his shirt. Gary tried to hold onto the counter top to keep from being dragged by Tod. Tod was shouting at Gary and delivering a battery of punches to the larger man. Tod shouted at Gary to tell him everything, tell him about Aimee and then also about Brittini. Gary couldn't stop crying enough to answer any questions, he was in pain and his face bled profusely.

Tod made an easy beating of Gary; the man fell to the floor and cried as Tod kicked at him. Tod grew tired quickly; his thirst gave him reason to pause for a few moments to step back to the cooler for another drink. Gary rolled in the pool of his own blood on the floor, his shirt soaked in beer and his pants in piss. Tod heard the sirens in the distance and suddenly he knew that they were headed for him. Tod grabbed his beer and headed over to kick Gary one last time, Gary was curled up in the fetal position, and Tod saw the reflections of the blue and red lights on the trees across the street as he left the gas station behind him. Tod poured himself into the Caprice and tried to get out of the parking lot before the police arrived. The police came flying into the parking lot and the bouncing lights lit up the area plenty. Tod knew he was in deep shit when a second car boxed him in; he dropped his head towards the steering wheel.

Big Ken was stirring on his floor, the commotion outside had dwindled down to a random noise or two, Wriggle could be heard loading his truck, the thuds of the speakers landing in the metal truck bed had raised Ken from his stupor, it was hard for him to raise up and get his head on straight. Big Ken heard a familiar noise, the ladders on the top of his truck were a distinct sound, the ladders rattled on the overhead racks, it gave him the suspicion that someone was breaking into his truck. Big Ken reached under his couch to get a pistol that was stashed hidden underneath; a piece he carried with him once in a while when taking loads into the harsher parts of the city. Ken leaned forward over his couch, there was a dark figure opening up the driver's door of his truck. Big Ken immediately assumed that one of the towel heads he fought with earlier had returned to rip him off. Big Ken had to prop his hand up on the back of the couch; he was tired and looking to pop off one shot to put out a steadfast warning. "*POP*" one shot rang out, Ken took a deep smell of the gunpowder in the air, the figure ran off to the distance and Ken fell to the couch to pass out.

The morning after the party was somber and quiet, hardly any bodies stirred, the streets were littered with cups, garbage, and clothing, the only real movement along the streets were stray cats scampering about. Big Ken snored away the sunrise and Carsey was slow to rise as Brodan was calling out for his mom. Brittini was out for an early walk, Tod never made it home overnight and she had to find the courage to talk to her mom. Brittini had been troubled with a problem and only Aimee could help her, except that Aimee had the same problem. Tod crept into her room one night, he had been drinking and zooted up on some pills, her mom was already passed out for the night. Tod took advantage of her, he raped her and she suspected her mother wouldn't believe her. Tod let his nasty breath steam up her face, she tried to cry as he pinner her down and each time she tried to cry loud he would kiss her and muffle her voice. Once Tod was done with her he reminded her how physical he could get with Aimee and he'd have no problem doing it again, or with her or her little friend Jonny. Brittini was upset that she needed Jonny last night, she wanted his comfort and he turned her down, she had hoped that he would have sex with her and that things might be OK. Brittini couldn't understand why Jonny didn't love her, it wasn't how she wanted things to happen, she wanted to tell him about Tod but couldn't find the right opening.

Angel rolled over to see Lamarc still asleep next to her. There was a moment of clarity that she had after her drugs wore off. Joey could be heard in the next room as he had just come home from work. Joey was bumping into drawers and making a serious ruckus. Angel tried to run her fingers through her hair in an attempt to untangle some of her hair; her left rings gave her some struggle to remove her hand as she exited her room. Angel wanted to shout at Joey, she wanted to rip his ass for making such noise, and she didn't want to wake Lamarc. Upon opening Joeys room she saw his bed covered in clothes, Angel stood in the doorway trying to make sense of what she was seeing; "hey what's with the noise dickhead?" she asked. Joey turned to face her, the look on his face was shocking, his mascara was running down his cheeks and he was pale. Angel was still mad at him, she kept herself drugged up to deal with her feelings and emotions about what was going on, it was a hard subject to confront and the inner turmoil trying to accept it was just too much.

"Your parents are in the living room" Joey told Angel, her heart rate dropped. Her parents had left Florida to come up, they had been trying to get ahold of her and got worried, they got ahold of Joey after a lot of inpatient trying to call, and he came clean to them. Angel was doing a lot to delude her reality, the drastic change of what she had envisioned for her life haunted her, it was too hard to let go of Joey but hanging onto him was impossible. Angel was lost and she was lacking her morning bump of cocaine, the realization of trouble was wearing on her already. Angel shuddered at the thought that her parents were sitting in her living room, she ducked them for months now and didn't want the ambush in her living room. Angel turned back into her room, she was trying to find clothes in a hurry, and Lamarc began to stir. Angel leaned in to tell Lamarc to sit tight, he had no idea what was going on or who she was talking to but he was drowsy and hung-over. Angel finished dressing, she wriggled into a bra then shirt and quick slapped her hands onto her face to try and reduce the puffiness by her eyes

Angel turned and headed towards the living room, she could see her father standing with a menacing look on his face and his arms crossed. Angel already missed her patches, she wanted to numb over her worry, and she felt nauseas and seeing a similar expression on the face of her mother only made it worse. Her parents asked her to come clean about why she was avoiding them, why Joey was becoming Lilly and why she felt she couldn't tell them. The conversation spanned many years of them being family and honesty and all the noise involved in a hearty scolding. Angel's parents decided that they were selling her trailer; it was in their name so it was their choice. Joey came out of his room; he had already been warned about how things were going to happen. Joey began packing his things right before Angle woke up and was going to start looking around for a new place to live, he also offered to help pack Angels things while she was gone.

Angel turned a shocked eye towards Joey; she didn't understand the inference "gone?" Angel was puzzled, there was so much she couldn't grasp, her head was clouded with a hangover and a small line of coke would certainly clear her head but she was out and with her parents looming over head, she wasn't sure if she could sneak a bump. Angel plopped herself down on her couch, she didn't fully understand the entirety of what her parents were plotting so she buried her face in her hands again. Angels father Roy spoke up, his deep voice resonated in her ears, making her blood pressure raise and beat in her ears. "You're coming with us today, we're selling the trailer and you're going to a rehab center for 6months" Roy began to inform his daughter. Roy was an ex-soldier, he ran a tight ship but knew that a good parent gave their children space the be themselves, Angel had plenty of space but now she was in trouble and he wanted to help. Roy set up a six month appointment for Angel, he knew she was struggling to deal with her past and what happened between her and Joey so he reached out to a facility that dealt with soldiers returning home with mass amounts of stress from war, there are many pros in the psychology field that were trained to help with traumatic stress syndromes and she was aligned to begin meeting with one while rehabbing off of her current way of life.

Carsey put Brodan in his high chair and gave him a handful of Honey Maid Graham Crackers, she had to take a pee after a night of drinking and staying out late, she didn't drink much because it messed with her meds but one or two still were still enough diuretic to make a full bladder painful first thing in the morning. Carsey sat on the cold toilet seat; the day already showed that it might get pretty warm so the cold seat on the back of her thighs was a bit of a relief so early in her day. Carsey stared around, Brodan's bath toys filled a basket in the corner of the tub, her feet left steam imprints on the dirty tile on the floor, she flexed her toes and watched her toe knuckles turn red and back to white again, something to pass the time for a quiet minute or two. Carsey turned to reach for some toilet paper and noticed a small unfamiliar object in her trash; it was neither a tampon cartridge nor floss box. Moving a piece of plastic out of the way cleared some writing on a small pink box wedged towards the bottom, Carsey knew exactly what she was getting ready to grab ahold of, and it made her heart stop. Carsey pulled out a small white piece of plastic; it was almost as long as her finger, Carsey pulled the box from the trash and studied everything she had in her hands. Two lines meant positive, sure as birds shit she was holding a positive pregnancy test that wasn't hers and wasn't there the day before.

273

Aimee finally gave into exhaustion, between coming off of the coke from the party as well as coming down from her surge of adrenaline when Brittini came hollering through the door. Aimee fell asleep with her daughter on the couch, Brittini hardly slept but being shrouded in her mother's arms finally made her feel safe in her own home for the first time in many years. Aimee didn't know what to do anymore, things with Tod started out pretty well, he was a guy she remembered being tall and handsome, and very athletic, his time in prison had degraded him, it caused his brain to rot and his desires to seep into vile depths. Tod needed more drugs or alcohol to remain satisfied, he cost her one decent part time job and most of her self-respect, be at least she wasn't alone. Aimee came to the conclusion that being alone was much worse than being with a guy that only occasionally slapped her around; he also meant a warm body to sleep next to. When Tod forced her to blow some of his coworkers he was on a lot of drugs she told herself, when he got physical it was because he messed up and when he was close to clean he could be charming. Tod took decent care of Aimee when he broke her jaw; she convinced herself that he could have been much worse to her.

Brittini rounded one corner on her walk, she was so lost in the world, Jonny was probably mad at her for getting upset, she couldn't bring herself to tell her mom that Tod raped her and was now pregnant by him, she wanted out of her life. Brittini looked off into parts of the woods that lined the sidewalk; it was much more serene than on the other side of the berm that attempted to mask the trailer park within. Up ahead on the sidewalk it looked like Jonny, he must have slept on the outside of the berm to avoid dealing with Big Ken overnight. "Jonny" Brittini shouted to her friend, this was her chance to come clean, to apologize and to make things right. Brittini picked up her pace to rush over to Jonny and greet him good morning. Brittini reached Jonny' side, something was wrong; he was curled up on his side and not responding to her calls. Brittini tried to roll Jonny over, his body was stiff, his eyes were glazed over and ice blue, and there was no life left in him. Brittini couldn't believe what she was seeing, seeing her friend with his eyes open but his body with no life in it hit her with a shock, she scanned her friend with her eyes and found that he was clutching his stomach because it had a bloody hole in it, he had been shot. Brittini didn't know what she was going to do now, she sat by his side and held his hand, he must have been trying

274

to sleep in Big Ken's truck when Big Ken shot out the window and hit him, he ran away and then bled to death hiding at the grass berm.

Tammi woke up, it took the girl a few minutes of searching to locate most of her clothes, Billy, Tuner and Karl took turns with her most of the night, it kept her warm enough through the night but when she woke up endlessly disoriented. Tammi's body hurt in so many ways, she felt like the streets of New Orleans during Mardi Gras, but it must have been one hell of a party. Tammi didn't remember much, her young body would recover from the hell she put it through and she was already planning on coming back for another one for Labor Day as she headed over to meet up with Dez'rae for the day. Tammi enjoyed her reputation, she was called every name in the book but her reputation was what made her popular, she had a nasal voice and an overweight body but men still lusted for her.

Tod was picked up by the officers responding to Gary's emergency request, two cars were nearby dealing with all of the fireworks and scouting to keep a safe watch out for fires or riff raff when the call came in. The shorter sheriff lady finished telling the oncoming junior deputy her report, the whole list of who was tied together within the *Heights* and how the night had gone after getting plenty of witness reports. "Turn to your right" the lady officer yelled to Tod as they finished the mug shots. "I was a junior detective when I arrested him for shooting up and selling steroids to the other boys in high school all those years ago" the officer told the younger deputy. The deputy began to lead Tod to the general holding cell when the lady sheriff spoke up to stop him; "he can't go in to general holding, he got AIDS back in high school sharing all those needles, he has to go to a private cell to keep from infecting anyone else." The relieving officer changed his direction; Tod hung his head and just remained silent.

www.ingramcontent.com/pod-product-compliance
Lightning Source LLC
Chambersburg PA
CBHW021953170626
46808CB00001B/141